The Wedding Party

The Wedding Party

SOPHIE KING

LARGE PRINT
Oxford

First published in Great Britain 2009
by
Hodder & Stoughton

Published in Large Print 2010 by ISIS Publishing Ltd.,
7 Centremead, Osney Mead, Oxford OX2 0ES
by arrangement with
Hodder & Stoughton
an Hachette Livre UK Company

British Library Cataloguing in Publication Data
King, Sophie.
    The wedding party.
    1. Weddings - - Planning - - Fiction.
    2. Divorced women - - Fiction.
    3. Women clergy - - Fiction.
    4. Large type books.
    I. Title
    823.9'2–dc22

ISBN 978–0–7531–8682–4 (hb)
ISBN 978–0–7531–8683–1 (pb)

X000 000 039 3035

Printed and bound in Great Britain by
T. J. International Ltd., Padstow, Cornwall

This book is dedicated to

My wonderful children William, Lucy and Giles (for richer, for poorer — and no, you can't have any more pocket money!)
Fresh starts (a new groom sweeps clean?)
My Dearly Beloveds (many of whom have continued the family tradition of divorce, proving it's perfectly possible to be Second Time Lucky).

This book is not dedicated to

Marriage wreckers (let no woman put us under)

Acknowledgements

Anthony Goff of David Higham for being my "Best Man"

Carolyn Caughey (Hodder & Stoughton) for accepting my (novel) Proposal.

Betty Schwartz for being my "Literary Matron of Honour"

Jane (in memory of our Friday coffees)

Emmanuel Church, in Chesham for lending me its funny notices (in return for some of mine)

Sunnyside Church, Berkhamsted for its love

Rachel and all the other vicars who helped with research

NINE MONTHS TO GO

CHAPTER
ONE

Becky

"Ohmigodwhereisshe?Stupidstupidsillywomanshouldhave beenherehalfanhourago.I'mgoingtobelateforwork.It'sabloody nuisance,that'swhatitis."

"Mummy." Ben was tugging at her sage green silk trousers, fresh from the dry cleaners. "Stop crying, mummy. Someone's knocking on the door."

Shit. So they were. It had to be Laura. Desperately hoping the nanny hadn't heard her tantrum, Becky swiftly opened it.

"Sorry I'm late."

Not for the first time, the laid-back Australian accent set Becky's nerves on edge. For God's sake. How could she be so bloody calm?

"Got on the wrong bus." Laura breezed in, slung an apple green backpack on the floor and knelt down to do up the shoelaces on her pink and silver trainers. "Still, it was reelly interesting. I went past this playground with some cool things for the kids."

Ben had already transferred himself from his mother's legs to Laura's and Becky's heart lurched. If her son didn't have any loyalty at six, what hope was there for him when he was old enough to date?

"Mummy said it was a bloody nuisance that you were late." Ben was climbing up Laura's skinny jeans now. Any minute now and he'd be swinging from her arms.

"No, I didn't," began Becky, feeling a line of sweat trickling down between her shoulder blades, newly-tanned from a series of six free sessions in return for a review on the beauty page. "I just meant that . . ."

"And," chirped Ben, swinging from Laura's arm, "she said you were a stupid stupid silly woman . . ."

Becky grabbed her slim black leather briefcase which had been waiting by the door below the beige and black painting Steve had bought the other day, even though it had been a ridiculous price. Still, it was certainly eye-catching with that triangular Picasso-like nude figure and it went with the polished floorboards that they'd had put in throughout the house in preference to carpet.

"Got to dash now. It's conference day and it's already — oh, shit — 7.30. Listen, Laura. Daisy's still asleep. I gave her a little something to help her get to bed last night after that cold."

The nanny frowned. "I thought the doctor told you not to do that."

"Well she's still not sleeping." Becky heard the words snapping out of her mouth, too late to take them back. "I've had to re-do the spreadsheet (inaminuteBen) because Daisy's gymnastics class has been moved to Tuesday but that clashes with the Wriggle and Giggle session so one of the other mums — can't remember

4

exactly which one now but you'll see when she gets here — is going to take it. WHATISIT, BEN?"

"Can I come to work with you? I could help you. Did you know that a flea can jump more than fifty times its height? It says so on Ask Jeeves."

"No, I didn't and please don't tug at my trousers like that. Laura, if that's not clear, text me but don't ring."

"Why not, Mummy?"

"Because it's conference day." Becky could hear her voice rising. If she didn't get out now and grab a taxi fast, she'd lose it completely. "See you later. If Steve rings, tell him to call me tonight."

Thank heavens. As soon as she walked into the chrome steel automatic rotating doors, Becky felt better. Here, at *Charisma* magazine, she was Becky Hastings, features editor, instead of Becky Hughes, hopeless mother who couldn't cope without a nanny.

Here — thank God — there was no one to shout at her. No one to scream when all she wanted to do was go to bed. No one who kept asking impossible questions like what keeps the clouds up in the sky and why don't they fall down. No one to throw temperatures of 103 like Daisy had last winter during Laura's day off and freak her out so she thought her daughter was dying, only to be leaping up and down the next day.

"I love my children," said Becky silently, as though to convince herself. And she did. No one — least of all her mother who'd been desperate for her to get pregnant — had told her it would be like this, that's all.

Flashing her ID card with a smile at the new boy on reception (not bad!), she stepped into the lift, checking her reflection in the mirrored glass. Glossy chestnut hair in a sculptured bob, thanks to the wonderful Michaeljohn; light-reflecting foundation courtesy of a freebie from Beauty and — no, no, no — the beginnings of eye bags due to all the late nights at the office. Better have a word with Beauty about that too.

Second floor. Going up. The lift walls were lined with promos that were on that week. A taster session in the kitchens of *Homes To Come Back To* which had been launched last month. Some talk by Annabel Karmel on how to feed the family for one of the parenting magazines. A sale of beauty products at another well-known monthly glossy in the building. She might go to that one if the conference finished on time.

Stepping out onto the fourth floor, Becky noticed the advertising people had changed the six foot high poster to show *Charisma*'s latest cover.

HOW TO HAVE EXPLOSIVE ORGASMS EVERY THREE MINUTES

She was quite proud of that. OK, it was bending the truth a bit but the coverline had pulled in the readers. Becky allowed herself a small smile at the pun. She'd have to try it out with Steve sometime when he wasn't away on one of his never-ending work trips.

Sliding her card down the security panel, she pushed open the door. It might only be 8.09 a.m. according to the neon flashing clock on the wall but the floor was packed. In the early days of her career as a journalist, Becky could remember little cubbyholes where there was a certain amount of privacy. Now it was all open plan; the idea being that there was little room for private phone calls and everyone could see what everyone else was doing.

"Morning," she said to Nancy, the editor's PA. Nancy smiled nervously. Everyone was twitchy on conference day and with good reason. Cat, the editor, hadn't brought *Charisma* magazine to its current circulation peak without demanding blood from her staff in return. In precisely 32 minutes, they would all be summoned into her spacious, glass-walled office (one of the few perks of being an editor as far as Becky could work out) and asked, in her dangerously silken voice, what each department head intended to suggest for the magazine that week. She'd probably be wearing an elasticated waist, even though the twins were two and she should have shed that post-preggie bulge ages ago. More Devil in Primark than Devil in Prada, as Becky sniggered to Steve in private.

That week, of course, wasn't the week they were in right now. Like most other weeklies, *Charisma* worked two-and-a-half months in advance, although if a story was hot — really hot — it got squeezed in earlier.

"Fuck." Becky was opening her emails. "Where's the 'I tried to sell my baby on eBay' copy? It was here last night."

"There was a powercut last night," offered Bel from Showbiz at the other end of the room. "We've all lost some stuff. IT's working on it."

Becky could feel the telltale sweat trickling down her back again. "But I need it for the conference."

"Did you print out a copy?"

No, she fucking hadn't because she'd been late getting home last night which was probably why Laura had been late getting here this morning as a none too subtle reminder that she was fed up with her employer's hours.

Bloody hell, she couldn't even remember exactly what it was about. Becky ran her hands through her short chestnut bob. Let's see. Some woman from some godforsaken village in the Midlands couldn't pay her credit card bill so had tried to sell her kid on eBay (it had been stopped in time). The woman blamed post-natal depression, though that hadn't prevented her from being interviewed and pocketing the £750 fee.

Maybe she could type out a few notes, although that wouldn't be enough. Cat would want to hear the whole story and she didn't have it to give. Stabbing the IT number into her phone, Becky could feel the panic curdling in her throat like a golf ball. "This is Becky Hastings from Features on *Charisma*. Yes, I know you're busy. What I want to know is how the . . . how I can get some copy out of this thing which was here last night and isn't now?"

Numbly, Becky listened to the techni-rubbish which the girl at the other end was spouting. She couldn't take much more. She really couldn't. Bleep. Glancing at her mobile, she saw Steve's name flashing. He'd have to wait. "What? When? Well that's not good enough.

I've got a conference in fifteen minutes and I need it now."

"No luck?" asked Bel sympathetically as she slammed the phone down.

"No." Becky could feel hot tears of frustration pricking her eyes. She'd have to take in another lead story but what? Scrolling down the list of features that hadn't been eradicated, she considered her options. The kid who was molested at the theme park by the known paedophile? No. It would clash with the piece on how to keep your kids safe on the street. The piece on the groom who slept with all six bridesmaids the week before the wedding? Too similar to last month's "True Hen Night Confessions".

The phone! Becky grabbed the receiver like a lifebelt. Dear God. Please may it be the woman from IT. Please . . .

"Becky!"

The very sound of his voice stopped her in her tracks, as it always did; transporting her back to another world when he'd been able to fix things. When he'd been there for her before he and mum had split up. When he'd been a real father.

"Dad. Look, I'm sorry but this isn't a great time."

"I know and I wouldn't have bothered you except that I tried last night and you didn't pick up and . . ."

"Please, Dad." Becky could feel the hysteria about to escape through her mouth. "I can't talk."

"I need to tell you something." His voice was low and steady. "I'm getting married, Becky. And I wanted you to know before anyone else told you."

Becky felt her fingers grip the receiver and her vision blur. On the screen in front of her, she thought she could see the headline *"I SOLD MY BABY ON EBAY"* suddenly popping up but it didn't seem important any more. Dad was getting married? Who to? When?

She could hear him taking a deep breath, as though he'd been practising this. "She's called Monique and I met her through work. We're getting married in November but I want you to meet her as soon as you can." He paused and she could hear his nervous excitement oozing through the silence. "I know we haven't exactly seen eye to eye over the years but I'd like your blessing, Becky. Please."

CHAPTER
TWO

Helen

Helen was planting late tulip bulbs in her head when the mobile rang. It was a trick of hers in spring. They'd come out in early summer when everyone else's had long faded away, so people would say, "Oooh, aren't you lucky that you've still got yours."

Normally, she'd start planting her second wave in January but with one thing or another, it had slipped her mind. Was it too late? Maybe not with the weather behaving as oddly as it had been. Blast, there it was again. Even if she wasn't driving, her mobile always rang when it was least convenient. Usually, she'd be on her hands and knees and then have to wipe her muddy hands on the side of her jeans in order to prise the wretched thing open.

One day, she promised herself, swerving into a lay-by, causing the lorry behind to hoot angrily, she'd get a new mobile which she could flick open one-handed without dropping her trowel. Maybe one of those blue tooths that her son-in-law Steve kept going on about.

It was all very well entering the Age of the Panty Liner but that didn't mean she couldn't keep up with other things.

"Hello?"

The person at the other end was gabbling so fast that if it weren't for the distinctive excited tone, she might have just shoved the phone in her jeans pocket and got on with her mental bulb planting.

"Becky? How lovely to hear from you, darling."

"Dad'sgettingmarriedagain."

For a minute, Helen thought her daughter was saying "Dad's getting buried again."

The little van rattled as another large lorry shot by. "Slow down, darling and say it again."

"I am slowing down. You should have heard me the first time."

"Well, I thought you said dad was getting buried again." She heard herself give a small nervous laugh. "But that couldn't have been right."

"Don't be stupid, Mum. I said dad's getting married again. To some woman called Monique whom he met through work. Do you know about her?"

Helen could actually feel her heart jumping up and hurtling itself against her ribs. At the same time, her throat tightened, her chest deadened and she wondered if she was going to be sick. "No, I didn't. It's all right, Dandy. Get back on the seat. I said, get back. Ugh — you've made another smell!"

"For God's sake, Mum, can't you give me two minutes?"

Helen glanced back at her aged, rather overweight Labrador with a tendency to fart at the most inappropriate moments due to his age. As though sensing her shock, he had jumped up from behind and was now frantically licking her face. "Of course, I can, darling. Are you sure Dad's really getting married and not just engaged again?"

What she really wanted to say was: "Your father always said he'd never marry again because he couldn't trust anyone else after what I did to him." Or maybe "Are you sure he's getting married? Because your father has had so many short-term girlfriends in the last ten years that he's incapable of settling down."

But there were some things — lots, actually — that a mother shouldn't say to her daughter. You just, as she'd learned over time, clamped your mouth shut and, if it made your feel better, said it in your head instead.

"Course I'm sure. He's just rung me at work."

"On conference day?"

"I'm impressed you remembered."

No need to be sarcastic. "Of course I do. If I try to ring you in the office on a Tuesday, you . . . you say it's not convenient."

"Well it's not." Becky's voice was sounding muffled now, as though she was cupping her hands round the receiver. "If you worked here, you'd understand."

Ah, there it was again. The constant reminder that she'd never worked in an office but had "wasted" her life through being a full-time mum. "I'm sorry. It must be difficult."

"Yes, it is." Becky sounded slightly mollified. "But what are we going to do about Dad? He can't just marry her — we don't even know her."

"Well you can't stop him." Helen continued stroking Dandy's ruff; it felt calm and soothing. She could remember choosing him as a puppy together with Geoff and the children when they'd been a proper family. "He's a grown man. Are you going to meet her?"

"He wants me to have dinner some time next week."

Tell me what she's like, Helen wanted to say.

"I'll tell you what she's like."

"Only if you want to," she replied too fast.

How old was she? What colour hair did she have? (Hers was still exactly the same colour as her daughter's but maybe Geoff wanted a change from naturally glossy chestnut.) What did she do? (Probably a model like the previous one.) If so, was she a size zero? Helen personally prided herself on the fact that, unlike many of her contemporaries, she was still a 12 below the waist and a 10 above it, thanks to all the gardening and dog-walking.

"Have they set a date?"

"Yes. That's another thing. November. November 25th."

How could they?

"Thoughtless, isn't it? You'd think he'd have remembered. Sorry, Mum. I've got to go."

Helen could hear voices rising urgently, as though her daughter was in an operating theatre instead of a weekly tabloid. Why didn't these people realise it didn't mean anything? That the only important thing was family and doing the right thing, which was exactly what she had failed to do herself over ten years ago. She wanted to fling her arms round her daughter who had got sucked so far into this mad world that she couldn't even cope with her own children.

"Just a minute. How are Daisy and Ben? I thought I might come over and . . ."

"Just coming, Cat. Yes I'm printing out the tried-to-sell-my-baby-on-eBay copy now. Sorry, there was an IT blip . . ."

Helen heard the phone crashing down. Selling a baby on eBay? That couldn't be right; she must have misheard again. But she hadn't misheard the news about Geoff. Burying her head in Dandy's neck, she tried to clear her head. Why shouldn't he marry again? As he'd said enough times, it was she who had left him. And she herself could have married, well at least a couple of times. Even so . . .

"No!" She pushed Dandy firmly back on the seat behind her, along with the packet of compost she'd just bought from the garden centre and turned the ignition key. Come on. Don't die on me now. That was better. The van hated these sharp spring mornings although she herself loved them; loved the resistance of the white frosted earth when she plunged in the fork to turn the sods and lose herself in another world.

It wasn't until she found herself on the Little Rington Road — past that church which always had interesting signs outside like "Anyone for Afters?" — that she realised where she was going. Part of her wanted to laugh out loud. It didn't need a psychologist to explain that the news about Geoff had somehow made her want to run back to the house they had shared since Adam was a baby; to the home where they

15

had, for a time, been happy. But why? She'd put her ex-husband out of her mind years ago. It didn't hurt any more. Besides, she'd been the one who had finally snipped the cord.

"It's all right, Dandy." The dog was whimpering, standing alert on the back seat, ears pricked up, as though recognising the lane, even though she'd gone to great pains to avoid it during the last ten years.

"Do you remember?" she asked him. She certainly could, despite trying her best to block it out. But it was all flooding back now. Watching the removal men leave in front of her; not knowing how to say goodbye to Geoff who was standing stiff by the back door; driving off herself with a sullen teenage Becky in the back, together with the dog.

And now, here she was, pulling up outside the beautiful stone Georgian rectory with that lovely honey wall cracked with ivy. Oh my God. How could she have ever left it? Dandy was beside himself now; nose pressed against the window as though he was going to break it. No doubt there that he recognised his old home even after all this time.

Helen found herself getting out of the van and staring up at the white sash windows. Whoever lived there now — and it had changed hands twice since she'd left — had kept her old bedroom curtains, she realised with a pang. They'd trimmed the magnolia too; rather badly it seemed from here. It would never flower at that rate. And why on earth had they left the roses to straggle against the wall? They should have been pruned ages ago. As for the ivy . . . if someone didn't thin that soon, it would ruin the brickwork. She'd been religious about doing it twice a year. But oh — there were the hyacinths against the wall; the same place she'd always planted hers. Unable to help herself, she knelt down to smell them. Heavenly! Absolutely heavenly!

"Can I help you?"

Helen jumped, flushing deeply as a somewhat heavy-jowled man — definitely in the "eligible for Saga holidays" category — suddenly threw open the door, with suspicion etched over his thick grey eyebrows.

"I'm so sorry. I was just admiring your garden."

He glanced at the van behind her with the bright pink logo "Lady Gardener" on the side. That had been Adam's idea before he'd thrown up advertising and gone to Australia. ("Some people feel safer, mum, if they're employing a woman gardener. Pity you're not a plumber as well — you'd do a roaring trade.")

It was certainly attracting this man's attention. "I'm a gardener," said Helen unnecessarily as she awkwardly shifted from one gumboot to the other. "I've got a new client in the village and I stopped to find the way." Why had she lied? He'd ask her now who the client was and, as she knew all too well, everyone in Little Rington knew each other and she'd be rumbled.

"I won't ask who," he said, looking a little more comfortable, "because I've just moved here myself and don't know anyone. Actually, as you can see, I need a bit of help with the garden."

He laughed, a rather nice warm crinkly laugh. "Never really had green fingers myself and my wife

17

isn't able to do any gardening now. Just as a matter of interest, how much do you charge per hour?"

She quoted her usual rate and he shrugged. "Seems reasonable enough to me. You wouldn't like to take a look around, would you? There's quite a lot at the back; you might find it too much."

Helen wanted to laugh. Too much? She'd done it all herself when the children were growing up as well as everything else. Often, she'd thought it was that which had brought their marriage to its knees; the impossibility of doing it all with a husband who commuted from the city and collapsed in the armchair at gone 9p.m., only to repeat the whole thing the next day, every day.

But it had been the garden that had saved her. Helped her escape from the heavy atmosphere in the house. Allowed her to make a difference without arguing back at her.

"I'm a hard worker," she said, leaving Dandy barking madly in the van and following him through the wooden picket side gate which she had put up herself when Adam had been a baby. Her phone began to bleep, indicating a text message. Glancing at it, she could see it was David and promptly slipped the mobile back into her navy-blue fleece pocket.

How could she have forgotten how lovely it all was! In front stretched the lawn with its long borders on either side. Shoots were already beginning to poke through; the irises she had planted when Becky was about six; the fuchsias which Adam tried to deadhead as a toddler; the bleeding heart which was growing wild. And at the bottom, the orchard. The wonderful apple orchard where she and the children used to play cricket with the little apples and where she'd gathered windfalls for pies.

"What do you think?" He was looking at her, almost pleadingly. "My wife's an invalid, you see. We were going to look in the book for some help but somehow you turning up like this seems rather fortuitous, don't you think?" He held out a hand. A strong hand with a firm handshake. "I'm Robin, by the way. Robin Michaels."

Tell him, said the voice inside her. Tell him you used to live here and you only turned up this morning because your ex-husband is getting married again and you, for some ridiculous reason, find this strange which is why — again for some unknown reason — you have come back to your old home. If you don't tell him, it's bound to come out. Someone in the village will see you and tell him you used to live here and then he'll wonder why you didn't tell him . . .

"I'm Helen." Her hand met his. "I could start next Tuesday," she added brightly. "Will that do?"

CHAPTER
THREE

Mel

Mel fiddled with her Portobello Road turquoise drop earrings — she always wore the largest and brightest she could find to cheer up her "uniform", even though it was a jeans day today — and stared blankly at her empty computer screen.

"Anyone for Afters?" was going to be hard to beat. When she'd first thought of catchy signs outside St Mary's to draw in passing trade, the archdeacon had been sceptical.

"I'm not entirely certain of the wisdom, Melanie," he'd said, sucking his breath in through his two missing teeth and disapprovingly eyeing her second-hand, high-heeled black suede boots underneath her cassock. (She'd come straight from a funeral and hadn't had time to change.) "I agree we need to be part of the modern world but there's a danger, don't you think, of becoming gimmicky, like certain other members of our flock."

"I disagree." Mel fought an overwhelming urge to nip out for a cigarette. The AD, as she called him, always did that to her, even though she'd given up five years ago. "It's not gimmicky. It's a USP."

He frowned. "I beg your pardon?"

"Sorry. It's advertising speak for Unique Selling Point." Swiftly, Mel drew out a sheet of paper from her briefcase. "These are the attendance figures for the past five years. You'll see that since I arrived last summer, it has gone up by ten per cent. I want to improve that but I can only do so with your help."

There had been a brief silence during which Mel could imagine the AD wondering — not for the first time — why he'd appointed a blonde mother of two in her mid-forties who had come somewhat late to the church after a varied career in advertising to be vicar of a traditional establishment like St Mary's. If they were both honest, thought Mel, it was probably because there had been a distinct lack of applicants, both male and female, for a rather dull rural patch stuck a good forty minutes outside Oxford.

"Very well." The archdeacon had sipped his Earl Grey delicately, leaving his lips moist and damp. Mel almost felt like dabbing them for him, as she would have done the children when they were little. "We will give it a six month trial to see if it improves attendance figures. But I would like to see each of your little signs before they go on the board, in case I feel they are unsuitable. Meanwhile, I'm afraid that I'm not getting favourable feedback about your drop-in coffee mornings instead of individual visits to parishioners. Or to your new idea to put up large television-size screens for the words instead of using the hymn book."

Now, as Mel continued to stare at her blank screen, she wondered if the contretemps with the archdeacon had been worth it. Despite all those years as a copywriter, she was finding it increasingly difficult to come up with weekly slogans which straddled the gap between the sexy vernacular and God as the archdeacon saw him. It might, she thought, irritably getting up from her desk, be a bit easier if it wasn't for that awful music screeching out of Amy's bedroom.

"Turn it down!" She heard the words screaming out of her mouth before she could make herself sound more reasonable. But the kids' music always did that to her; made her feel capable of doing the kinds of things which no mother in her right mind would consider.

"Chill out, Mum." Amy's cool distant voice cut into her, instantly making Mel feel like the naughty child. "There's no need to yell like that. The neighbours might hear."

Mel pushed past to shut the window which wasn't easy. The vicarage had been built in the sixties when the church had sold off the beautiful Old Rectory and plonked the incumbent in this soulless box made of yellow piebald bricks and metal windows which were always getting stuck. It was cold too with its 1960s vented central heating system that had, at the time, been new but which was now in dire need of being overhauled just like the melamine kitchen with the sticky drawers.

"I can't think," Mel tried to explain. "I'm trying to write this week's slogan and after that the sermon and I can't concentrate with that noise." She sat down on the bed, next to Amy who was sprawled on her stomach, lying on A-level textbooks which she should be reading instead of that trashy magazine.

Amy turned over a page showing yet another celebrity wearing scarlet thongs and a brassy belly ring. "Well don't take it out on me."

"I'm not. I'm just saying that I need peace just like you do when you should be revising . . ."

Oh, God, she hadn't meant to say that.

"Stop nagging, Mum. I'll revise when I want to. I'm a teenager. We all have different ways of doing things like your God. You should know that, of all people."

Your God . . . Amy was going through a phase when she refused to go to church ("you can still believe without going to some boring service") but both Mel and Richard had decided not to push it, even though certain parishioners were always asking where the children were at Sunday morning communion. "Faith" to Amy meant shoe shops rather than an uncomfortable pew seat.

"Can I look at your magazine?" Mel reached out for it, desperate to rebuild the bridge she'd just smashed. "What's it called? *Charisma*? I haven't heard of that one before."

Amy snorted. "It's only one of the biggest weekly selling magazines."

"Really?" Mel's old advertising instincts were beginning to take over. "What's the circulation?"

Amy eyed her with distrust. "What's that?"

Mel sat on her daughter's bed, back against the wall. "It means how many people buy it. It's the kind of thing you ought to know if you're serious about being a journalist." Damn. She'd done it again.

"All you do is criticise me. You really put me down. Josh says the same."

"I don't." Mel was stung. "I'm just trying to give you some guidance."

"Nag, you mean." Amy jumped off the bed revealing at least two inches of bare midriff between the bottom of her t-shirt and top of her jeans.

"What aren't you wearing?"

"Very funny, Mum. I'm off, anyway. Sharon and I are going to Oxford."

"Hang on." Mel leapt off the bed. "How are you getting there?"

Amy gave her a pitying look. "Sharon's driving."

"But she's only just passed her test."

"So that means she can drive, doesn't it?"

Mel's mind shot back to last month's funeral of a local boy who had been killed when his best friend overtook on a bend. "But she hasn't got much experience yet."

"Tough." Amy was applying lip gloss in front of her mirror. Nice colour. She wouldn't mind borrowing that. "Well I am going. If you hadn't dragged us out of London to this pathetic village in the middle of nowhere, I wouldn't have to go miles to get to the shops and see my friends, would I?"

She had her there. Even after four years, the kids still missed their old home — and so, if she was honest, did she. But vicars couldn't be choosers. On the whole, you went where the church sent you.

24

"Ring me when you get there."

"Maybe." Amy slipped into a pair of pink flats which were totally unsuitable for the weather. "If I've got enough credit."

Mel ran her hands through her hair which badly needed trimming. That morning, she'd noticed a stray grey hair behind her ear, even though she'd only just passed forty. Hopefully, it would merge into the blonde bits but any more and she'd need to do something about it. "I only topped you up last week. Where did it all go?"

"On making calls to you, Mum, cos you always want to know where I am."

She was out of the door now and running down the stairs.

"Have you had breakfast?"

"I'll grab a banana. Stop fussing."

Dear God, asked Mel returning to her study, what were teenagers like in your day? And why couldn't she be more reasonable instead of letting it all come out. Hang on. "Let it all come out," she typed. No, that wasn't right. "Let it be." Not bad. "Let Him Be." Would they get the allusion to the Beatles? Some of them. And if they didn't, it didn't matter because it still made sense. Well, it would do. Now for the sermon and after that, with any luck, she could have her run. When she didn't have her daily jog, she always felt something was missing. It gave her time to think. Space to be.

Downstairs, she could hear the doorbell. Probably Sharon. Part of her wanted to leap up and say something like "Be careful" or "Watch out for that nasty bend before the Headington Roundabout". But if she did that, Amy would be livid. She had to learn to let go, as Richard was always saying. Easy for him. He didn't see the things she had to see. Didn't live through the pain of the woman down the road whose new (second) husband had just died of a heart attack. Didn't . . .

Hang on. It wasn't Sharon. That sounded like a male voice. Surely it was too early for Richard to be returning from his interview because, if it was, it meant he hadn't got it. No. Definitely not Richard. Please God, not another parishioner or she wouldn't get this sermon written by lunchtime.

Good. No one was calling her downstairs. Amy must have explained she was working, although now she felt guilty because a good vicar — one who didn't yell at her children — would be able to receive callers and write sermons at the same time as well as having sex at least once a week.

Mel's fingers began to race across the keyboard. That was it. That was the key, the kerygma to her sermon. "We want to do it all but is that what God wants? Sometimes we have to cross the line . . ."

An hour later, she leaned back exhausted. It was always like that when she wrote. She had no idea where the time went. Heavens. She should have got Joshua up by now. Why was it that fifteen-year-old boys could sleep in on Saturdays until gone lunchtime?

"Josh." She ruffled his head. "Josh. Get up. It's almost bedtime."

Groaning, he turned away, so she pulled back the duvet. "Come on, Josh. You ought be doing your homework."

"Fuck off, Mum. Can't you see I'm sleeping?"

Mel lived in dread of one of the parishioners overhearing this kind of conversation. "Josh, don't say the f-word. It's not nice."

He was asleep again or at least pretending to be, just as she tried to pretend she didn't notice the girly magazines under his bed which, she told herself, weren't that awful; in fact, healthy providing her son stuck to the paper version rather than explored the real thing at his age.

Stomach rumbling, Mel went downstairs to put a baked potato in the microwave. If she ate, she might feel better. Passing the hall table, she saw a note which Amy had left: "Some old bloke called in about his wedding. Gross! How can people think about That Sort of Thing when they're that age? Can you ring him? PS Sorry about the argument."

Instantly feeling both repentant and comforted at the same time, Mel rang her daughter's mobile.

"Hi, this is Amy. Leave your message and I'll try to find time in my busy life to call you back."

A gulp of fear grabbed her. Surely they'd have got there by now? Or was she refusing to pick up? Maybe a text would be less obtrusive. R u ok?

Amy was always teasing her for her limited text vocabulary. It was true. No chance of her getting "text thumb" as Amy called it. She only had a few stock sentences, including "Dnt dnk 2 much" and "Wn r u comng hme?"

Hang on, her mobile was bleeping. Mel's heart swooped in relief. Amy had texted back.

"There nw. C u ltr."

Phew. Now she could relax. Maybe have her two squares of Galaxy as a treat after the baked potato and . . . hang on. Wasn't that Richard's key in the lock?

"Hi." She brushed her cheek against his. "How did it go?"

Richard shrugged. "Waste of time. They made it plain within five minutes they were looking for someone younger."

"But they're not allowed to say that nowadays. And they'd have seen your age from the CV."

"Probably hadn't read it properly." Richard spoke with the resigned tone of someone who'd been unemployed for nearly a year. "There's always next week's interview."

"It's not fair." Mel put a cup of coffee in front of him. "Dragging you up to town on a Saturday for nothing when . . ."

"Come on, Mel." Richard put a hand on hers. "There's no point going over that again. Isn't that your mobile ringing?"

"Yes. Bother. Where did I put it? It's stopped."

"It's started again." Richard picked up the *Telegraph Weekend* section. "Look. It's under this. Hello? Sharon? Yes, this is Amy's dad. What?"

He turned and looked at her with the kind of look that their son used to give her when he'd hurt himself and expected her to fix it. "Can you say that again?"

And somehow, just by looking at her husband's face, Mel knew exactly what he was going to say.

CHAPTER
FOUR

Janie

"There's been a bit of an accident apparently, towards Cornmarket," said Janie, pretending to study her list even though the words were — as usual — making funny shapes on the page. "So the wedding car was almost ten minutes late picking up the bride."

"Not very good, is it?" snapped Linda.

That's right, Janie wanted to say. Blame me for that one too. "Well, there's not a lot we can do about it, I'm afraid. Maybe it will give the groom a chance to do a runner. Sorry — only joking."

Sadly, Linda's sense of humour was the Limited Edition variety. "Anyway," continued Janie quickly, "the problem over the glasses at the reception has been sorted. The flowers look lovely — I popped in this morning to check — and the taxi's booked to pick up the new Mr and Mrs Foster to take them to the airport."

Linda sniffed unwillingly, as though hoping Janie had got something wrong. Ever since that last warning, Janie felt Linda couldn't wait for her next mistake which would definitely ensure the boot. It wasn't fair. As she'd told Becky during their last heart to heart, it wasn't as though she'd done anything really awful. Just a series of small problems like ordering deep red roses instead of white freesias.

If it hadn't been for the fact that the bride hated red roses because her groom used to send them to his previous fiancée, it might not have mattered so much. She sighed. Working for a wedding organiser should be fun not stressful.

"What time is the flight?"

Janie glanced down at her list, trying to make sense of the figures. "Eighteen hundred hours. They only have to be there two hours before with these tickets because . . ."

"Eighteen hundred hours!" Linda screamed, her blue vein standing out in the middle of her forehead. The stress vein, Janie called it. It always sprang to attention in an emergency or a potential disaster. "But that's six o'clock. They'll need to be picked up by 2p.m. at the latest, which means they're going to miss most of their wedding reception."

Janie felt a cold prickle of fear. Why did people have to use a twenty-four-hour clock? It was so confusing. What was wrong with saying 6p.m. instead of 18.00 which made you think of 8p.m.? And why couldn't she remember that "recepshun" was actually spelt "reception"?

"I'm sorry. I honestly don't know how that happened. Look, I'll re-book the taxi and . . ."

Linda's vein threatened to burst its banks. "But what about missing their wedding party? What kind of start is

31

that going to be to their married life, let alone the impact on our business?"

Her fists were clenched so tightly that for a moment, Janie felt in danger of being assaulted. "Look, I'm sorry." The words seemed woolly as they came out of her mouth. Confrontation always did that to her. "It's my mistake. At least, I think it was. Let me just check the airline hadn't changed the flight at the last minute in which case we could claim compensation and . . ."

Linda was so close now she could smell the mouthwash on her breath. "There won't be any compensation either for us or for you. Because it was your mistake. You're fired, Janie. And don't expect any references."

When this sort of thing happened, Janie had learned, the best thing to do was to take a walk. Not a hike, as Linda and previous bosses had suggested, but a nice calm walk along the river. At this time of the year, only hardy tourists or inebriated students were out there punting but there were plenty of ducks to look at and the odd brave naked swimmer at Parson's Pleasure. She and Becky had swum there naked once, after their A-level results had come out. It had been freezing cold but worth it just to be shocking.

It had been soon after that that Becky had met Steve at uni, got a job on a magazine and had two children in her early twenties, all in such quick succession that everyone — including Janie who'd never felt as old as her birth certificate — was taken aback. "Just because your parents have split up, doesn't mean you have to do all this, you know," she'd tried saying. "You can make your own security. It's much better because you won't let yourself down."

The irony, mused Janie, as she sat down on the river bank and got out her sketch pad, was that some people would think that it was Janie who had let herself down. Lots of people had problems reading and writing, as Mac was always saying, but still managed to get decent jobs. Besides, she didn't always make mistakes. What about that nice couple, the Wilsons-to-be who'd come in last week and been really impressed by her suggestions?

Blast! If she hadn't been so stupid, she might still have a job which she actually didn't want, apart from the fact that it paid the bills on the tiny cottage which she and Mac rented. How could she apply for another job when she couldn't even fill in an application form without someone helping her?

"Laid back, that's what you are," her mother used to say exasperatedly. But what was wrong with that? Too many people were all het up like poor old Becky who hadn't been the same since that magazine had taken over her life. They hadn't had a good old natter for ages now since Becky couldn't take calls at work and when she was at home, she was always flapping over the kids.

Kids. Janie watched the pencil sketching an outline of the bridge above with an imaginary figure on it, looking down on her. That was the only thing she wouldn't mind being committed to. Recently, she'd caught herself looking at a pushchair or two and thinking that actually, she wouldn't mind a little thing like that with a wispy top knot. After all, she'd been a pretty good godmother, hadn't she, apart from the time when she'd mislaid Ben on the London Eye? Even then, it had only been twenty minutes before she'd found him and promptly bribed him with a Hamleys trip to never ever tell his mother.

Not bad, she thought, glancing down at her sketch. The imaginary figure had acquired a face. A rather kind face with the suggestion of a beard. Why was it that she could draw — and paint a bit — but not understand the words that jumped out at her from the page?

An ambulance screamed by, and she could almost feel the wind of its movement as it shot down New College Lane. Really, thought Janie, walking on back up to Cornmarket, they shouldn't go so fast and wasn't it weird that its lights looked so pretty — like sapphire blue Christmas tree lights — when it actually meant something so much more serious?

"Hello, my friend!"

A small dark woman, wearing a headscarf and what looked like a bale of rust-brown and grey-striped cloth around her, waved a copy of *Big Issue* at her.

Friend? She'd never seen her before.

"Sorry. I don't have any money. I've just been sacked."

"Please, my friend, come here."

She spoke in a heavy accent (Turkish?) and reluctantly, Janie drew near. The *Big Issue* lady was sitting on a small stool outside Boots. Surprising she hadn't been moved on.

"You have a nice face."

Janie was always surprised at the way some people looked at her. Not that she considered herself particularly pretty but there were those — like Mac — who seemed to find her dark looks very striking. Or maybe they stared because of those pink highlights she'd put in herself last week. She usually changed the colour to suit her mood. Next month, she rather fancied midnight blue or perhaps bright green.

But compliment or not, she still wasn't parting with £1.50.

"Please give me your hand."

Something made her hold out her palm. The *Big Issue* lady turned it over, stroking the creases. "You have a boyfriend. You have had him some time but he is not the one."

Although Janie had been telling herself the same thing, she nevertheless felt a slight flutter of disappointment. "New opportunities will open up and you mustn't say no. You must be brave. Very brave."

She was holding her hand more firmly now and looking into her eyes. It was all Janie could do not to burst out laughing.

"You do not believe me." The *Big Issue* lady gave her the kind of look that Becky's mum's dog did when she wouldn't give him some food from her plate.

"Yes, yes, I do. Here. Take this."

The *Big Issue* lady tucked the coins into the voluminous cloth dress. "Thank you, my friend." She waved the magazine. "See you next week perhaps?"

Now why had she done that? It wasn't as if she could even read the thing. Crossing the road, she just stepped out of the way of the ambulance which was now screaming its way back from Cornmarket and up towards the hospital. They'd closed the lane, she could see. Must have been a nasty accident.

New opportunities will open and you mustn't say no? Her mobile began to vibrate in her pocket and she fumbled for it, hoping it was Mac rather than Linda.

"Becky! How amazing! I was just thinking of you. How are my godkids?"

"OK."

"Well you don't sound OK. What's wrong?"

Becky's voice was flatly quiet. "Dad's getting married again."

"Really?" Janie struggled to remember when she'd last seen Becky's dad. When they'd been at school, they'd lived in each other's houses, even after her friend's parents had split up. Then she'd seen much more of Helen who had been so much warmer and approachable than her own mum. Their house had been her second home until Becks went to uni. "Do you like her?"

"I'm meeting her this week. No one's met her. No one knows who she is or what she's like or why Dad's doing this so fast — he's only known her for two months. It's ridiculous. She could be an axe-murderer or after his money."

Even though she was her best friend, Janie had always considered Becky to be rather selfish. Maybe it was because Helen had overcompensated after the split; always trying to give Becky what she wanted whether it was a new CD player or a pair of designer jeans. But

36

she'd known Becky for so long and, besides, Becky was one of the few people who instead of feeling sorry for her, treated her the way she was. "Come on, Becky, you want him to be happy, don't you?"

"Course I do but he won't be with her."

Janie laughed. "You don't know that. Make up your mind when you meet her."

"I suppose so. How are you doing, anyway?"

"Me? Well, I've just been sacked from the wedding shop because of some confusion over timing so I'm out of work again. But don't worry. Something will come up. And I've just had this weird encounter with some . . ."

"Stop!" Becky's voice was squeaking with excitement. "I've just had this fantastic idea! You can arrange Dad's wedding. You've had enough experience. It will give you a job and . . ."

"But I don't work for a wedding company any more."

"So? Start your own. He doesn't have to know you're his first customer. And to be honest, Janie, the reason none of your jobs have worked out is because you're not good at working for anyone else. I've told you that before. You need to set up on your own. You can do it from home to begin with and you've got all the contacts . . . It's a brilliant idea."

Don't turn down new opportunities . . . Was this what that *Big Issue* lady had been referring to? "But suppose your dad and his fiancée don't want me to do it?"

"They will." Becky's voice sounded grimly determined. "He owes me. Besides, they're not getting married until November. That gives you nearly nine months to practise. And if they do cancel it, I'll make sure you get paid in full. Go on, Janie. You can't lose. Can you?"

CHAPTER
FIVE

Becky

He wanted her blessing! For God's sake. Sure, Dad. I really approve of you marrying a woman you've only known for two months — and who I haven't even met — who's fifteen years younger than you, according to the yarn she's spun you.

Becky's fingers sweated as she scrolled down the cursor. Monique. What kind of name was that anyway? Sounded like one of those lurid paperbacks she'd devoured as a young teenager.

Monique Brown. There were plenty of Browns in that part of London so it was just as well she'd got the full address out of dad under the pretence of agreeing to see her the following week. One of the pluses about working for a tabloid magazine was that staff had access to data such as the electoral roll or other less uptight institutions, which could tell you not just where someone lived but what they did, how old they were and other vital statistics if you were checking out your father's future bride.

Bride! The word made her want to retch. "Don't you think you're overreacting?" Steve had asked at breakfast in between wiping Ben's nose and feeding Daisy spoonfuls of over-sugared cereal (the only kind the kids would eat). "Your parents have been divorced for years. They're entitled to get married again."

"I know that but . . ."

"Mum? Did you know that bees can have sex? It said so on the Discovery Channel."

"InaminuteBen. I don't mind Dad getting married — no, Daisy, don't smear that stuff in my hair — although I suppose it would take a bit of getting used to. But we don't know her, do we? She could be anyone!"

Which was exactly why an hour and twelve minutes later she, Becks, was sitting at her screen when she should be getting ready for the emergency conference with the editor, trying to find out as much about this Monique Brown as possible. There she was! Becky leaned forward, as the small print leapt out at her. "Age: 39. Address: 32a Stanhope Terrace." Sounded like a flat. "Sole occupant."

Bloody hell. She'd heard of her. In fact, they'd got a press release from her the other day about some celebrity. A pushy company with — no doubt — a pushy owner.

What had Dad got himself into this time?

The only good thing was that she'd managed to get a job out of it for Janie. Becky never thought of her friend without a wry smile and an automatic shake of the head. Janie, with her perky, elfin looks and mismatching colours; always smiling; always getting into scrapes; always choosing the wrong man; always acting and looking at least ten years younger than her age;

always loyal. Friendships like that could be more lasting than marriages. In fact, that might make a feature.

"Becky!" Nancy, the editor's PA, was beckoning her. "We're ready for you!"

Shit. "Just a sec. I need to print this out for the meeting." She couldn't stop now. There was a link to the agency's web page. Fuck. Was that what she looked like? Monique Brown smiled coolly down at her from the screen as Becky gaped back. It wasn't just that Monique really was brown — possibly a splash of Caribbean blood there. It was more that she was gorgeous. Really gorgeous with thick eyelashes and the sort of heavy eyebrows that only women like Bianca Jagger could get away with.

But it was the eyes that got her. There was a harsh, worldly look about them which spoke quite clearly. "I know what I want and I get what I want." Becky's heart fluttered. This woman was as different from her own mother as she could imagine. She didn't just spell danger. She positively oozed it . . .

"Becky!" Nancy's voice had an edge of panic about it. No one ever kept the editor waiting and under any other circumstances, Becky wouldn't even have dreamed of it. But, as she hit the Print button, even the threat of annoying Cat, wasn't enough to stop her. She needed to know more about Monique. Maybe if she sent one tiny quick email to Clarissa on *Vogue* who owed her a favour, and whose brother-in-law was a gossip columnist for one of the tabloid papers, she could . . .

"Someone printed out something on Asian babes?" Bel from Celebrities was holding up the picture of Monique from her website. Fuck. The printer was used by the entire office. She should have got there first.

"She's not Asian, she's from the West Indies," retorted Becky, leaping up from her chair to grab it. "Thanks. Sorry, Nancy. I'm ready now."

"So you see, we have a problem." Cat tapped her immaculate finger nails on the desk. Pity the editor couldn't keep the rest of herself in such good shape, thought Becky. She'd personally ensured through rigorous exercise and diet that she'd got back to a decent size 10 after the children but Cat didn't seem to have made any such effort. Oh, God, children. She needed to find out if Monique had any.

"Becky, perhaps you could let us know what your opinions are on this?"

What? Fuck. She could vaguely remember something about a bidding war which wasn't unusual. Every now and then, a story came up — usually involving some heart-wrenching tale about a mother and child — which every tabloid magazine wanted as an exclusive. So the heartbroken mother would be inundated by offers, each of which was more obscenely high than the other, and — sometimes with the help of a PR firm to "guide" her — would take the most money on offer.

"Er, well, obviously we want the story but we do need to watch our budget."

Cat nodded and Becky thanked her lucky stars for her innate ability to think on her Manolos.

"I mean, after we got the piece on the quads, we said we'd hold fire for a few months."

Cat nodded again, as did most of the others round the conference table. The quads, all of whom had been conjoined at the elbows and hips before their operation, had cost the magazine an arm and a leg as Brian, their MD, had joked.

"But don't you think we ought to splash out on this one?" demanded Lavinia, Cat's deputy, a red-head who hated Becky's guts.

"Why?" Becky returned her gaze steadily.

"Because of the national importance. Sally Smith is an example of today's single mother." Lavinia's eyes flashed dangerously. "You have read the cuts, haven't you?"

Becky was suddenly aware of all eyes on her, including Cat's. "Well of course, I have. And yes, I know she's an example of . . . of today's single mother. But I still think . . ."

"We haven't time to think," Cat cut in sharply. "Do we raise our bid to twelve grand or do we risk losing to someone else?"

"We raise it," said Lavinia firmly.

"We . . ." Becky faltered. If she agreed with Lavinia, she'd look weak. If she disagreed and one of their rivals' circulation rose that week as a result of their exclusive, she'd be blamed. "We get her to do it for nothing."

Lavinia snorted. "Sure and that's going to work, isn't it?"

"Why not?" Becky steeled her voice. If she was going to go down drowning, she'd do it in style. "We'll appeal to her better nature. Tell her that we're not going to prostitute ourselves like other magazines but that we will give her copy approval and tell her story as it is."

Cat nodded thoughtfully. "Go on."

"We'd promise to put at the end of the feature the fact that she hasn't received any money for the feature or that the fee has gone to charity."

"Rather you than me," muttered Lavinia.

"All right." Cat was writing something on her notepad. "Give it a go, Becky. But be quick. I want an answer by the end of the day."

"By the way," Lavinia said as she pushed past her, going out of the office. "You do know that Sally Smith used to be a man, don't you?"

Becky didn't miss a beat. "Of course I did."

"Good. Off you go now. And make sure you read the cuts so you really know what you're talking about."

Shit, shit and double shit. Becky returned to her desk, forcing herself not to make any more Monique Brown queries.

"Sally Smith," she typed in on Noosequest. Of course. How could she have been so daft. This was the woman who used to be a bloke and had adopted fifteen children over the last five years from all over the world. Almost put Madonna in the shade. What's more, this Sally Smith had given up a high-powered career to do so. So she was going to take some persuading.

OK. Time to call in some favours. Maybe Max could help.

"Becky!"

What now? Nancy could be a bloody nuisance at times.

"Did you see those two messages I left? When you were in the meeting?"

"What? No. Where?"

Shit. Nancy had scrawled them on a Post-it note, stuck to the side of her coffee mug.

"Ring Laura. Urgent."
"Your dad says next Tuesday is fine."

Urgent? Nothing was ever urgent in Laura's book. Ignoring Lavinia's beady gaze, she rang the nanny's mobile. "What's wrong?"

She could hardly make out what Laura said with all the screaming in the background.

"I've had enough, Becky, that's what," drawled Laura. "I'm packing my bags. Or, as you English say, handing in my notice."

CHAPTER
SIX

Helen

"Mum, what should I do? I can't afford to lose Laura. She's the only one who's stayed this long."

Long? Is that what you called three months, wondered Helen as she snipped away at Doris Evans's clematis with the mobile wedged between her shoulder and ear. When Becky and Adam had been little, Helen had had au pairs and each one had stayed at least a year; one, she seemed to recall, for nearly two. But then again, you needed to envelop them into the family; make them feel wanted; spend time on them rather like a child. Not expect them to work a fifteen-hour day as Becky and Steve did.

"Tell her you'll cut down her hours." Bother. She'd taken that stem too far back now. "And give her a week's holiday."

"But how can I?"

Becky was close to tears; she could sense that. She could also hear frenetic voices in the background and some high-pitched woman shouting for something that sounded like "copy". Or was it coffee? What a life! Couldn't Becky see she was trying to do the impossible? "I'll come over one day a week," she heard herself saying. "Ask Laura which day she wants off and I'll change my jobs."

"Oh, Mum. Thanks so much."

Becky's grateful voice — so different from the usual sulky you-don't-understand-mum tone — made her feel better, although heaven knew how she was going to fix it. She had more clients than she could deal with as it was and she really shouldn't have taken on the Old Rectory. It was madness. Sheer, utter madness. Maybe she should ring up and cancel. "You'll never guess where I was last week," she began.

"Yes, Nancy, I'm just coming. Tell Cat I'll be one second. Sorry, mum. Got to dash. I'll ring tonight."

Helen heard the phone click and tried not to feel deflated. It was her job; she couldn't help it, poor kid. It wasn't the kind of life she'd have wanted at that age and it certainly wasn't the sort of future she'd have hoped for for her daughter. But they all did things so differently nowadays. Look at Steve. He was never home either but somehow they seemed to manage.

Helen gave the clematis a final clip. In some ways, she was secretly relieved to have been part of that last generation where women weren't expected to work. Yet she couldn't help wondering if Geoff would have found her more interesting if she'd had a career of her own. And perhaps she'd have been less bored herself . . .

"Like a cuppa, Helen? I've just put the kettle on." Doris Evans appeared at her back door, wearing her blue and white checked pinny which she had never been seen without. Doris was one of Helen's regulars: she used to "do" for her in the old days when the children had been small but now, riddled with arthritis, she could barely do anything for herself. Helen did her garden as a favour, not feeling able to take anything. Besides, Doris was looking after her sick brother at the moment. Money was probably tight.

"Ridiculous," David called it. But then again, he hadn't known Doris for as long as she had.

"Love one. Thanks, Doris." She accepted the mug gratefully.

"Hear your Geoff is getting married again."

Helen spluttered slightly on her tea. "That's right," she said, dabbing the stain on her shirt with a tissue. "News travels fast."

"Went to see the vicar, I hear." Doris was nodding with urgency as though in agreement with herself. "Just before that poor girl was knocked down."

Sometimes Helen wondered if Doris didn't make sense on purpose. "What poor girl?"

"Didn't you hear?" Doris's eyes glinted with the anticipated pleasure of delivering news which hadn't been heard before.

"That woman vicar's daughter. Knocked down by a hit and run, she was. In Oxford. Still on a life-support machine, she is."

Helen felt a cold shiver running through her. God, how awful. How had the poor mother found out? Maybe she'd had one of those calls that every parent dreaded . . . Even now her kids were grown up, she still panicked if Adam hadn't emailed for a few weeks or if she couldn't get hold of Becky on her mobile.

"She's not very old, is she?"

"Just seventeen." Doris clearly knew all the facts. "Your Geoff apparently spoke to her when he called at the vicarage to arrange the wedding. Soon is it, then?"

The clematis zoomed in and out of Helen's vision like a distorted painting or badly focused photograph. "I don't know. How awful. I mean, that poor girl. Do they think she'll make it?"

Doris clucked her tongue. "Touch and go, I heard. Still, that's life, isn't it? The way these kids drive nowadays. It's a wonder they don't all kill themselves." She peered at the clematis. "You've taken that back a bit, haven't you?"

"It needed to be." Helen's sharp tone surprised herself. "It will soon grow and you'll get more flowers. Thanks for the tea."

She put the still-full, slightly chipped mug down by the step.

Doris glared disapprovingly at the slosh of grey liquid which had had at least two sugars, even though Helen had said on countless occasions that she didn't take it. "But you haven't finished."

"I know. Sorry. I've got to dash. See you next week."

Helen found herself almost running to the comfort of the van. That poor vicar! She'd met her once at the local show and been struck by how young and pretty she was. Tears pricked her eyes. She'd die if anything happened to her two, and yet it happened. A vision shot into her head of how she'd feel and how she'd have to tell Geoff: Geoff whom she had hardly spoken to for years.

Amazing really, thought Helen, as she tried to get the van heating to work, that they didn't bump into each other, considering they only lived a few miles apart in neighbouring villages. And if Doris knew about the wedding, that meant God knows how many others knew about it as well. People who could still remember Helen and Geoff being married; people who had been born and bred in these parts, whose world revolved around Little Rington and its orbit.

Helen picked nervously at her frayed cuticles; often a casualty of the job. Perhaps she should text him. Something very casual. Congrats on yr marriage. Yes, that would do. She'd deliberately stopped herself from asking Becky how their meeting had gone. After all, it was nothing to do with her now. Nothing at all.

She stopped off at the cottage before the next client, partly to make herself a cheese sandwich and also to change her shirt which was splattered with mud. Yanking off her boots against the black metal shoe scraper, she put them next to the much larger pair which had once belonged to Geoff. It didn't do any harm, she told herself, to have a man-sized pair of boots outside the house, suggesting to strangers that there were two people inside, instead of one single woman with a live-out boyfriend.

"Hi." David looked up from mending her kitchen cupboard which had come off its hinges last night and which, annoyingly, she hadn't been able to put back herself. "You're early." He spoke with a mouth full of nails. Such an annoying habit! Supposing he swallowed one?

"Just thought I'd make a sandwich. Want one?"

"No, thanks." David spat out a nail before hammering it in. "I'm going back to my place after this to pick something up."

She felt an absurd flutter of relief. Occasionally, one of them would suggest moving in together but then the other would make some weak excuse. It wasn't that they were averse to the idea; more that they never seemed to have the inclination at the same time.

Quite why, Helen wasn't sure. On paper, David was a rare man. Not currently married — most important — although twice divorced which was one time too many in Helen's book. Tall. Capable. Loyal (as far as she could tell). A man of his own means although carpentry hadn't been his first career. Like her, he had come to his love late; before that, he'd been a frustrated accountant which was useful because he could do her books.

"Geoff's getting married again," she said, casually, cutting herself a wedge of mature cheddar and nibbling the crumbs as they scattered on the bread board.

"Really?"

She could feel his interest burning from where she was standing.

"Mmm. Not sure when but he's already been to see the vicar. Talking of who, did you hear . . ."

"Yes, I did."

Shit. She should have thought. One of the reasons that David's first marriage had broken up was because his son had been killed in a car crash on the school run. It had been years ago but there were some things you could never forget. His wife had gone slightly loopy apparently which wasn't surprising.

"Anyway, she's called Monique. Geoff's bride, that is. Probably some French model."

"And what does Becky think?" He spoke stiffly, hurt at her crass thoughtlessness about the vicar's daughter. She could apologise but two years of knowing — or rather not knowing — David had taught her it was best to ignore it.

"She's not keen." Helen laughed shortly. "As you might expect."

"Indeed." David gave the screwdriver a final twist. Becky didn't approve of David either, a fact she barely bothered to conceal. It was, he joked, as though she expected her mother to remain celibate for the rest of her days. "Well, maybe it's time she learned that other people have a life of their own."

Helen nodded. "Maybe."

"I'll be off then." David brushed her cheek and for a minute, she felt herself stirring. Pulling him to her, she felt him responding too.

"Unless . . ." she began.

David looked down on her, his face softening. "I haven't time. Sorry. But I could come over tonight. My turn to make supper and I'll bring some logs for the woodburner too."

She nodded, feeling strangely disappointed. "OK. See you later."

* * *

Robin Michaels opened the back door just as she was about to knock. "Sorry. Did I startle you?"

He had but she was too polite to say so. "No. It's fine. I just wasn't quite sure whether I should have come to the front."

He laughed; a nice rich warm laugh like the home-made onion soup she'd just gulped down from the thermos in the front of the van. "If there's one thing I've learned since moving to the country, it's that no one uses their front doors. Another thing is that it's never your house; it's always the name of the previous owner. People keep saying to me: 'Oh, you've bought The Old Rectory, haven't you? The Jenkins' house.'"

Helen stiffened. Surely this was where she ought to tell him that before the Jenkins and before the Wilsons, it had been her house. Hers and Geoff's . . .

"I don't know where you want to start." He was striding ahead of her now, pulling on a rather newish-looking Barbour. "It's all so overgrown. I'm sorry."

"Don't be. It's what I'm here for." Her eyes were darting around, greedily, drinking it all in. There was the magnolia which she'd planted to mark their fifth wedding anniversary. And there was the buddleia which the children used to hover over, trying to catch butterflies. How that had spread! But where was the lilac tree? She could hardly ask.

"We've got a pond over there but it's horribly overgrown."

Helen had a sudden flash of hauling out a drenched six-year-old Becky. ("I was only catching tadpoles,

53

mum.") "We'll get to it, in time. How about starting with this border? Those irises need thinning out."

"Wonderful." Robin glanced up towards the house and Helen followed his gaze. For a second, she thought she glimpsed a face but then it vanished. "My wife." He shifted awkwardly. "She likes to look through the window."

"Pity it's not warmer or she could come out."

"I don't think so," Geoff sounded flustered. "She likes to stay inside — at least, she has since she got ill."

There was an awkward silence. Helen put on her gloves which were stiff with dried mud. "Right, I'll get cracking then, shall I?"

She waited until he walked back to the house, before kneeling down on the grass and getting out her small fork. "Hello," she whispered softly. "I'm back."

CHAPTER
SEVEN

Mel

Richard's words were coming at her like a distant lifeguard's tannoy from across the bay, rather like the one at Brighton where they'd taken the children on holiday one summer. She could hear the urgency in her husband's tone but there seemed to be some blockage in her ears so she could only make out the odd word and phrase.

Accident. Driver didn't stop. Sharon jumped out of the way just in time. Amy was texting on her mobile phone. Didn't see car coming. Coma. Intensive Care.

They were going that way now. At least, her legs were trying to but it felt as though they were pushing their way through seaweed or something undefinably thicker; something rather nasty. The bit below her breasts and above her navel felt as though it had been shot away and she glanced down, expecting to see a large bloody gaping wound. At the same time, she felt an enormous weight below her collar bone like a mass of food which had to be brought up when you don't want to be sick but know you have to be, in order to feel better.

"This way." Richard was trying to guide her by the grip on his arm and she tried to shake him off.

"I know the way," she wanted to say but nothing would come out. Of course she knew. Didn't she come here every week as part of her pastoral duties? Last month, it had been to sit by the side of an elderly parishioner who had fallen down the stairs while staying at her daughter's home. The daughter had been beset with guilt (the top stair carpet had been loose) and she, Mel, had sat with her, holding her hand and trying to explain that in God's eyes, no one needed to feel guilty any more. The woman had died the following week and the funeral had, apparently, been a large, jolly affair with lots of well-rounded ladies from the Women's Institute with several jam scones afterwards and no mention of stairs or loose carpet.

They were walking now, down the long corridor with its little yellow arrows on the floor and bright posters on each side of the wall, exhorting you to tell the x-ray department if you were pregnant or to contact the local authority if you were ill in hospital and couldn't pay your rent.

Amy had been on her mobile, Richard had said. That's why she hadn't seen the car. Mel could visualise it all too clearly. Her daughter was always walking around, mobile clamped to ear. "You'll get radiation poisoning," she'd said countless times. Had she ever warned her not to use it while crossing the road in case it deflected her concentration? She couldn't remember.

Past the Chapel of Rest. Mel knew that one all right. Some chapel! A bare room with pale beech chairs; as pale as the parishioners or rather non-parishioners which Mel had sat with and comforted after someone had died. For some reason, very few visited before the death so by the time they got there, there were no more "It might be all rights" or even "I'm afraid it's touch and go" which did at least contain some margin for recovery. The only hope she could offer then was the higher variety, when all her "clients" craved was a modern-day Lazarus miracle.

"She's not dead," Mel said and this time it came out aloud. Richard's grip on her arm tightened and she suddenly realised he wasn't guiding her after all. He was hanging on to her for support. Was that in her role of a mother or a spiritual advisor, she wondered. Richard had always had a slight problem with her vicar status. He'd never admitted it, despite probing on her part, but she could see his point. It couldn't be easy — even in today's age — for a man to accept his wife was virtually "married" to Someone Else.

Round the corner and into Intensive Care. A nurse immediately glided from a side room as though she'd been waiting. "Mel," she said simply and Mel recognised her as the sister whom she'd sat with last month while the old lady who'd fallen down the stairs slipped away. Mel always encouraged her parishioners to call her by her first name, even though the older set sometimes took some persuading. It was alien to them, just like the drop-in coffee mornings or the word screen at Sunday service.

"Mel," the nurse repeated or maybe she didn't; perhaps it was her ears. "I'm so sorry."

57

Sorry? Was it over then? Mel began to tremble and she could feel a trickle of urine oozing into her pants. "She's not . . . she's not . . ."

Why couldn't she say the words? God, what are you doing to me? *Talitha cumi. Talitha cumi.*

"Mel, Mel." Richard's voice was booming now as though he had that tannoy close to her ear. "She's not dead. She's still in a coma. Hold on to me. That's right."

And suddenly there she was on a bed in a room on her own. A pale face, lying on her back laced with wires and machines. Her daughter. Her little girl who she'd given birth to all those years ago. Her firstborn whom she'd cradled in her arms, wishing desperately she didn't have to go back to the office in three months time.

In a flash, she could see it all. Amy riding her bike for the first time without training wheels, her blonde plaits — exactly the same honey colour as her own — flying out on either side. Amy grinning after the tooth fairy had left a shiny 50p to make up for the ugly gap. Amy shutting herself away in her bedroom to "do her homework" when she was really on her phone.

Dear God. The mobile. "It was me! Christ, Richard. It was me. It was my fault."

Richard didn't even turn to look at her; he was, she could see even in the middle of his distress, rooted to the mass of white sheet and sharp wires in front of him. "What are you talking about, Mel?"

"I phoned her. I wanted to know she had got there safely because Sharon had only just passed her test.

58

Don't you remember? Then I texted because I was worried that her answerphone was on. She texted me back and that's why she wasn't looking properly when she crossed the road . . ."

"Shhh." The nurse was holding her other arm, stroking her skin rhythmically with her thumb as though she was massaging it. "These kids are on their mobiles all the time. My son's the same."

Her son. Mel could remember now. While the old lady had been dying, she and the sister had talked in hushed tones about their children and how hard it was bringing up teenagers. And now God was punishing her for complaining; for moaning about Amy and Josh because they wouldn't get up on time or ran up huge phone bills or answered back.

"Is she going to be all right?"

Richard's voice cut through the stroking and Mel reached out, craving the calm comforting movement to continue. "We don't know." The sister's voice was calm, smooth and falsely reassuring. "She's got severe head injuries, I'm afraid. The next few hours are going to be crucial. The neurologist will hopefully be here before long and he can tell you more."

She was pulling up two blue plastic seats. "Sit down. Talk to her. It might help."

The daughter of the old woman who had fallen down the stairs had talked to her mother. She'd spoken about the memories; the hot summer days when they'd picked blackberries in the fields and gone home to strain them through muslin suspended from an upturned three-legged stool. She'd spoken about how

59

important her mother was to her and how she'd always loved her. Afterwards, to her disappointment, the daughter had requested a male vicar to do the funeral. She was sorry, she said, but her mother wouldn't have felt comfortable with a woman. So Mel had had to ask the archdeacon to find someone from outside the parish.

"Amy," she began awkwardly. "Amy, can you hear me?"

No answer.

"Amy, this is Mum. I'm sorry I called you this afternoon. I'm sorry I distracted you while you were crossing. I only did it because I love you."

Someone was putting a soft white tissue in her lap; a tissue so insubstantial that it disintegrated in seconds. "Amy, please wake up. Don't die. God, listen to me. I'm telling you. You're not to let my daughter die. Do you hear me?"

It wasn't until she felt Richard nudging her in the ribs that she found she must have fallen asleep. For a second's grace — if that — she "forgot" about Amy and then it all came flooding back.

"Amy," she began.

"Nothing's changed." Richard's tone was flat. "The neurologist hasn't turned up either. Been called away apparently to an urgent case."

But Amy was urgent, wasn't she? Mel looked at her daughter's pale face, obscured as it was by white bandages. Outside, it was dark; how could that have happened so fast?

"Mel." Richard was speaking again. "One of us needs to get back to Josh. He's on his own."

My God! Josh! "Does he know?"

Richard shook his head. "We agreed to tell him together when we got back. Remember?"

No. She didn't.

"He's got to come in here. See her." It was a gigantic effort to find the words in her head, let alone get them out.

"Is that wise?"

She nodded. How many times had she seen this before? Distraught relatives at a hospital bed, crying and weeping because they "hadn't been told" in time.

"All right." Richard rubbed his eyes. They looked red and paper-thin. "I'll bring him in."

After he'd gone, Mel pulled her chair closer up to her daughter. "Amy. Amy. Listen to me. It's Mum. It's time to get up. Please."

Again, she must have dozed off because when someone touched her shoulder gently, she sprang up so fast that something clicked in her neck. "Amy?"

"No, Mel, it's me."

Surely the sister should have gone off duty by now? Perhaps she'd stayed. Mel could imagine the whispers in the nurses' office. Vicar's daughter. Run over. Such a shame.

"Mel, can you hear me? That's a good girl. There's a policeman here to see you. They think they've got the driver who ran Amy over. He needs to see you."

The driver? "No!" Mel leapt to her feet. "Why should I see him? What's he got to say that could possibly bring my daughter back? What kind of a sonofabitch doesn't stop when he knocks a kid over?"

Appalled, Mel heard a string of obscenities tumble out of her mouth as though someone else was saying them. Obscenities she never knew she knew; words which she'd only occasionally heard the children using.

But if she was shocking herself, it was nothing compared to the horrified expression on the sister's face. "Not the driver, Mel. It's not him you need to see. It's the policeman. He's waiting outside. Are you ready?"

CHAPTER
EIGHT

Janie

A wedding business! Her own boss. Janie Jones' Wedding Services. No, that didn't sound right. Janie's Wedding Belles. Too twee. Still she'd think of something. Maybe she'd be like that wedding planner in the film and end up with the groom. No. She didn't need that. Not with Mac.

Janie almost skipped through the little wooden gate, the bag of warm croissants (bought to celebrate after Becky's brilliant idea) under her arm. After working so late last night, Mac would probably still be in bed even though somewhere she could hear a church striking three. For a second, a vision of the disappointed bride and groom, deprived of their reception, flitted through her mind. Oh, well. It would be a test for them to see if they could get through the honeymoon without a major argument. When she ran her own business, she promised herself, she'd make sure there were no more mistakes.

"Mac!" she called out, flinging her coat on the little rack he'd put up the other month. "Mac. Guess what! I've . . ."

Later, Janie couldn't even remember exactly what she said after that. All she can recall is one lump —

Mac — on the side of the bed, his large hairy arm flung over the side the way he always slept. And curled up beneath the other arm, was an extremely small, extremely blonde and extremely naked woman.

At precisely the same time that Janie heard the scream coming out of her mouth, the blonde sat bolt upright, croaked "Shit", grabbed a t-shirt (which turned out later to be one of hers) and scooted out of the door.

Mac, meanwhile, continued snoring; great heavy nasal snores which shook the creaky bed springs.

"Wake up, you bastard." She shook him furiously. Still no reaction. Mac was notoriously hard to wake up, whatever the time of day. Right! Janie's eye fell on a quarter-full bottle of Speckled Hen, perched perilously on the rug next to the bed. She was always telling him not to bring drink to bed but this time, it seemed more than fortuitous.

"Fucking hell." Now it was Mac's turn to sit bolt upright, wiping beer from his eyes. "Fucking hell, I'm soaked and all. What did you do that for?"

"What did I do that for?" Janie repeated the words in disbelief, noting with satisfaction that his hair was saturated. "How can you even ask that? And don't rub your face with my sheets. Who was she? And how could you?"

Light, she could see, was beginning to dawn in Mac's eyes. "Who was who . . ." he started to say weakly.

"Don't give me that." Janie was yanking the sheets off him now. "Get up and out. I told you the last time.

I'm not standing for it again. I was an idiot to take you back before. Now go."

"Where?" Mac stood there shivering, like an overgrown school boy. Why was it, thought Janie, that men looked so weird when they were naked and unaroused. And how extraordinary that that funny little thing hanging down between their legs, caused so much trouble with the world. She reached for a handy pair of scissors.

"What you doing with those?" Mac looked terrified now, as well he might.

Janie snipped the scissors open and shut. "I'm going to give you a trim if you don't beat it right now."

"You're mad, know that? Not just dyslexic but mad as well."

One snip. That was all it would take.

"Ouch!"

Janie brandished the lock of greasy black hair, dripping with Speckled Hen. "It will hurt a lot more next time if you're not out of here."

"I'm going. I'm going. I'll come back for my stuff later."

"Forget it," she yelled just as he slammed the door. Sinking down on the bed, she promptly jumped up again, forgetting it was wet. The funny thing was that she wasn't really surprised. Mac had never been right for her. Marjorie, her neighbour, was always saying that. But somehow she'd thought that after eight months — her record — he might just be as near to right as she was ever going to get.

I should be crying, she thought, as she went through the little back door and climbed over the small wooden fence which separated her garden from her neighbour's. I should be angry or numb with shock or . . . well, something.

"Afternoon, dear." Marjorie raised her bifocals. "Did I hear a little rumpus going on inside your house, just now?"

"Mac was in bed with someone else." Janie took the chair that Marjorie proffered. "He didn't even say sorry."

Marjorie sniffed. "Well I'm not and nor should you be. I've told you before, dear. You can do much better than an out of work artist. Cup of Earl Grey? There's plenty in the pot. Besides, if you'd asked me, I could have told you about her. Small and blonde, was she? Or was that last week's?"

What?

"Come on, darling — you're not deaf like me. Yes, I probably should have said something but you wouldn't have listened. It was better that you saw it with your own eyes. Looked as though she was the type who needed her five a day, don't you think? And I'm not talking fruit and veg here. Talking of which, have a slice of lemon with that. Why don't you find someone in the paper? The newspaper does a rather good dating service one day a week."

It wasn't easy, thought Janie, as she took the neatly folded copy of the *Daily Telegraph*, to keep up. Marjorie had this habit of leaping from one subject to the other, often without any apparent link. Now she

66

was gesticulating at the open Obituary column. "No one in it today, for a change. Rather dull compared with last week's."

Janie took a small sip of tea. She hated Earl Grey but didn't like to offend Marjorie who presumed everyone drank it. "Two, wasn't it?"

"Three. It had been two the previous week."

How did Marjorie know so many people who were important or grand enough to be seen dead in a posh paper? She began sketching a face of an imaginary professor in the margin of the paper. "When's next week's funeral?"

"Tuesday." Marjorie's face brightened. "Thought I'd wear that rather nice purple outfit from the Jaeger sale. What do you think? You're good on colours."

It was Marjorie's habit to wear very loud funeral outfits. When it was her turn, she insisted, Janie would have to put "Wear Purple" on the invitations.

"Nice one." Janie helped herself to a slice of walnut cake, wondering why she still had an appetite and why she was so bad at choosing men. How could Mac have been so mean?

"It's because he wasn't right for you." Ever since they'd met, some five years ago, when Marjorie had moved in next door, she'd had this uncanny knack of knowing what Janie was thinking.

"Maybe." Janie was chewing thoughtfully. "Just before all this happened, my friend Becky rang."

"Nice girl." Marjorie nodded approvingly. "Tense but nice."

"She wants me to set up a wedding service."

"On your own?" Marjorie frowned. "But your boss wouldn't like you taking business away, would she?"

"My boss? Oh. Yes. Forgot to tell you." Janie took another slice of cake. "I got sacked over some kind of timing issue."

"What did you say, dear?" Marjorie twiddled with her hearing aid. "I'm afraid this is playing up today."

"I got the time wrong. For today's wedding." Janie shuffled awkwardly in her seat. "Well, not the wedding itself but the honeymoon. So I got sacked."

"Tracked? Who's tracking you?"

"I got fired."

"There's no need to shout, dear. I heard you the first time. Dismissed. Oh dear. That's a shame. What will you do now?"

"I told you. Set up on my own. Becky's dad's getting married again and she wants me to organise it."

"Well don't get it wrong or he won't ask you again. That was a joke, dear, by the way, although my generation seems to be getting married again much more than they used to. You'd think they'd learn, wouldn't you?"

Marjorie, Janie had learned, had been married many years ago before being widowed at the age of forty. ("One of those things, dear. You just have to get on with it.")

"What do you think about starting my own business?"

"Have you got enough money?"

Janie had thought about that briefly. "I'll ask for a deposit up front from each client."

"Pity you can't do funerals, as well," murmured Marjorie. "I'm not looking forward to Tuesday. I just know it's going to be a really drab boring affair. In fact, I wouldn't go except that the reception is at the White Hart and they do a wonderful chocolate pudding."

Janie jumped up excitedly. "But we could! We could do funerals. You're always saying they need livening up. Well we'll do it. I was reading an article about green funerals the other week. We could get in wicker caskets."

"And rock groups!" Marjorie's eyes lit up. "That church music gets so predictable. What's that group you're always playing?"

"The Wattevers. We won't get them in person, of course, but we could rig up a music system."

"A what, dear?" Marjorie fiddled with her hearing aid again.

"A music system. Like a tape recorder but bigger." Janie reached across the table and grabbed Marjorie's frail liver-spotted hand. "You know, Marge, we really could be on to something here!"

"But what about the embalming bit?"

Janie's face wrinkled in disgust. "We won't do that side. We'll just organise the service and the reception and the nice bits. I suppose it will mean hob-nobbing with some of the undertakers . . ."

"We can use my personal contacts!" Marjorie's eyes brightened. "And the great thing is that even if we make a couple of cock-ups, the customers can't complain because they'll be all boxed up! Pass me my mobile, can you? It's in my bag."

"What are you doing?"

"Ringing Doris. Her brother's been terribly ill for the past six weeks. I'll tell her not to book anywhere until she's spoken to us."

"You can't do that. He's not even dead yet."

"Well he will be soon. Doris says it will be a relief in more ways than one. Doris? It's me, Marjorie. How's Maurice? Still hanging on. Excellent. Now listen. My young friend Janie and I have had rather a good idea . . ."

CHAPTER
NINE

Becky

Everyone, Becky knew, was itching to leave the office but no one wanted to be the first. It was only 6.30 p.m. and Cat, whose male Finnish nanny would be putting the twins to bed now, showed no signs of emerging from her goldfish bowl.

Could she risk going to the loo again for a nap? She was still shattered after being up half the night with Daisy's new tooth since Steve — who was so much better than her at getting up at night — was still in Dubai.

Stifling a yawn, Becky forced herself to reread the copy on her screen which had been sent in by a news agency. God, it was crap. Really badly written, although the story itself was right up *Charisma*'s street.

"We built up £10,000 worth of debt because we wanted to look like Chantelle" screamed the headline. The story was about three readers who were so desperate to copy celebrity lifestyles and looks that they'd spent thousands on cosmetic surgery and flash clothes despite the credit crunch.

It might have worked if the pictures hadn't been so awful. The "readers" which the news agency had claimed to have found were still so frumpy after all that cosmetic work and new clothes that they looked worse than the "before" shots. Cat would throw it out before conference even started. The only solution was to find some different case histories who looked good — but how? It had to be in by the end of the week.

"Becky? Mind if I go now?"

"What?" She looked up from her screen to see Maddy, a work experience student from a local journalism college hovering nervously next to her. In some ways Maddy reminded her of herself ten years ago; desperate for experience and keen to learn at all costs. Quite pretty too and wearing something that looked rather like that skirt/scarf which Chantelle had been photographed in last week on the front cover of *Closer*.

"Course you can. But just before you do, tell me," she eyed Maddy's skirt again. "Is that designer by any chance?"

"Are you kidding?" She laughed, giving a twirl at the same time. "Got it in Portobello."

Damn. Still . . . "Maddy, would you like to earn a bit of extra cash?"

Silly question. "You bet. I'm skint this month."

"Great. I mean, it's not great you're skint but great that you'd like to do some extra work. It's not that difficult although it will involve you being photographed for the magazine."

Maddy's eyes shone as Becky knew they would. "Fantastic! What's the piece about?"

72

"Oh just something about shopping habits." She'd fill Maddy in later when it was too late for her to change her mind. "You'd need to find me a couple of friends to be in the piece with you. We could pay you each about a hundred quid."

"A hundred quid!" Maddy looked like she'd just picked a winning lucky dip ticket. "That's amazing. Thanks so much."

This was proving easier than she'd thought. "I need some pictures of your friends so we can check them out. Bring them in tomorrow morning, can you? And just one little tiny thing. Don't mention this to Cat. We're not really meant to have staff in the magazine as case histories so I'm doing this for you as a favour."

Maddy frowned. "But won't she recognise me?"

"She probably doesn't even know you're here. Don't take that the wrong way, Maddy. Cat's a very busy woman. Besides, you're only around for another week, aren't you?"

Maddy nodded. "Yes but I was hoping I might be able to come back in the holidays."

Not now. "Let's see how this goes first, shall we? Now off you go and make sure you bring in those pictures tomorrow."

Becky watched Maddy walk jauntily out of the office, swiping the door with her security card. A flicker of guilt flashed through her. Still, it wasn't the first time they'd roped in pretend readers to make up the case histories. But what was a girl to do when the deadline was only 48 hours away? As long as Cat didn't find out, it was worth the risk, especially after that

73

disappointment over losing the bid on the Sally Smith story.

"Still here?" Becky jumped as she suddenly realised Cat was by her shoulder. Had she heard anything?

"I just want to finish editing this copy." She smiled brightly.

Cat smiled approvingly. Her smile was so rare that when she did allow it to crack her face, everyone got scared. "That's what I like to see. Well, I'm off now. See you tomorrow."

There was a tangibly silent air in the office as everyone waited for the click of the security door. By unspoken agreement, no one moved for five minutes until Becky stood up; the signal for everyone else to do the same. There was a chorus of See you tomorrows and a rustle of shoe changing as most of the girls, including Becky, exchanged their high heels for the trainers necessary to negotiate their way through the London rush hour. Becky glanced at her watch. 8p.m. If she was lucky, she might just be home by 9p.m.

"Sorry," she panted, throwing her jacket on to the hall chair next to Steve's suitcase. "The tube stopped for ages between stops. It was awful. No one could move and the air was so stuffy that I could hardly breathe."

"Poor you." Steve, still hot and sweaty from his own journey home, hugged her briefly. He smelt of airports and one-bedded hotel rooms. "How's it been?"

She tried to remember when Steve had left. "Daisy had her jab . . ."

"She had that before I went."

"Right. Course. And Ben went to his iPod party — Laura made him a great costume."

"I know. I took him there."

Had he? Oh, God, it was so hard to keep up. "Oh and Laura threatened to hand in her notice again so mum says she'll come up one day a week to give Laura another day off."

Steve frowned. "Just as well. I only got back myself a few minutes ago and Laura was waiting by the door with her coat on."

"Oh, God. Well, I would have been back earlier if it hadn't been for that tube and some problem at work."

"Becks, there's always a problem at work. What's for dinner? I'm starving."

Fuck. She'd meant to drop in at M&S on the way back but with the tube delay, she'd forgotten. "Well, there might be some eggs so I could whip up an omelette. Sorry. It's been a bit hectic."

"That's OK. An omelette would be great. By the way, your dad rang. He wants you to ring back."

Becky, who was halfway up the stairs to check on the children, stopped. "What did he want this time? To make another Meet Monique date after cancelling the last one?"

"C'mon, Becks. Give him a chance. I told you. He probably blew out of last month because he was nervous. It can't be easy for him."

They'd been through this before. "You mean, I'm not making it easy for him."

Steve shrugged. "You said it. And by the way, don't wake the kids. Laura said it took her ages to get them settled."

Settled? Laura had either been lying or over-optimistic. Daisy was leaping up and down from her bed and had managed to rip her new blue and white spotted Boden PJs in the process, while Ben had clearly never been in his at all and was, instead, glued to his AppleMac. Maybe her mother was right; perhaps it hadn't been a great idea to get him his own PC, even though he only had access to educational games.

"Mum!" Daisy stretched out her arms and Becky gathered her daughter to her, smelling her hungrily. Ugh! What was that smell? "You've done another poo, haven't you? For heaven's sake, Daisy, you're too old for that. No, don't start crying. Shit. Steve — come and give me a hand, can you? Steve?"

Next door, in their bedroom, she could hear the shower. Great. She'd have to do this one on her own.

"Ben, don't touch that. It's Daisy's dirty pull-ups. Ben, I said don't touch!"

Now her mobile was going. Reaching out for some baby wipes to clean her hand first, she knocked the phone on to the floor right into the middle of the filthy nappy. For a minute, Becky thought she was going to be sick. "Now look what you've made me do!" she yelled at Daisy who promptly began yelling even louder.

"What's going on?" Steve stood in the doorway, towel round his waist.

"Can't you see?" Becky glared at him. "Daisy's had an accident. She's nearly four, forcrissake — isn't it time she was clean? I told Laura to talk to the health visitor about it. And I've just dropped my mobile right in the middle of her dirty nappy. *No, Daisy, don't touch it!*"

"Mum, did you know that ostriches are bigger than eagles? It says so on my computer."

"NotnowBen. Oh, Christ. Look she's got it all over her!"

"It's all right." Steve bent down, picked up the mobile, wiped it and handed it to his wife. "Come on you lot, let's get you cleaned up."

"I can't use this!" Becky regarded her slim silver handset with horror. "It's been in shit."

"Well it hasn't stopped it ringing," Steve pointed out. "You'd better answer it."

Gingerly, Becky put it to her ear. "Hello. Yes, Dad, I'm back. Yes, it has been a long day. What? Tonight? Well, I was just going to make supper."

She glanced at Steve who was nodding and putting his thumbs up. Why was her husband so keen to accommodate her father? "I suppose so, although it's very last minute and it's only an omelette. All right. See you then."

Great. That was all she needed. "Come on, you two, off to bed."

"Why?" Ben glowered at her. "You're always saying Dad's never at home. So why can't we stay up and see him?"

"I'm never at home?" spluttered Steve. "Actually, it's your mother who . . ."

"Bed," repeated Becky, shooting him a not-in-front-of-the-children look. "Not in a minute. Now."

"But, Mum! Did you know that the average person has over a million hairs on their head and . . .?"

"I said NOW!"

Dad was passing, he'd said. A likely story. As Steve said, he'd probably summoned up some Dutch courage after a couple of drinks and decided to get the introductions over and done with. Typical of Dad to be so thoughtless! Becky opened the fridge door. It was empty apart from two and a half fromage frais yoghurts and three eggs which were three days past their sell-by date.

That would have been fine for her and Steve but could she stretch it to four omelettes? Fuck. If her father had given her proper notice, she'd have been able to cook a proper meal. She might not want to meet this Monique woman but she didn't want her realising she was a complete domestic disaster.

"Three eggs?" Steve came up from behind her, giving her a let's-make-up cuddle. She knew what that meant but he could forget it after the sort of day she'd just had.

"Why don't I nip out to the deli round the corner?"

Why was he always so nice? And why did she end up sounding like the wicked witch in front of the kids? No wonder Daisy had pushed her away just now. "Sure you don't mind?"

"Course I don't. It will only take me a second."

"Thanks."

She heard him open the front door and at the same time, heard a chorus of voices. Bloody hell. They were early.

"Hi, Dad. Steve's just popping out to get some more food . . ."

Her voice trailed away as she took in the small squat woman standing next to her father. She was wearing a dull grey jacket over a black skirt that wrinkled at her hips, indicating the wearer was at least one size bigger if not two, judging from the undulating waves of fat, rippling under her cherry red blouse. Her hair was longer than in the picture, as though she was trying to look younger. And those legs! Talk about hourglasses strung like hammocks. Despite the way she held herself straight, (as though an ice cube was stuck between her shoulder blades), this woman bore no resemblance at all to the glamour puss she'd seen on the website, apart from her massive and almost indecently huge boobs which were peeping out above the blouse, despite the weather. There had to be some mistake!

Becky tried to find her voice. "Hello, Monique."

The woman was pumping her hand and her double chins were flying up and down at the same time. "It's really nice to meet you, Becky. I've heard so much about you!" Her eyes met Becky's in a don't-fool-with-me look. "And I'm sure we're going to be great friends."

CHAPTER
TEN

Helen

She'd parked round the side so the Davies — who'd always been nosy — would hopefully not see her. Sooner or later, she'd have to come clean with Robin and explain she used to live here before one of the neighbours recognised her and told him. But not yet. She had this funny feeling that he wouldn't want her any more for the job when he knew the connection and he'd definitely think her weird for not telling him in the first place.

But now she was here, back in her old garden, running the soil back through her fingers and tenderly touching that wonderful fucshia she'd planted all those years ago, not to mention the lilac bush and the peonies — oh how they'd blossomed! — she couldn't bear to risk losing it all over again.

It's a bit like Miriam, she told herself, kneeling on the damp grass and deftly weaving her fork in and out of the lambs tongue. Miriam in the Bible who had to leave poor little defenceless Moses by the river only to find — through some stroke of luck — that the queen who had found him then hired her as the wet nurse. Now, here she was, wet nurse to the garden which had kept her going through all those long unhappy years with her then husband.

"I can't talk now," she used to say during those arguments so many years ago. "I need to get on with the garden."

Geoff's eyebrows — which hadn't grown grey then — would rise in disdain and his nostrils curl, the way they always did when someone in the family didn't fall into line with his way of thinking. "Ah yes, the garden. Every woman's escape. Off you run, then. It won't solve anything, burying our problems and thinking they don't exist."

What exactly had been their problems? Helen had often pondered this while pruning her roses or planting baby courgettes which she'd grown from seed in the greenhouse that was now, she noted with disapproval, lying in neglect with cracked panes and long-dead tomato plants languishing inside. If they had been able to pinpoint them, maybe they could have solved them.

But all she knew was that Geoff was always home late (he blamed work but who knew?) and they went to go to bed early because he had to be up at 5 a.m. the next day to commute to London. In the meantime, there were the twins to bring up; both of whom were poor sleepers which meant that she, Helen, was the one who had to get up in the night because she didn't have a proper job to be awake for during the day. At weekends, Geoff was too exhausted to do anything apart from the occasional trip to the cinema or maybe supper with one of the neighbours whom he always described as dull or too up-their-behinds.

By the time the twins had gone to school and Helen began to wonder about where she could find a job that would fit in with holidays and unexpected bouts of illness, the damage had been done. Only the garden saved her. The garden which never answered back. The garden which, unlike the house, didn't get into a mess the minute she'd tidied it. The garden which everyone cooed over when they dropped in (usually when Geoff was out at work because it was always more welcoming then) and whose praise made her feel worth something.

"But that's still no excuse for doing what I did," she told herself, replanting a sad little daffodil bulb which was lying on its side on the damp earth, rather like a little bird that had fallen out of its nest. "No excuse at all."

Sitting back on her heels, she surveyed the work she'd done that morning. Only two hours, yet already the border was looking tidier. You could see the winter jasmine now the bindweed had gone; see the mellow worn golden brick wall at the back that divided her — them — from the Davies. When the children had been little, they were forever sending their football over the wall and then climbing over to get it, much to the Davies' displeasure. The memory sent a sharp pain shooting through her chest and, as it did so, a bird flew overhead, calling.

She looked up, momentarily blinded by the sharp glare of the spring sunlight and, shielding her eyes, turned towards the shadow of the house. Something moved away from the top window; she wasn't sure but she was pretty certain it was Robin's wife because it hadn't been an upright person; it had been something lower down. The same sort of height as someone in a chair.

"Like a coffee?"

Helen jumped as a tall longer shadow fell across the grass.

"Sorry, did I startle you?"

She picked up her fork to cover her confusion. "Not really. I heard the bird — I mean I looked up and . . . well the sun's quite bright today, isn't it?"

"It is." He plonked a steaming mug next to her on a tray with a bowl of sugar. "Sorry, would you rather have tea?"

"No, really. Coffee's marvellous." It smelt good. The real stuff. Blue Mountain or something similar.

"Goodness." He was taking in her border — his border. "That looks amazing. What's that green stuff on the wall?"

"Winter jasmine. It has very delicate white flowers but you probably couldn't see it because it was being choked by the bindweed. Horrible stuff."

"You've done a brilliant job. Thank you so much."

He spoke as if they were at a cocktail party instead of him delivering coffee to the gardener. He was wearing, she noticed, those brown corduroy trousers again but this time, there was a slight rip at the waist as though he'd caught it on something. For a second, he reminded her of Geoff when she had first gone and he'd been so hopeless at looking after himself until finding a string of replacements. That reminded her. Becky had left a message on her phone this morning;

something about having met this Monique woman. She needed to call.

"There's a lot more to be done," she added. "But we'll get there."

He nodded. "I don't suppose you could come for another couple of hours later this week, could you?"

She tried to remember her diary. "I'm not sure. I promised my daughter in London that I'd go up and help look after my grandchildren — she works full time and has got nanny problems. But I'll check when I get home and ring."

"Thanks. I'd appreciate that."

He seemed reluctant to go but something inside her wanted him to leave; something that made her feel both comfortable and uncomfortable. "I thought I'd have a look at the artichokes next."

"The artichokes? What artichokes?"

"The ones in the vegetable garden." Whoops. "I mean, I thought I saw them when I looked last time."

"You're probably right. As you can tell, I'm not much of a gardener. There's probably all kinds of stuff in here that I don't know about."

Very true. "I also wondered . . . I mean, please tell me if I'm talking out of turn. But your wife. She likes looking out of the window, doesn't she? If it's warm when I come next, would she like to sit next to me for a bit?"

Something imperceptible flashed across Robin's face. "How very thoughtful. I'll think about it. She can't talk now, you know. Just sounds which mean nothing to anyone else. It's horribly frustrating for her."

"But she can look," intercepted Helen urgently. "She can see and smell. Gardens are healing places." She stopped, conscious she was gabbling but he didn't seem offended.

"I agree. As you say, let's see what the weather's like, shall we?" He looked up at the sky. "The radio forecasts rain."

She'd always, she thought, getting out of the car and fishing in her bag for the housekeys, been slightly suspicious of people who listened to the weather forecast. It suggested someone who had nothing better to do; people who were so sheep-like that they would actually put off a shopping trip or a day out because someone in authority had said it might rain or worse.

Funny. Robin hadn't struck her as one of those people, which showed how wrong you could be. Of course, she hardly knew him but even so. Then again, how well did you know people; even those whom you really thought you did. Geoff . . . Alastair . . .

She shivered as she turned the key in the lock. No. Don't go down that road now.

"Hi. You're back early."

David was wrapping something up on the kitchen table. When he heard her voice, he slid whatever it was he was wrapping under the *Telegraph*. "What's that?" she asked.

"Nothing." He laughed nervously. "Well, it is but it's a surprise."

It wasn't their anniversary, was it? Certainly not her birthday although one of the odd things about getting older was that you often forgot until it was almost there — so different from her grandchildren who actually had birthday advent calendars. Yet at the same time, she still — ridiculously — felt like a girl rather than a woman in her early fifties. "A surprise? That sounds fun."

"Yes." David looked distracted and she wondered, not for the first time, if swapping housekeys had been such a good idea. He'd suggested it last year ("An in-between step until you agree to move in with me") but she still didn't like it when he caught her out by coming into her home unexpectedly.

Kicking off her shoes, she put the kettle on the Aga. She loved her cottage which she'd bought all those years ago when they'd finally sold the Old Rectory. It was less than a quarter of the size of her old home but it was her cosy refuge which she'd made into her own with its comfy squashy sofas and worn rugs, the Victorian pine kitchen table with its turned legs and her own small bedroom with lavender hanging from the beams over the cast iron bed. She would never again, she told herself, have to wait with a sinking heart for the sound of Geoff's car on the drive.

"So come on then." She ran her finger down the back of his neck, briefly wondering why it didn't give her that delicious shiver it used to. Was it because the contraception the doctor had recommended destroyed spontaneity? And did she really need it at her age? Mid-fifties was still a borderline area; just look at that sixty-three-year-old woman in Italy who'd had her first baby? "What's the surprise?"

David frowned. He was a tall, good-looking man, always brown from working outside. They'd met when he'd come to mend her roof soon after moving in and she'd been struck — rather snobbily, she'd told herself — by his well-spoken voice which seemed at odds with his occupation. "If I tell you, it won't be a surprise."

"It's not any more," she pointed out. "Never mind, I'm sure it will keep. Cup of tea?"

"You're right." She was aware of him standing next to her at the Aga, holding out a small box. Her heart gathered pace inside her throat. Not this. She hadn't been expecting it. Hadn't really thought that . . .

"I wanted to wait." She could hear his words swimming at her through the steam of the kettle. "But maybe now is as good a time as ever. Please, Helen. Open it."

Her fingers fumbled on the catch. It was an old box, faded through velvet-blue time.

"It was my grandmother's engagement ring." He was watching her face so intently that she felt like a picture rather than a person. "If you don't like it, we could get another. And of course, if it doesn't fit, we can get it altered. God, I'm babbling, aren't I? Helen, what I'm really trying to say is will you marry me?"

CHAPTER
ELEVEN

Mel

He was older than she'd expected. Not a teenager but possibly only just in his twenties with a boyish face, a floppy fringe and a habit of saying "like" in every sentence. Amy did the same. She was always telling her off for it.

"You see, like, I didn't have a chance to stop like." The boy — Kevin he was called — wriggled awkwardly in one of several black plastic chairs which were studded round the station interview room. "She just stepped in front of me like and I slammed my brakes but there was this thud and . . . Oh, Christ."

"It's all right, duck." His mother was putting her arm around him, pulling this great grown boy towards her and Mel had to resist the urge to leap up and prise them apart because it wasn't all right. It wasn't all right at all. This stupid little woman with her little gold hoop earrings and black polyester skirt had her son in her arms. He was talking, walking, breathing — all the things he had taken away from Amy.

"I know I should have been insured like . . ."

The boy's solicitor — a wiry worried-looking middle-aged woman — frowned. "Kevin, I would rather you didn't say any more at this stage."

"But I want to!" The boy's face shone up at her — at all of them — with an almost religious zeal. "I want to explain to the vicar why I didn't stop like." He turned directly to Mel. "I was scared, see. And I wasn't sure. I mean I felt the bump and I saw this . . . this sort of thing flying over the front of the car but I thought maybe it was a big bird like or some kind of rubbish in the road."

Mel started to shake. She should have allowed Richard to come with her instead of insisting he stayed next to Amy's side in case something happened.

"Then I pulled in, like, and I saw this blood stain on the bonnet and . . ."

"Please." Mel staggered upright. "I don't want to hear any more of this."

The policeman — the same one who had come to the hospital — nodded gravely. "I understand, Mrs er . . ." He didn't know how to address her; the vicar bit had confused him from the beginning, even though she'd told him to call her Mel. If she'd been a man, he'd have probably called her "Rev" without hesitation. "We'll carry on taking statements now and I'll find someone to take you back to the hospital."

Someone was clutching at her coat. It was the mother with her white pinched face and heavy eye make-up. "But you've got to forgive him, vicar. That's why our Kev wanted to talk to you. Don't you remember us?"

Remember them? Mel's head began to swim.

"We came to your midnight service last Christmas." She was staring accusingly at her now with little pink piggy eyes bursting with reproach as though Mel had run her daughter over instead of this Kevin. "All right, we don't come regular but we made a big effort to get there for midnight mass, especially as you were new." She pronounced the word "new" like "noo". "Thought we'd support you, like."

Was she meant to thank them now?

"I'm sorry. I don't remember. People. There were so many people there."

She tripped over her words, conscious of the woman's narrowing eyes.

"But you do forgive our Kev, don't you?" She tightened her grip round her son's shoulders. "You've got to. You're a vicar."

Forgive? Mel's mind shot back to an interview she'd heard on *Woman's Hour* some years ago about a woman vicar whose daughter had died in one of the London terrorist bombings and who'd tried hard to forgive the killers. At the time, Mel herself had been disturbed to find herself wondering what she would do.

"I . . ." She wanted to say the words but they stuck in her throat. At the same time, she knew with an overriding certainty that, even if she did get them out, they would be meaningless. How could she forgive this horrible lanky greasy-haired youth for not stopping when he had run over her beautiful vibrant laughing Amy?

"I'm sorry. I've got to go. Got to get back to my daughter."

And as she almost ran down the corridor, the policeman close behind, she could hear the woman's indignant tones rising after her. "Call herself a vicar? What kind of Christian is it, what can't forgive?"

"No chnge," read the text on her mobile. "Pls cme hme. Josh needs us. Am there now. R."

Josh. Of course he needed them. Was Richard waiting for her to come back so they could tell him together, as agreed, or had Richard already broken the news? Mel resisted the urge to put her foot down, even though every bone in her body was screaming to get home as fast as possible; sort out Josh and then get back to the hospital. If anything, she drove extra slowly, aware of the impatient driver behind who couldn't wait to overtake. "Don't go so fast," she wanted to say. "My daughter's just been knocked over by some maniac like you."

Had the boy been going too fast? No one had mentioned that. If he had, would there have been proof? And if there was, what difference did it make to Amy, motionless, like a swaddled broken butterfly on the hospital bed? What kind of Christian is it that can't forgive? Dear God, where are you? Listen up, will you? I need some help here.

Josh and Richard were slumped on the sofa in what was known as the den. There were two reception rooms in the vicarage and the smarter one with the Parker Knoll furniture from the previous incumbent was kept for visitors; people wanting help in getting married, getting divorced, having babies, losing them, finding parents, wanting to leave them. Mel far preferred the cosy den with its slightly saggy Sanderson sofa, the roomy matching armchairs with the faded autumn colours and the scattered newspapers with half-full mugs of tea and a packet of Rich Tea biscuits, Amy's favourite.

One look at Josh and Mel knew Richard had told him. She slid next to him on the sofa, pulling him to her. "Are you all right?"

She was aware of a silent sniffling in her shoulder before he pushed her away. "What do you think, Mum?" His eyes were raw red. "She is going to live, isn't she?"

Mel glanced at Richard who gave her a slight nod so fast that she wondered whether she'd caught it right. "We hope so."

Josh leapt up, kicking aside the local newspaper on the carpet and knocking over a cup of tea which someone had left recklessly on the floor. Mel watched the dark brown liquid seeping into the carpet. At any other time, she'd have been fussing around, soaking it up with kitchen roll. "I don't want any of your hope stuff, Mum. And don't you dare suggest we start praying either. I want my sister back. I want to know she's going to be all right. So tell me. Will she or won't she?"

"We don't know." Mel heard Richard speaking at the same time as her. She allowed him to continue. "We don't know, Josh. I'm sorry. Amy has had serious head injuries. We're still waiting for the neurologist to examine her and when we know more, we'll tell you."

Josh nodded and Mel realised with a pang that that was all he'd wanted. He needed the facts.

"Do you want to see her?" she heard herself saying.

He was standing at the doorway looking like a small child again, as only teenagers can do, Mel thought. "Yes. No. I don't know. I'm scared."

"Oh, darling." She was up in an instant, holding him tight, feeling his warm skin, determined not to make the same mistakes she'd made with Amy.

"Getoff, Mum." He pushed her away, walking up the stairs to his room. "She wanted to borrow my iPod for the journey to Oxford, you know. And I wouldn't let her."

"It's not your fault," Mel called up but the door slammed and she didn't know if he'd heard her. She started to run up the stairs.

"Leave him," said Richard below her. "He needs time to himself. Come here, love."

When had he last called her that? Mel allowed herself to be held stiffly for a second before breaking away. "I'm going to ring the hospital," she called out. "To see if there's any news."

There wasn't. Richard insisted that he would do the night shift with Amy. "Someone needs to be at home with Josh. You get some sleep."

But she couldn't. Everywhere she went, were reminders of Amy. The bath oil in the bathroom which she wasn't allowed to use. The kitchen radio which her daughter had turned to Radio 1 instead of her usual Radio 4. The Scissor Sisters CD on the deck in the den. And her bedroom. Dear God, her bedroom.

Mel slumped down on the edge of the bed with its garish purple duvet cover that Amy had insisted on buying. Around her was a sea of clothes, indicating that her daughter hadn't been sure what to wear when she was going out. There was that ridiculously short little white skirt they'd argued over last week.

"Tarty," Mel had pronounced at the time.

"That's because you're old-fashioned and boring," Amy had retorted.

So many words which she wanted to take back. So many words which she should have said.

Downstars again, her eye fell on the list of messages by the phone which Richard and Josh must have taken. Goodness knows how many people had rung with sympathetic can-I-do-anythings; her curate, the chair of the cleaning rota, the chair of the flower-arranging rota . . . And right at the top, before any of these other messages had been taken, Amy's clear bold loopy writing that she'd seen earlier before any of this had happened: "Some old bloke called in about his wedding. Gross! How can people think about That Sort of Thing when they're that age? Can you ring him? PS Sorry about the argument."

Below, was his name and number. Amazing that Amy had taken both. Usually the kids were hopeless at messages, even though she'd explained how important it was to get it right in her job. She'd even, she remembered now with a pang, had another nag about message-taking the other week. And this time — maybe for the last time — Amy had got it right.

This Geoff Hastings was possibly the final person Amy had spoken to before getting in the car with Sharon. She'd wanted to talk to Sharon too but she was still asleep at home after the sedative the doctor had given her, Sharon's mother had said earlier and Mel had winced at the relief in Sharon's mother's voice; the relief that said silently "Thank God it was your daughter and not mine."

Mel glanced at the old clock on the wall which she'd inherited from her parents and which was always ten minutes slow. Ten to ten which meant ten o'clock. Was that too late to ring?

Watching her fingers punch the numbers as though they belonged to someone else, Mel counted the rings. She'd give it six. No, five. If he hadn't answered by then, she'd leave it . . .

"Hello. Geoff speaking."

He had a bold, assured but warm voice which knocked Mel down on to the kitchen chair. She could see him quite clearly in her mind, even though they'd never met. Shortish for some reason. Jolly face. Slightly rotund face with glasses and a beaming smile because he hadn't expected to find love again at his stage in life. (It was what they all said to her.)

"Mr Hastings? I'm so sorry to ring rather late but it's Mel Thomas, the vicar. I'm afraid I was out when you called. Listen." She stopped, wanting to ask him about Amy's last moments — but she couldn't. Not on the phone. Far better face to face. "I know this sounds a bit strange but I wonder if you could do me a big favour . . ."

EIGHT MONTHS TO GO

CHAPTER
TWELVE

Janie

Janie sprawled back on Marjorie's comfortable mustard-coloured Dickins & Jones sofa (a "snip" apparently, at one of its sales before Janie had even been born) with *Yellow Pages* in one hand and a china mug of Russian Caravan, from one of Marjorie's vast array of Fortnum & Mason teas, in the other.

Setting up your own business wasn't quite as easy as she'd thought. In her head, she'd imagined finding a friendly off-licence — an essential for both marriage and death — a printing company which didn't charge the earth but which could also produce advertising material by yesterday and, of course, lots and lots of contacts.

"Well, I've got those," Marjorie had pointed out. "The trouble is that we don't know exactly when they're going to need us. If only people knew when they were going to die, it would save so much trouble. It should be like those things which you young girls go in for nowadays. What is it now? Scissoreans?"

"I think you mean caesarians," Janie had giggled.

Now, trying to make sense of *Yellow Pages* while Marjorie was in the kitchen (ringing her OAP chums and asking if they fancied a funeral with a difference), she wondered how to drum up business for the wedding side.

How had her old boss done it? Janie tried to think as she sketched the outline of a bride in Biro on the front cover. They just sort of came in through the door as far as she could recall but brides to be were hardly likely to do that, given that Marjorie's cottage wasn't exactly a high street spot. They'd have to advertise and maybe start hobnobbing with local vicars. That might be tricky — when had she last been to church? Still, maybe now was the time to start. She might even find a handsome sexy young curate with a cream-coloured old rectory and honeysuckle growing up the front. There he was now, next to the Biro bride. Tall and slim with a hint of that beard again.

"I was engaged to a vicar once," announced Marjorie, coming in from the kitchen and plonking a tea tray on to a rather beautiful mahogany side table which was crammed next to a Chinese-looking cabinet stuffed with Limoges china. Marjorie's cottage — rather like its owner — had far too much in it ("I can't bear to get rid of the memories, dear") but somehow, it all seemed to go together.

A vicar? Janie swung her legs over onto the ground. "What happened?"

"He was absolutely hopeless in bed." Marjorie lit a cigarette. "I could have put up with the parishioner stuff but not that. It wasn't easy to get divorced from vicars in those days, although I believe it's happening more and more now. They go off with rich old ladies like that vicar in the paper the other day." She chuckled. "I should be so lucky."

Sometimes Janie wondered exactly what Marjorie's financial position was; not that she would ever have asked. But there was something a bit strange about an old lady in her seventies who lived in a small two-up two-down cottage but whose (deceased) brother had been to Eton and whose furniture clearly belonged to a more well-off era in her life.

"The first thing we need is a brochure." Marjorie nodded at the *Yellow Pages*. "Did you find a printing firm in that thing?"

Over the years, Janie had become adept at making up excuses to mask her reading and writing deficiencies. "There are so many that I can't make up my mind." She handed it to Marjorie. "What do you think?"

Marjorie re-adjusted her bifocals. "How about this one in Summertown? It says it has a forty-eight-hour service. Here's the number?"

Janie felt her palms sweat. "Can you ring it?"

"Still finding it hard to read, dear? Oh dear, it's engaged. You must get your eyes checked. Hang on — where are my own glasses?"

"You're wearing them. Listen — what do you think about 'For Weddings and a Funeral' as our business name? It's a pun on the film — do you think they'll get it?"

Marjorie pursed her lips. "Wasn't that the film with that actor who was found with a prostitute in a car?"

Janie nodded. She still couldn't quite forgive Hugh for that one and if she ever met him, she'd tell him so.

Marjorie's eyes sparkled. "I like him! 'For Weddings and a Funeral'? Maybe we could add 'Make this a day you will never forget!' Mind you, they're going to be dead anyway so they can hardly remember, can they, although I did once have a friend who believed . . ."

"Marje. I don't mean to be rude but we need to work out the wording for an advert. Here's a pen. My writing's terrible. I was thinking about something like this. 'Make this a day you will never forget. Marjorie and Janie have had several years' worth of experience with both weddings and funerals.'"

"Is that strictly accurate?" interrupted Marjorie. "I've been to, let's see, about seventy funerals so far. How many weddings have you clocked up?"

"About five as guest. And I probably disrupted at least twenty in the last job."

"Fair enough. Several years' worth of experience, then." Marjorie's pen looped across the page. "Should we give out both our numbers?"

"It will have to be my mobile — the landline's been disconnected again."

"Fine, dear. If I get a prank call on my landline, I'll tell them where to go. Do you know, the other day, some joker rang my friend Doris at our Salsa for Over-Seventies and spent ten minutes telling her what he'd like to do to her body. When he'd finished, she said, 'I'm afraid I'm a little deaf so would you mind saying all that again?' He couldn't put the phone down fast enough."

"Brilliant! I'll have to remember that one. Anyway, if you think this is OK, I'll cycle round to those printers."

"Wonderful, dear." Marjorie was already lighting a second cigarette and Janie wondered if she should remind her she already had one in her mouth. "By the way, how's that wedding for your friend's father going?"

"Ah, yes. That one." Janie spoke as though it was just one of many bookings instead of the only one. "I need to ring her dad to make an appointment. You will come with me, won't you?"

Marjorie stuck the second cigarette in her mouth, next to the first. "Certainly. At my age, you never say no to anything new which is probably why I can't make up my mind whether to join the Writing the Mass Market Novel Leisure For Pleasure class or Silver Surfing for the over-fifties. What's he like?"

Janie tried to keep up. "Geoff, you mean? Quite jolly. Can't do enough for Becky although she's never forgiven him for her parents' divorce."

Marjorie took out both cigarettes with one hand and exhaled two lots of blue smoke. "But I thought you told me that Becky's mother left him?"

"She did but Geoff was a really difficult man to live with. The irony is that he's sort of mellowed now. Becky used to hope they'd get back together one day but then Helen, her mum, met some bloke and now Geoff's getting married. I don't think she's very pleased about it, to be honest."

Marjorie's lips pursed. "How very selfish of her. When I got married, Angus already had children and they didn't take to me at all, even though their mother was dead. They made life extremely difficult for me, especially when he died."

Maybe that explained why Marjorie was living in such reduced circumstances.

"By the way, dear, feel like a spot of dinner with me tonight? I've got some smoked salmon in; it was on offer at Waitrose."

"That would be lovely." Smoked salmon! The last time she'd had that was with Mac last month when he'd treated her. In more ways than one.

"Still miss him, do you?"

Janie shrugged. "Not really. I sort of expected it, to be honest. Men never stay long with me."

Marjorie held out her arms to give her a brief hug. "That's because you don't have enough confidence in yourself, dear. When you meet the right man, it will be different. Meanwhile, why don't we switch on the television. Isn't it time for *Loose Women*? Such a funny programme. I'd never have discovered it if it hadn't been for you, dear."

Sometimes, thought Janie, as she cycled towards Summertown, narrowly missing a white van, she wondered if it was her or Marjorie who got more out of their friendship. It was amazing how easily they could talk to each other, bearing in mind their age difference.

Blast. The printers had some sort of notice outside — probably gone to lunch. Parking her bike outside, she sat down on a grassy patch and prepared to wait. Just as well she'd brought a cheese sarnie with her, hastily wrapped in cling film. She could also use the time to ring Becky's dad.

"Geoff? It's me, Janie. Becky's friend."

"This isn't Geoff."

With a jolt, Janie realised that the rather deep voice which sounded so affronted was actually a woman's. "This is Monique, his fianceé. Can I help you?"

Shit! What a start. "Thanks. Like I said, this is Janie. Becks said . . . I mean I believe that . . ."

"You're the girl who's meant to be arranging our wedding."

"Exactly!" Janie felt a surge of relief at the fact this woman actually knew about it. Mind you, she'd heavily accentuated the "meant" bit. "We're really experienced!" Horribly aware she was babbling, she couldn't stop herself. "We do funerals too. Of course, you don't need that yet, although we'll all do eventually . . . what I really mean to say is . . ."

"Perhaps we should meet." Monique's voice was icy cold. She really did sound like a bitch. Shit. Had she messed up before they'd even started? Letting down herself was one thing but letting down Marjorie was another. She'd also be messing up Becky who'd tried so hard for her: Becky who had befriended her at school and helped her when the others had tried to bully her, just because she was such rubbish at reading and writing. OK, so Becky was self-centred at times but she'd always been loyal and she, Janie, would never forget that. Even her brother Adam had helped her out with homework. "You've just got a certain way with words," he would say kindly. "No sweat. We'll help you."

Monique's crisp voice egg-sliced the memory.

"I'm coming down to Oxford next weekend. Let's meet at the Randolph, shall we? Two o'clock on the Saturday?"

"That would be lovely but . . ."

"Good. We'll see you then. And Janie — it is Janie, isn't it? — please bring your company brochure with you."

Brochure! Even more need to have one. Where the hell was the fucking printer? How long did it take to have a lunch break anyway? Janie shuffled on her bottom as the grass beneath began to itch. The day had started off warm for this time of year but now it was getting cold. If he didn't turn up within half an hour, she'd leave it and . . .

"Hi. Been waiting long?"

She looked up to find a tall swarthy man staring down at her with amusement. Sometimes when people looked at her like that, she'd look down just in case she'd forgotten to get dressed (it had happened once). Actually, she was wearing her favourite apple green mohair jumper from Oxfam's new designer shop and red leggings which were just thick enough to pass for trousers.

"I have actually. I kept ringing and you were engaged."

"Well, I'm here now. Is this what you want printing?" He read Marjorie's notice as she followed him through to the office. "Excuse me for asking but why just 'a' funeral? Can't you do more than one?"

"It's a pun." Janie began to feel hot even though she was cold. "A pun on the film title. You know, *Four Weddings and a Funeral*."

He sniffed. "Never saw it myself although Lily, my wife, did."

Wife? Typical. They probably had his and her email addresses in the way people used to have their names on the car windscreen. She could see it now. LawrenceandLily@hotmail.com. For God's sake, Janie, stop seeing every handsome dark stranger as a potential boyfriend.

He was still reading the ad. "What font do you want it in?"

"We're not doing christenings."

He grinned again, showing very even white teeth. "Font means what kind of type do you want it in. Have a look at the list. I'd suggest Arial in 16 point."

Janie spent the next half hour talking through peculiar words which she'd never heard of before — she'd never been very computer literate because of the word problem.

"Right. I think that's all sorted then. We'll get it done for you by next Wednesday then."

"But your ad says you can do it in forty-eight hours."

"Sorry. We had to take on another job. An emergency."

"Well so is this." Janie began to feel irritated. "I definitely need it by Saturday, otherwise I could lose a client."

"Don't worry." He seemed amused by her distress. "It'll be sorted."

Just as she got on her bike, the mobile bleeped, indicating a voicemail.

"It's me, Marjorie. Great news. Maurice has popped off. Peacefully apparently, although they all say that. Anyway, Doris wants us to sort out some unusual music and put together some poems. He was very keen on poetry; that sort of man, if you get my drift. So come back now, dear, can you. Then we can get started on our very first client. Exciting, isn't it?!"

CHAPTER
THIRTEEN

Becky

Becky looked at her father and tried to imagine him as
Monique — or some other predatory woman — would
see him. To her, he was just Dad. A distant shadow in
her childhood although, ironically, they saw more of
each other after her parents had split and he'd made
this concerted, if artificial, effort to see her every
Sunday; taking her out to this restaurant or that and
asking her how the week had been.

Now, after marrying Steve and having the children,
the weekly visits were monthly and usually at Becky's
for Sunday lunch or maybe a drink at the local wine
bar. Becky didn't like going down to his modern
town flat near Headington in Oxford. It was too
far for a start and if she did, she always felt she
had to see Mum who was only a couple of miles
away and then they'd get back late and the children
would be grizzling and it would be work the next
day . . .

"So what did you think of her?"

Her father was looking at her with that "I want the
truth" look which she recognised so well. He was sitting
back in the chair at El Vino's (which had recently

replaced their comfortable sofas with upright barrel-back chairs), his long legs crossed and his arm sprawled across the neighbouring empty chair. He'd lost weight, she noticed. Not that he needed to. With a huge frame like his, he could easily put on half a stone or so without anyone noticing.

"I thought . . ." Becky hesitated, toying with her mozzarella salad. (Why was it that mozzarella was so tasteless yet everyone, including her, kept ordering it?) "I thought she was very interesting."

"Interesting!" Her dad's eyes glittered with amusement. "I always think that's such a bland word, don't you?" He took a slug of red wine — they'd already nearly finished the first bottle between them — and leaned forward. "So you didn't really like her?"

"I didn't say that." The words came out in a more brittle way than she'd meant. "She just wasn't what I'd expected." Becky cast her mind back to that evening when Monique and her dad had turned up so unexpectedly. It hadn't been the best of times, what with Steve getting back from a trip and her having had another bitch day at the office. Then there was the meal which had been disastrous thanks to the deli being closed — her omelettes had been as floppy as a lettuce leaf, probably due to the fact she'd only had three eggs. But even so, Monique had eaten hers with gusto as though she hadn't had a square meal for weeks.

Her dad beamed as though she'd said exactly the right thing. "Not like the others, is she?"

Becky thought of the previous stringy leggy blondes (all of whom could have had door handles on them

110

saying "Pull Here") and was about to agree when Dad ploughed on enthusiastically. "And that's why I like her. She's intelligent — did you know she had a double First in Classics from Cambridge — and she listens instead of going on about herself. Runs her own business, you know."

Becky nodded. "I, er, looked her up. In fact, I think we might have used her agency to get cases for work. Have you seen her website, Dad?"

He laughed. "You know computers and I don't go well together."

"Well, try and look it up. Get your secretary to do it. You ought to look at her picture."

Geoff frowned. "Why?"

Fuck. Perhaps she shouldn't have said anything. "It's just that it's well . . . not very up to date. She looks different. Sort of . . ."

She broke off as a shadow fell across the table. "Monique!" Shit. Had she overheard?

Her father was all smiles, fussing over the bloody woman and taking her coat as though it was something precious instead of a rather dull grey mac. Migod, what was she wearing beneath? Some ghastly track suit with a stripe down the side that made her look like a square chocolate Liquorice Allsort. "Darling, you made it. I'm so glad."

Made it? So this had been arranged. Becky felt sick. When dad had rung to suggest an after-dinner drink (something which Laura had gone into an Antipodean strop over, because it meant her staying late), she'd presumed it would be just the two of them. He

111

hadn't said anything about Monique dropping in. Why couldn't he have just come clean instead of pussyfooting round the truth?

"I've come straight from the gym but I so wanted to see you again as we had to dash off so early last time."

The gym! What a hoot. And how dare she pull a chair up beside her and pat her on the arm like that, as though they were close friends?

"We would have rung last week, wouldn't we, Geoff, but we've both had terrible stomach bugs."

Was that Becky's imagination or was she giving her a look that said "thanks to your out of date eggs". She felt a twinge of guilt, remembering how she and Steve had both had the runs for a couple of days too.

"I'm so sorry. How are you feeling now?"

"Not great."

You don't look it either.

"Still," said Monique rearranging her ample rear on the seat and giving her a smile that contradicted the serrated edge to her voice, "it wasn't your fault, was it?" Another grin followed by a brief glance at Becky's dad. "Now what are we all drinking? I don't know about you two but I've had a hell of a day."

She reached over for the wine list — without asking someone to pass it to her. Those nails, thought Becky enviously, looked immaculate (definitely acrylic), while her hands (one of her better features) had the soft pampered look of someone who did very little manual work.

"Becks, another bottle of wine?"

"Sorry, Dad, but I've got to go. Laura didn't want to stay late and I've got to be in the office early tomorrow. We've got a crisis on."

"Really?" Monique was looking round impatiently for someone to take her order. "It's all right, Geoff — someone's coming now. What kind of crisis, Becks?"

It's Becky to you! Gritting her teeth, she briefly explained about the bidding war which the magazine had lost which had now taken another twist. Sally Smith had changed her mind and was now open to new offers. "We've got to decide whether to pay serious money or lose again to one of our rivals."

When it arrived, Monique seized on the new bottle as though it was water after a week in the desert before leaning back in the chair and resting her head against Geoff's shoulder. Ugh!

"That's better. Sally Smith, you say? What a coincidence! She's just signed up with me. Didn't like her previous PR. I've advised her to turn down the deal with the other magazine because it wouldn't give her copy approval."

Geoff frowned. "What's that, Bitsy-Boo?"

Bitsy-Boo?

"The interviewee gets to see what's being written about them before publication and can ask for changes," said Monique swiftly, just as Becky was trying to decide whether to explain or throw up. "Would your magazine do that?"

Cat loathed copy approval. She said that if they were paying a lot of money for a story, it was up to them

113

what they'd do with it. On the other hand . . . "I think I could get my editor to agree."

"Well then!" Monique sat back in her chair with a satisfied expression rather like Dandy when he had been for a run. "If you can, the story's yours."

"We wouldn't have to bid any more?" Becky could hardly believe it.

"Absolutely not." Monique was examining the wine list again. "My client just wants the chance to put her story forward so people can see what she's really like. Geoffrey, darling. Shall we order? I'm famished. And after that, Becks — you don't mind me calling you that, do you? — I want to hear more about this friend of yours who organises weddings. It's my first time, you know. And before we definitely give her the job, I need to make sure she's the right person."

Becky felt sick as Monique reached out for her father's hand, gazing up at him with a pathetic puppy-dog expression. "After all, it's going to be the most important day of our life. Isn't it, darling?"

CHAPTER
FOURTEEN

Helen

It was all because Geoff was getting married again. Bloody wedding fever.

"Helen, will you marry me?"

That's what David had said while she was still staring in disbelief at his grandmother's ring in its velvet blue box. And what had she done? Gone bright red and mumbled something about it being a bit of a shock and weren't they too old for this sort of thing and what was wrong with the way they were right now?

And then David had gone all quiet and said "Fine" and snapped the box shut, shoving it deep in his jeans back pocket. No, he wouldn't stay for lunch thank you and yes, he'd call tonight or maybe tomorrow. But apart from one terse phone call last week, she hadn't heard from him.

"Do you miss him?" a small voice kept persisting inside her. Yes and no. Of course she missed his company; he made her laugh and it was nice to know that if she picked up the phone, he'd come round and she'd cook spag bol or maybe he'd bring a curry over and they'd have a glass of wine and end up in bed. But if he was still there in the morning, she felt this

115

overwhelming urge to shove him out so she could get on and maybe, but not necessarily, see him the next day.

"I've been on my own for too long," she told herself, getting out at Angel station and waiting for the lift. "I'm used to doing things my way; eating when I like and going to bed when I like and not talking when I don't feel like it. How could I possibly get used to living with someone else's likes and dislikes? Really, how on earth do people actually make marriage work?"

Frankly, she had her doubts at times about Becky's. She'd never thought easy-going Steve was the right person for her over-energetic daughter. What had made her so driven? Maybe school, which had pushed her in a way that Helen had disagreed with but which Geoff, who'd hauled himself up from humble beginnings, had thoroughly approved of. Helen had never wanted to be more than a wife and mother in those days. It was only when she . . . when *that* all happened, that she began to reassess her future.

Helen walked briskly along the high street, trying to avoid the rubbish on the pavements, towards Becky and Steve's modest terrace. "Can you be there at eight o'clock, Mum?" Becky had pleaded on the phone. "Otherwise I'll be horrendously late for work. If I don't give Laura the day off, she'll definitely leave."

Horrendously late? What time did they start? And what kind of life was that for a tired mother of two young children? Well, she was sorry but it was nearly nine o'clock now already. She might have got here earlier if the van hadn't broken down last night which meant she'd had to get a train from Oxford (peak rate too) and made her way over on the tube. God, she was exhausted already but also so looking forward to seeing Daisy and Ben.

"Mum, you're late!" Becks was already on the doorstep, hauling her in. "Their lunch is in the fridge and there are clean nappies up in Daisy's room. Only ring if it's an emergency. Steve will be back before me. Bye."

She was off without a thanks or a how kind of you! Helen looked around the house which was strewn with toys and dirty washing up in the sink. She'd deal with that later. In the meantime, where were the children?

"Daisy? Ben?" she called up the stairs. "Granny's here!"

Was that the sound of a television coming from Daisy's bedroom? Surely not! But yes. An enormous wide screen — new since she'd been here last — was actually on the wall and there, in front of it, were her two grandchildren, riveted to a pair of teenage presenters with earrings in their nose.

"Hello, darlings!" she cooed, crouching down and holding out her arms, her heart melting at the sight of Daisy's little thumb in her mouth and Ben's new short haircut which made him look so grown up. "Granny's here. Aren't you going to give her a cuddle?"

Neither child moved. They didn't even look as though they'd heard. How ridiculous! Helen strode across and turned off the screen although it took a few wrong buttons to do so.

117

Immediately, there was a loud roar. "You stupid idiot!" Ben was jumping up and down. "Turn it on. Now!"

Stupid idiot? Where had he got that from? "Ben dear, you mustn't call Granny that . . ."

She felt herself being knocked to one side as a small body shot past, hurling itself at the screen. Immediately, the loud coarse tones of the teenage presenters filled the air. "Daisy, don't do that!"

Helen tried to turn the button off again but Ben was there this time, pulling her arm away so it hurt. She'd never seen anything like it! What was wrong with these children?

Geoff, she remembered, used to get cross with Becky and Adam when they played up but she'd usually get them to calm down by reasoning with them. "If we turn the television off, we could go to the zoo," she suggested brightly. "Wouldn't that be nice?"

Daisy, who was sitting down again so close to the screen that surely her eyes were hurting, shook her head violently. No wonder she wasn't reading much if all she did was watch television. Helen suddenly realised her granddaughter was still in her pyjamas with a bowl of cereal sitting half-eaten next to her. How could Becky let them eat upstairs?

A bleeping sound emerged from her mobile, indicating a text. Grateful for the interruption, Helen opened it. "Meant to say thanx," Becky had texted. "Lv u mum."

There were times, sighed Helen, as she sat herself down on a mauve bean bag between her two grandchildren, an arm around each, that you just had to give in.

By the time the train pulled back into Oxford station that night, Helen was exhausted. It had taken all her efforts to get the children to sit up at the table to eat, let alone do anything creative. All they wanted to do was watch television or play some computer game. Her suggestion of building a castle out of cereal boxes — something she used to do a lot of with Becky and Adam — wasn't even considered. Frankly, it had been a relief when Steve had come home ("early" apparently) at just after 8p.m.

Blast the van for breaking down. That was something else she'd have to get fixed. Now she'd have to get a taxi, as she had done this morning; it was simply too far to walk.

"Like a lift?"

Swinging round at the familiar voice, she took in David standing awkwardly, both hands in his pockets. Where on earth had he got that loud jumper? "I rang you at Becky's, because I couldn't get through on your mobile. Steve said the van had broken down so I thought you might like a lift."

"How did you know what time I'd be here?"

"I didn't." David was looking at her, his eyes pleading. "I've been waiting. It wasn't any bother. I had the paper to look at."

She was touched. "That's really kind. Like your jumper."

Now why had she said that?

"Thanks. Got it today from a stall in the market. I nearly got you a matching one."

They fell into line together as they walked towards his car and he fumbled for her hand. It felt surprisingly reassuring. "Did you have a good day with the kids?"

"In a way. Different. Look, David, about the other day . . ."

He was already starting the engine and looking ahead. She could feel his hurt burning into her. "You don't have to talk about it."

"But I want to. It was a shock, that's all. All this wedding stuff. Geoff and . . . well you know what I mean. It's catching. One person does it, even at our age, and that gets other people thinking about it. It doesn't mean that what is right for one person is right for another."

Silence.

She reached out to touch his knee. "All I'm saying is, can you give me some time, please? To think about it?"

Briefly, he turned his head towards her, his eyes lit up with a flash of hope. "Sure. If that's what you want."

"It is. Thanks."

"Stupid idiot!"

For a second, she thought he was referring to her and then, as she found herself being thrown forward with her belt cutting into her, she realised David meant the red Saab which had cut them up in front in its hurry to get out of the car park.

"Are you all right?"

"Fine." She smiled wanly as she reread the number plate in front to make sure. Even if it hadn't been, she would have known from the outline of the driver's back exactly who it was. Not that she was going to tell David. Besides, what she was more interested in — despite herself — was the outline of the woman sitting next to her ex-husband.

Too late. The Saab had swung out to the left and sped off down towards the Ashmolean whereas they were turning right. It left her with a strange feeling in the pit of her stomach; even after all these years, she still had the odd feeling that she should be going home with her husband and not sitting next to another man who hadn't fathered her children.

"Thought we might stop off for a bite to eat."

She was about to make an excuse but stopped. It wasn't fair. Heaven knows how long the poor man had been waiting for her. "That would be nice but I can't be late. I've got an early start tomorrow morning."

Briefly, she thought of the gardens lying ahead for her tomorrow. Doris who was too arthritic to manage with her aching joints and whose brother had just died; Miss David who was never there but who liked the garden neat every time she returned; and of course, her garden which wasn't hers at all but Robin's. A brief vision of his wife, sitting at the window, flashed into her head. This time, she determined, she'd definitely ask if Sylvia wanted to come outside and join her, providing the weather was warm enough.

"Me too." David's tone made her realise she'd been too brusque and immediately, she felt embarrassed at her thoughtless rudeness.

What's wrong with me? How many other women of my age have someone who wants to be with them for the rest of their lives? "Don't take that the wrong way." She touched his knee again. "I'd love something to eat. Really."

CHAPTER
FIFTEEN

Mel

God, it was good to run. Feel the ground under foot. Pitch her face against the wind. Shut out the world. Jesus had needed time alone, hadn't he? Did he too need to forget?

"No change," said the nurse when, after her jog, she went to the hospital again, just as she'd been doing now every day for the last six weeks. Why expect any different, Mel asked herself as she sat by the side of her motionless daughter, holding her hand punctured with all kinds of tubes and colourless liquid which were keeping Amy alive.

The neurologist had been quite clear. Amy had a blood clot in her brain as a result of the head injury. It was too dangerous to operate at the moment. It might — and he'd seen this before — simply disperse on its own. Or it could get worse and then that wouldn't be so good.

"Talk to her," the consultant had said. "There are all kinds of cases showing this can make a difference. Play her favourite music. Chat about anything that she'd want to hear about."

Did this man have teenagers? Mel thought not. The one thing that was destined to make a teenager stay in her coma was for her mother to ramble on for 24 hours a day. She allowed herself a small smile at that one. Now if Amy wasn't in a coma but was actually in one spot and willing to listen — another thing which teenagers avoid — she'd say, "Will you please tidy your room? You promised to do that weeks ago and I can't even see the colour of the carpet because there's so much on it."

Or she might say something like, "Amy, why don't you get a holiday job? I can't afford to keep giving you handouts and besides when dad and I were your age, we always worked."

Or, "Haven't you got any holiday homework? You've got your exams coming up soon, you know."

Dear God, have you forgotten her AS exams? The ones which under this new educational scheme happened at the end of what she used to call the lower sixth. Mel clasped her hands, bowed her head, scrunched her eyes shut and tried to get through. How could you do this to her? Six weeks ago, I took it for granted that my beautiful seventeen-year-old daughter could argue back and talk and jump into friends' cars. And now, here she is, motionless and cabbage-like thanks to some stupid boy who didn't stop.

All right. She could almost hear the words in her head. Kevin hadn't been able to stop, just like she wasn't able to forgive him. "Please give me the grace to do that," she prayed. "I know you're testing me and I know I'm failing but just give me the benefit of the doubt. Please."

Mel looked through the chink of her fingers. Nothing. Amy was still lying there, silent, white, thinking God knew what. "Sharon sends her love," she tried. "She's got tickets for that band you like; you know the Wattevers. It's not until Christmas so you've plenty of time to get better. Sharon says she was really lucky to get them."

Nothing.

"Like a cup of coffee, Mel?" One of the nurses was sympathetically hovering at her shoulder.

"No, thanks." Mel had drunk enough insipid hospital coffee over the years. She put her hand over the nurse's and squeezed it back. Over the last weeks, she'd felt as though God had put her on show. If she revealed her true feelings of despair, it would look as though she was being hypocritical and failing to draw comfort from the very person whom she was trying to advertise.

"Actually," she added, standing up. "I've got to see someone; make a visit."

The nurse had nodded understandingly. "It must be difficult to get your work done."

"It is." Mel flashed her best Vicar-of-Dibley smile. Dawn French had actually done a great favour for the church by making it more human. And you couldn't get more human than this, could you?

"Lucy — that's my curate — is filling in and one of the other vicars in the diocese took the sermon for me last week but I'm still taking the service this Sunday. Do come if you like."

"I might do that. To support you." The nurse's eyes filled with tears. "You're so brave, Mel. I don't know how you do it."

He was going away for a week, he'd said. After that, Mel was very welcome to come and see him. Geoff Hastings worked partly from his home in Jericho and partly from his offices in Wilton Street. Which was most convenient for her? She'd chosen the office on the grounds that there would be other people around and she'd have to stay composed.

What would Mr Hastings be like? She'd pictured a short bald little man who was probably marrying some babe and couldn't believe his luck. Until he'd given her the name of his firm, she hadn't realised he was a solicitor. According to the smart brass plaque on his door, he specialised in matrimonial law.

The secretary was sitting next to a smart electric blue fish tank. "Can I help you?"

Mel felt her gaze go straight to the white plastic collar round her neck. For a minute, she almost giggled. It was clear from the girl's face that she thought a vicar might have come about a divorce. "I've got an appointment. With Geoff Hastings. I'm afraid I'm a bit early."

The girl glanced at the diary on the desk. "Please. Take a seat."

She'd only just settled down on the red plastic sofa, unable in the circumstances, to pick up one of the glossy magazines (something she'd normally home in on) when a door opened and a very tall jowly baldish

126

but somehow extremely good-looking man strode in. So much for her mental image.

"Vicar?"

She knew that look. It said "How can a woman who looks like you, possibly be a vicar?"

Being pretty had, in Mel's experience, been more of a drawback than anything else. When she'd been in advertising, the other women had seen her as a threat and the men had either patronised her or tried to get her into bed. Now some parishioners found it hard to take her seriously until they knew her better, while her male colleagues tended to call her "dear".

Geoff was shaking her hand. "Is it all right to call you vicar? I'm afraid I'm a bit out of practice. Oh dear, I probably shouldn't say that, should I, considering I'm asking you to bless an old divorcee. Stop looking at me like that, Katie." He winked at Mel. "She thinks I'm far too long in the tooth to get married. Her generation doesn't do it any more, you know."

Gently touching the small of her back, he ushered her into his office and closed the door behind her. "Hope you didn't think I was being unsympathetic then. But I had a feeling you'd had enough of people saying how sorry they were and how dreadful it was."

Mel nodded vigorously. "I have."

"They probably expect you to take it in your stride, too, bearing in mind your job."

She smiled. "They do."

"Please sit down."

He poured her a glass of water with a slice of lemon in it. "I've banned coffee from the office. It's my new attempt to get fit for the wedding, you know." He fixed her with a pair of startlingly blue-grey eyes. "That's why I came round to your rectory. To see if you would bless us. I was married before so I wasn't sure you'd be able to actually marry us in church."

"It might be possible." Mel began to feel awkward. "I'd need to ask you some questions first. But . . ."

"But you need to talk about something else first, I believe." He was looking at her kindly. "You mentioned a favour. How can I help?"

It was usually her asking that question. "You were the last person to see her — Amy, my daughter — before the . . . before the accident. The last person apart from Sharon, her friend, and she hasn't been able to say much. She's still shocked, poor kid."

"Understandably so. Then again, in my experience, teenagers never say much anyway unless they want some money!"

Somehow she was surprised. "You've got your own then."

"Grown up now. But I remember it all too clearly. I used to worry like hell about them driving . . . sorry, I didn't mean to say that."

"It's all right." Funnily enough it was. She hadn't known what to expect about this man but somehow it wasn't this extremely approachable (for a solicitor) chap, leaning back against his ergonomic chair, voicing things that she felt but didn't think anyone else thought. Was he flirting with her? No. Surely not.

"I just want to know if she seemed all right when you saw her."

"All right?" he repeated.

She shifted awkwardly in her chair. "We'd had a bit of an argument. About her going out in her friend's car and about what she was going to wear."

He grinned. "Typical teenage stuff again."

"She and my son are always saying 'I'm a teenager, mum.' As though it's an excuse. But now I feel guilty for not understanding more."

He leaned towards her and for a second, she thought he was going to take her hand in his. "Look, Mel, I don't know you but I have a funny feeling for some reason that we're on the same wavelength. And I also know how guilty I used to feel as a dad — still do actually. But often, there's no need to. Your daughter seemed like a normal teenager to me. In a rush. Dressed in a skirt that barely covered her bottom. Too much eye make-up, heavy foundation to hide a few adolescent zits and genuinely happy. Does that make you feel better?"

She nodded, unable to speak and horribly aware of the hot tears pricking her eyes. He pushed a box of tissues towards her. "Please. Help yourself. I keep them for my clients. When you're a matrimonial lawyer, there are a lot of tears in here. Don't suppose you want a divorce at the same time? I'm doing them cheap this week! That's better. It's nice to see you smiling. Seriously, Mel — you don't mind me calling you that, do you? I always used to say to myself that if anything happened to one of my kids, at least they'd die doing something they enjoyed. My son, Adam, is having a gap year in Australia. In fact, it's been ten gap years and he still hasn't got a proper job. Every time the phone rings and I hear the long distance pause, I wonder if he's all right. But you've just got to have faith, haven't you?"

She laughed ironically.

"I don't necessarily mean your kind of faith. Just faith in," he swept the air, "in whatever."

"Thank you."

This time he did reach out for her hand and she clasped it gratefully.

"But I can't forgive him. The boy who didn't stop. The one who ran her over."

"Why should you? He should have stopped. Teach the little blighter a lesson not to do it again. As for you, you will actually learn to forgive him in time. Maybe it's your God testing you."

She nodded. "I thought that too. You sound like a great father."

Something dark flickered across his face. "I doubt if my ex-wife would agree. I wasn't there enough for the kids when they were growing up which is probably why I'm trying so hard now. But it was difficult. I was based in London then and commuting."

"I used to do that."

He raised an eyebrow. "A commuting vicar?"

Mel smiled weakly. "In my previous life, I used to be in advertising."

"Did you now? That explains your lively adverts outside St Mary's. More water? Go ahead. It's good for you. Speaking of the church, would this be an insensitive time to have a chat now about my wedding and whether or not we can make it to the altar, given my wicked past?"

His eyes flickered down to her feet. "By the way, I know I shouldn't ask this. But I couldn't help noticing your trainers. Has the evangelical dress code changed since my day?"

How embarrassing! She'd forgotten to change.

"I've been on a run — sorry, I forgot to put my ordinary shoes on."

He grinned. "Don't apologise to me. I like jogging too. Where do you go?"

She felt so much better coming out of his office. But then a picture of Amy shot into her head and she immediately felt guilty for smiling; laughing even. Switching on her mobile, it immediately began to bleep. A message? No. A call. Stephen.

"What's happened?"

"Nothing." His voice was taut and in the background, she could hear loud music. "Nothing with Amy anyway. It's Josh. I think you'd better come back."

Oh, God. Visions of her son crying his heart out for his sister or locking himself into his bedroom, refusing to come out until she was all right, came into her mind. "What's he done?"

"He seems to have upset one of the neighbours." There was a slight pause. "Someone who knows that boy's mother."

CHAPTER
SIXTEEN

Janie

If getting married was — according to a survey in Becky's magazine — one of the most stressful things in life, so was getting buried, thought Janie, as she cycled along to the printer's. The only advantage was that you could be the centre of attention without having to do anything. Doris, who hadn't got on particularly well with her brother during his life time, was obviously determined to make up for her lack of sisterly love now he was dead. Talk about picky!

"I want the thanksgiving sheets to be on cream paper; not white," Doris had announced when she and Marjorie had visited her to receive their briefing. "Maurice was always keen on cream. He used to pour jugs of it over strawberries when we were children. Never left enough for me of course but that was Maurice . . ."

Her voice trailed off as she turned over another page of the photograph album. "Mustn't speak ill of the dead, must we?" Look, there's Maurice holding the handle of my pram when I was born. Mother told me that he once tried to tip me out of it because he resented having a baby sister. Of course, we can't prove anything but between you and me, I wouldn't be at all surprised.

"Now we must have 'Jerusalem' because he always loved that; we'd try and out-sing each other in church, even when we were quite grown up. And we need watercress and egg sandwiches for lunch because those were his favourite and mine too, as it happens. He always accused me of copying him but I haven't because he's gone and died now, hasn't he, and I'm still here."

Marjorie took her hand but Doris pushed it away. "I'm quite all right, thank you. Although I do wish he was still here so I could tell him that I've beaten him at one thing because I'm here and he isn't. He always used to win at Scrabble, you know but then again, he wasn't averse to a little cheating. That reminds me. We must have Psalm 27 too."

All this was still running through Janie's mind as she dismounted off her squeaky bike outside the printers. Whatever relationship Maurice and Doris had had, at least it was something. It must be so nice to have a brother or sister; she'd hated being an "only", which was why Becks was so important to her.

"You're early."

Startled, she looked up to see the printer lounging against the door of his PortaKabin which doubled up as his office.

"No, I'm not. We said midday."

"Well it's not ready yet. You'd better come inside and wait."

Janie peeped inside the dark office where, in the corner, a large machine was churning out a rush of blue and white brochures.

"I've got another job to finish first." He was looking at her with mild amusement. Janie hated it when people did that. It was usually when they were in the wrong and made you feel silly to compensate for it.

"I'll wait outside, thanks." Taking a seat on the verge, she pulled out a cheese sandwich from her pocket which she'd made before leaving. Why was the wretched man still standing at the door, watching her?

"Don't you have work to do?"

He grinned. "The machine's doing it for me."

"How long is it going to take?"

"Not sure. Half an hour. Maybe an hour."

Janie attempted a rough calculation in her head (always dodgy), while doing a pencil sketch of some wedding flowers on the sandwich bag. They didn't need the service sheets until this afternoon; after all, Maurice's service didn't start until 4p.m. So she could nip into town and buy a few more flowers. The church was looking decidedly bare which wasn't surprising since Maurice hadn't been a regular church-goer so there weren't the usual hordes of dedicated flower-arrangers at the ready. Marjorie was liaising with the funeral firm which wasn't very pleased at someone else being commissioned to do the service sheets. Then she needed to make sure that Doris had her reading in hand and . . . damn, not her mobile again.

"Is that Janie Jones?"

134

For a minute, Janie thought someone was putting on a posh voice. But it sounded vaguely familiar.

"Yes." She swallowed a mouthful of cheese sandwich. "Who's talking?"

"This is Monique Brown. I was expecting you at the Randolph half an hour ago."

Monique? The Randolph? Half an hour ago? But she had her down in her head for next week. "I think you've got the date wrong." Damn, the cheese sandwich had stuck in her throat in her rush to get it down and she began coughing. "Excuse me, Miss Jones, but I never get dates wrong."

Why couldn't she stop coughing? To her annoyance, the printer was handing her a tumbler of water in a none-too-clean-looking plastic cup. There was nothing else but to swig it back. "I've got you down for next Thursday."

The voice sliced down the phone like a cheese-cutter. Shit, that reminded her. Marjorie had asked her to get some Stilton in for the buffet. "Of course, if it's not convenient, I can find someone else."

"No, no, it's fine." Janie glanced at her old watch which always ran ten minutes slow. "I can be there right now . . . well, in a couple of shakes. See you. And, er, sorry."

Leaping on her bike, she drained the last drop of water from the tumbler. The printer held his hand out, indicating she should throw it to him, so she did. Well caught! "Bit of an emergency," she called out. "I'll be back for the service sheets in an hour. But you will make sure they're ready, won't you?"

Monique was waiting in the foyer of the Randolph. Standing up, rather than sitting down, which was a bit ominous. Pity Geoff wasn't there; she'd always got on well with both of Becks' parents. Too late, she wished she'd put on something smarter than a pair of old jeans and a pink, green and blue candy-striped shirt made out of an old pillow case. And she hadn't realised how bad her nails were; that must be charcoal from her sketch this morning.

As if reading her mind, Monique gave Janie a cool lanky handshake. "This isn't a very good start, I have to say."

She waited, clearly expecting Janie to apologise but somehow she couldn't find the words. All she could do was stare. What was Becks' father (who'd always been quite dishy for his age) doing with a woman with lumpy sausage legs under a navy sack dress? And as for her podgy round face with little black beady eyes — it was the kind of face she'd be tempted to put out with the bins. And not the green one.

"Sorry. I thought . . . I mean I'm sure I had it in my diary for next week."

"Well, since you're here, let's get on with it, shall we?" She withdrew a bulging brown leather Filofax from her bag and fixed Janie with a pair of cold grey eyes. "I want a wedding which is going to be noticed by everyone. And I mean everyone. I want music that will make people sit up — not the kind of stuff you hear on Steve Wright's Sunday morning love songs — and I want white doves to be released from the door of the

136

church when we leave. Are you writing this down? And a flautist too."

A flowtist?

"Someone who plays the flute. Surely you know that? I specifically want 'Where e'er you walk' by Handel. We always used to sing it at school. Handel used to live there, you know. Now at the reception, I want . . .'"

Janie's hand was aching madly by the time the wretched woman had finished. What she did and didn't want was clearly something she'd been planning since she was a child of six. Right down to the last napkin. Pity, she thought, as she absentmindedly cleaned her nails with her door key while Monique pored over one of the cake catalogues which she, luckily, just happened to have on her. Pity brides never selected their grooms with as much care. Frankly, she'd always thought men should be like Ikea products. If you didn't like them when you'd removed the packaging, you could take them back, even though it meant you lost 30% of the full price. Seemed fair to her.

"I will expect a progress report twice a week." Monique handed over a slim silver and white business card. "Email me, will you?"

"I'll need a deposit," said Janie quickly putting the door key back in her pocket. She and Marjorie had agreed to ask for 50% up front.

Monique stood up. "I'll talk to Geoff about that and get back to you." Her eyes held Janie's challengingly. "Be very clear on this, Janie. I'm only giving you this job because Geoff is doing it as a favour to his daughter. But if anything, anything, goes wrong, I will immediately go to a proper weddings organiser. Do I make myself understood? And another thing. Do get your nails done properly. It really doesn't project a very professional image, does it?"

Bitch! Quickly, Janie tucked away her page of notes before Monique spotted the not-very-complimentary sketch she'd made of her in the margin. Do this, do that, do this, do that. What had Becks' father got himself into? And the awful woman had left her Filofax behind. Now she'd have to find some way of getting it back. Flicking through to find an address, her eye fell on the diary section.

She knew it! Their appointment had been for next week. It had been Monique who had got it wrong and not Janie. Something inside her made her wonder if she'd done it on purpose just to keep Janie on her toes. Shit. Not her mobile again.

"Janie? Where are you?" Marjorie's voice boomed down the line. "One or two people have begun to arrive early and we haven't got the service sheets to give them."

Fuck. Was that the time? "I'm on my way. Don't worry. I've just had a bit of a hiccup. Oh and Marjorie, I couldn't get any Stilton so we'll just have to manage without."

To give the printer his due, he was standing by his gate, service sheets at the ready in a bag to hand over to her. "Thanks," panted Janie, throwing them in her bike basket. "I'm in a bit of a rush."

She zoomed past but not before glimpsing a rather pretty woman inside the office who was probably his wife. Why was it that everyone could find someone — even the horrendous Monique — except her? A flash of Mac flew into her head, followed (inexplicably) by the *Big Issue* lady.

"Thank God you're here." Marjorie virtually pulled her in through the church door, grabbing the sheets. "Bloody hell, Janie. These are purple, not cream!"

"They're what?"

"Didn't you check?" Marjorie's liver spots were gleaming with panic.

"Sorry. There wasn't time. I got a phone call from that woman Monique and . . ."

Marjorie frowned, although whether it was at the sight of Janie's dirty white t-shirt or the purple sheets, Janie wasn't sure. "Never mind. Look, something awful has happened. The organist hasn't turned up."

"We've still got another ten minutes. Can't you ring him?"

"The vicar's still trying to get hold of him. Besides, look! They've all turned up early. I blame those motorised scooters they're all on. In fact, I wouldn't mind one myself."

It was true. Despite Doris's disparaging remarks about her brother not having any friends, there were several old crocks in the church, together with an assortment of zimmer frames and motorised scooters at the door. What a noise! They were nattering together as though at a party. Presumably, funerals were one of their main meeting places now.

A tall pretty blonde woman in a cassock, came towards them. How could a vicar have such a flawless peach complexion? "I'm afraid there's still no sign of our organist. I don't understand it; he's normally so reliable."

Janie nudged her landlady. "Marjorie, you can play the piano. Why don't you do it?"

"It's completely different from the organ, dear."

"Well, as it happens, we do have a piano here." The woman looked relieved; close up, she wasn't quite as young as she'd first looked. Striding to a corner, she proceeded to pull off a plastic wrap. "It hasn't been tuned for a while but it works."

Marjorie turned pink under her purple velvet cloche. "I don't have any music and there's only one piece which I know off by heart."

"What's that?" Doris had come up. "What's the delay? Where's the organist? And what's the only piece you know off by heart?"

Marjorie took her friend's arm. "Doris dear, there's something I need to explain."

Together, Janie and the vicar watched the pair of old ladies launch into a lively conversation, both turkey necks bobbing madly as they spoke. Hang on. Wasn't that her new padded bra, Marjorie was wearing? She could see the plastic straps showing.

Eventually, they looked as though they'd come to a compromise.

"Twenty-five per cent discount?" Doris said.

"Twenty."

"All right. Done. Quick, here's the coffin."

140

Marjorie flew to the piano and lifted the lid. Janie took a rear seat as the vicar scooted to the front to beat Maurice making his last journey. Omigod, what was that? Surely it couldn't be? Everyone turned round with astonished expressions on their face. One or two began to giggle. And no wonder.

Maurice was going home to the sound of one of the most well-known musical pieces in the world. "Don't worry," said Doris, nudging her in the ribs. "I always said he'd never get to hear the Wedding March before me. Well now I'm making it up to him. Better late than never, don't you think?"

CHAPTER
SEVENTEEN

Becky

"Great news," said Becky, hovering at Cat's door. One never knew whether to go in or not when it was half ajar like this. Cat's back was facing her so she couldn't gauge the mood of the day.

No answer.

"Would you rather I came back later?"

The chair swivelled round sharply. Cat's eyes were steely as she held out a copy of *Charisma* magazine. "What do you call this?"

God, she hated Cat's trick questions. She smiled bravely. "Looks like this week's copy of the magazine."

"Don't try and be smart with me, Becky. I'm talking about this." She stabbed a stubby finger at the double page spread. Fuck. Fuck, fuck, fuck. It was the feature on ordinary women who got into debt by copying celebrity lifestyles and there, in the centre, was Maddy, the work experience student.

"Who's this girl?"

Becky forced herself to sound steady, hold back the bile that was rising up her throat and hold Cat's eyes. "She's a reader."

Well, that was true enough. If the bloody girl didn't read the magazine, she shouldn't have been here as a work experience student.

Cat's eyes narrowed. "Don't I know her from somewhere?"

Becky did a quick mental calculation. Maddy had left one, no two weeks ago. There were so many people who passed in and out of the office as temp and work experience girls. There was a new one now, a skinny boy with a mop of white hair and Harry Potter glasses. Surely Cat would have forgotten Maddy by now?

"Wasn't this the work experience girl we had in the other month?"

Quadruple fuck. "Sort of."

"Sort of?" Cat's eyes were almost boring through her head and out the other side. "You do know the rule, don't you?" Her voice was tight and clipped with intentionally small pauses around each word as though to emphasise them. "We don't use staff as case histories. Not after the last time."

It was coming back to her now. One of the other magazines in the group had used the entire editorial team for a feature on how many men they'd all slept with because they couldn't find any real case histories to be daft enough to agree. The editorial team had been promised a grand each to do it (presumably this was to compensate them for the fallout with family and friends) and had been heavily disguised with make-up. But somehow the scam had got out, the editor-in-chief had been sacked and a warning had been sent round the entire group that if anything like that happened again, the editor's bum would be on the block — not to mention the culprit behind it.

"But she wasn't staff." Becky could feel herself sweating. "That's why I thought it would be all right and besides, I was desperate. We couldn't find a case history . . ."

"Couldn't find a case history," Cat repeated, clipping each word like her mother clipped the holly bush at home. "That's another phrase we don't use or have you forgotten that one too? My staff at *Charisma* can do anything. That's why they're here. No matter how challenging our features, we can always find case histories; real ones who aren't work experience girls or staff or made up. That's why we have the reputation we have and frankly, Becky, if you feel you can't match that, maybe it's time for you to think about your future."

How unfair! She'd been on *Charisma* for longer than Cat had been; in fact, she'd applied for the editor's job and been really miffed when an outsider from a rival magazine got it. "You can't be serious."

Cat's lips tightened. Pity her stomach couldn't do the same thing. "Oh but I am. I'm not having my position threatened because you've broken a major rule."

"I'm sorry. Perhaps I shouldn't have. All right, I was wrong. But I didn't think it mattered and . . ." she stopped, conscious she was making it worse. "But I can get Sally Smith for you. That's what I came in to tell you. They'll give us the feature and we don't even have to pay them."

144

"Sally Smith?" Instantly, Cat's eyes managed to narrow even further yet brighten at the same time. "The Sally Smith who wouldn't sell us her story before?"

"I've got a contact. My father's future . . . his girlfriend. She runs a PR agency and Sally has just gone to her as a new client. Apparently, we can interview her without a fee because she wants to put her story across." She faltered. "The only thing is that we have to give her copy approval."

"Which we don't do."

"But it's the only way we can get her."

Cat looked out of the window. "I see. Well, that puts a slightly different complexion on matters. How quickly can you get them?"

"I don't know. I'll have to ring Monique. She's the PR."

"Well what are you waiting for?" Cat's back was already facing her again. "If you can file copy by Monday, I won't take further action over the celebrity cock-up. Unless, of course, someone else notices." She swivelled round again and the expression on her face made Becky tremble. "Because if they do, my head will be on the block. And be in no doubt that I'll take yours with me."

Something garlicky floated out from the kitchen. Something that smelt of fried peppers and onions and maybe vegetarian lasagne. On any other occasion Becky would be on her knees with thanks that a) Laura had cooked an adult supper and b) that Laura was still there. But the scene with Cat had totally eradicated her appetite. She'd written a feature, not long ago, about the Secretary Diet where women whose husbands went off with their secretaries lost a stone almost overnight. She'd have to do something about the Boss Diet too. Want to lose weight? Simple. All you have to do is work for a bitch like the editor of *Charisma* magazine.

"Laura, that smells great . . ."

Her voice tailed away as she took in her husband Steve wearing his blue and white striped pinny (a present from her mother last Christmas) and bare feet (something he liked to do at weekends and on the rare evenings when he was home). "You're here. I thought you were in Frankfurt until tomorrow." A sudden panic gripped her. "Omigod, don't tell me you've been sacked too."

"No." Steve was intent on chopping onions to a fine moon shape. "Frankfurt was last week. I was in Paris, if you remember, and I was meant to be back last night but the plane got delayed. I left a message on the answerphone."

"God, I'm so sorry. I haven't had time to listen to it."

"Or to my work schedule apparently." Steve continued chopping up the onions into even slimmer slices; he always did this when they had one of these "Where were you?" discussions.

"And what do you mean 'sacked too'?" He looked up at her for the first time since she'd come in and she was struck by the dark shadows under his eyes. "Cat hasn't really given you the boot, has she?"

Briefly, she explained what had happened. "Then it's just as well Monique can bail you out, isn't it?"

"But I don't want her to." Becky took a large slurp out of Steve's wine glass next to the cooker. "I'm not owing that woman any favours."

Steve tipped the sliced onions into the pan, emitting a spatter of butter. "I don't think you're being very fair on 'that woman', as you call her. She seems perfectly nice to me."

"How can you say that?" Becky almost choked on her second slurp. "She's fat and ugly — nothing like her website picture — and she's far too young for him and . . ."

"And he looks a lot happier than I've seen for a long time," finished Steve. "Far happier than he looked with all those leggy blondes."

Becky sniffed. "I don't trust her. There's something fishy there if you ask me."

Steve shrugged. "I don't think you want your father to get married at all."

"That's ridiculous!"

"Is it?" Steve tipped some freshly chopped tomatoes into the blender, followed by a tub of yoghurt. "Just like you don't want your mother to get married."

"Well any fool can see that she and David aren't suited."

"Becky, love." Steve pulled up one of their new Conran kitchen stools and took her hand. "I think it's time you realised something. Your parents have been apart for years. They're never going to get back together. They're both great people in their own right, even though your dad's a terrible flirt — yes he is, don't deny it. Like father, like son if you ask me."

Difficult to argue with that one.

"He and your mum just weren't good together," continued Steve gently, still stroking her hand. "Surely you don't want them to be lonely for the rest of their lives, do you?"

"No. No, of course not. But . . ."

"But what? But you'd like to choose their partners for them?"

Becky reached out for the bottle. This bloody wedding of her father's was causing so many problems; it was even making things worse between Steve and her. "Maybe. After all, look at all those cultures that arrange their children's marriages. Why can't kids do the same?"

They both smiled and for a second, Becky felt like she used to feel all those years ago when she and Steve didn't have conversations like this and didn't have children and . . .

"Shit." She leapt up. "Where are the kids?"

"In bed." Steve gave her a pitying look. "I wondered when you'd ask."

The familiar wave of parental guilt washed over her. "It wasn't that I'd forgotten . . . It's just that I didn't expect you home and then we started talking and then . . ."

"I know." Steve sounded sad. "I got back about four so Laura went early. Just as well from the fed-up expression on her face. Are you going, then?"

Becky dipped a finger into the lasagne sauce. Mmmm. Delicious.

"Upstairs. To see the kids?" Steve was giving her a funny look. "You know. Ben and Daisy, I believe they're called."

"No need to be sarcastic." She was already halfway up the stairs, fishing in her pocket for her mobile as she spoke. A quick peep inside the kids' rooms showed they were fine as they always were every night. Wide awake and on their mobiles. Mum disapproved of that, of course, but they all had them nowadays in case they got abducted or something went wrong on the school run.

"Daisy! Ben! Stop talking to your friends now."

"Why? You are."

"That's very rude, Ben."

"Laura says you're rude. She says you treat her like shit."

"Ben!"

Right. She'd definitely have a word with Laura about that in the morning, except that she'd be gone before she arrived, wouldn't she. Maybe a note. "Dear Laura. Don't you dare say I treat you like shit." Second thoughts, she'd get Steve to sort it.

"Mummy, can I have another ice cream?"

Another? At this time of night? "Course you can, Daisy. Just as long as you don't say anything while Mummy makes a phone call."

Good. She was answering now. "Monique? This is Becky. No, Becky Hastings. That's right. Geoff's daughter."

Ouch!

"Yes, sorry it's a bit late. I hadn't realised. Look, about Sally Smith. We'd love to interview her. And of course we can give copy approval . . ."

They agreed to meet the following day not, as Becky had hoped, in Monique's offices but in a rather run down sandwich bar close to the magazine.

"Hope you don't mind coming here," said Monique after kissing Becky on both cheeks and pricking her in the process with those stray hairs on her chin. Yuck!

"We're not likely to be seen by anyone and I'm sure you understand that I don't want anyone else to know about our deal."

Deal?

Monique was already pushing a piece of paper towards her. "It simply states that *Charisma* promises to show my clients the feature before it goes to press, in return for which, Sally Smith will give her full story and be photographed."

A picture of Cat flashed into her head. What the hell? Fingers sweating, Becky took the Mont Blanc pen Monique was holding out (what a cliché this woman was!) and signed.

"Good." Monique sank back into her stool as though forgetting it wasn't a chair and then had to grab the edge of the counter to heave herself up. The bloody woman was like a whale. A heavily red-lipsticked whale who was grinning at her inanely.

"I expect you're wondering."

Becky was still looking at the piece of paper, wishing now she'd made some excuse about taking it back to the office first. "Wondering what?"

"Wondering why I look as I do when my website picture is so different."

Her direct factual tone took Becky completely by surprise. "No. Well, yes. I mean . . ."

"Your dad said you'd mentioned it."

She'd kill him.

"No, it's all right. You're not the first one." She leant towards her and Becky could smell the coffee on her breath. "The truth is, Becky, that it's my hormones."

"Your hormones?"

Monique nodded. "Sadly so. About a year ago, I was as slim as you. But then I hit my late thirties and started to put weight on and grow a few hairs on my chin (you wouldn't know it, thanks to electrolysis) and lose some hair (you can see how thin it is) and . . . well, everything began to go a bit pear-shaped."

She leaned even closer and out of courtesy, Becky desperately fought the urge to move away. "I was having problems with my personal life too; the man I'd been dating for some time, wasn't as trustworthy as I'd thought."

"I'm sorry."

Monique shrugged. "Me too. God, I wish I could have a cigarette. Mind if we leave this coffee and go outside?"

Without waiting for an answer, she lumbered off the stool and headed for the square outside. "I wasn't going to change my picture on the website, mind. Why should I? Would you?"

Becky found herself agreeing. For a large person, Monique could walk very fast and she was almost stumbling in her heels to keep up.

"I suppose you're wondering what your dad sees in me?"

Yes, yes, Becky wanted to scream.

"I make him laugh." Monique dug her in the ribs with her elbow and began to wheeze. Once Becky had recovered from the shock of the rib-digging, she realised Monique wasn't actually having an asthma attack. She was chuckling in a loud uncouth way that made passers-by turn round and look. "We make each other roar with laughter actually and, of course, there's that incredible physical attraction."

That was it! The very thought of her father in bed with this lump of lard made her want to throw up. "Monique." She stood still, forcing the other woman to do the same. "I'm very glad for you that you've found happiness. But I would ask you to consider one thing."

"And what's that?" Monique's eyes were narrowing now.

"How long have you known my father for?"

"Three months but . . ."

"Exactly." Becky clutched the agreement in her hand, in case Monique tried to snatch it back. "My mother thought she knew him for fifteen years but it turned out that she — none of us — knew him at all."

"Really?" Monique's eyes weren't just narrow. They were as cold as gun metal. "I understood that your mother . . ."

"Stop right there." Becky could feel her colour rising. "You know nothing about my mother and I forbid you to make any assumptions."

152

"Becky." Monique was trying to touch her arm but she angrily shook it off.

"I don't want to discuss this any further." She folded the paper in half and put it in her pocket. "From now on, Monique, our relationship will be strictly business. Understand?"

And without waiting for a reply, Becky marched off, horribly aware that this time, it might not be so easy to patch up things with Dad.

The office was eerily quiet when she returned. Shit. She hadn't forgotten a meeting again, had she? Even Nancy wasn't at her desk. In fact, where was everyone? There was a note on her desk. "Please go straight to Brian's office."

Brian? Fuck. He was the big chief. The real big chief, even though he was a small man who looked as though he was still waiting for a growth spurt. The one that hired and fired. He might as well have had his hanging cap on — clearly he'd found out about the fake case histories. Cat had told him. Bitch. Almost unable to walk, Becky forced her legs to jelly their way to Brian's office.

It took three knocks for him to answer. "Ah, Becky, there you are."

Her eyes took in an empty office. The others weren't there. It was just her. Shit. How would they pay the mortgage on just Steve's salary?

"Please. Sit down, will you."

She'd only once met Brian before when he'd taken her on after a gruff hauled-over-the coals interview which she'd been convinced she hadn't got. Everyone knew Brian was only polite when he was about to chop off someone's P45.

"You might wonder where everyone is." He spoke as though his words were constipated, enunciating each one clearly.

She nodded numbly.

"I sent them out to Starbucks. To celebrate."

He was watching her face and Becky hesitated. This was clearly a test. If she laughed, she could be out on her ear too. If she failed to laugh, it might be the same result.

Instead, she cleared her throat. "I'm not quite sure what you're getting at, Bri."

Fuck. No one called this man Brian. Legend also had it that his wife (his former secretary) still called him by his surname.

"Cat's gone." He was looking straight at her. "I fired her. Hadn't been happy with her for some time."

"But . . ." Becky struggled with her conscience. If he'd fired her because of the case histories, she ought to tell him the truth. It wasn't fair.

"I ought to say she split on you about your case history scam."

The trail of sweat trickling down Becky's back was accumulating in the little dip at the back of her buttocks. "Of course, I don't approve but it showed initiative. It's not as though the work experience girl was staff."

"Exactly," burst out Becky.

"And that's why you're here, Becky. I like your initiative. I like your willingness to work hard. I like your ideas." Brian thumped the desk. "So, do you want it or not?"

Quadruple fucks. He didn't want to leap into bed with her too, did he? That was another thing this man was legendary for.

"You're disappointing me already, Becky. I thought you'd be with me by now." His eyes were boring into hers. "I'm offering you Cat's job. As editor. Well, what's your answer?"

SEVEN MONTHS TO GO

CHAPTER
EIGHTEEN

Helen

"So you see, I want a white garden to remember him by. Not a big one; just a little patch by the apple tree. We used to climb it as children, you know, although that's how I broke my arm. Maurice pushed me, although he said he didn't."

Helen nodded. Poor Doris with her arthritic arm and her only living relative so recently buried. Life didn't go on for ever. David had said something similar the other night and she had to agree. One more reason why she ought to consider his proposal. Did she really want to be alone for the rest of her life?

"I thought white roses and maybe a white lilac tree?"

Helen knelt down to feel the soil's consistency. "Possibly." Not that there was anything wrong with being alone; at times, she was positively grateful for the solitude. But at other times, like bank holidays when everyone else was busy being a family or on Saturday nights when there was nothing on television (why, when everyone had been saying this for years, did no one do anything about it?), she rather liked the idea of being married. And, there was no doubt about it, all the fuss about Geoff's wedding — which she'd picked up from

159

Daisy and Ben who were going to be "flower fairies" as they'd put it — was beginning to get to her.

"Your daughter's friend Janie did the funeral, you know." Doris was sitting down on the little garden stool by the summer house, her thin Stilton-blue-veined legs bare since the weather, for April, was surprisingly warm. "She and her neighbour Marjorie who can only be a bit younger than me. Everyone's going back to work, you know. I always fancied being on the telly myself as one of those weather girls but I suppose they'd say I was too old. Should have done it ten years ago."

Helen smiled. She'd known Doris since the children were little and considered her old then. Never in her wildest dreams did she think her life would turn out like this, grateful to have her small core of loyal customers to pay the mortgage (and their company too, which was strangely comforting, especially when it came to Doris whom she'd known for so many years). She might not have a husband or financial security but her life had broadened into wider horizons than she'd ever thought possible.

"Hear they're doing your husband's wedding too."

Helen busied herself in the roses catalogue. Husbands were like houses in Doris's book: they belonged to you, long after you'd left and it took several years for the real incumbent to be known as the rightful owner by the locals.

"Is she?"

Doris's chin wobbled in affirmation like three turkey necks in one.

"For Weddings and a Funeral, they call themselves. After some film apparently. They suggested 'Come on, Baby, Light My Fire' for Maurice's crematorium bit. Went down a treat it did. Your Geoff's bride's having the works, Janie said. Real fussy, she is. Met her, have you?"

"No. No, I haven't." Helen turned over a page. "If I were you, Doris, I'd recommend Peace. They're a creamy yellow with a beautiful scent. I used to have them at the Old Rectory. In fact, they're still doing quite nicely . . ."

She pulled herself up just in time but Doris didn't seem to have noticed. Luckily Candlewick Cottage, where Doris and Maurice had lived since birth, was a good five miles away from her old home so hopefully she hadn't been spotted. But it wouldn't be long before she was (in fact, she was on her way there now) and she simply had to work out what to say to Robin.

"You could have some stocks too. They're a lovely colour. And I'll drop into the garden centre to find out about lilac bushes."

Doris nodded as if expecting no less. "Right you are. Matter of fact, I've been meaning to ask you something else." She nodded at Helen's hands; normally she had her gardening gloves with her but today she'd left them in her van. "Nice ring."

Helen flushed.

"Let's have a look. Sapphire, is it?"

"Yes. It's a sort of family ring."

Doris's chins wobbled. "A family ring, eh? For a minute, I thought you'd gone and got yourself engaged seeing as how your husband's getting married again."

Helen managed to laugh gaily. "What, me? I'm far too old for that."

Doris's face gleamed with disapproval.

"I mean, no one's really too old for marriage of course but I've got quite set in my ways — you must know what I mean . . ." Horribly conscious she was getting into even deeper water, Helen snapped the catalogue shut and whistled to Dandy who came bounding up, reeking of the manure pit. Hopefully, it might disguise his fart smells. "Well, must be getting on now. I'll ring about the lilac to give you the price. Bye, Doris. Take care."

She shouldn't have worn the ring. It was mad. She'd only tried it on again to make David happy; grateful that he'd picked her up from the station; grateful that he was still there and hadn't seen her rejection of his proposal as a rejection altogether. "I'd love to see it on your finger again," he had said. And then, when he had admired it — and it did really look rather nice — he'd added: "Why don't you keep it on for a bit. Just see how you get on with it?"

So she had. And to her surprise, she rather liked it. Even after all these years since Geoff, her left hand had felt horribly naked. It was the one thing she'd found hard to get used to. Sometimes, she'd tried wearing a costume jewellery ring but they'd all looked like a cheap excuse; like a little lie pretending to be something it wasn't.

In Debenhams this morning, the sales assistant had glanced at it and treated her, or so it seemed, with a little more respect. How ridiculous, thought Helen, pulling up outside the Old Rectory, that in today's day and age, marriage should still be seen as the "right thing to do". Or was it? Was it simply her old stupid traditional values which she somehow couldn't shed?

And if so, why was it that — even though she couldn't imagine getting back with Geoff — she still felt she couldn't possibly be married to anyone who *wasn't* him? How could anyone else ever fill the shoes of a man whom she'd spent most of her life with and had two children by?

"All right, Dandy. I'm coming."

He was barking excitedly, desperate to get out of the van and shoot down the garden he'd known so well as a puppy and into the paddock at the bottom. She too, thought Helen, as she carted her tools out of the van and down the side gate, was beginning to get used to it. In fact, if she closed her eyes, she could easily imagine that . . .

"Ah, good. Helen. How are you?" Robin was outside the greenhouse, wiping down the panes of glass with a cloth. "Don't mind me. I won't get in your way. Thought I ought to sort this out; the previous owner didn't bother with it and it's got into a terrible mess."

Geoff had given it to her when they'd moved in. She'd always wanted a greenhouse and her subsequent prize-winning tomatoes had usually come first or second in the village fête. Helen swallowed hard and automatically twisted her ring. Was it her imagination or did Robin glance down at it too? Something inside her made her turn it again so the stone faced inwards.

"Thought I'd start on the vegetable patch," she said, turning away. "By the way, I hope you don't mind me asking but, as it's such a lovely day, I wondered if your wife wanted to sit next to me."

Robin's head jerked up towards the house where a face sat, looking through the window just as it always did. "I'm not sure." The jaunty tone in his voice had gone. "I could go in and ask her. Are you sure you don't mind? She can't talk, you know. She won't be any company."

Helen didn't normally get angry but she resented the patronising tone in Robin's voice. "It's not the company I was thinking of. I just thought it might be nice for your wife to see her garden. But if you don't think it's a good idea . . ."

"No. No. It is. I'm being thoughtless. I suppose I just get used to doing things my way and usually she's in the house while I'm dashing around, doing the shopping or the gardening or whatever else needs doing. You're right. It is a warm day and it could be just what she needs. Thank you, Helen."

And he was gone, marching sturdily up the incline of the lawn towards the poor woman who was waiting inside.

Robin — who'd abandoned the greenhouse to do "a few chores inside" — was quite wrong. Sylvia was excellent company. In fact, Helen thought with a wry smile, she was the perfect companion. She listened (or seemed to) without butting in because she couldn't talk. Helen had always talked while she dug, although it

164

was usually to herself and often out loud which made her feel slightly mad. Now, she had a perfect excuse.

"These artichokes will be fine given time. I put them in, you know, when the children were little."

Helen looked back but Sylvia's face, if surprised, showed no emotion. "I used to live here, you see, when I was married. Your husband doesn't know that. I should have told him when he first caught me snooping over the fence but somehow the time didn't seem right. And now it's a bit late so I'm telling you instead."

Gosh, the soil was heavy. It needed mulching. "We brought up the children here. In fact, we were here for nearly fifteen years. It was my dream house and this was my dream garden. I used to come down here to escape from my husband."

This time, there seemed like a flicker of something akin to recognition in Sylvia's thin pale face framed by her short rather reddish-auburn hair and Helen had one of those intuitional flashes; something which told her that all had not been right with this marriage before this poor woman was in a wheelchair.

"I could grow things here which I couldn't grow in my real life." Helen's fingers worked their way deftly across the soil, yanking out weeds with long, unwieldy umbilical cords. "And then something happened."

She stopped. For years, she hadn't allowed herself to think of it. To think of the one stupid, stupid thing which she'd done that hadn't seemed at all stupid at the time but which had changed her life for ever.

"I . . ." She stopped, trying to find the words. "I . . ."

There was the sudden sound of barking and from the distance, Dandy tore up the garden, racing towards them. "Stop," shouted Helen, standing in front of the wheelchair; for a minute, she thought he was going to knock it over. "What are you doing, you daft dog." Dandy stood, panting before her and she prayed he wouldn't start farting again. "He must have been chasing the rabbits again. I'm sorry. He always used to do that."

Sylvia was looking down at the dog who, sensing her needs, began licking her hands voraciously.

"I'm sorry. I hope you don't mind."

Was that a gleam in her eye? A gleam which definitely hadn't been there before?

"How are you getting on?" Robin's jolly voice strode down the lawn towards them. "Getting a bit chilly now, isn't it?"

Helen was about to disagree but something stopped her. "Shall we go in now, dear? Thanks, Helen. You've done some sterling work. Like a cup of tea in the kitchen before you go?"

He was glancing down at her hand again but the stone was still out of sight.

"No, thanks. Think I'd better get going. I need to get to the nursery before it closes. See you next week, Sylvia. And you, Robin."

"I've got your money here."

He handed her a brown envelope. Accepting it graciously, she felt awkward; how weird to be paid for doing your own garden. She'd almost have paid him for the pleasure.

166

"By the way, do you mind if I make it Wednesday next week instead of Tuesday? My daughter's just been promoted and I've promised to help out her nanny."

"Wednesday? That's fine. Every day's the same to us, isn't it dear?"

She used to feel like that until she made herself do something and a wave of sympathy for Robin and his wife washed through her. "The greenhouse looks better."

"Do you think so?" He sounded brighter.

"I do. I could bring you some cuttings if you like from mine."

"That would be wonderful." He left the wheelchair at the back door, rather to Helen's consternation, and walked with her to the van. "Thank you," he said in a low voice. "I don't just mean for the garden. I mean, for Sylvia. I should have thought of that myself. It was selfish of me."

"No. No, it wasn't." Helen almost wanted to pat his arm in reassurance. "It's just that sometimes it takes someone else to point something out. Besides, I liked having her there. We had a good chat."

He laughed sadly.

"No, really. I meant it. Come on, Dandy. Time to go."

CHAPTER
NINETEEN

Mel

It had been a while now since the "little problem with Josh", as Richard called it.

Little problem indeed, thought Mel to herself as she stood in her underwear, ironing her cassock ready for the Sunday service. (It was unseasonably warm today so she wouldn't bother wearing anything else under it.) Is that what you'd call the filthy row they'd all had when Richard had called her back from the hospital because Josh was, as he put it, "in some kind of trouble with the neighbours".

Josh had locked himself into his bedroom again and it had taken all her powers of persuasion to get him to unlock it. When he finally did, he refused to look her in the eye and went back to his laptop, his back resolutely towards her.

"Josh," she'd said, placing her hands on his shoulder.

"Gerroff." He moved his chair away from her, knocking over a bowl of half-eaten cereal. Honestly! He wasn't meant to eat breakfast up here. He usually ate it standing up in the kitchen which was bad enough.

Don't sweat the small stuff. "Look. I know this has been a difficult time but can you tell me exactly what

168

happened? Dad said you punched Alex from next door and made his nose bleed."

No answer. Josh was scrolling up and down Facebook as though he couldn't hear.

Some kids should come with subtitles.

"Is that true?" she persisted.

"He deserved it."

"Why?"

"He's friends with that kid. You know, the idiot that ran Amy over. He said you wouldn't forgive him so you shouldn't be a vicar any more." Josh turned round and she could see his eyes sparkling with tears. "Is that true?"

Yes, yes, yes. "Well," began Mel carefully. "It's not exactly right . . ."

"Do you forgive him or not?"

Dear God, give me a hand here, will you? "I'm trying, Josh. But it's difficult."

"Random."

"Sorry?"

"It's like random, Mum."

They'd had this discussion before — and with Amy too. As far as she could work out, "random" meant anything you wanted it to in teen-speak. Very useful for an entire generation that had grown up grunting instead of articulating. Still, now definitely wasn't the time to argue.

Josh was still talking to his screen. Why did eye contact end after the age of twelve? "Just cos you're a Christian doesn't mean you have to forgive everyone.

169

And that's why I hit him. I was defending you, Mum. You should be pleased."

Pleased? Because her son had hit another boy who had, quite rightly, accused her of acting in an unChristian way?

Josh had turned back to his screen. "He says his mum says everyone is talking about you."

A wave of unease washed through her. "Are they?"

"But I don't care. I think you did the right thing. 'Sides, what goes round, comes round. That's what the Buddhists say. Amy was going to become a Buddhist, you know. I'm thinking of it too."

Christ didn't dismiss other religions, Mel told herself. He listened to them respectfully; told his followers to give Caesar what Caesar was due.

"Hang on. What have you got in your ear?"

He grinned. "It's an ink cartridge. I lost the one I ordered on the net so I put this in to keep the hole open." He glanced back at the screen.

Dear God, what was *that*? Facebook. She knew that much. But she'd never seen those pictures before. Mel caught her breath as Amy beamed out at her. "Lovely, healthy, happy wide-awake Amy. Loves dancing, the Wattevers, her best friend Sharon and shopping."

"Why don't you visit her?" she suggested softly. "The doctors say it might help to talk to her."

"I am visiting her. On the net."

"I mean go to her. Visit her."

"What's the point? She can't hear, can she?"

"She might."

"I'm not a kid any more, Mum. I'm a teenager."

"Exactly. And you've got GCSEs next year. If you've got the time and energy to go on the computer, you can do some work."

Was it possible to sue Facebook for destroying your son's school career?

"Just open your school bag and do some work." She picked it up. Lord it was heavy. "Josh! You've got beer cans in here!"

"Sowot?" Josh scrolled down the page. "Least it's not vodka. Amy used to drink that, you know. 'Sides, I'm going to leave school as soon as I can and have a gap year or two. Then I might go to uni. Can I have a Prince Albert, by the way?"

"I thought you'd given up history for geography."

"It's an earring, Mum. Don't you know anything? You have it put on your thing. You know."

No, she didn't. But she could take a horrible guess. What had got into him? Was it Amy or being a teenager or . . .

"Get out of my room."

He was almost pushing her now. "Get out, Mum. I need my space."

Since then, Josh had stayed either in his room or gone out, slamming the door behind him, to be with friends. Meanwhile, life had to go on, even though there was no change with Amy. Richard had to find a job and she — here she gave the iron a sudden angry push — had to take the Sunday service. Yet another packed service where everyone would be looking at her just as it had been since the accident. The vicar who couldn't say "I forgive you".

★ ★ ★

Mel almost laughed when she took her place at the front. The church was packed; even more so than it had been last Christmas. She'd been right. Everyone had come to gloat or wallow in her grief.

The first bit of the service wasn't too bad; lots of jolly post-Easter hymns during which she realised that one of her regular parishioners whose name she couldn't remember (either through stress or the usual middle-age memory loss which seemed to be happening more and more recently) was staring at her chest. Blast! Two crucial buttons down the front of her cassock were undone which wouldn't have mattered if she'd remembered to put on her surplice. Only a man, with time to spare, could have designed a coat-dress with thirty-two buttons down the front.

Oh, God, time for the sermon. Every topic that was recommended for this part of the church calendar seemed to have some link with forgiveness so in the end, she'd plumped for the Good Samaritan, realising too late it would be construed by some as a criticism of Kevin who had failed to stop for her daughter in her hour of need.

And then the Lord's Prayer. "Forgive us our sins as we forgive . . ."

Mel made her lips move but somehow couldn't get the words to come out of her mouth at the same time. She lifted her head slightly while keeping her eyes shut, but not so tight she could not see out. Sure enough, several pairs of eyes were on her — and not just because of the open buttons.

Say the words. Say the words. He was a young boy. He was too scared to stop. Yes, he should have done but he lacked the maturity to do the right thing.

At the door, she had to steel herself to cope with the flood of "I'm so sorrys" and the more challenging "How are you doings?" One woman, whom Mel hadn't seen before, had shaken her hand limply, looked at her oddly with a squint that might or might not have been the sun in her eyes and said, "It can't be easy for that young boy either." Mel had managed to nod her agreement.

"Hi," said someone else.

It took her a moment to recognise the kindly tall burly man shaking her hand firmly, holding it for a second.

"Geoff. Geoff Hastings," he said as though she might have forgotten. "I haven't been here for years but I thought I might give it another go. This couldn't have been easy for you."

She grasped gratefully at the words. Not an inane enquiry on how she was doing (how could the mother of a teenager in a coma be doing?) but a simple acknowledgment that this service was one of the hardest she'd ever had to conduct.

"You're right," she said quietly. "It wasn't."

"If you ever need to talk," he'd let go of her hand now, "just give me a ring."

Mel was suddenly conscious of a short plump woman behind wearing thick make-up and heavy expensive gold earrings. "May I introduce my fiancée, Monique."

Trying to hide her surprise, Mel held out her hand. "Congratulations. I'm looking forward to our talk about the wedding."

"It's on the sixteenth, isn't it?"

The woman's voice was squeakier than she'd expected; rather like a little girl. She had a squeaky voice now! Yet it had sounded gruff before — was one an affectation? The squeak certainly didn't fit the heavy frame.

"I can't remember offhand but it's in the diary. Your fiancé spoke to my daughter about it before . . . before . . ."

Why had she said that? Why had she felt the need to slip in the phrase "my daughter" as though to convince herself, if no one else, that Amy was still there. Still alive; properly alive.

"Sure you're all right?" Geoff's voice was coming at her like a sound through water.

"Yes, thanks." She followed them as they made their way down the path; the funny little short squat woman hanging on to Geoff's arm as though worried he might escape. The queue was dwindling now. Just another couple of minutes and she could get out of these ridiculous clothes (something she'd campaigned about at theological college along with other radicals, even though they hadn't got anywhere) and have a couple of peaceful minutes in the vestry before she got on with the process of tidying up. Lucy usually helped her but she'd had to go early to cover another service.

Weaving her way past the gravestones, she headed with relief to the cool calm of the church.

174

"Well, God, I did it."

Her words echoed into the high vaults.

"As you'll have heard, I'm still working on the confession; in fact, it would have been nice to have had more help."

Silence. Then again, what did she expect? Sighing, Mel's eye fell on the silver communion wine cup, still half full with the usual bread lumps left by those who liked to dip their wafers in, together with God knows how much dribble and germs.

Dear God! What was she doing?

Mel looked down at the empty chalice and dabbed her mouth with the sleeve of her cassock. It was a warm, not unpleasant and surprisingly guilt-free experience. Mel looked up at the beautiful stained-glass window which had been donated by a grieving widower in 1897. "Was that your idea of help, God?"

No answer.

Amy drank too much. Amy. Hospital. Mel's head began to throb. She'd promised Richard that she'd take over. But she couldn't drive; not after the equivalent of at least two glasses. Fuck. Mel heard the unfamiliar word coming out of her mouth at the same time that she heard the heavy clink of the church door.

"Who's that?" she called, horribly aware her voice sounded slightly slurred as she made her way out of the vestry.

"Geoff."

His fiancée, she noticed with relief, wasn't there unless she was part of that pillar next to him.

175

"Hope you don't mind but I was concerned about you so I came back to see if there was anything I could do."

He must be able to smell the drink on her breath. She certainly could.

"I had some wine." She was definitely feeling giddy now. "I shouldn't have done. And now I can't drive to the hospital. I need to see my daughter . . ."

The tears were spilling out now. "I need to see Amy."

Dimly she was aware of a strong arm guiding her towards a pew. The thought flashed through her that Geoff was what her mother might have called "a bit of a ladies' man". Still, he was being extremely kind.

"You sit down, Mel. That's right. Now where can I get some water round here?"

She tried to think. "From the tap at the back. For the flower-arrangers."

Seconds later, she was aware of a plastic tumbler being put in her hands. She drank it and then another.

"It's what I used to do when I had too much. Do you want me to drive you to the hospital now or do you think you need to go back home?"

"To the hospital, please."

She must have fallen asleep in the car, even though it was only a twenty-minute drive. But when she woke up, she was aware of him saying her name.

"Mel? Mel? We're here now. Are you sure you're all right to go in?"

She nodded.

"I can't take what I used to either. After my wife left, I stopped drinking because I didn't want to be one of

176

those sad men who drink alone. But I must admit to enjoying a few drinks with friends every now and then."

She fumbled with the car door. "Thanks for understanding."

"It was a pleasure." He leaned over to help her and his arm brushed hers. Scorched, she leapt out.

"See you at our meeting," he said, leaning across the passenger seat to speak through the window. "Let me know if there's any change with your daughter."

Richard had just left, the nurses said. He'd left a message; something about seeing her back at the house. Silently, she took her seat at the side of the hospital bed.

Amy was lying there, head on one side, as though asleep. Leaning over, she gently brushed a strand of her daughter's blonde hair away from her face. As she did so, her other hand leaned on something hard under the pillow. What on earth was Amy's mobile doing there?

"Your son left it."

The nurse — the same kindly one who had been on last time — had come into the room.

"My son?"

"He visited last night after you'd gone. Left his iPod too and his sister's mobile. He said she couldn't live without her phone and when she woke up, she'd feel better if it was there. We all thought it was terribly sweet. You've obviously got a lovely son, there, vicar. A real credit to you."

CHAPTER
TWENTY

Janie

Maurice's funeral had been such a resounding success that the phone hadn't stopped ringing with Marjorie's friends putting their names down.

"I don't want the usual boring service," boomed one octogenarian down the phone. "I fancy going out with a bang, not a whimper. Mind you, I'm not sure about the Wedding March. Personally. I fancy something by Vera Lynn. Can I come round and discuss it?"

"You don't think it's a bit soon?" ventured Janie.

"At my age, nothing's too soon or too late." The old boy chuckled. "You'll find that out if you ever get as old as me. I can put down a deposit if you like."

Janie reported the conversation when Marjorie returned from her Salsa for the Over-Seventies. "So like Godfrey. Always wanting to be in control. I'm not surprised he wants his send-off organised in advance. Knowing his family, they'd have him cremated in double fast time so they could read the will."

"How do you know him?" Janie was sitting in one of Marjorie's wonderfully comfortable deep armchairs which seemed to sink down for ever.

"Bridge." Marjorie airily lit up a Marlboro. "The card type — not the dental. His wife was a friend until she dropped off on the golf course."

"How awful."

"Rather. Can you imagine being found in flagrante on the rough with the coach? Godfrey had no idea. None of us did." She chuckled. "He was a bit under par after that."

"I'm not surprised." Janie lit up one of her roll-ups.

"Of course, every single woman over the age of fifty in the Tuesday Club has been after him since." Marjorie chuckled; a deep low chuckle fuelled by her 30 a day. "Men never last long when their wives go. They're snapped up like two for one at Tesco and before you can put in your falsies, they're married again."

Falsies? "Teeth, darling. Not your padded bras although I was rather intrigued by yours when I emptied the washing machine the other day. It's almost obscene the way women launch themselves at their dead friends' husbands. 'Stay mean; keep 'em keen' is what I say. Now, let's get back to bookings. How are we doing?"

"Five funeral provisionals but only one wedding."

Marjorie sniffed. "That's because we all know our funerals are inevitable in the end but a wedding is something one can avoid. Now tell me a bit more about this wedding. The bride sounds rather demanding."

"She is. Tried to pretend I'd got the time wrong for our meeting. I can't think why Geoff — that's my friend's dad — is marrying her. She's not pretty and doesn't seem to be a particularly nice person either."

179

Marjorie stubbed out her cigarette. "Talking of not very nice people, I saw Mac today."

Janie's heart began to pound. Ever since she'd thrown him out of bed, she'd refused to allow herself to think about him. Instead, she'd pulled a mental shutter down every time the words "How could he?" and "I trusted him" came into her head. Mental shutters, she'd discovered many years ago at school, could be extremely useful.

"Where?"

"In the underground market. To give him his credit, he came up and asked how you were."

Marjorie was looking at her quizzically.

"And what did you say?"

"That you were getting on very nicely with your new business and that you had several young suitors in hot pursuit."

Janie giggled. She could just see Marjorie standing there in her plum velvet hat, using wonderful old-fashioned words like "suitors". Mac, who hadn't been the brightest of sparks, probably thought she was being headhunted by Burtons.

"Thanks."

"Not at all. You know, dear, you deserve much better than that."

Janie hated it when Marjorie spoke like that. Becky used to say the same at school to be kind. But what was the point? She hadn't been as clever as the other girls — which was why she hadn't got anywhere with a career — and she couldn't even get a boyfriend to stay.

"And don't think it's because you're not very hot at reading or writing." Marjorie was narrowing her eyes which could get very black when she was in one of her you'll-be-fine moods. "No, don't deny it. I'm not daft, dear. I've noticed."

Janie began to feel that usual horrible feeling creeping over her.

"It doesn't mean you're stupid — far from it. And it doesn't mean you have to resort to followers like Mac. There are lots of nice young men still left out there. It's not like the Great War, you know."

"Isn't it?" Janie kicked off her trainers and began sketching a face on the back of her hand with a Biro. "In my experience, men might not be dead but a large proportion are either gay or married. 'Sides, I'm going to stop looking for someone and concentrate on my career." She examined her sketch. It was a man all right but nothing like Mac. "I simply can't afford to go wrong any more."

Marjorie chuckled. "You'd have to sack yourself. Don't look like that, dear. I'm only joking."

One of the joys of being your own boss was that you're entitled to a day off, argued Janie to herself as she made her way through the underground on the way to Becky's office. Besides, it had been ages since they'd met up and when Becky had called to suggest lunch, she'd jumped at it. It wasn't as if she and Marjorie were busy yet.

Making her way to Becky's building — which threatened to pierce the skyline — she negotiated her

181

way through revolving doors and made her way to reception.

"I'm here to see Becky," she stumbled.

"Becky who?"

She almost gave her married name but then remembered Becks was known at work by her maiden name. "Becky Hastings."

The man glanced appreciatively at her shiny black plastic zip-up jacket — another Oxfam buy which went rather nicely with the short red skirt and peacock blue tights. "Sign here, can you? And put the time."

Tongue pressed against her cheek in concentration, Janie gripped the pen with terror. The signature bit was all right — she'd perfected that after years of practice — but the 12.15 p.m. came out as a 21.51. Hopefully, he wouldn't notice.

"Take a seat over there please. Mzzz Hastings will be down soon."

Janie didn't need asking twice. There was a great pile of magazines on the table and anyway she could sit for hours on this deep comfortable leather sofa and look at all the glamorous people going in and out. That girl who'd just come out of the lift, simply had to be a size zero! In fact, she looked as though she was going to snap as she walked with that enormous black portfolio under her arm.

And as for that long-haired chap behind her with the yellow ochre Worzel Gummidge hat. What was he? A photographer? An editor? Janie began to wish she was safely back in her little cottage, pretending to run a business. It was at times like this that she realised how far her world was removed from her friend's.

"Janie! Sorry I'm late." Becky emerged from the lift in a flurry. She almost didn't recognise her in the smart black trousers with the skimpy lime green top that was surely too cold for this time of year. Still, it was baking inside.

"Had a meeting with my deputy," Becky was saying. "You haven't been waiting long, have you? I thought we'd go next door to the salad bar. I've only got ten minutes; you don't mind do you? But otherwise we'd never have got to see each other. Gosh, that's a great sketch of the receptionist. It's just like him."

Janie followed her through the street, which was teeming with other women all in proper jobs with proper suits and proper career expressions, into a glass restaurant with high-backed beech chairs at counters. Great, she was starving.

"Just the rocket salad for me," said Becky when the waitress approached.

Bloody hell, what kind of prices were these? "Same for me. Thanks."

"So!" Becky glanced at her mobile and then back at Janie. "How's it going? Want to show me your business plan?"

"Not quite now, thanks. Marjorie and I are still working on it." She shrank back into her seat, feeling increasingly out of her depth. This sharp-trousered Becky with the dark wine-coloured Prada handbag, wasn't her Becky any more. Not the one she'd grown up with. "Starting your own business can be a bit slow at first."

"But you've got Dad's wedding."

"Yeah. Thanks for that. And there are a few other irons in the fire too."

Becky picked at a lettuce leaf which probably cost about four quid. "What did you think of her?"

"Monique? She wasn't what I expected to be honest. I mean she's not like any of your dad's other girlfriends, is she?"

Becky snorted. "You can say that again. I don't get what he sees in her. It's not as though she's got the personality to make up for her lack of looks. She just sits there like a blob of lard when she's with my dad. The only time she gets animated is when she talks about her work. Talking of work, I haven't told you my news." Becky leaned towards her, eyes sparkling. "I've been made editor! Isn't that amazing! Mind you, I've never worked so hard in my life. I'm shattered."

"Thought it was all that hot sex with Steve."

Becky snorted again. "Sex? What's that? I haven't seen him for six days. Know what the earliest is that I've been out of this place? Ten o'clock. I'll be bringing my bed in next."

"What about the kids?"

"Well, I wake them up when I get back so I can see them but then Laura — you know, the nanny — doesn't like that because it means they wake up later in the morning."

Janie reckoned she knew slightly less about kids than her friend but even she wondered about Becky's

184

child-rearing skills. "Is it a good idea to wake them when you get back?"

Becky stared at her. "How else would I see them? Listen, I'm really sorry but I'm going to have to go now. I've got a meeting with Pictures and then a briefing with the editor-in-chief and then . . ."

Janie allowed herself to switch off as the details of Becky's impossibly busy day wafted over her head. It had taken an hour and a half to come up here just for ten minutes of her friend's time.

"I said, how's Mac?"

Suddenly aware that Becky was actually addressing a question at her instead of focusing on her own life, she jolted awake. "Oh, he's gone. It didn't work out. Well, it did for him in one way but not with me."

Becky was rifling through her bag. "Can't say I'm sorry. He wasn't the brightest of sparks, was he? You couldn't lend me £20, could you? I seem to have left my purse in the office. By the way, I've got something here that might interest you."

She shoved a piece of paper into Janie's hands. "It's some new research by a private clinic on dyslexia — no, don't give me that look. I know you can't bear talking about it. But it might be worth investigating."

Janie spent an hour or so browsing round some shoe shops in Knightsbridge, knowing she couldn't possibly afford anything. The train fare and the twenty quid for ten lettuce leaves had wiped out her spending money for the week.

185

Then there was the rent to pay for the cottage which was due next week. As for that dyslexia treatment Becky had told her about, it cost a fortune. Besides, what if she had it and it still didn't work, like those exercises they had given her at school? Then she'd feel even thicker than ever.

Janie spent the train journey from Paddington feeling slightly sick. Perhaps she should just have gone on the dole instead of recklessly starting her own business. A business plan, Becky had said, but what was the point in that when you didn't have enough business to start with? At this rate, she wouldn't be able to afford to live unless she asked her parents for money and that was out of the question. They were, she thought, getting off the train at Oxford, disappointed enough in her as it was.

Shit! Janie eyed the cycle rack with horror. Who could have done that to her bike? That front tyre looked as though it had been slashed deliberately and . . .

"Something happened to your bike, miss?"

A couple of kids in black hoodies — one with a large gold cross round his neck — were talking over their shoulders to her before running off, giggling.

"Come back," she yelled. "Come back . . ."

Too late. Shit. It wasn't fair. It wasn't fucking fair.

"Hello, my friend!"

No! "Sorry, I can't give you anything right now. Look! They've slashed my front tyre."

The woman was shaking her head. "Did you do what I said? Broaden your horizons?"

What was she? Some kind of fortune teller?

"Well, I've started a wedding and funeral agency with a friend."

The woman nodded. "You get grant for new business. Go to Job Centre."

Why hadn't she thought of that? "Brilliant. Thanks very much."

Shit. She could hardly walk away now. "Here." She pressed a £2 coin into the palm of her hand. "Do you have change?"

"Sorry, my friend. See you next week."

Janie was still bubbling with excitement when she got back, holding a wodge of leaflets that the kind middle-aged woman at the Job Centre had handed her. She'd just pop to the loo and then go round to Marjorie with the information and then . . . blast. What was that? Brown envelopes addressed "To the Occupier; do not throw away" were not, in her experience, good news.

"Dear Tenant, We are writing to inform you that, as of next month, your rent will be increased by . . ."

Appalled, Janie skimmed the rest of the letter. How could she afford another £100 a month without Mac's contribution. She'd have to move. But where?

SIX MONTHS TO GO

CHAPTER
TWENTY-ONE

Becky

Becky barely looked up from the pile of proofs as Nancy dumped another pile next to her. From the day she'd accepted Brian's offer, she hadn't been able to see one inch of free space on her desk. One day, she thought, downing the cold Starbucks coffee — no time to drink it before — they'd find her underneath a tomb of papers, still trying to belt something out on the keyboard.

But she loved it, didn't she? For fuck's sake, Becky, that's what being an editor is all about.

"You've got half an hour for those — max," said Nancy apologetically on her way out. "They're late already and Pics is in a foul mood. More coffee?"

"Great." Becky was already trying to look at the second pile at the same time as the first. Fuck, were they on June already even though it was only May? When she'd first started on magazines, they were a good two months or maybe three ahead. Now the lead time was getting shorter and shorter in the frenetic race — shared by all other ambitious magazines — to get newsy-angled features in. Like Sally Smith.

Becky felt a nervous muscle twitch in her right hand. The interview with Sally was a real coup, which they'd never have got without Monique. To be fair, she had followed her promise. She'd shown the copy to the woman and she (he?) had approved, providing a few small changes were made. But then — and this was when she began to feel slightly nauseous — then she'd added just a couple of little points. Nothing big. Well not really and Brian had insisted on her putting back the bit about . . .

"Phone call on line one," said Nancy, poking her head round the door.

"I said I wasn't to be disturbed." Sometimes you'd think it was Nancy who'd been promoted, thought Becky irritably.

"It's your dad's fiancée. Says it's urgent."

What? "Monique? Is dad OK?"

"Yes but I'm not."

Her cold voice serrated the air and instantly Becky knew the game was up.

"Why?" She could hear her own voice wavering. "What's wrong?"

"You changed the wording in the Sally Smith piece. It's nothing like the original and she's extremely upset."

This hadn't been the first time this had happened in Becky's career. Bloody hell, it happened all the time in journalism. But this was different. Monique was, though she hated to say it, almost family. "I wouldn't say it's nothing like the original," she faltered. "As you know, these pieces have to be cut . . . ."

"But not added." Monique was audibly spitting. "You referred to Sally Smith's sex change even though that was off the record."

"Yes but . . ."

"Even worse, you referred to the accusation that she had killed her first husband — even though it was never proved."

She'd told Brian that shouldn't go in but he'd insisted.

"I'm afraid that the final decision about what should and shouldn't be mentioned, was down to my editor-in-chief so . . ."

"Then I'd better tell him that we're going to the Press Council."

Fuck. "Please, Monique, don't do that. I'm new in this job and it really wouldn't look good." To her dismay, Becky felt her eyes filling with exhausted tears. "Is there nothing I can do?"

"Print an apology."

That was just as bad. An apology discredited the entire publication; made it look as though it couldn't do its job properly. For a new editor, it was the kiss of death.

"On the other hand," continued Monique, "I'm not sure an apology would help. The damage has been done now. There is one alternative."

"Yes," she gasped.

"Pay me £2,500."

Had she heard her correctly? "£2,500?"

"That's right."

"To go to Sally Smith?"

There was a slight hesitation. "Partly to her and partly to my business for the problems this is going to cause me. I might well lose clients over this, Becky."

"But we don't have that sort of money."

"You have a budget, don't you? Use it."

The phone went dead but Becky continued staring at the receiver. Her father's future wife — bloody hell, her future stepmother — was threatening to blackmail her. But what choice did she have?

Monique was right. She did have a budget but if she parted with this kind of money, it would mean that there wouldn't be much left if there was another bidding war for another vital case history that they simply had to have to stay ahead of the game.

And that's what she did, wasn't it. What she'd always done. Stay ahead of the game. Becky stared at the screen in front of her, seeing her own determined reflection staring back. And she wasn't going to stop now.

By the time she'd got back that night, the house was dark, apart from the kitchen which was spotless. Steve or maybe Laura had obviously cleared up the debris of the day and the black and white marble-effect surfaces were neatly wiped down and the floor clean. The house almost looked as though it belonged to someone else.

Becky's stomach was rumbling but she couldn't be bothered to eat. Opening the fridge door, she couldn't see one thing which appealed. Packets of cheese and a couple of half-opened tins were neatly sealed with cling film and labelled in her nanny's loopy writing. Did she, Becky, really live here?

There was a note on the kitchen table. "Ring your dad. Urgent. He'll be up late." Late? What was late in

194

ordinary people's language? Becky glanced at the neon kitchen timer. 11.56p.m. She hesitated. Urgent. Did that mean "Monique urgent" or "something else urgent". She hadn't thought Monique would have told him about their conversation because she wouldn't want to mention the money but on the other hand . . .

Fingers shaking, she punched in her father's number. By the fifth ring, she was just about to put it down when he answered, sounding sleepy. "Dad, did I wake you?"

"It's all right." He sounded cool and her heart lurched with apprehension. "I'm glad you rang. I have to say, Becky, that Monique told me what happened and she's very upset."

Upset! With two and a half thousand! "Well I'm sorry, Dad, but I have to say that this is between Monique and me. It's business and . . ."

"You're wrong, there, I'm afraid, Rebecca."

Ouch. He hadn't called her that for years and only then when she'd misbehaved as a child. "Whatever upsets Monique, upsets me too. I must say that I'm surprised by your behaviour. I know journalists get a bad press but I thought your mother and I had brought you up to be more responsible."

This wasn't fair. "It wasn't like that. My boss changed a few things and then the subs . . ."

"I don't want to discuss this any more. It's late and I'm tired."

"So am I."

"That's another thing. Do you think it's fair on Steve to come home from work and have to cope with the kids while you're out?"

This was too much. "Dad, I was working. Just as you did when Adam and I were growing up. Mum had to hold the fort then, didn't she?"

"Exactly." He sounded sad now, rather than angry. "And that's just what I'm talking about. Good night. We'll discuss it in the morning if you want."

How dare he patronise her! Becky shook with anger as she thudded up the stairs. Her father had always been so narrow-minded; only seeing things his way. No wonder her mother hadn't been able to stay. It would have been different if it had been Steve coming in late; her father wouldn't have seen anything wrong with that. But things had changed since his day and there were countless numbers of women like herself, working all hours to pay the high mortgages and school fees (their nursery bill was staggering) and nannies and God knows what else before other essentials like food and holidays.

"Sshhh." Steve turned over in bed. "You'll wake the children."

"Sorry." She began to undress, draping her clothes over the ottoman which had been re-covered in a beautiful blue and gold Designers Guild fabric when they'd had the bedroom refurnished last year.

"Did you get the issue to bed?"

"Only just and then Brian wanted to see me about . . . about something. I'm exhausted. Just going to have a quick bath. Are the children all right?"

"Fine."

"Did they ask for me?"

There was a slight hesitation. "Yes."

So they hadn't. After her bath — literally in and out — she looked through their bedroom doors. Two blonde heads in two separate rooms, each breathing heavily. Two lovely looking children who could so easily belong to someone else. If she kissed them now, would they think it was the nanny in their sleep?

Becky bit her lip as she made her way back to the master bedroom, sliding in between the silk sheets and cuddling up to Steve's back. He turned over, taking her in his arms. "Did you ring your dad?"

Instantly, all the anger came flooding back. "I did. You'll never believe it."

Briefly she told him what had happened, playing down the "necessary alterations".

"But you promised to stick to the original."

Not him too! "Oh, for God's sake." She rolled away. "Don't get all pious, Steve. We live in a business world. Decisions have to be made and they're not always easy. Besides, it's got nothing to do with him."

"Hasn't it?" Steve's voice had a strange, unsettling edge to it. "If someone upset you, I'd be upset and I'd like to think you'd do the same."

"Well, of course I would." Becky wriggled uncomfortably. "But there's more to it than that. I wouldn't be surprised if Monique might be in trouble financially."

"You're not suggesting she's marrying him for his money?"

"Well they're a very unlikely match, aren't they?"

She could sense Steve shaking his head in the dark.

"I can't believe you can say something like that, Beck."

197

"Shh. You'll wake the children. And I can't believe that you aren't supporting me more."

"Daddy." A small blonde figure flew into the room, past her side and straight towards Steve.

"Daisy, it's me. Mummy's home." She reached out towards her daughter but Daisy pulled away, burying her head like a limpet into her father's chest.

Becky felt like she'd been slapped in the face.

"Shh, Daisy. It's all right."

Under the covers, Becky felt Steve's hand reaching out for hers, squeezing it reassuringly. She took it away. Forget sex. Even hand-holding took time and energy.

"Don't be hurt," whispered Steve.

"Wouldn't you be?"

She turned away from the two of them, feeling totally and utterly excluded. The neon light on the bedside table showed it was nearly 1.15a.m. Just four hours sleep until she had to get up again.

And she hadn't even told them about New York.

CHAPTER
TWENTY-TWO

Helen

"Of course I can come up, darling." Helen tried to sound reassuring but inside she was panicking. How was she going to fit it all in? Now she had taken on her old garden — or rather, Robin and Sylvia's — she had ten regulars, which meant a full working week and sometimes the odd Saturday morning.

But her daughter needed her. A picture of the vicar's daughter, still apparently in her coma, flashed through her head. Poor, poor woman. Helen had only been to church a couple of times in the last few years when there had been a rather old world-weary vicar before the new one. Mel, wasn't she called? Rather a contemporary name for a vicar but also fitting, considering she wore make-up and was rumoured to wear black leggings under her cassock.

What she must be going through now . . . It didn't bear thinking about. How would she cope if anything ever happened to her two? It was bad enough Adam being on the other side of the world.

"Thanks, Mum." Becky actually sounded grateful instead of taking her mother's availability for granted. "It's hectic here."

It certainly sounded like it. The background noise resembled a zoo; something Helen could recall all too well from when Adam and Becky had been a similar age. Looking back, she didn't know how she had done it, although, as she'd told herself countless times, that was no excuse . . .

"Steve's not very happy about my trip to New York."

Becky's voice sounded strangely vulnerable; rather like when she'd been little and had sought reassurance over some homework that had gone badly.

"Well . . ." Helen found herself searching for the right words. "You do live a busy life. Both of you, that is," she added hastily.

"It's the real world, Mum. It's what people do."

There she was. Back to the old acrylic Becky. Defensive. Determined to get to the top. Certain of having it all. How exhausting it must be, to be young nowadays.

"When you're an editor of a magazine like *Charisma*, you don't just sit on your haunches all day long."

Ouch. Clearly a reference to her gardening which Becky was always referring to in the kind of tone that made it seem like a hobby rather than a late career. "I know that, darling, and we're very proud of you."

"We?"

"Your dad and I." There she went again, talking as though she and Geoff were still together. But even after you'd been apart for all those years, there were some things you always shared, like children. Besides, it gave her an odd sense of security to refer to him every now and then, despite the ring on her left hand.

That was something else. She ought to tell Becky. Email Adam.

Becky made a dismissive noise down the phone. "Dad doesn't understand what I do at all. Look, getting down to practicalities, can you come up for two days?"

"Darling, I would but I've got my gardens and . . ."

"OK, make it just the Monday then. I'll find someone to fill in for the next day until Laura's back."

The nanny had taken a much-needed long weekend break which was what had thrown Becky's week out. To be fair, it wasn't her fault there was this big editorial conference in New York for magazine editors worldwide. As Becky said, it was a fantastic opportunity to network.

"I'll be up as early as I can," promised Helen. "See you then."

But Becky, amid much background screaming, coupled with the sound of a deeper male voice shouting (Steve?), had already put the phone down.

"Children can be such a worry." Helen sat back on her haunches (Becky had been horribly correct about that) and surveyed the border. Those gladioli bulbs which she had planted only a few months ago, were already beginning to send up hopeful green shoots.

She glanced sideways at Sylvia who, as usual, was looking straight ahead. It was getting warmer now with no need of the red tartan blanket which Robin usually draped over his wife's knees before leaving to "potter about".

201

"Sorry, Sylvia. I didn't mean to be thoughtless. I know you don't have any but . . . well, what I really meant was that children are a great blessing but you don't stop worrying about them."

She was making it worse. It was even more unnerving that the poor woman couldn't speak. Until then, she'd rather enjoyed their one-sided, almost-therapeutic conversations. Better change the subject.

"Isn't it lovely now the weather's a bit warmer? When the children were younger, we'd put a rug down on that patch of grass over there, by the wall and have all our meals out here. Sometimes we'd have a barbecue on the terrace. I see you've got one in almost the exact spot . . ."

"How are you getting on?"

Helen jumped. She hadn't noticed Robin's long shadow across the lawn. How much had he heard?

"Fine. These glads are coming up nicely and I've sorted out the irises round the pond."

Was it her imagination or was he looking at her in a strange way?

"It's looking wonderful." He crossed over to his wife who remained stoically looking ahead. Something inside Helen made her wonder if this was deliberate. What had their marriage been like before this cruel illness had struck? It reminded her of an uncle who'd been engaged to a girl but then met another. Just as he was about to post a letter (how quaint was that!) to inform the first that he could no longer fulfil his obligations, he received one from her saying she had

TB. Feeling honour-bound, he married her. They had lived unhappily ever afterwards until he died first.

Helen shivered. Don't be so ridiculous. Robin and Sylvia might have been perfectly happy; might still be happy. She stood up, stretching. It always felt so good to do that, yet her exaggerated motions suddenly made her realise that Sylvia must yearn to do the same.

"See you next week then."

"Excellent." He began walking with her towards the side entrance in what was becoming a routine. Any minute now and he'd suggest a cup of tea. She'd politely refuse and then make her way home to an empty cottage which was becoming increasingly attractive now the prospect of living with David was a distinct possibility.

"Like to come in for a cup of tea?"

She glanced at her watch out of politeness. "I don't think I've got time, thanks."

Something crossed his face and she found herself hesitating. "Actually, a quick one would be lovely if you don't think me rude if I dash off after that. I promised to go up to my daughter's again next week so it's all a bit hectic."

"Wonderful." He looked genuinely pleased. "I bought a lemon drizzle cake from Waitrose and could do with someone to share it with. Sylvia didn't seem that interested."

"Shouldn't we bring her in?"

They both looked down at the wheelchair, facing away from them. "In a few minutes," said Robin quickly. "I rather think she enjoys sitting out there. I don't know why I didn't think of it before. Thank you."

"Not at all."

Watching him busy himself round the kitchen — her kitchen — she began to wonder if she'd done the right thing in coming inside. The Aga was exactly the same, although it needed a bit of a clean. Did he know how to do it? Unless you were used to one, it could seem daunting at first.

"Amazing contraption, isn't it?" he said, noticing her look. "We don't use it, of course. The electric cooker is much easier and quicker."

"But it's not!" She heard the dismay in her voice before it was too late to take it back. "I had one just like that, once. You must use it; it's so easy. It is lit, isn't it? Good. Look, you just lift this left-hand lid if you want to boil something fast and the right-hand one is for simmering. The top right oven — you open it like this — is for roasting and the bottom one is a little cooler for baking."

She carried on explaining, conscious that Robin was watching her with an amused smile on his face. "I used to use an enamel cleaner which you can get from the Aga shop in Oxford or online. And look, here's my — the old toasting grid. Aga toast is brilliant! My children used to love it. You just put a piece of bread inside and then lift the lid and put it on top."

"Won't it burn?"

"No. Look. I'll show you. Have you got some bread?"

And somehow, before she knew it, they were sitting round the farmhouse table — spookily like her old one and in almost the same position — eating toast and honey and cake and nattering away as though they'd known each other for ever. He was, reflected Helen, so easy to talk to.

"They want to have the village fête in the grounds this summer," continued Robin. "I felt I had to say yes although I'm a bit concerned about security."

"You don't have to worry about that." Helen reached over for the honey. "This village is incredibly quiet. Always has been."

"Really?" Robin was looking at her quizzically again. "I thought you said you lived a few miles away."

"I do but I used to have a friend here. She's moved now."

Funny how the lies got easier.

"They're planning the fête for the third weekend in June."

"They always do — I mean, a lot of villages round here do the same. What about Sylvia? Will she mind all these strangers coming round to her garden?"

A dark shadow slid across his face for a second until Robin replaced it with his usual perky expression. "She wasn't particularly sociable before she was ill but it might do her good, just as you do. Another slice?"

"No, thanks."

He was standing up, his back to her, fiddling with the toaster rack which he still hadn't got quite right. "It's good that you talk to her so much, you know. Very few do that now. It's like 'Does she take sugar?'"

Helen could see that.

"I like it too." His back was still to her and for a minute she wondered if she'd heard him right. "It's nice to have some company."

"Thank you." She wasn't sure what to say. "But you must see people here, in the village."

"Yes but they keep themselves to themselves and I think they're a bit embarrassed about Sylvia. They don't know what to say."

She could see that. "Robin, can I ask you something? Why did you move from London out here? I only ask because the countryside isn't always as welcoming as the picture postcards would have you believe and I just wondered . . ."

"I needed to get away." He was facing her now; his eyes fixed on hers and she felt her skin tingle. "Our house in Fulham had too many memories. Sylvia and I . . . well, we had a chequered relationship. A lot went on and . . . never mind. But after she was diagnosed, it got worse."

"What got worse?"

Robin looked away, down towards the garden. "Everything. Look, sorry. I've said too much. And I must get her in now. It'll be getting cold. Besides," he glanced at her left hand, "you have people to get back to, I expect."

So he'd noticed the ring. "Yes." Helen nodded. "Yes. I must be going."

The conversation haunted her all weekend, including the fact that this time, Robin hadn't walked with her to the van. "What's wrong?" David had asked, not unreasonably as they made their way back from the cinema on the Saturday night. "You're very quiet. Didn't you enjoy the film?"

She had — it had been a remake of a classic Hitchcock — but somehow she couldn't get Sylvia and Robin out of her head. She'd often wondered, after the divorce, if she and Geoff would have stayed together if one of them had been ill. Probably. Indeed, until Monique's arrival, she secretly thought that if Geoff had fallen sick with something serious, she would have moved in to look after him. The thought hadn't displeased her; it had made her feel useful, if anything. Now, of course, there was no need.

"Do you have to go up to Becky's on Monday?" continued David, taking her arm in his as they crossed the road. "She's a grown woman. Can't she sort out her own childcare? It's unbelievable."

David had never had children and if her own had still been at home, the step-parenting rows would be — she could imagine all too well — horrific. "Besides, I love spending time with Daisy and Ben. And it's the nursery's half term so Becky's desperate."

"But you've got so much work on. You're looking tired."

"You're right. Actually, David, I won't come back tonight. I think I need a good night's sleep. You don't mind, do you?"

Of course he had, but that was too bad. In a way, the ring had made her more determined to keep her own independence. The next day, while doing her own garden, she'd taken it off, forgetting to put it on again — something she didn't realise until she was on the train the next day up to London. Too late now to go back and, besides, it would save having to explain anything to Becky. Now didn't seem a great time.

"Granny!" The children hurled themselves at her as she arrived on their doorstep. Steve had opened the door promptly, briefcase in hand, clearly desperate to be off. "Becks left hours ago and I've got a plane to catch to Frankfurt."

"But what about tonight?"

"I think one of the neighbours' au pairs is coming over. Can you ring Becky on her mobile to check?"

And with that, he was gone. Poor kids. Was this what family life had come to? They weren't alone if newspaper reports were anything to go by and, to be fair, Ben and Daisy seemed very well adjusted happy children.

"Who wants to play hide and seek?"

"Me, me!"

"Fantastic!" Helen clapped her hands in delight. "You go first, Ben but don't lock yourself in the wardrobe again, will you?"

An hour later, she was exhausted. Seven hours later, she was almost on her knees but at the same time, wonderfully exhilarated. It was so nice to be wanted again; so lovely to have little Daisy clambering on to her lap in front of tea-time television. So amazing to feel Ben's small hand creeping into hers.

"Mum says you're really old."

Well thank you, Becky.

"Actually, darling. I might seem old to you and maybe your mummy but I'm still quite young really, compared with many grannies."

His little face looked earnestly up at her. "You won't die soon, will you? We've been doing death at school."

"No." She touched wood. "I won't die soon. Although," she hesitated (just how much do you tell a child about death?), "everyone has to die one day."

Ben's face lit up. "And then they go to heaven or hell. We've been doing that at school too. Mum says she wishes Granny Mona would go to hell."

Helen froze. "Granny who?"

"You know. Grandad's new wife." Ben's little face shone with seriousness. "Well, she's not his wife yet and mummy says she hopes she won't be cos she's always moaning. That's why we call her Granny Mona. I hope she won't be his wife either cos she wants us to be flower fairies at her wedding."

"Really?" Helen stared straight ahead at the television. "And do you see a lot of her?"

"A bit." Ben started playing games on his mobile. Ridiculous having one at his age. "Mum says she's younger than you. Is she?"

"Slightly." Honestly! That reminded her. She still had to get hold of Becky to see who was looking after the children that night.

"The doorbell! The doorbell!"

"No, Daisy, don't go. Let Granny."

But her granddaughter was already there, standing on tiptoes to reach the handle. On the other side was a couple. The man was tall, but not quite as tall as she remembered. How long had it been since seeing him close up like this? And how could she have forgotten the way his hair flopped to one side?

Next to him, hugging his arm tightly, stood a small tubby little woman with thin reddish hair (obviously dyed) and heavy black eye make-up. That oversize liquorice-pink trouser suit — what a colour! — made her look like a giant Teletubby and she was wearing a long knotted scarf down the front, in the mistaken belief that it suited her.

Both sides stared at each other in disbelief. "I didn't realise you'd be here," said Geoff tightly.

"What are you doing here?" Helen heard herself saying.

"Becky rang us." The Teletubby was eyeing her coldly. "Asked us to take over."

"My daughter," (she pronounced the words clearly to establish ownership) "didn't tell me." She stepped back, holding open the door reluctantly. "You'd better come in."

CHAPTER
TWENTY-THREE

Mel

Mel couldn't take her eyes off the boy in the dock. Gone was the black hoodie with the skull and crossbones on the back and where were those three earrings in his nose? That cheap dark suit was clearly new from the crisp polyester creases and the white collar and cuffs and even his shoes shone as he'd walked past, eyes respectfully on the floor, to take his place.

When she'd been informed that Kevin's hearing was finally about to take place, she'd felt a mixture of relief and apprehension. What did it matter now? Nearly three months had passed and there was still no change in Amy. Her life — all their lives — had fallen into a pattern which she could never have imagined before the accident. Every day, she'd get up at 6.30, say her prayers, make breakfast, get Josh up for school, cheer up Richard ("you've got another interview next week") and then head for the hospital.

She always spent half an hour with her daughter, brushing her hair, wiping her face, doing her nails — doing everything in fact which she hadn't done for Amy since she was about eight and her daughter had decided she didn't need a mother to look after her any more.

Then back to the office in the vicarage or to the vestry or to yet another meeting with her curate or the PCC or whichever organisation needed her time.

"Any change?" they'd ask, not expecting one. So she'd shake her head briefly with an "I don't want to talk about it" expression and off they'd embark on to the real business of the day.

Until now. Facing Kevin, she was forced to confront the reality; the stark, terrifying remembrance of what had happened that day on 15 February.

"So can you tell me, Kevin, why you didn't stop?" The solicitor, a young woman in her late twenties or possibly early thirties, sounded sympathetic even though she was meant to be acting for the crown prosecution.

"I should've done, I know now." The boy looked up at her from under his lashes almost in a Lady Di fashion. "But I got scared, see. She came out so fast like and I thought fucking hell — pardon — what's that? Then I felt this thump and I just went on."

Mel felt Richard reaching out for her hand. A thump. Her daughter made a thump. *She came out so fast.*

"But you came back?"

"Yeah," Kevin was nodding enthusiastically. "Then I saw something lying in the middle of the road. I was going to ring but my phone didn't have any credit like and I heard an ambulance anyway." The boy's voice trembled. "So I went home to Mum and she said I ought to go to the police station."

It all sounded so horribly plausible. Mel could almost imagine Josh doing the same. The kid was

212

scared. He was only a teenager. So he went back to his mum. She made him do the right thing.

They were calling for witnesses now. Sharon came up, in a short skirt and long earrings, plastered with make-up. "Amy was checking her voice messages," she started saying. "There was one from her mum. I don't think she was concentrating cos she just carried on listening while she was walking across the road. I called out to her but she didn't hear. Then ..." Sharon started crying. "Then this car came up. I don't think it was going fast but it went straight into her. She just kind of flew over the bonnet and crumpled up on the ground. I couldn't believe it was happening."

There was one from her mum.

Her fault. Her need to constantly check on the kids to make sure they were all right, had led to this. Amy. Motionless. In a coma. A coma from which she might never come out and, even if she did, might never be the same again.

"He's going to get off, isn't he?" hissed Mel to Richard. Her husband made a shussing noise but there was no need. There was so much shuffling at the front of the court that hopefully no one had heard her. Mercy. That's what God believed in. So why did she find herself desperately hoping that Kevin wouldn't get any.

The judge was talking but the words were washing over Mel's head. Something about Kevin coming back, as though he should be praised for this. Something else about Amy not looking and having to take some responsibility. Mel heard herself taking a sharp intake of breath. Taking responsibility! How was she meant to do that, lying motionless in a hospital bed. And then something about a year in some open prison somewhere.

Richard's hand was squeezing hers even tighter now, as though he was the one falling from the cliff and not her. At the front of the court, there almost seemed to be a small party. A large fat woman with rolls of neck and cheap gold earrings was shouting out to Kevin. "It's OK, love! It's going to be OK!"

OK? Mel wanted to run up and grab her by those rolls of fat. "My daughter's not OK," she wanted to yell. "My daughter's the victim of this; not your stupid son in his cheap polyester suit."

"No. Stop." Richard pulled her back. "Don't say anything. It's not worth it."

But the woman was looking at her now and Mel knew what she should do. Knew as clearly as if God was talking to her right now. She ought to go up and take Kevin's hand; the same hand that had been on the wheel of the car which had hit her daughter. She should go up and say "It's all right. I forgive you."

But she couldn't. She just couldn't. And then, as she turned her back, walking towards the exit, she saw a tall skinny youth in a black hoodie with a large gold cross and a Jewish star round his neck.

"Josh?" she called out. "Josh! Come back."

"You didn't tell me you were going to court."

He'd got back before them — heaven knows how — and was in his room as usual, glued to his laptop.

His eyes didn't leave the screen. "Yeah, well she's my sister, isn't she?"

His eyes didn't leave the screen.

"Why didn't you sit with us?"

"Maybe I didn't want to."

Could children be done for emotional GBH to their parents? "I would have felt comforted if you had."

"I thought that's what parents are meant to do to their children."

He was right. Instinctively, Mel wrapped her arms around her son. "Sorry."

"Gerrof." He put something in his mouth.

"What's that?" She picked up the packet, heart pounding.

"Caffeine tablets, Mum. Everyone takes them. Now leave me alone. This is my room and only one person is allowed into it, apart from me."

"Who?"

Stupid question.

"Amy. Now piss off, Mum, can you?"

He was upset. And understandably so. This wasn't the time or the place to have a go at him about his language although it had got worse long before Amy's accident.

Richard was in the kitchen putting on the kettle, morning post on the table.

"I didn't get that interview."

She looked up. "Which one?"

He laughed hoarsely. "Next week's. They wrote to say the vacancy is no longer available which means they must have found someone already."

215

"I'm sorry."

He plonked a mug of steaming Redbush in front of her. "You sound as though you're sorry for someone else. It affects all of us."

"So does Amy."

"I know." He sat opposite her on an old kitchen chair which had come with the rest of the furniture of the house with its peeling yellow and white formica seat. "Listen, Mel. Now the case is over, we've got to move on and I've been thinking. I'm going to apply for that job in Leeds."

"But it means you living away during the week."

"I know." Richard moved towards her as though to give her a hug. Neatly, she sidestepped it. "But we can't manage on your salary alone."

Ouch. Richard had been very understanding when she'd first told him she needed to enter the church. But every now and then he'd remind her of what they'd chosen to give up. Two holidays a year. A Smallbone kitchen in a four-bedroom Victorian terrace in Wandsworth which they now rented out and was worth a good deal less than they paid for it, thanks to a hostel for the homeless which had since been built next to it. Would she have entered the church if she'd known Richard was going to be made redundant?

"I probably won't get the job," Richard was saying, "but it's worth a shot."

"Whatever." Amy's phrase slipped out of her mouth and it made her feel comforted as though, just by saying it, she could summon up her daughter's presence.

216

Upstairs, a door slammed and there was the thudding of feet down the staircase. Josh pushed past, grabbed a slice of bread from the packet — ripping it so she couldn't reseal — and headed for the back door, his music still blaring from upstairs.

"Where are you going?" called out Mel.

"Out."

"But it's school."

"It's half term, Mum."

Was it? She must be worse than she'd thought.

"Leave him." Richard sat down again, the Leeds application form in front of him. "He'll be all right."

Without even saying goodbye — what was the point? — she followed Josh outside and sat in the front seat for a few minutes before fumbling in her bag for the phone.

"Geoff? It's me. Mel. You don't fancy a run, do you?"

CHAPTER
TWENTY-FOUR

Janie

"It makes perfect sense, dear," Marjorie had said, pouring Janie a double g and t (though she'd have preferred a Stella) on hearing the news. "I've been thinking of getting a lodger anyway and I'd much rather have you than a stranger."

Janie had made some polite noises (Are you sure? Shouldn't I pay you more than that? Won't I get in your way?) before accepting gracefully. And now, here she was, three weeks later, moving what little stuff she had into Marjorie's cottage next door.

In truth, when asking if she'd get in Marjorie's way, she was really wondering whether Marjorie would get in hers. Much as she loved the old lady, what would happen if she found another boyfriend and wanted to bring him home? Mind you, Janie hadn't found one person she liked since Mac and, if she was being really honest, his main attraction had been that he had liked her, although clearly that wasn't the case any more.

"What a sweet little chair," enthused Marjorie, eyeing one of her market finds approvingly. "Why don't you put it in the sitting room?"

"I couldn't possibly. That's yours."

218

"My dear, I expect you to treat it as your own. And by the way, don't worry about bringing back any young men if you feel like it." Her eyes twinkled. "I'm very good at turning a blind eye — you should have seen what we got up to at house parties during the fifties — and besides, I'm deaf." Her eyes sparkled. "Can be quite handy at times!"

Not like her dyslexia. How was she going to get anywhere if she couldn't even write telephone messages properly? It wasn't as though she hadn't tried — years ago, one of the kinder teachers at school had tried to help but it hadn't made any difference. Face it, Janie. You're thick. No wonder Mac had found someone else.

"Goodness, haven't you made that room cosy!" exclaimed Marjorie, peeping round the spare room door. "I love that bedspread; it looks as though it belonged to your grandmother."

Janie shook her head. Not only were her parents abroad but her grandparents — both sets — had died before she was born. "I got that from the market too."

"It's exquisite." Marjorie was running her finger over the fine antique lace and blowsy rose chintz squares. "I'll have to go there myself. And I adore the way you've stacked your shoes in those brightly coloured plastic crates; so artistic. Gosh! Is that one of your paintings? Magenta and red — how unusual! Now, have you got enough wardrobe space?"

She hadn't but she could pile stuff under the bed and maybe get some chiffon lengths from the market to drape over the pole. In fact, thought Janie, looking around, it wasn't too bad. Not home but something rather like it.

"How about some supper?" Marjorie was rubbing her hands together as though she was going to light her own fire. "I've got some rather nice pasta in" (she pronounced it like "parsta") "and I make quite a nice tomato sauce if I do say so myself."

Janie hadn't thought she felt hungry but her stomach seemed to kick in on hearing the words "tomato sauce". "I thought we were going to do our own cooking so I didn't get in your way."

Marjorie looked fleetingly disappointed. "As it's your first night, it would be nice to eat together. We can have a chat about the business over supper too. I was rather hoping we'd have some more bookings by now."

Janie followed her new landlady with mixed feelings. Yes, she was hungry and yes, she needed a home. But was it really a good idea to share her life with one of her few good friends? And what would happen if they fell out?

The mobile rang just when she was standing at the Debenhams counter the following day, trying out some new foundations under the guise of pretending she needed to replace her usual Boots brand. Janie had found, long ago during teenage shopping sprees with Becky, that if you pretended you wanted to switch brands, the assistant was only too keen to give you free samples.

Now, one of the few advantages about crossing the thirtieth birthday boundary was that sales assistants took you more seriously. "I rather like this shade," Janie was saying. "Do you have a sample of this and also one for my sister? She's the same colouring."

The sister ruse had been one which she'd dreamed up in order to get two lots. "Thanks. Sorry, I've just got to answer this call. Hello, Janie speaking."

"It's Phil. The printer."

Blast. She'd thought it might be a new client. "Listen, this isn't a great time actually. Can I ring you back?"

"You can but you might lose some business. A friend of mine is getting married and he wants a rather unusual wedding in a hurry. But if you're too busy, I'll tell him and . . ."

"No, don't. We'd love to do it."

"Good. Here's his number."

Not numbers! "Actually, I don't have a pen on me at the moment but could you ring back and leave the number on my mobile? Thanks."

Ten minutes later, Janie was cycling back with a bag full of free cosmetic samples plus a squirt of free Chanel perfume behind her ears (golden rule — never pass a perfume counter without spraying something on) and a possible new client. Marjorie was never going to believe this one!

"Marge! Marge!" Racing in through the front door, she stopped. Marjorie was sitting very upright on the sofa with her face rigid.

"If you insist," she was saying. "Although I don't know what your father would have said . . ."

On seeing Janie, she gave a small nod. "Please ask your solicitor to put it in writing. Goodbye."

Janie put down her bags. "I'm so sorry. I didn't mean to interrupt."

"No, I'm glad you did."

Marjorie looked as though she was going to say something but then stopped.

"It didn't sound like a very nice conversation," ventured Janie.

Marjorie stood up and brushed some biscuit crumbs off her not inconsiderable chest. "It wasn't. Don't marry someone who's already got children, Janie. It can cause all kinds of problems, especially when your husband goes and dies on you."

Fleetingly, Janie thought of Becky who seemed to think Monique was after her father's money.

"Want to tell me about it?"

"No thanks, dear. Now, would you like some shortbread biscuits and a nice cup of tea? These biscuits are absolutely delicious. I treated myself when I was last up in Fortnum & Masons."

It was a polite way of telling her not to intrude, thought Janie. And quite right too. Clearly, there was going to be a lot they both needed to learn about living together.

"Actually, I've got some news," she said excitedly, putting on the kettle while Marjorie opened the silver and pale blue biscuit tin. "Phil, the printer, has a friend who wants us to organise his wedding."

"Excellent! Two biscuits or three?"

"Just one please. I've already put on a few pounds since moving in."

"You needed to if you don't mind me saying. Now, what kind of wedding does Phil's friend want?"

"That's the thing." Janie sat down at Marjorie's small but rather lovely mahogany table, taking care to use a coaster for her cup of tea. "They're gay."

"Well so should everyone be when they're getting married. The misery usually sets in afterwards."

"No, I mean gay as in well . . . you know, that way inclined."

Marjorie frowned. "What are you talking about, dear?"

"Well my father used to call it queer or bent." She struggled over the words which seemed so unkind now.

"Oh, you mean homosexual!" She pronounced "homo" like "Hoe-moe". "I see! Goodness. I did read somewhere that homosexuals could get married now. That's going to be a challenge. What will the church think of that one?"

"Bill and Len — that's the couple — have already been turned down by some vicars and I wondered about Becky's dad's vicar; if she's agreed to marry a couple who've been divorced, she might be fairly broad-minded."

"Good idea. Do you want to ring her?"

"OK. Bill and Len also want us to meet with them to discuss themes. Apparently they've got their heart set on Midnight Ice because they met ice-skating."

Marjorie helped herself to another biscuit. "How charming! By the way, a letter arrived for you this morning."

"Looks a bit formal." Janie was already tearing it open. Oh, God, what did it say exactly?

"I've . . . I've lost my glasses so I can't read it very well."

"I didn't know you wore glasses."

"They're new."

"Well dear. If you'd like me to read it for you . . ."

"Thanks."

"Good gracious."

"What?"

Marjorie beamed. "Looks like you've got that business grant we applied for! How absolutely wonderful. Well done, dear."

"It wasn't me." Janie had a fleeting glimpse of a small dark woman on a stool and began drawing the outline in her head. "It was a friend."

"Well, why don't you pop down and thank him." Marjorie's enthusiasm was all too obvious. "Was he wearing a wedding ring by any chance?"

"It was a she."

"Pity. By the way, that former suitor of yours had the nerve to call round again. Apparently he has something to tell you, although personally, I'd ignore him. Anyone who gets caught in bed with someone else isn't to be trusted."

Janie nodded.

"In my day, we had the decency and foresight to lock our doors. Now, if you'll excuse me, dear, I'm going to have to ring my lawyer." She sniffed. "Stepchildren! Who'd have them?"

224

CHAPTER
TWENTY-FIVE

Becky

Becky stretched out in the middle of the huge double bed with its heavy sage silk cover, looking through the net curtains framed by heavy green and pink drapes. The view down on to the street was incredible; like one of those paintings which had been turned sideways to give the impression of height even though you were on the same level.

In fact, she was on level 59; something that would have freaked her out if she'd had Daisy and Ben with her. They'd be clambering at the window right now, if they were here, insisting on having a look at all the traffic (even at 3 a.m. in the morning, it was teeming) and she'd be saying, "Don't go so near. Steve, can't you stop them!"

Just as well they weren't here, then. Besides, even if they were, they wouldn't want her. They'd demand Steve or Laura. So why feel guilty? Becky shifted herself to a more upright position, grabbed the remote control and scrolled through the various channels, ranging from Godpox to a sharply-featured newsgirl, earnestly updating them on a typhoon approaching Bermuda.

The distraction almost helped to eradicate the memory of Steve's expression. "New York?" he'd questioned when she'd told him about the trip. "For a week? Who's going to cover for Laura when it's her day off?"

"Mum's coming up," she'd retorted, even though at that point she hadn't had time to ring and check. "I've got to go, Steve. It's my job. It's not as though you're not always away."

"Too much," he said quietly. "OK. I understand. Have a good time."

"I'm not going for a good time." Becky heard her voice leaping into a crescendo like Daisy at the Wiggle and Giggle class she loved so much. "I'm going for a bloody editors' conference because, just in case you've forgotten, I've been promoted."

Steve had given her a look which had made something jolt from her chest up to her neck and then back again. "How could we forget? We never see you nowadays."

"And we don't see you. What about all your business trips?"

So she'd gone, expecting a "sorry" call or text while at the airport. But nothing. She'd managed to obliterate it from her mind on the plane when she'd found herself sitting next to another (much younger) editor who was delighted to be leaving her boyfriend behind for a week. And now she was at the hotel with a full programme of social events revolving around the four-day conference.

Was it too late to ring Steve? He might be able to wake up Ben or Daisy to say goodnight.

"Hi. This is the Hughes family . . ." Her married name always sounded unfamiliar and she didn't remember asking Laura to record the message. That Australian twang made them sound like a family from *Neighbours*. "Sorry but we're not in at the moment. Please leave . . ."

Sod it. She'd ring tomorrow. Besides, they knew where to get her if they needed to. And when she did get back, she'd have a word with Laura about that message.

"Why can't Americans make a decent cuppa?"

Becky turned to face a freckly grinning male face which, if she had to guess, was roughly her age and definitely of her own inclination when it came to tea. "I know. All they think they have to do is hand you a mug of warmish water with a tea bag."

"I read somewhere once that they don't give you boiling water in case you scald yourself and then sue them. Dan Smith, by the way. I edit *Heated Issues*."

"*Heated Issues*?"

"No one else has heard of it either." He grinned again. "It's a trade magazine for electrical goods. Dead boring but a stepping stone to greater things." His eyes glanced down to her wedding ring. "And you're . . ."

"Becky. Becky Hastings. I edit *Charisma*."

"*Charisma*! Wow. My other half will be really impressed."

Becky felt a thrill shooting through her; a thrill that almost made up for the fact that she still hadn't been able to get hold of Steve, even though she'd sent him several texts. It was lunch time in the UK. Where was he? "Thanks. Actually, I was only made editor a few weeks ago so it's still all quite new."

Dan looked around the breakfast bar which was on a raised mezzanine surface next to the restaurant where they were due to eat tonight. "All this is pretty new to me. I've never been on one of these things before. In fact, I'm surprised we were asked. Most of you lot edit proper magazines for real people instead of retailers who want to know what to buy for their discerning customers."

"Sounds like the sell on the front cover."

"How did you know? God, this tea's undrinkable." He stood up, pulling on a crinkly brown leather jacket. "Think I'll get a mocha at Starbucks opposite. Want to come?"

Of course it wasn't the first time she'd been chatted up since getting married. Although most other editors tended to be female, Becky had been approached or sounded out, as she would put it to Janie, a few times by male photographers, subs and — once — rather a well known editor-in-chief in the lift after a Christmas party.

But never once had she been tempted. Nor was she now, she told herself, after roaring with laughter over Dan's story about his new series "My Hot Buy" which featured a different recommendation every week. One of his picture editors, who was leaving, had substituted a picture of a pair of slinky red thongs instead of a toaster just before going to press.

"Did you get into trouble?" asked Becky, thinking of the Sally Smith fiasco.

"You know the funny thing was that I thought I would but so many readers rang or emailed to say they loved it that my editor-in-chief let it go."

"Who is your editor-in-chief?"

"Me!" Dan's eyes twinkled. "I told you. We're a small set-up. I'm the editor and heaven knows what else. I suppose *Charisma* is so big you don't even know everyone on the staff."

She swallowed her croissant before answering. "I know them by name although I don't really know them. It's dog-eat-dog in my world."

And somehow she found herself telling him about Sally Smith and Cat getting sacked and how she saw herself only lasting a year or two at the most before the same happened to her because that's how it worked.

"That's awful." His eyes grew serious for a moment. "And is your husband a journalist too?"

"No. He's in sales so he's away a lot."

"Can't be easy. Do you have kids?"

"Two. Ben's six — no, seven — and Daisy's four, going on ten."

"Lucky you. I'd have liked kids but it never happened." He glanced at his watch. "Better make a move, don't you think? Aren't we all meant to be going to the Museum of Modern Art for a pre-conference dash of culture?"

Slightly to her disappointment, she lost sight of Dan in the museum after Beatrice, the editor of a glossy house magazine in the same group as *Charisma*, pounced on her in delight. "Becky! Didn't know you were coming. Fantastic. You can give me all the goss on

Cat. Rumour has it that she's got her eye on the editorship of *Dressing Up*."

"Really?" Becky had always fancied that magazine herself. "I didn't know it was going."

"It's not but that wouldn't stop Cat from having her eye on it. How's everything, anyway?"

It was, thought Becky as she found herself sharing titbits with Beatrice on the way round some amazing pictures and sculptures (none of which had anything to do with the conference), really refreshing to get away from both the office and home. This was normal life. This was what Janie could do, lucky thing. This was what ordinary people could do if they weren't tied down by an eight to ten job, driven by the fear of not being able to pay the mortgage and school fees.

Steve still hadn't answered her texts. Well, sod him. He was off to Belgium tomorrow — or was it Belize? She was sure it began with "B". Either way, she'd be back before him and then she could maintain the moral high ground about not being around for the kids. She might even have a quick cat nap before dinner. Now that really would be bliss.

"Forgot to come, did you?" grinned Dan as she slid into the only empty seat left on the table that night.

Becky blushed, hoping no one else had noticed her late arrival but also pleased she was wearing her cream sheath dress since everyone else had also dressed up. "To be honest, I thought I'd have a quick lie down but I didn't set the alarm."

230

"Lucky you woke up when you did, then." He handed her a pudding bowl. "Here, have some of this. It's mouth-watering." His eyes rested on her dress. "Like you."

The compliment slid out so quickly that she almost missed it, especially as Beatrice then caught her eye from the other end of the table. "Becky! You made it," she called out in a voice indicating she'd had rather a lot to drink. "Come here, darling. We've still got so much to catch up on!"

She turned back to Dan. "See you later."

"Sure."

It was the right thing to do, Becky told herself, making her way through the crowd of diners who were beginning to stand up now the meal was over and mingle. The last thing she needed in her life right now, were any complications. So why couldn't she stop that little niggle of regret just above her top rib?

Partly for that very reason, she took care to stick with Beatrice and a couple of other acquaintances the following day. Of course, this was the whole point about conferences. It wasn't just to debate worldly matters such as editorial responsibility. It was a glorious Who's Who and Where which, she had to admit, was rather nice to be part of.

It was when she still hadn't been able to get hold of Steve by the end of the third day that she began to get really worried.

"Mum? It's me. Look, sorry to bother you but I can't get hold of Steve. The answerphone's always on at home and he isn't replying to my texts."

"Really? He's fine, darling. I called last night and had a long chat with Ben and Daisy."

Becky's chest lurched. "How nice."

"There's no need to sound like that, darling. I know it must be difficult being away but they'll be thrilled to have you back."

Would they? And why was it that her mother could always read her so well?

"You are using Steve's new number, aren't you?"

"New number?" Becky went cold. Shit. Of course. Steve had changed his phone last week. (Daisy had dropped the last one in her orange juice.) So she'd been sending all those text messages to a phone that didn't exist . . . "Yes. Course I am but I might just try it again. Bye. Oh and thanks for looking after them the other day."

"I need to talk to you about that."

"Not now, Mum. I've got to make a call. Speak later. OK?"

This time she got through immediately. "Hi, this is Steve. Please leave a message."

"It's me. Becky. Your wife." Immediately she regretted the last bit but it was too late to take it back. "I have been trying to get through to you although I thought you might have rung me. You're probably on your way to Belgium — I mean Belize. Anyway, just to say I'm on my way back. See you on . . . well, see you."

The conference continued the next day although most of them, Becky included, skived off towards the end to do some serious shopping. She'd glimpsed Dan a couple of times and given him a cheery wave while making it quite clear that she was sticking to Beatrice and the others. If I was single, she told herself en route to Bloomingdales in a taxi with Beatrice, it might be different. But she was a grown woman with responsibilities although it was lovely, really lovely, to have a break like this away from the office and everything else.

They had a glorious couple of hours in Fashion but just as they were leaving, her mobile sang.

"Steve!" She could hardly hear him above the noise and chatter of the others. "Is everything all right?"

"Not really."

Oh, God, Daisy was ill or Ben had got hit by a car or . . .

"Laura's left."

Shit. That was almost worse. No, of course she didn't really mean that but on the other hand this was seriously bad news.

"Can't you get her to stay again? Listen, with my increase we could pay her a bit more."

"Too late." His voice was cold and distant. "She's already gone."

"But why?"

"Why do you think, Becky? That note you left, accusing her of being rude didn't help. But the real reason is that we were asking her to do too much. Christ, we're asking ourselves to do too much."

She felt a tremor of unease pass through her. "What exactly do you mean by that?"

"We'll talk when you get back. Or rather, when I get back. And by the way, it's Luxembourg I'm going to. Not Belgium or Belize."

Did he just ring off or did they get cut off? She could have sworn it had been a "B". Maybe it would be easier if they just tagged each other.

"Come on, Becks, we're here." The taxi had already stopped outside the hotel. "We're just going to drop this lot off and then hit Greenwich Village. Coming?"

"No, thanks." She glanced down at the skinny lime green jumper she'd bought from Bloomingdales. At the time, it had seemed perfect for conference or even a casual supper with Steve. Now it seemed irrelevant. "I'll catch up with you later."

She ought to find out who was looking after the kids. Probably her mum but Steve hadn't said. Walking back into the hotel foyer, she caught sight of Dan sitting in a chair reading the *New York Times*. "Hi, stranger," he grinned. "So you bunked the rest of the conference too. Had a good time?"

"It was all right."

He stood up. "All right is the kind of word I use when it's the opposite. Tell you what, I was thinking of getting one of those horse-drawn cabs round Central Park. Naff thing to do, I know, but it's my first time in New York and all that. Want to join me?"

CHAPTER
TWENTY-SIX

Helen

"You could have warned me." Helen was conscious that she sounded unusually cross but when Becky still hadn't rung after being back for over three weeks from the New York trip, she began to think that David was right. Much as she hated to admit it, her kids could be selfish at times — even Adam, who hadn't emailed for ages. "How do you I think I felt," she continued, "when I opened the door to find your father and his . . . his fiancée, standing on the doorstep. I had no idea they were coming."

"Sorry, Mum." Becky sounded genuinely contrite. "I thought I'd asked Steve to tell you. There's been so much to do that I don't know if I'm coming or going."

That had been one of her own phrases years ago, she realised with a jolt, when the children were little and she hadn't even had a job. How did her daughter manage? How did the rest of the family cope? Not very well from what she had seen during her brief nannying stint.

"Have you ever wondered," she said gently, "if you're doing too much?"

"Don't you start!" Becky's previously contrite tone immediately gave way to the old strident voice she knew so well. "Steve's been banging on about that as well. But he was the one who wanted to buy this house. He was the one who said we could manage a mortgage like this with two salaries. So it's a bit late to start suggesting I give it all up and become a domestic goddess. It's not like it was in your day, you know."

Ouch, thought Helen, pulling up outside the Old Rectory, grateful not for the first time for the new blue tooth that David had bought her. Otherwise she'd never be able to work and sort out her family problems at the same time. "No one's suggesting you become a stay at home mum like I was," she said coolly. "I'm just trying to say that maybe you've bitten off more than you can chew. Now I'm sorry, Becky, but I have to get on. I've already missed one day of work through looking after your children which, I have to say, I'm quite happy to do. But in the meantime, I've got clients to look after."

"Fine. Ring when you have time for me."

Helen felt like putting her head down on the wheel and closing her eyes. But Dandy was inching forwards from the back seat, putting his nose into her lap and making small whining noises as though to say: "Come on, it's all right. Let's get out into the fresh air and we'll both feel better."

Thank God for her garden, thought Helen, opening the boot and getting out her tools. At least it didn't answer back like kids or ex-husbands or ex-husbands' wives.

"You can imagine how I felt when I opened the door." Helen looked up from the asparagus patch at Sylvia whose face, unusually, was turned towards her instead of straight ahead. "I mean, of course, I don't feel anything for him any more. Although when you've been married to someone for that long, it's difficult not to have some feelings. I don't mean physical feelings; more root feelings like this bulb here. We've shared so much history and it's ongoing with the children, isn't it?"

She dug her small fork fiercely into the dry soil, mentally noting to ask Robin about getting a sprinkler system like her old one. "Sorry. I'm rambling on here, I know. But it was a shock, seeing her. Monique she's called. Did I tell you that?"

Something in Sylvia's eyes suggested she had. "Such a common name, don't you think? And she wasn't in the slightest bit as I'd expected. Very short and squat; definitely on the plump side with the most appalling taste in clothes. She looked like a pink Teletubby. They're on children's television — you might have heard of them."

This time she could have sworn there was a slight lift to Sylvia's mouth, almost like the beginning of a smile.

"But the worst bit was when she marched in and took over the children. That's when I felt sick; quite sick. She'd obviously met them before — although I don't remember Becky telling me — because Daisy actually ran up to her and clung to her legs."

The earth was definitely too dry.

237

"Of course, they were quite easy to cling to. She probably thought they were tree trunks."

Sylvia's mouth definitely lifted then. Just on one side so it gave her a slightly crinkly grin.

"Ben was more loyal, bless him. He stayed next to me and got a bit upset when I said I had to go. Geoff didn't suggest I stayed. I think he felt as awkward as I did. Then again, he was never very good at handling tricky situations. I remember once, when we'd been here for about three years, he . . ."

"Helen! That looks absolutely amazing."

Robin was striding down the garden towards them in his green Barbour boots, admiring her handiwork. He stood next to Sylvia's chair, looking down on his wife. "It all looks so much tidier, doesn't it, darling?"

She really ought to be more careful.

"Enjoying the fresh air, Sylvia? Not too cold for you, is it?"

That upturn in her mouth had gone now. So too had the twinkle in her eye.

"I think we'd better get you in."

"Are you sure?" Helen couldn't stop herself. "It's getting warmer now and she seemed to be quite happy."

Was she mistaken or was that a slight nod? If so, Robin hadn't noticed. "No, I think we'll play safe. Can't afford to get a chill, can we, darling? Helen, I don't suppose I can tempt you with a cup of tea and some scones? I'd like to say I made them myself but I have at least heated them up in the Aga. Did I tell you,

Sylvia, that Helen has shown me how to use it now? It really is much more user-friendly than it looks."

The way he spoke, thought Helen, you might almost think they were having a proper three-way conversation. Yet at the same time, there was a stiffness in his speech; the kind of polite stiffness you heard between couples who'd been quarrelling which was, of course, given Sylvia's condition, quite impossible.

"That would be lovely." She took off her gardening gloves, noticing as she did so, that some dirt had somehow got into the blue stone of David's ring.

"Excellent." Robin beamed. "I've got one of the villagers coming round shortly to discuss this fête they want to hold here. I can introduce you. She's got a very posh name; Angela Ponson-Ponsonby, I think she said."

Shit. Helen hardly ever swore but if ever there was an occasion for swearing, this was it. Angela Pee Pee, as the children used to call her, was the worst kind of snob possible. She and her husband — who sounded as though he had swallowed an entire set of crystal glass — had moved in at about the same time as she and Geoff had bought the Old Rectory. Turned out that they had also put a bid in but been unsuccessful, so instead they'd moved to the Old School House but never forgiven her or Geoff for having got the house they really wanted.

Angela had also thrown herself into village life, worming her way on to the village committee with indecent speed. The last thing Helen wanted to do was see that woman again. Besides, she'd blow her cover in front of Robin and Sylvia.

"Second thoughts, I think I'm going to have to pass on that cup of tea," she said, gathering up her tools. "I'm a bit behind with some of my clients after taking a day off last week."

"Ah, yes." Robin was looking at her with concern. "Your daughter had to go to New York, didn't she, while you went up to London to look after the grandchildren. I must say, Helen, you really are a good mother."

She laughed shortly. "I'm not sure they'd agree. Well, maybe Adam but he's been away for so long that he hasn't needed me for years."

"No." A shadow of something like sadness passed through Robin's face. "Children always need you. Well, darling, we'd better be getting on."

For a second, she thought he was referring to her. "Make ourselves tidy for Mrs Ponson-Ponsonby. I feel like calling her Mrs Pee Pee but that would be awfully rude, wouldn't it?"

"Not at all! I think that sounds absolutely perfect for a woman like her — I mean, someone who has a name like that. I'll see you next week then."

"Aren't you going to come back with those roses? The ones you were going to pick up from the garden centre? Unless, of course, you'd like me to get them for you if you're short of time."

She'd completely forgotten. "That's really thoughtful but I've got things to collect for other customers too. I'll be back late afternoon, if that's all right."

★ ★ ★

"You're taking on too much," said David when she'd said no, sorry, but she couldn't go out tonight because she'd be working late now the evenings were lighter.

"I can't help it. I promised one of my old clients to mow her lawn. It's my job. And I have a mortgage to pay."

"When we're married, you won't have that to worry about. As you know, I'm all paid up at my end."

She thought of his plain 1930s semi in a village that wasn't nearly as nice as hers and failed to suppress the shudder that ran through her. "I didn't think we'd discussed where we would live if . . . when we get married."

"Well it makes sense to be at my place, doesn't it? For a start, I've got more room."

Helen leaned against her Aga and looked round at her cosy kitchen with its low wooden beams and pitch pine cupboards. The back door was open and the smell of lavender from her tubs on the tiny patio drifted in. There was a pile of sheets in the washing basket which she'd just brought in from the line. Impulsively, she picked them up, breathing in that heavenly mown grass smell on them — she loved it when the weather was fine enough for them to dry naturally before being aired off on the Aga. Did she really want to swap all this for his horrid semi, increasingly bland chat and automatic-parking sex?

"We'll have to talk about it sometime. Listen, David, I'm sorry about tonight but I really have to dash. I've got an order from the nursery to pick up."

"By the way, I meant to ask what Becky said when you spoke to her this morning."

Helen groaned. "I told her I wasn't very happy she hadn't warned me about Monique coming and she said she thought she'd told Steve to tell me and . . ."

"I'm not talking about that. I meant, what did she say about us getting married?"

"Oh. That."

"Yes, Helen. That, as you put it."

"Sorry. I was thinking of something else."

"Clearly."

Oh, dear, she'd upset him and quite understandably too. "Well, of course I will tell them — I'll have to email Adam — although we haven't got a date, have we?"

"Thought we'd agreed late winter. Just before Christmas. You said, if you recall, that you couldn't possibly take any time off work until then."

"Right. Fine. I'll tell them."

"You do want to get married, Helen, don't you?"

Her chest quickened with fear. She loved David, didn't she? At least, she liked him being around — at times — and yet . . .

"Of course I want to get married," she heard herself saying. "I'll call Becky right now."

"I'm busy, Mum. I'm about to go into conference."

"But you're in charge, aren't you? Can't you be one minute late?"

She was desperate now. Wanted to get it over and done with.

"Go on then."

242

"I'm getting married."

"What? To David?"

"Yes. To David."

"Shit, Mum. That's all I need. First Dad and then you."

"Becky, I can't believe you just said that. It's so selfish."

"Yes, well maybe I am selfish. When are you going to do it then?"

"Mid November. Probably the eleventh."

"You do realise that's two weeks before Dad's wedding, don't you? I suppose you did it on purpose."

"No but . . ."

Too late. She'd put the phone down.

By the time she'd picked up the roses, it was nearly six o'clock. Much later than she'd intended. She wouldn't get to Doris now until seven and then she wouldn't be home until at least nine. Perhaps David was right. She was doing too much.

"Helen." Robin answered the back door almost immediately. "Thanks so much. Here, let me take them. Want a hand with the digging?"

Her instinct was to say no but she felt tired. So very tired. "If you're sure. I am a bit short on time."

"Absolutely. Sylvia's watching television; well of course I don't know exactly how much she takes in but it does mean I'm free to help out. Where do you think we should put them?"

"Along the wall. That's where I . . . that's where they'd look best."

"Where you what?"

His eyes held hers and she tried to look away.

"Sorry."

"You were going to say something else."

"Was I?"

He reached towards her. The warmth of his touch sent something down her, something indefinable. "Come on, Helen. I think it's time we were honest with each other, don't you? That's where you had your climbing roses when you lived here. Wasn't it?"

CHAPTER
TWENTY-SEVEN

Mel

"C'mon, vicar, knock 'em for six!"

What on earth, dear God, was she doing here, trying to hit a coconut at the parish fête in the garden of a house — big enough to almost house an entire East London street — when her daughter was lying comatose in Intensive Care?

"Fantastic, vicar. You've got quite a punch there!"

She didn't even know the short squat man who was talking as though he knew her. Certainly wasn't one of her regulars. Of course I've got a punch, she wanted to tell him. I was pretending that bloody coconut was the yob who didn't stop after running over my daughter.

"Here you are then, vicar!" The paunchy short man was handing her a hairy coconut as though she'd won the lottery. "Take it back for the kids!"

Someone nudged him and there was a horrible silence for a second until everyone started talking again.

"He didn't mean it," said a voice at her shoulder. It was Lucy, her curate.

"I know." Mel's voice came out strained like an elastic band. "I might take it to her anyway on the way back. Tell her about the fête. She and her friends came here last year just before you arrived. They were eyeing up the local lads."

The curate giggled. "That's what fêtes are for. I remember doing the same at Amy's age."

They walked together towards the second-hand book stall. "I like it when you refer to her by name," added Mel quietly as they flicked through the paperbacks. "It makes me feel as though she's still with us."

Lucy patted her briefly on the shoulder. "She is. You know everyone is praying for her, don't you? Not just the prayers we say in church but in our house groups too."

"I'll make the next one. Promise."

"Only when you're ready. We can manage until then."

She couldn't expect them to carry on, thought Mel, handing over 60p for a tattered copy of a Mary Wesley novel. It had been four months now. She had to get back to normality. Had to pick up the pieces for the sake of her congregation, for her curate. Not to mention Josh and Richard.

"Richard not here?" asked Lucy, as though reading her mind.

"No. He went up to Leeds yesterday for another interview and stayed over as they wanted to take him out to dinner with the other applicants." She allowed herself a small laugh. "Probably wanted to see how he performed as part of a team. Teamwork is the buzz word nowadays."

"Well it's great he's got a second interview."

"We've been there before."

"Look, Mel, I hope you don't mind me saying this but . . ."

There was the sound of shouting from the other end of the garden. "What's happening?"

"I don't know. Hang on. What's that up there?"

Mel put her hand above her eyes, squinting into the sun.

"Looks like some kid has climbed a tree. What an idiot!"

"There's two of them. They seem to be holding something. Looks like a banner."

Mel was still trying to see. "What does it say?"

"I'm not sure but they're pretty high up. Oh, God." Even as she spoke, there was a scream. "One of them has fallen. Come on. Quick!"

Even as she ran towards the tree — a handsome chestnut that had probably been there for ever — Mel knew it was Josh. It wasn't just the black hoodie which seemed to be standard uniform nowadays for anyone under seventeen. It was the fact that she knew she'd lose him too. First Amy. Now Josh.

"Dear God. Please. I'll do anything. Just don't let him be hurt."

Breathless, they arrived just in time to see a tall skinny youth getting up from the ground and brushing himself down. Mel recognised him as one of Josh's friends and, to her shame, felt a flood of relief.

"Are you all right?" someone asked.

"Piss off."

There was a murmur of disapproval. "Honestly," said the woman who was in charge of the fête. Angela

247

someone, Mel seemed to remember, with a posh double-barrel name. "How very rude. Isn't that your son, vicar, who is still up the tree?"

She looked up. Sure enough, sitting on a thick branch several feet up, was a spiky-haired Josh, glaring down at them. In his hand he still held the banner which read, she could see now, "SAVE OUR TREES!"

"Save our trees?" Mel repeated. "Josh, what on earth do you mean? Come down at once."

"Fuck off, Mum."

There was an audible gasp. Mel felt herself burn with embarrassment. It was one thing having to deal with rude teenagers in the privacy of your own home but quite another when it was in front of your parish.

"Josh. That's very rude. Please come down at once."

"Make me."

What was she going to do? Call Richard? He'd still be on the train. A crazy part of her wanted to ring Geoff but that was silly. "Josh, please."

Angela whatever her name, sniffed. "In my day, we didn't plead with our children. We told them what to do."

Mel swung round. "I'm aware of that but you might not realise that my son has been through rather a lot recently. His sister is in hospital. And he's only a teenager."

"It's OK. I'll sort this out." A tall good-looking man in a rather distinguished way with short grey hair and a green Barbour was at the bottom of the tree looking up. "Listen, young man. If you want to stay up there, that's fine. We'll leave you to it. Come down when you're ready." He turned to face the crowd. "Why don't we all move on to the tea table? There's some delicious lemon drizzle cake and scones which the ladies committee has made."

"Who's that?" whispered Lucy as the crowd reluctantly dispersed.

"Robin Michaels. He owns this place." Mel was still staring up at Josh, willing him to come down.

"Seems a decent sort of man."

Mel hardly heard her. She wanted to climb up the tree herself and bring him down. "Josh, what do you mean about this saving trees stuff?"

"I told you. You just don't listen." His voice was spiked with anger. "They're cutting trees down everywhere round here. It's bad for the environment."

"But climbing trees and swearing at me isn't going to help."

"Fuck off, Mum. Why don't you go and see Amy? She won't answer back now, will she? You can make up for all the arguments you used to have with her by being nice for a change."

Mel felt as though she'd been punched in the ribs. It was true. She and Amy had rowed a lot and God knows, she'd apologised enough for that to her daughter even though she might or might not be able to hear her.

"Leave him," whispered Lucy. "He'll come down when he's ready."

"But what if he falls?" Mel heard her voice rise hysterically. "I can't cope if something happens to him too."

"Don't look now but he's coming down. No, don't look. Pretend you're walking away. There. He's down now."

Mel swung round. "Josh, how dare you scare me like that? You could have hurt yourself."

Her son scowled as he readjusted the large gold cross round his neck that had got caught up in his Star of David chain. "And what do you care? All you're interested in is Amy and how it was all your fault for texting her. Know what?" He glared at her. "You're so negative nowadays that you're not fit to bring me up."

The force of the words hit her like a concrete boulder and, for a second, she couldn't breathe.

"Josh, that's really unkind," she heard her curate saying.

Something flickered across her son's face. "Sorry. Didn't mean it."

Mel watched him running off out of the garden, trailing the banner behind him.

"You heard him," said Lucy urgently. "He just said it in anger. Teenagers do that kind of thing."

"But it's true," she said quietly. "It's really true."

There was only one place to go after that.

"Amy's having a lot of visitors today!" said the ward sister brightly, as though Amy might actually be sitting up, receiving guests. "Isn't that nice?"

Who else was there, wondered Mel, making her way to the room which was becoming so familiar now.

"Hi," said a young voice cheerily.

She stared. Amy was still lying motionless in her bed but all around her, her friends were sitting and nattering as though they were having what her daughter used to call a "chillaxing" session in her bedroom. Sharon was carefully painting her finger nails and another girl, whom she vaguely recognised, was doing the same to her toenails.

Jackie, another chum, was plaiting her hair and a fourth was fiddling with a CD player on the side of the bed.

"You don't mind, do you?" asked Sharon. "We thought she might like this. It could even wake her up."

She slid on to the seat that one of the girls found her. "I think it's fantastic."

"Can I get you a cup of coffee from the machine?" asked another one.

"That's really kind."

Mesmerised, she watched Amy's friends nattering and chattering around her like bees in a hive. That was the amazing thing about today's generation, she mused. She'd had friends too but not like this. They were there for each other; maybe that's why Amy had always been on the mobile or emailing them. Friends, like that article she'd read in some magazine the other day, were the new family.

She'd lost touch with most of hers because of work and children. But there was one person who understood . . .

"Glad you phoned," puffed Geoff, running alongside her.

"You didn't mind?" She turned to look at him. "Rather last minute."

"I need the exercise if I'm going to get fit for my big day."

"I need the exercise to get through the day I've just had."

"That bad, was it. Want a rest?"

They both sat down together on an old fallen branch in companionable silence, although the wind had just started to whip up again.

"Lovely here, isn't it?" Geoff looked around at the woods with the leaves just beginning to break out in green and white buds. "Really peaceful."

She nodded. I want to stay for ever, she felt like saying. "I've got to be going. Thanks for the company."

He looked at her as though wanting to say something else.

"Next week?"

Shut up, God, will you? I'm not doing anything wrong.

"Great."

"By the way, I've thought of something for your notice-board. How about 'Check out your destiny. Get your psalm read here.'"

At times, this man took her breath away. "Know what, Geoff? That's really good!"

"You're back."

Richard was opening a bottle of special-offer Australian wine, his back to her. "Your fête went on for a long time."

Should she tell him about Josh? What was the point? "I went on to see Amy afterwards."

"Of course."

The unspoken question ("Any change?") hung between them.

"How did the interview go?"

He brandished the corkscrew. "That's what this is all about. I got it. I actually got it!"

His face shone with such excitement that for a minute she wondered if she'd got it wrong. "Is it still in Leeds?"

"Yes, but I've worked it out. If I get up really early on Monday morning, we can still have the weekend together. I'll find a bedsitter — in fact, I've already got a list — and you'll be so busy with work you won't even notice I've gone."

She stood, silent, looking at him.

"Well I know it's not perfect but it's a job, Mel, for pity's sake. And isn't that what you've been banging on at me to do?"

"But how am I going to manage on my own? I haven't even begun to tell you what Josh did this afternoon."

"I know. He came back earlier. It's OK, Mel. I did things like that at that age. So did you. Remember that anti-nuclear march we went on?"

She took a slug of wine. It was sharp; cheap and nasty. "I didn't tell my mother to fuck off in front of everyone."

"He's upset, Mel."

She wanted to scream. "We're all upset. It's impossible for all of us and now you won't be here to help and . . ."

"Sssh. There's the phone." Richard seemed vastly relieved. "I'll get it, shall I?"

She waited, half-hoping, half-praying. Even now, after all these months, her heart still stopped when the phone rang in case Amy had "woken up". Amy had taken a turn for the worse. Amy had . . . Sometimes, she even hid her mobile in her cassock during services.

"It's for you." Richard's face was taut as he handed over the receiver. "It's the archdeacon."

The archdeacon? Mel felt a football of apprehension in her chest. The archdeacon, ringing on a Saturday?

"Mel!"

His deep gravelly voice, which belied his small stature, made her hold the phone away from her ear. "I do apologise for bothering you over the weekend but I wondered if we could arrange a meeting in the not-too-distant future. I've heard some rather disturbing news concerning your village fête . . ."

CHAPTER
TWENTY-EIGHT

Janie

Bill and Len were thrilled. "Bill had set his heart on getting married in a church," boomed Len down the phone. "But we'd given up finding anyone to marry us. It was so clever of you to think of Mel. How do you know her?"

"I don't." Janie was sketching a face on the wall — whoops! — and at the same time, wondering how anyone with such a sexy Green & Black voice could possibly be gay. "But a friend's mum lives in her village and I heard she was . . . well quite broad-minded."

"You were right. We went to see her last night for the pre-wedding chat." He chuckled. "She said we seemed like a very well-matched couple. Now about the flowers. Marjorie said you could get those sorted for us."

"Sure," said Janie, licking her finger and trying to rub out the pencil sketch. Marjorie had suggested that, to cut costs, she did them instead of employing a professional florist. ("I used to run the church flower rota when I was married, dear.")

"As we said, Bill has set his heart on a Midnight Ice theme so we were thinking deep blue irises . . ."

"No problem." If she didn't stop him now, they'd be here for ever. "I'll pop down to the market right now to check them out."

"Hello, my friend!"

Some mate, she was. What happened to the someone she was meant to have found, according to the *Big Issue* lady's promise all those months ago?

"You want some tea, my friend, from my Thermos? It is green. You like green tea?"

Well yes but not from a cracked plastic Thermos cup. She'd been into green tea for years, before it got popular and she'd almost got Marjorie round to it. It was rather nice the way they'd introduced each other to new experiences. Her landlady's pile cream was so much better than any eye stuff she'd used. And they both — by agreement — shared that "holiday lotion" moisturiser which gave them, as Marjorie put it, a "rather fetching glow". It almost made up for her landlady's irritating habit of rinsing her false teeth in the dishwasher.

"Thanks for the grant advice. We've actually got some money! It's not a lot but it's a start."

"Good. You want magazine?"

She'd walked into that one, all right. At least she had the right change, this time.

"You want to buy crystals too?"

She held out a string of wonderfully coloured clumps; heather mauves, brilliant peacock blues, port red.

"Sorry. I really can't afford them."

256

The woman made a regretful face. "They are healing crystals. Shame. But now you drink."

The *Big Issue* lady had made the tea with leaves; it was lukewarm and Janie drank it quickly, not realising how thirsty she'd been.

"Leave a little liquid in the bottom and swirl it around. Then I read your leaves. That's right. Good. I see now. There is a man. He has hurt you but he is sorry."

Janie snorted.

"No. Please. To forgive is to get rich in spirit. Yes? But there is someone else." She tipped the plastic cup sideways. "Someone very different. And I can see a woman. I do not like her. Be careful."

"What kind of woman?"

"I'm sorry, my friend. I do not know. But be careful."

She was pressing something hard into the palm of her hand. "Take. Please. It is a gift."

How ridiculous, thought Janie, making her way through the teeming shoppers on the way to the underground market. Anyone could say that sort of thing. *There is someone else.* Well, there would be eventually and he probably would be different. They all were until they all ended up doing the same thing — chucking her.

Janie's hand closed round the small bright blue crystal in her pocket. As for the woman, well, that could be anyone. Linda, her old boss who had fired her? Monique? She was probably the most obvious candidate. Becky? No that was ridiculous although she hadn't phoned since they'd had that really short lunch

257

when Becky probably hadn't even realised how rude she'd been.

"Hello, you!"

Shit! Only one person always said that. Yet for a minute, she wondered if it was him. Gone were the scruffy jeans and ripped t-shirt with sloppy untied trainers. He'd cut his hair too and got rid of the earring. Bloody hell! Mac was actually wearing a suit.

"Sorry." She forced herself to sound cool and unruffled, even though her heart was pounding. "I didn't recognise you."

"That's what everyone says." Mac beamed. "I've got myself a job and all. A proper one. Know what I mean? At the estate agents on the corner."

Janie made to move on. "I'm very pleased for you."

"No, please. Wait." He reached out as though to touch her on the arm but she stepped back just in time. "I don't blame you, Janie, for being mad at me. But I'm sorry. Really sorry. It was one of those stupid spur of the moment things."

His eyes were pleading with hers. "I haven't met anyone else since you. No one I feel the same way about, anyway. Couldn't we give it another chance?"

Had that *Big Issue* woman somehow set this up? Think about forgiving people, she had said. Why not? Mac had made her feel good about herself until the end which she honestly hadn't seen coming. He made her laugh. He accepted her for what she was.

And then he'd jumped into bed with someone else when she was slaving away, trying to pay their rent.

"Sorry, Mac. I can't forget what you did."

She walked on but he was striding along next to her. She'd forgotten how tall he was, how persuasive he could sound. "Just think about it, will you, Janie? Please?"

"No. Maybe. Sod it, Mac, I don't know. I've got a wedding to organise — well, two actually. So just leave me alone, will you?"

"About to commit bigamy, are you?" His eyes twinkled.

"No. I'm working. I'm a wedding planner, remember. And since you buggered off, I've started my own business. We do funerals too and if you don't stop pestering me, I might just have one more booking on my hands."

Mac grinned. "That's my Janie. A right old fighter and all."

She stopped and swivelled round, facing him. "I am not your Janie. You lost me when you fucked someone else. Now beat it, Mac. I'm glad you've got a job but I'm nowhere near forgetting what you did."

"But you might someday?"

Something in his voice made her stop, waver. "Maybe," she heard herself saying. "But not now."

"I can wait. Know what I mean? I can wait for ever."

"Well, I can't. I've got to get to the flower stall before it closes."

The wedding was a rushed one. Just three weeks to get it all sorted. "You'd think it was a shotgun affair," joked Marjorie who'd been practising on irises for days.

"Mind you, it probably won't be long before the Americans work out how to get a man pregnant."

In the meantime, Janie had been fielding calls from Monique who was constantly ringing about minor details such as hymn sheets and the colour of napkins or "serviettes" as she called them.

"I want them in the shape of a swan," she'd said on the phone that morning. "You do know how to do that, don't you?"

"Sure." Janie made a mental note to get a library book on napkin shapes. Marjorie would be able to read it.

"And of course, I want the ice sculpture in the middle of the table to match."

Ice sculpture?

"You do remember us discussing that, don't you, Janie? I made that quite clear during our first meeting at the Randolph. The one you were late for."

She was 99% certain that they hadn't discussed a flipping ice sculpture, let alone a swan. But, as her old boss had always said, the customer was always right. Right off her head.

"Janie, are you writing this down?"

How could she do that? But she'd remember instead, the way she always did.

"Yes, Monique. I am. Just leave it to us. We won't let you down."

Thank God, Bill — who turned out to be the bride — and Len were less demanding, although it didn't stop

260

them being so nervous that both arrived at the church half an hour early.

"What amazing flowers!" Bill gasped as he took in Marjorie's arrangement

"I'm so glad you like it." Marjorie glowed. "I spent some time practising."

Len looked at them sideways. "I wonder if you'd mind if we moved them ever so slightly over here. Whoops!"

"Careful," called out Bill.

"Shit," said Janie.

"Oh, dear," said Marjorie.

They all stared in horror as the Midnight Ice display lay in a heap on the floor by the bride's feet.

"I'm so sorry." Len squeezed Bill's hand. "How very stupid of me."

"It's all right." Bill spoke in a small voice. "Actually, I feel a little faint."

"Don't sit there!" called out Marjorie.

Too late. Bill was already sitting on a chair which she'd used for the flower arrangements.

"Oh, dear." Bill stood up again, turning round and trying to examine his bottom. "I feel rather damp."

"Looks as though you've wee'd yourself," giggled Len.

For one awful moment, Janie thought Bill was going to cry. Then, to her huge relief, he grinned. "Never mind. It will dry off. Besides, all that matters is that we're going to be forever."

The couple gazed at each other and Janie couldn't resist sneaking a look at Marjorie. Her face said the same. This was love. Real love. The kind that didn't get into a flap over ruined flower arrangements. The kind that transcended social boundaries.

"I think your guests are beginning to arrive," whispered Marjorie as the couple continued hugging each other.

"I'll go and sort them out," offered Janie. "Looks like the ushers are a bit late. Shall I do the honours until they arrive?"

The ushers, in the event, didn't turn up until the service had started so it was Janie who was saying "Bride or groom?" as the guests entered. After a few minutes, it didn't seem so strange and although there was the odd tricky relative, including a rather snooty looking woman in a large pink hat who almost choked at the word "bride", most seemed to take it in their stride.

It really was, as Janie and Marjorie agreed later, a beautiful wedding. The best man was Bill's sister and the bridesmaids were her children. The reception, back at Bill and Len's house, went almost without a hitch, partly because Bill and Len had chosen to get takeaway curries for everyone.

"It's our favourite dish," confided Len. "We had it after our first date." He blushed. "The curry, that is."

"You know," said Janie, flopping back into Marjorie's sofa at the end of the evening when the boys had given them a cheque, including a generous tip, "it makes you wonder, doesn't it? Love strikes in the most unlikely places."

Marjorie nodded sleepily over her nightcap of whisky and lemon. "It certainly does. By the way, poor old Ned popped off this morning. There was a message on the answerphone from his wife. He was on our waiting list, remember?"

Janie did. Ned had had dementia for so long that his demise really was a blessed release. "She wants a green funeral. Apparently, he turned green long before his time and had a thing about wicker caskets. Do you think you could do some research into that? Maybe that nice modern vicar woman might help. He also left a tape, apparently. But I'm not quite sure what that's all about . . ."

FIVE MONTHS TO GO

CHAPTER
TWENTY-NINE

Becky

"What do you mean, you need to take a week off? You've only just got back from a week in New York on some press beano. It's hardly fair on your staff to go swanning off immediately you returned."

Brian cold-eyed her from the other side of his mahogany editor-in-chief desk. Becky, who'd had her strategy all worked out, felt herself wavering in the face of Brian's granite face. Rumour had it that Cat had only slipped out of her La Senzas to appease him over a proof problem. At the time, she'd been revolted. Now she was almost tempted.

Hold your nerve. Stand up to him. Bullies hate that.

"The press beano, as you put it, Brian, was something — if you remember — you specifically asked me to go on. I believe you used the phrase 'We need to keep *Charisma's* eye in the market place.'"

The flicker in his eye suggested he did indeed remember, but the thinning of his mouth (Mum had always told her to beware of men with thin lips) suggested he didn't appreciate being reminded.

"I'm well aware," she continued hurriedly, "this isn't the best time to take a week off. But I'm afraid I have a slight domestic issue."

Brian sat back in his green leather chair, arms folded with an "I thought as much" expression. "When I offered you the job, Becky, I specifically asked you about childcare back up. And you — if you remember — assured me that you had that organised. Naturally, at *Charisma*, we're well aware of our employees' rights but at the same time, we need staff who are going to be reliable and not take a week off at the sign of a child's cold."

Horrible, horrible man. Second thoughts, there was no way she'd even touch his hand, let along anything else. "I hardly think a hysterectomy is a child's cold," she heard herself say.

"A hysterectomy?" Brian's eyebrows crocheted together in one. "My dear girl, I'm so sorry. My wife had one last year and it's quite a serious operation. You're going to need at least three weeks, you know. If not four."

"If you're sure. Thanks very much." She'd phoned up so many nanny agencies that she was bound to get a replacement for Laura by then. And then she could be back at her desk after her so-called op with no one any the wiser. "They're doing a new procedure on me. It's meant to help people recover even faster. I might even write a feature on it — if it works of course."

Whoops. Maybe that was a bit ambitious.

"How very interesting." Brian leaned towards her, his eyes almost melting with the thought of the coverline. "We are a bit low on our Health stock. Still, don't think I'm being personal here, Becky, but normally hysterectomies are performed on women who are, shall

268

we say, much older than you unless there is a serious problem." His voice dropped. "Maybe even a life-threatening problem."

"Oh, no." Becky laughed gaily, thinking of how she'd dearly love to threaten Laura's life for getting her into this mess. "I'm fine. Really. You don't need to start advertising for my replacement yet!"

The guilty look that shot into his eyes confirmed that that's indeed what Brian had been thinking. "Becky! What do you take me for? I hope it goes all right, dear."

Dear?

His hand crawled out towards hers and she steeled herself as his large, damp hand encircled hers. "And if there's anything I can do — anything at all — please let me know."

Of course, she felt awful about it. Especially when she had to lie to Nancy and her deputy too. Lavinia, far from looking pissed off, seemed over-enthusiastic. She'd see it, Becky knew, as an opportunity to prove she was just as good, if not better, than her boss. *Charisma* should carry the strapline "Dog Eats Bitch", Becky thought bitterly as she cleared her desk of essentials she needed to take home.

If only they knew that she'd much rather stay in the office than be stuck at home with the kids, until the agencies had come up with someone. "I don't think we have anyone suitable for Daisy and Ben yet," one of the managers had told her only that morning.

"What do you mean?"

"To be frank, Mrs Hughes, certain children require a certain kind of nanny. Someone who won't take any nonsense."

"So you're saying my children are difficult?"

"Not difficult, Mrs Hughes. Just, shall we say, challenging."

Well, sod that. She'd look after the kids herself for a bit and then, when they finally found her a nanny, life could finally get back to normal.

"What did the big boss say about you taking time off?" asked Steve who was in his bath as usual when she got back that night around 10p.m. Half an hour earlier than usual, thought Becky smugly. He could hardly complain about that.

"He was quite understanding, actually."

Becky deliberately looked at Steve's face rather than the rest of his body. If she did, he'd take it as an invitation for something else and frankly, she was exhausted.

"Really?"

He stood up in the bath and Becky felt the slight stirring of a long-forgotten feeling in the pit of her stomach. No. It had gone. Just as well. She really was pooped. "Course, I couldn't say I needed the time to look after the kids while every agency in town is trying to find a nanny that can deal with two 'challenging' offspring."

He was putting on his once-white bathrobe now, which reminded her — Laura hadn't done the laundry before sauntering off. "Why not?"

270

"Because he wouldn't have understood. So I told him I was having a little operation."

Steve frowned. "What kind of operation."

Becky turned her back and pretended to examine her face in the bathroom mirror. "Just a hysterectomy."

"A hysterectomy?" Steve gaped. "But that's a really big operation. My mum had one. Remember?"

Becky smiled. "That's why they're going to be so impressed when I come back, nice and rested after some time at home. Do you know, I'm actually looking forward to it. By the way, what time does children's television start in the morning?"

"Early." Steve joined her at the mirror and she looked at them both, as though seeing them from someone else's point of view. They almost seemed a happily married couple with two young children. "You have remembered that I'm going to be in Germany all week, haven't you?"

"What?" Becky spun round. "You didn't tell me."

"I'm sure I did."

"Well can't you get out of it? You can't leave me alone with the kids all day and all night! What if they both wake up or one is ill or I can't find the remote control?"

"Very funny."

She hadn't been joking.

"Can you get your mum up to help?"

Becky plonked herself down on the bathroom stool next to a pile of *Vogues*. "Not after my last conversation with her."

He knelt down beside her, putting an arm around her. If she hadn't felt such a heel, she might have been tempted to have rested her head on his shoulder. He smelt so nice, so secure.

"I know it's tough, Becks, having both parents getting married again. But aren't you happy for them? You don't want them to be alone for the rest of their lives, do you?"

"No." She hesitated. "But I don't like David much. He's so dull. And Monique . . . Ugh! She's hideous."

Steve laughed. "I agree she's hardly an oil painting but she makes your dad happy and that's what counts. Who can account for chemistry and besides, she's very good with the kids, isn't she?" He stood up. "By the way, someone called Dan called a few hours ago. Wants you to ring him back about some deadline."

When Becky woke the following morning, her first thought was that Steve had acquired two extra pairs of arms and legs. By the time she realised it was actually Daisy and Ben, wrapped up on each side of her body, the second thought had struck. Shit! It was eight o'clock. She was two hours late for work.

No, hang on. She wasn't going into work. She was going into hospital or rather pretending to be. Instead, she was going to have her very first full-time week at home with the kids. Becky began to shake. What was she going to do with them? Even at weekends, either Steve or Laura had been there. She'd hardly ever — although she would have died rather than admit this to anyone — been on her own with both children for more

272

than a few hours. Last year, she'd taken Ben to the zoo for a whole day and he'd thrown a tantrum because the keeper wouldn't let him move into the elephant cage.

But two was a different matter and how the hell did women manage with three or more? No wonder alcoholism amongst the over-thirtysomething working mothers was rising according to a feature she'd just put to bed. They hadn't needed to make up any case histories for that one . . .

Becky glanced down at her sleeping children; their chests rising and falling with reassuring rhythm. It was so much easier when they were like this. It was almost tempting to pop them into a specimen jar, put them on the new glass and chrome display shelf from Conran and admire them when convenient.

Fuck! The doorbell. It would wake the kids unless she got out quickly and stopped it from ringing again. No! Not so loud. Daisy stirred. "Laura," she murmured.

Thanks a bunch. And now Ben was waking up! "Stay there, both of you. I've got to get the door."

The courier was about to leave when she finally opened it. "Sign here, please," he said sulkily.

Flowers! Fuck. Not from Dan. Please from Dan.

GOOD LUCK FOR YOUR OPERATION. LOVE FROM EVERYONE AT *CHARISMA*.

For a second, she almost felt guilty.

Sod it. They owed her. If she added up all the extra hours she'd put in — had been expected to put in without extra pay — she could demand a bloody florist's shop from them.

"Mum, Mum! Daisy won't let me watch my programme."

Right. If she could organise an entire magazine team, she could jolly well organise two minors. "Daisy," she said, marching in. "You're to let Ben watch his programme . . ."

Her voice tailed away as she stared at the enormous screen which she and Steve had had installed when they'd moved in. Somehow Ben had managed to override the "Not Suitable For Children Switch" which they'd put on as a precaution and now here he was, sitting, cross-legged, thumb in mouth, staring at a larger than life picture of a woman sitting on a man's lap, facing him and wearing . . . well, very little. "Ben, turn that off immediately." Grabbing the handset, she stabbed the red button in disgust.

Immediately, there was a loud roar. "Turn that on, Mum. Laura always lets me watch it."

"She watched it with us," lisped Daisy. "Said it was efu-cational."

Becky could see the headline now. "HOW SAFE IS YOUR NANNY?" She'd have to email that one in to Lavinia for conference, except that might be a bit difficult considering she was meant to be under the surgeon's knife right now.

"Well you're not watching it anymore." She looked at her watch. At least eight hours, 42 minutes until bedtime. "We'll get dressed in a minute and go to the park instead."

"Boring." Ben lunged at the handset.

274

"You're not having it." Becky held it above her head and Ben started leaping up and down. This was ridiculous. Who was the adult round here?

"Laura says I can have wot I want because I'm a spoilt brat."

She might just have a point. "Tell you what." Becky felt a huge relief at the thought which had just rushed into her head. "We'll ring Auntie Janie. See if she'd like us to go down to Oxford for the day."

Both children looked mildly interested. They adored Janie who did all kinds of daft things with them like letting Daisy go through her make-up bag.

"OK," said Ben reluctantly. "But only if you let us go in our pyjamas."

Sod it. "It's a deal."

CHAPTER
THIRTY

Helen

She'd been trying to make the phone call for weeks. But somehow, she just hadn't been able to find the words. "Yes, Robin, you're right. The Old Rectory was my home and yes, I've missed the garden dreadfully. So when you asked if I'd help out, I jumped at the idea although I should have told you I used to live there . . ."

Or how about, "Sorry, Robin. I've got a terrible perimenopausal memory and I'd quite forgotten where I used to live . . ."

Or, "OK, I've been coming into your garden on false pretences but to be honest, I felt it was my destiny."

That wouldn't do either, even though she'd been quite taken with that destiny/psalm reading notice outside the church the other week.

What was it she always used to tell the children? The truth is always best because if you don't come clean, someone somewhere will find out what really happened. And that's exactly what had happened. Even though the kitchen was too hot — she ought to turn off the Aga now for the summer — Helen shivered at the memory of her last conversation with Robin.

"You used to live here, didn't you?"

It was the look in his eyes, rather than the words, which had struck her. That look which said "I trusted you, Helen. I've let you into my home and my life but you haven't been honest with me."

Honesty! She'd always liked to think she was reasonably honest but in the end, it was her inability to be totally honest with her husband that meant she'd had no option but to leave Geoff.

Just as she wasn't being honest with herself by staying with David.

Sod it. She'd ring Robin. Remind him that today was the day she usually came to him — as if he wouldn't have remembered — and then say she totally understood if he didn't want her to come again.

He answered on the second ring, as though expecting her.

"Robin?"

"Hi, Helen."

He didn't sound surprised or angry or particularly pleased to hear her. Just pleasant in a distant sort of way. Her chest knotted again.

"I just wondered if . . ." She faltered, willing her well-rehearsed sentence to come into her head.

"Wondered if I still wanted you to come over today?"

"Yes."

"I don't think so."

Helen leaned back against the Aga, feeling the soothing warmth on her back. Never again would she see her garden. Never again would she sit by the pond which she'd cleared of weeds. Never again would she

277

trim her artichokes. Never again would she see Robin or talk to Sylvia, whom she'd become quite fond of. "Of course." She fought to keep her voice even. "I understand . . ."

"I'd rather we met somewhere neutral instead. Somewhere out of town, perhaps. So we can talk." She could hear the hesitancy in his voice. "You did rather rush off last time. There's quite a lot I'd like to ask, although of course, you don't have to."

"I want to." The words came rushing out of her mouth. "I want to explain. It wasn't the way it looks. I didn't mean to spy on my old house."

"I know. There's a rather nice pub just outside Summertown." He named the place and instantly memories shot back to lunches she and Geoff had shared there when they'd first moved in. "It does good food, apparently," he added.

It always did. "Fine. I'll meet you there. About one o'clock?"

"Perfect."

People who were early, Helen had always thought, didn't have enough to do with their lives. But it had proved impossible to work that morning.

"Going already?" enquired Doris who'd come out with a cup of tea (proper china on a doiley-lined tray) as Helen finished tidying up her small dahlia patch and tied up some stray roses.

"It's actually time," said Helen gently, as she looked around for Dandy who'd been exploring the compost heap. They both knew that she normally stayed at least a good ten minutes or more longer than she was paid for. "I've done all I need to today. What do you think?"

"Very nice." Doris wasn't looking at the dahlias. She was looking at Helen and possibly taking in the fact that she'd put on foundation for a change and even eyeliner. "Want to come in and brush up before you go on your lunch date?"

Helen stared at her.

Doris chuckled. "Don't worry. I won't tell that boyfriend of yours. Besides, you might be meeting a girlfriend although I must say that I wouldn't have gone to all that trouble myself unless he was someone special."

"It's just a friend," Helen managed to say.

"Surely." Doris shrugged. "Still, the offer's there if you want to come in and put on that pretty summer dress you've got hanging up inside that van of yours. And don't forget to squirt on some of that Chanel you've got on the front seat."

No wonder Robin had found out about her past. With villagers like Doris and Angela Pee-Pee, she must have been mad to have thought she could have kept it quiet. She should, she thought, as she topped up Dandy's water and took a seat in the pub garden — such a lovely day! — have told him right at the beginning.

"Hello!"

A tall substantial shadow fell on the ground before her. She looked up. Dandy was already jumping up, excited to see him, his nose — so embarrassing! — nuzzling Robin's groin. "Dandy! Get off. Oh, God, I'm so sorry. He's made another smell. I'm afraid he does that now, at his age."

"I've noticed. Thought it might have been you, the first time. Don't worry, I'm only joking." He took a seat next to her. "I'm glad you've found an outside table. This place can get really busy."

She suddenly realised. "Where's Sylvia?"

Something flitted across his face. "At home. I have someone from the agency who comes in every now and then if I need to go out."

She hadn't realised that.

"About the other week," she began.

His hand briefly touched hers. "Not yet. Let's have a drink first, shall we and look at the menu." His eyes locked with hers. "Then you can tell me all about it."

He'd been right. It was much easier to talk with a glass of cool Chardonnay and a plate of delicious smoked salmon with peppercorns and rustic cranberry bread. He'd chosen the same ("My favourite too") and asked the Polish waitress if she could possibly spare some sausages for "their" dog. Dandy had polished them off within seconds but she was still toying with the salmon, desperate to begin.

"I'm sorry, Robin. This looks wonderful but I can't eat until I've explained."

He nodded. "Go on."

She took a large slug of Chardonnay. "I didn't come looking for work at the — at your — house. To be honest, what really happened was that my daughter had just rung to say my ex-husband was getting married again." Another slug. "And it got me thinking. I mean,

I don't feel anything for him anymore. Not in that way, although he'll always be the father of my children. But it made me feel a bit sad, I suppose, because there had been some good times. And somehow I found myself driving back to the house where we'd brought the children up."

He nodded. "I can see that. Think I might have done the same."

"Thank you. Well then I was being nosy by getting out and having a bit of a look and you came out and offered me a job." She was horribly aware she was gabbling. "I should have told you then that I'd lived there but subconsciously I think I thought that if I did, you might think I'd interfere. So I thought I'd tell you later but there never seemed to be a right time."

In her nervousness she stuffed a too-large forkful of salmon into her mouth. "Just what I thought. I suppose Angela Pee-Pee from the village told you?"

Robin laughed. "She'd seen your van a few times, so when she came round she couldn't wait to pump me for information. I had my suspicions though."

"You did?"

He sat back in his seat and stroked Dandy who had settled down in a shaft of sunlight next to him. "Well you made the odd slip every now and then, like when you called the vegetable patch 'yours' and when you were explaining how the Aga worked. I thought then you seemed unnaturally attached to it."

"That Aga, I might tell you, cooked some amazing rusks for Adam when he was teething. It saved me — as

281

did the garden. They both gave me comfort at a time when I desperately needed it."

Robin's eyes softened. "Sounds like you've been as unhappy as me."

Oh, God. There she was, wittering on about her own problems when he had more than enough of his own.

"No, I don't mean Sylvia's illness. I'm talking before that."

"Somehow when someone is, well, is like Sylvia, it's hard to imagine what life was like for someone before it happened," she found herself saying.

"Very true. Do you mind if I tell you?"

She shook her head.

Robin leaned back again and closed his eyes briefly. "Sylvia and I didn't meet until our early forties. We knew it might be pushing it to have a child but we tried, nevertheless. It didn't happen and, although I hadn't thought it would, to be honest, she took it badly."

"I can understand that. I can't imagine life without my children."

He smiled wryly. "That's why Sylvia began exploring other options."

"IVF?"

"That as well." He looked away but not before Helen had caught the pain in his eyes. "She also began having relationships with other men to see if they could come up with the goods since I hadn't."

Helen gasped. "I'm so sorry."

Robin nodded. "Infidelity is the one thing I can't handle. My own father had liaisons and it caused my mother a great deal of pain."

282

She nodded. *If he only knew*

"But why didn't you just leave her?"

His voice changed into a flat, dispassionate tone, as though distancing himself from his words. "One day, I came home from work early, specifically to say that I couldn't take any more. The lights were on and the radio was blaring from the kitchen but she wasn't there. I went upstairs . . ."

"Oh, no." Helen could hear what was coming.

Robin shook his head ruefully. "I'd almost rather I had found her in bed with someone else. She was lying on it all right, but there was no one there. Her eyes were open but her mouth was bent at a strange angle, as though someone had smashed her face in. Her leg was hanging limply over the side of the bed and her arm looked as though it was twisted."

"She'd had a stroke."

Robin nodded. "I was hysterical."

She could hardly believe that; he always seemed so calm.

"I called the ambulance and she was rushed to Intensive Care. She's too young to have a stroke, I kept saying. But what I really meant was 'I can't leave her now. I'm trapped just as she was trapped inside her body.'"

"How awful." Helen pushed away the salmon.

"I found the best specialists in the field but nothing could be done. The only option would have been for me to send her into a home but I couldn't." He looked pleadingly at her from across the table. "You've seen how her eyes can talk. I've watched you speak to her.

They looked at me like that, afterwards. They were as clear as if she'd been able to speak herself. I'm sorry, she said. I shouldn't have behaved like that. I just wanted a baby and now I'm reduced to being a baby myself. Don't leave me."

"Of course you couldn't. I wouldn't have left Geoff if he'd been ill." She found herself putting out her hand to touch him briefly on his bare arm in sympathy but the surprised look on his face made her withdraw it fast.

"I've often thought," she continued, draining her glass, "that if Geoff was ill, I'd look after him. Of course, now he's getting married again, there's no need."

"That must feel weird after all this time."

She nodded. "But you know what the strangest thing of all is? Monique — that's her name — is nothing like the kind of person I thought Geoff would marry. She's not at all attractive, although my daughter tells me she's had hormonal problems, and she's really pushy. It makes me wonder why Geoff ever picked me. I'm so different."

"Maybe that's the point." He smiled sadly at her. "If I ever married again, I would find someone very different from Sylvia."

There was a brief silence.

"If you don't mind me asking," Robin continued, "why did you and Geoff break up?"

A prickle of unease washed through her. How, after what he'd told her about Sylvia, could she tell him the truth?

"I'd rather not say."

"Sorry. I shouldn't have asked." He glanced across at the ring on her left hand. "Mind me being even nosier and asking if that's an engagement ring?"

"Sort of." Helen felt herself flush. "We're probably getting married in November."

"Isn't that when you said your ex-husband was tying the knot?"

Had she?

"I'm afraid I overheard you telling Sylvia one day."

She nodded. "It's not intentional. It's just that, well, as David said, we're not getting any younger so . . ."

"*Granny!*"

"Ben? Daisy?" She held out her arms as two small children hurled themselves at her. "Ben, don't push Daisy like that. Becky! How lovely to see you. And Janie too. It's been ages. How did you know I was here or was it coincidence? Anyway, let me introduce you. This is Robin whom I garden for. That is, for him and his wife Sylvia. Robin, this is my daughter and her best friend Janie who lives near here."

"Actually, Mum, we didn't know you were here."

She should have realised.

"I've taken three weeks off work because Laura's left." Becky sat down beside her, looking even more stressed out than ever. "I was going to tell you but it all happened in a bit of a rush. So I thought I'd come down and see Janie but she had a meeting so we arranged to meet . . . meet the client here."

Helen was still cuddling the children; breathing them in hungrily as they clung to her neck. How she loved the way they smelt of butter and June sunshine and sunflower seeds all in one, just as Adam and Becky had done at this age.

"Mum said she hoped we wouldn't see you cos you always tell her off."

"Ben!"

Her daughter's face had turned puce. Stung, Helen turned away to hide the hurt. "We won't get in your way, will we, Robin? In fact, we were just about to go. I must get back to the dog."

"Ah dogs! Such a tie, I've always thought. Mind you, you could say the same about husbands, couldn't you!"

No mistaking that voice.

Helen felt her breathing begin to race and her palms start to sweat as a large woman, carrying a trayload of drinks, bore down on them. She looked at Becky but her daughter was looking in the other direction. So that's why she'd hoped they wouldn't bump into each other!

Meanwhile, Janie was looking decidedly awkward and Robin was clearly confused. There was no getting out of it.

"May I introduce Robin, a friend and client." God, how stiff that sounded!

"And Robin . . . meet Monique."

CHAPTER
THIRTY-ONE

Mel

"I hope," said the archdeacon, tapping his long, thin fingers on the sherry glass, "that you take my meaning. I'm not merely concerned about the — how shall I put it? — same-sex wedding although you should, of course, have sought permission for that. It's all the other issues as well."

Mel crossed and uncrossed her legs nervously, wishing she could stomach a glass of Harvey's Bristol Cream on an empty stomach, if only to give herself some Dutch courage. Oh, yes, she took his meaning all right. It had been quite clear. Phrases from the last hour's conversation still resounded in her head.

"Not the type of behaviour we expect in a vicar's family."

"We all have our crosses to bear but one's flock expects one to bear them with dignity."

"Forgiveness is an essential in a Christian's life, especially in a vicar."

Mel leaned forward and picked up the glass. Just a sip. Ugh! "I understand your meaning perfectly, Tom." She faltered, feeling as though she'd stepped out of line in calling him by his first name as invited. "But I cannot be responsible for everyone else's behaviour."

The archdeacon's eyes narrowed. He was a thin angular man with a nose that matched the shape of his fingers. "I'm afraid you must, my dear." The "dear" bit belied the sharpness of his tone. "We all have to act in an appropriate fashion in our position."

"Appropriate" was one of the AD's favourite words; in fact, he ought to put it on his list of Favourites if he knew what that was. What would Josh say if she told him his behaviour was inappropriate? Probably tell her to fuck off.

"What about your husband?" the AD was continuing. "He must be a great support at a time like this."

Support? Nowadays, Richard merely turned off the light, rolled over with a peck and goodnight and went to sleep without so much as a conversational fumble.

"My husband has been unemployed for some months," she began.

"Ah, yes, I remember now."

"But he's just found a job."

"Excellent news."

"In Leeds."

Was that a flash of relief crossing the archdeacon's face? "So you will be leaving us, my dear?"

"No. He'll commute and come back at weekends."

The archdeacon's fingers tapped even faster on the stem of his glass. "That won't be easy for you."

"No, but we've always been fairly independent."

Not like you, she felt like adding. She'd only met the archdeacon's wife twice but she wouldn't mind betting that the AD wouldn't even know where to find the Andrex if his wife suddenly hopped it.

"I see." The archdeacon's tone suggested that being independent was decidedly unwise. But isn't that just what Jesus had been? Suddenly, a slogan popped into her head. "Dangerous Book for Boys: Read at your own risk." She could run a picture of the Bible below.

"I'm afraid there's one more rather awkward situation I need to bring up."

She knew it. Forgive us our trespasses, as we forgive them. Unless, of course, it happens to be a scrawny kid who didn't stop when he should have done.

"Of course, I know how terrible it must be for you, with your daughter in hospital."

How did he know? Had he been through it himself? His three children had all grown up and become teachers. Well done. She could just see the chirpy Christmas round-robins.

"But I've heard a disturbing report that you have failed to show compassion to the young man in question who was driving the car."

"The young man, as you call him, did not stop. Now my daughter is in a coma and may never recover. Have your children ever been in hospital, Tom?"

"Well, yes." He was stumbling over his words. "One of them once had, er, her bunions operated on."

"Poor her." Mel stood up. "Well Amy's situation is, I'm afraid, somewhat more serious. And yes, I know I ought to forgive Kevin. But I find that I can't forgive. I can say I will but I don't mean it. And that's what counts."

"My dear girl, I do understand. That's why I wanted to have this little chat. We have support systems for this kind of issue, you know. I'd like you to talk to someone. It might help."

"Will it?" Mel felt dizzy. She really shouldn't have had that sherry. "I'm not sure that talking will do that unless, by some miracle, Amy starts to talk again."

The archdeacon nodded. "I've been praying for her."

Oh for God's sake. "Me too, but nothing's happened yet."

"These things can take time. Might it help to remember why you became a vicar in the first place?"

She'd often thought about that. It hadn't been a sudden conversion: just a slow steady realisation that nothing else made sense in life (especially her crazy hours in advertising). She'd always gone to church as a child and had continued as a teenager and through university. At mother and toddler, where other mothers would often ask her advice for some unknown reason, the vicar had suggested she might have a calling.

"I love the way you use your copywriting skills to make our newsletter funny," she'd said. "Have you ever considered the possibility that God wants you to use your gifts for Him?"

It hadn't been easy. The selection process and the training had been tough on all of them. And now, here she was in her first post after her curacy and everything was beginning to crumble. Had she made a terrible mistake?

Mel's hand was on the door handle. "Faith? And what happens when you start to lose it? I'm sorry, Tom, but I can't go on. I'd like to hand in my resignation."

CHAPTER
THIRTY-TWO

Janie

Of course, she'd been to wedding fairs before. In fact, she was due to go to one next week. But this was different. This was, Janie thought, looking around her in awe, really weird.

"A funeral fair?" Marjorie had guffawed when she'd first announced she was going. "What on earth is that?"

Janie looked up from the brochure. "It's where everyone who makes anything to do with funerals gets together and sells to the trade. And that's us. We could make all kinds of contacts, like where to find willow caskets or anything that's slightly unusual."

They'd already had quite a few requests for those following an article on green funerals in *Saga* magazine.

"Can't the local funeral parlours sort that out?" Marjorie had asked, sifting through her own post with a rather worried expression on her face.

"They gave us a really high quote. That's why I'm going to the fair."

And now, here she was. The funny thing was that it wasn't that dissimilar from the wedding fairs she used to go to for her old boss, apart from the fact that they were obviously selling different things. Janie ran her finger along the heather-coloured velvet lining of a king-size coffin. Quite inviting really, especially after getting up so early for the train. She was almost tempted to have a nap.

And look at all the things she could take in with her! Rather like a party bag for the next life! Janie paused at the next stall, with the chirpy name of Accessories for Afters. It almost looked like a normal craft shop with little flowers and tiny dolls and heart-shaped cushions.

Ah, there was the wicker casket stand. Honestly! Marjorie had something not too dissimilar herself to put the logs in next to the fire, although obviously hers was a bit smaller. Janie took off the lid. You'd never suspect it was really a coffin. In fact, it would be great as a huge toy box for Becky's kids.

"We are lining them of course," said a deep voice. "You can have fleece, silk, wool or even a floral design."

Janie looked up at the bluest pair of eyes she had ever seen. "Do you do Cath Kidston?"

"Cath who?"

Definitely a foreign accent. Maybe Scandinavian.

"I'm only joking. She's a designer. Love her stuff, although I can't afford it now." Janie looked shyly sideways through her fringe at the wicker casket seller. "Is this what you bury people in, then, in Norway?"

He nodded, glancing at her jeans. Maybe she'd overdone it a bit with the pink sequins this time. "You are reading my brochure?"

If only she could. "A bit of a guess, actually, although you might have been Danish or Finnish."

His eyes smiled. "It is good that I do not take offence. So. What brings you here? You do not look the type, if you do not mind me saying so."

Janie appraised his floppy blonde fringe, bead necklace and bare sandals. "Nor you."

He nodded energetically again. "Me, I am a student. An old student." He grinned, revealing a perfect row of white teeth. "But my father, he is ill. And my brother, his wife is exporting another baby. So I am here to run the stall for my family."

"Handy." She ran her finger over the wicker casket again. "If you don't mind me saying, these look pretty flimsy for a body. What if they fall out through the bottom?"

The casket man's eyes twinkled. "Our bottoms are reinforced. It will not happen. They are not so grave as wooden coffeens. And of course, they are eeeko-friendly. Very important today." His tone softened. "You are looking for one for a member of your family?"

"No." Janie was flicking through the hanging range of rainbow-coloured linings. "I run a funeral business. Well, we don't do the ghastly stuff like handling dead bodies. We just organise services for people who want something different. And weddings too!"

Shut up, Janie, shut up. Just because a tall, impossibly handsome blond and hopefully heterosexual stranger is chatting you up, doesn't mean you have to make a complete fool of yourself. He's only trying to sell you a flipping wicker casket.

"You are doing weddings in addition?" He raised his extremely fair and pelvic-melting eyebrows. "Before or after they have died?"

"Very funny. We organise wedding services for people who haven't died although I have to say that some of them are so scared, they would rather die than go through with it."

"But if they do not desire to get married, why do they do it?"

"Very good question."

"In my country, we frequently live together."

Janie laughed hollowly, remembering Mac. "I've tried that and it didn't work out either."

"Me too. There are no guarantees, as you say." He patted the casket. "Whereas this, it has a ten year guarantee."

"Against what?"

He shrugged. "Against anything going wrong."

"But that's ridiculous! No one's going to know if it falls to bits or doesn't do what it's meant to, because it's underground."

He grinned. "Precisely. It is why my father is a very rich man." He held out his hand. "My name is Lars. Please, I have failed to partake of breakfast yet. Will you come with me and we can divide a coffee together?"

She hesitated. There was still so much she needed to do before getting back. On the other hand . . . "Just give me two secs and I'll be with you."

"Two sex?" Lars' eyes glinted. "Just one will be very nice at present although I am not oppositional to more if you are desirous."

Wow! "I'll be back really soon. Just need to check out another stall. See you in a minute."

By the time Janie got on the train home, her mind was reeling and her fingers hurting from her carrier bags of freebies. Sachets of lavender which were destined for coffins but which would fit nicely into her underwear drawer. Swatches of fabric for coffin linings which Marjorie might be able to use for one of her quilts. A little toy bear and a tiny doll — more coffin accessories — which she'd give to Ben and Daisy, as well as the little sketch she was making of them now. And a lovely cushion embroidered "Forget Me Not" which she'd put on her bed, not to mention Lars' mobile number which he had insisted she'd punched straight into her phone. When she'd fumbled, making a terrible fool of herself, he'd done it for her without asking any questions, thank goodness.

"I do not have my mobilay with me," he had said when they had finally finished talking over breakfast which had lasted right through to mid-afternoon. "And if I write it on a scrap of paper, I will lose it. I am not, how you say, very organised."

Janie knew the feeling.

"It is why my English is not as good as other Norwegians. I keep failing my exams." He flashed her one of his charming smiles. "I am lazy. I think it is best to make these things plain at the start. Yes?"

She could almost hear Becky snarl, "Great boyfriend material."

"My English isn't good either," Janie heard herself admitting. "I . . . well, a friend used to say I had a certain way with words."

He frowned. "A way? Please explain."

She felt her skin prickle, the way it used to in class. "I find it hard to read and write certain stuff."

"Stuff? What is this stuff?"

Never mind. There was something about him — apart from the fact he was male and seemed to like her. She hadn't laughed so much for ages and he also seemed interested in her life.

"Your friend Marjorie," he had said. "She is hot, yes?"

Janie hesitated. Was he into OAPs? "Well, she's very well preserved for her age."

"Yes but she is kind. Is that not right? She opened up her hearth to you."

"Oh, you mean she's warm!" Janie felt a flood of relief. "Yes, she is."

"I would like to have a close encounter with her when I come to visit."

When he came to visit? The words still rang round Janie's head as the train pulled into Oxford. Of course, Lars hadn't said when he might come. But he'd told her to call. As soon as possible.

"Marjorie, I'm back!"

"Hello dear!" Marjorie placed a mug of Russian Caravan into her hand and Janie thought, not for the first time, how nice it was to come back to someone. "How was the funeral fun fair?"

297

She could feel herself still glowing inside. "Quite lively!"

Marjorie clapped her hands. "Wonderful! You met someone nice, didn't you?"

"Sort of. He's going to help us with wicker caskets and various other knick-knacks too."

"Just as well Ned's wife is putting his body on ice until the relatives can get over from Australia. Even so, we need to get it sorted. Talking of ice, that wretched Monique rang — something about swan sculptures. And before I forget, did I give you Ned's tape?"

"What tape?"

"Oh dear, maybe I put it somewhere."

Janie felt in her pocket for her phone. "I said I'd ring Lars — I mean the wicker casket man — when I got back. Blast. Did I put it down here?"

"What dear?"

"My phone."

She looked around. "I don't think so."

Janie felt a wave of panic rising up her chest. Where had she had it last? On the train. When she'd got out, she remembered, a crowd of youths wearing crosses had barged on without waiting for her to get off. Had she dropped it on the platform?

"Sorry." She put down her mug of tea. "I've got to dash back to the station. With any luck, I might find it there."

CHAPTER
THIRTY-THREE

Becky

She'd been at home now for precisely two weeks, three days and six hours. One more minute and she could very easily lose it. Really lose it.

You'd think that with all these kids' channels on digital, Daisy and Ben would have something to do. But instead of sitting quietly on their bean bags in front of the wide screen, they were leaping round on the sofas — strictly against the rules — or fighting on the floor. As for the noise! It even beat Cat on full throttle.

"Mummy, Mummy! Can we go to Kidzone?"

"Inaminute."

Shutting the sitting-room door on them, Becky retreated into the kitchen to make her third coffee of the morning, even though it was only 9.35a.m. That was another thing. At least, she'd thought, she'd be able to lie in now she didn't have to go to work or maybe sunbathe in their expensive six foot by 15 foot concrete garden. Wasn't that what you were meant to do after an operation, even if she hadn't actually had one?

No chance. The kids got up at the crack of the dawn, even before Steve had left for work or rather not left for work, as his business trip in Sweden (or was it Italy?) had been extended to ten days instead of a week. No wonder she was going nuts.

For two pins she'd ring mum but she hadn't liked to pick up the phone since bumping into her in Oxford. Such bad luck! It looked as though she'd been meeting that bloody Monique woman on the quiet instead of it being a horrible coincidence, as she'd tried to explain. It wasn't her fault that Janie already had an appointment with her on the day she went down. Or that Monique had insisted that Becky and the children joined them for lunch so she could "get to know them a bit better".

Besides, if she hadn't, she'd have offended her father. And now, instead, she'd offended her mother. It was, thought Becky, putting on the kettle again and opening a large packet of chocolate digestives, impossible to please everyone. So why keep trying?

"Mum, Mum!" Daisy burst into the room, her pigtails flapping with indignation. "He bit me!"

For God's sake, was it impossible to get five minutes peace?

"Then bite him back." Wasn't that what *Charisma's* child expert had recommended the other month. Second thoughts, maybe that's what the old advice had been; she seemed to remember they'd run an article on modern parenting strategies compared with what their mothers had done . . .

"Mum!" howled Ben from the next room. "She's murdered me!"

Oh for fuck's sake. Hang on. It almost looked as though he was right. Blood was dripping from Ben's arm and Daisy was smirking from the corner. A pair of kitchen scissors was lying on the floor. Quick. Where were the plasters?

"My arm!" screamed Ben. "It's falling off."

"Don't be silly. Of course it's not." Sod, sod, sod. But it just might need stitching . . .

Never again, vowed Becky as she struggled to keep Daisy on her knee away from the tramp on the other side, would she take a taxi to Casualty at this time of the morning.

"Afraid there's a bit of a wait," the receptionist had told them when they arrived.

"Why is it so packed?" asked Becky looking around for a seat.

The woman shrugged. "We'll try to get you in as soon as possible. How did you say he'd done it again?"

"He fell." Becky was still pressing the cotton wad against the wound. "On something sharp."

"Fuck, it hurts."

"Don't say that, darling."

"Why? You do."

"I stabbed him cos he bit me," interrupted Daisy.

The woman gave her a sharp look. "I didn't realise the scissors were there," said Becky, "and . . ."

"Save it for the doctor."

Becky felt herself being categorised in the same bracket as the tramp with the beer bottle gash on his

301

cheek. "Please, find a seat and we'll call you as soon as we can."

"I'm hungry," wailed Ben.

"And don't give him anything to eat," added the woman. "Just in case he needs an anaesthetic."

"But I haven't had breakfast." Ben's stomach gurgled loudly as though in league with his mouth.

Hadn't she fed them? Becky could distinctly remember looking for the cereal in the cupboard and then remembering she hadn't had time to go shopping because she'd been too busy looking after the kids. That's right. She was going to take them out to Starbucks when they had that argument.

"Not dressed either, I see." The receptionist's eyes narrowed as she took in Ben's Power Boy pyjamas. "As I said, take a seat, please."

What was she writing? Neglectful mother allowed son to fall on scissors after not giving him breakfast or getting him dressed? At least Daisy had a dress on, even if it had come out of the fancy dress box, complete with tiara and now bent wand that Janie had given her for her last birthday.

Two hours later they were finally shepherded into a cubicle and left to wait for another ten minutes before a teenager put his head round the curtain. "Miss Hughes?"

"Mrs," said Becky firmly. She might be acting like the stereotyped single mother but she wasn't one. Yet.

"Can you tell us when we'll be seeing the doctor? We've been here for hours."

"I am the doctor." His tight tone suggested she might not have been the first to have mistaken him for a youth experience student. He was already sitting next to Ben and examining his arm. "Can you tell me how this happened, please?"

Daisy, who'd been playing peek-a-boo with the curtain, ran up importantly. "Ben was being a little bugger, so Mum told me to bite him but when I did, he tried to push me and then he fell into the television and on to the scissors."

No, no, no!

"It wasn't quite like that," began Becky hastily. "The children were arguing, as kids do . . ."

She looked at the doctor for reassurance. His face remained impassive.

"So I told Daisy to stick up for herself."

Fuck. This was getting worse.

"I was trying to open a packet of biscuits," butted in Ben. "Mum hadn't given us breakfast and we were hungry. Our nanny normally does it when mum's at work but she's gone back to Australia and Mum's pretending to be ill so she can look after us."

"That's not exactly right . . ." She could hear her voice shaking.

"Your son is going to need stitches." How dare he speak to her in such a patronising tone. He was probably doing O-levels when she'd got married. "And after that, I'd like to have a little word."

So embarrassing! Becky kept replaying the conversation all the way home in her head. Was she finding it hard to cope with the children? Had she talked to the health visitor about it? Had she read their *Safety in the Home* leaflet?

Shit. She'd written enough stuff about it. She didn't need to do it herself. Besides, if Laura hadn't left and Steve wasn't still away in Sweden, none of this would have happened.

"Can I have some breakfast when I get home, Mum?" whined Ben.

The taxi driver looked around.

"Shutup," hissed Becky.

She smiled wanly at the taxi driver. "He's already had some but . . ."

"No, I haven't."

"I had Dolly Mixtures instead," butted in Daisy.

For God's sake, prayed Becky. Let's just get home. Fast.

For one amazing moment she thought it was Steve standing at the doorstep. Thank God. Another person. Another human. Someone who could take over. Someone who could . . .

"Dan?"

"Becky!" She couldn't help noticing how his eyes shone as she walked towards him. "I was just about to go home. Are you all right?"

"We've just got back from the hospital," sang Daisy, dancing up to him.

"I heard." Dan was clutching, she suddenly realised, a huge bunch of stargazer lilies, her favourite. "Your office told me when I rang. Surely you shouldn't be up? They said you'd had a major operation."

"Oh that." Becky felt herself flushing as she opened the door. "I'll explain later. Come on in. I'm afraid Ben's had a bit of an accident as you can see . . ."

Ben elbowed his way past with his good arm. "She tried to kill me with the scissors."

"Not me." Becky wanted to sink down on the floor and go to sleep. "His sister. Just give me one second, Ben, and I'll sort you out."

"Mum! Did you know crocodiles can't stick their tongues out? It said so on Ben's computer."

"Not now, Daisy."

Dan was already helping her take off her coat. "You look exhausted, Becky. Listen, why don't you sit down and I'll cook them some breakfast. I know what it's like with kids. My sister had three and she's permanently on a drip." He grinned. "Of chocolate biscuits and g and t's. I'll find my way round your kitchen. Just put your feet up."

God, it was nice to be looked after. Dan insisted she should rest ("You're meant to be recuperating") and now clearly wasn't the time to tell him the truth. Besides, he was doing such an amazing job in the kitchen. Not only was there a tantalising smell of bacon and egg but she could actually hear him making the children laugh.

"Feel like a coffee?"

She opened her eyes dreamily. "That would be lovely."

He sat on the arm of the chair, close enough for his arm to brush hers. "Ben seems a bit brighter now."

Shit. She'd almost forgotten about that. How could she? What kind of mother was she? And what kind of wife, come to that? Dan was getting closer. His arm was across the back of her chair. Nothing had happened in New York, she reminded herself. But it could have done. It could so easily have done. And now . . .

"Hi! Anyone at home?"

Becky sprang to her feet. "My husband," she gasped.

Instantly, Dan leapt up from the chair at the same time but not before Steve came into the room. The look on his face made Becky's chest tighten with an odd bottomless feeling.

"I thought you were in Sweden," she managed to say.

"Italy." He was looking at Dan. "And you are . . .?"

"Dan."

He was holding out his hand but Steve ignored it. "I'm a work colleague of Becky's."

"At *Charisma*?" His voice was cool.

"No." Dan gave a short laugh. "I write for *Heated Issues*. You won't have heard of it. Becky and I met in New York at that editors' ball."

Fuck. Fuck. Fuck.

There was a nasty silence. "I was passing." Dan was gabbling now. "Thought I'd pop in to see how Becky was doing after her operation."

"Ah yes." Steve was giving her another unreadable look. "Becky's op. By the way, darling. How are you feeling?"

Sick, actually. Very, very sick. "A bit weak," she managed to say.

"You do look pale." Dan glanced at his watch. "I'd better be off now. Hope the kids enjoyed breakfast."

"Breakfast?" Steve's tone was deadpan without its usual cheery lilt. "You were here for breakfast?"

"No." Becky was shepherding Dan to the door. "Not exactly. It's a bit of a long story. Thanks for coming over, Dan."

She'd shut the door on him before he had a chance to reply. "Look." She turned round. "It's not what it seems."

"Really?" Steve was still looking at her as though they hadn't met.

"Daddy, Daddy?"

The kids had heard him now and were swinging round his legs. "Look at my arm," chanted Ben. "We had to go to Casualty and then Mummy's friend cooked us breakfast."

Any minute now and she'd wake up.

"Mum said they were the best fried eggs she'd ever had." Ben was tugging at Steve's arms. "But I think yours are yummier."

"Actually, I . . ." Shit. Not her mobile. Not now. "Becky?"

Instantly, her entire body prickled.

"Brian?" She signalled at Steve to keep the kids quiet. "Hi! Thank you so much for the flowers. I was going to write when I felt . . . when I felt better."

"Actually, Becky, we need to arrange a meeting." Brian was wearing his crisp snake skin voice that made

307

her skin prickle with apprehension. "There appears to be some confusion over a rather large payment you made to a Miss Monique Brown. And we need you to come into the office to discuss it."

CHAPTER
THIRTY-FOUR

Helen

Why was it, Helen asked herself as she clasped both arms round a sack of manure (Rich Extra Large, rather like Dandy's farts now he was getting older), that every now and then she still wondered whether she should have left Geoff.

Would it, she wondered, heaving the manure into the back of the van, have been easier to have stayed put as a trade-off for security?

Of course, it would have meant not being "true to herself" which is, after all, why she had left. But there were pluses in favour of staying, which she hadn't fully considered at the time. Like having someone there; someone with whom you had a shared history; someone you could ring up and say, "Our daughter's really hurt me"; someone who helped pay the bills so she didn't have to work every hour God sent, even though she loved her job.

Very few of her friends, she had grown to realise over the years, had up-sticked as dramatically as she had done — even though enough had talked about it. Now, with their children gone and only each other left, they had the time and money for grown-up pursuits like cruises and houses abroad.

Not many of them had kept up with her; she didn't know if they had done so with Geoff but she suspected not. It was quite usual, or so she had read in a recent weekend newspaper piece, for friends to desert split-up couples either because they didn't want to offend one or the other or because, as the columnist had put it, "their lives might be catching."

Over the last few years, she had got used to it. But now Geoff was getting married. She, herself, had just got engaged. Family dynamics were changing. All over again. And it was, thought Helen as she finally slammed the doors shut, somewhat unsettling.

"Do you like being alone?" Robin had asked during that lunch just before Monique had turned up.

"Yes and no," she'd replied. And it was true. It had taken a while but there were times when she loved sitting down on the sofa with a glass of wine and a good book with no one to turn on the television or ask what was for supper.

But then there were the mornings when she woke up, her heart sinking at how much she had to do that day and wondering still — even after all this time — how she had ended up like this. Alone. On almost the wrong side of 55.

Her phone bleeped to indicate a text and glancing down, she saw it was from David. It was almost as though the phone was trying to remind her of something. Of course she wasn't alone. She was wearing an engagement ring, for heavens sake. An engagement ring that didn't feel right; not in the way it

310

had done when Geoff had slipped one on her finger just before her graduation ceremony.

And now he had given someone else a ring. A rather loud sparkling ruby affair that Monique had taken care to flash in her direction when she'd bumped into her the other week.

Dandy barked as she turned the ignition key. "I know," she said, glancing in the back as he settled down on his old red tartan rug. "Feels weird, doesn't it?"

In a funny way, it might have been easier if Monique had been her type. The kind of woman whom she could have chatted with or had a latte. Not Monique with her hairy upper lip and rolling waistline and little girl voice, which could be gruff when she chose — all of which added up in Becky's mind, to her future stepmother's affectations.

This time, the mobile rang instead of bleeping. Becky. Helen felt a mixture of relief and hurt. Pulling in, despite the angry signs from the Porsche behind, she flicked open the handset.

"Mum! You're there."

"I've had to pull in."

"You didn't have to."

Count to ten. "I thought it might be urgent. Can you be quick? I've got cars whizzing past."

"Forget it. Ring me when you have time for me."

"Becky . . ."

She'd gone.

Well done, Helen. That's another person you've managed to annoy. David would no doubt be cross that

311

he hadn't been able to get hold of her either, judging from the number of missed calls on her screen.

Sod it. If she didn't get a move on, she'd be late for Robin.

He was waiting by the beautiful sash windows framed by those elegant damask sage green drape curtains which she had once put up in the drawing room that faced the lane. She could see that as soon as she swerved into the drive. It was a tricky sharp turning which required skill and practice, both of which she'd perfected over the years of living at the Old Rectory and which had now returned in a rather alarming way.

You'd think, she thought, that Dandy also felt he was coming home. "Down, down," she protested as he stuck his nose out through the small gap in the window.

As soon as she opened the door, he was off. Streaking down across the garden and towards the paddock as though he owned it once more.

"Leave him." Robin was at the back door, smiling nervously. "He'll come back when he's ready."

He spoke, Helen noticed, almost as though Dandy belonged to both of them rather than to her.

"I've brought the manure." She stammered over the words, wishing she could feel that easy familiarity which they'd had before. But ever since that lunch in the pub where they'd spoken so openly, she'd felt nervous about seeing him again. "Sorry it's a bit late."

He ushered her into the kitchen. "Thought you might have been putting me off."

Was he joking? It was difficult to tell. "I've been really busy. Haven't stopped actually. And then . . ."

"Helen." He was standing in front of her. So close that if she'd reached out her hand, she could have flicked that bit of thread off his left shoulder. "Helen, this is tricky for both of us. We've told each other things that very few know. It should make us feel closer. Not awkward. Now, how about a cup of tea before you start? Look. I've actually bought myself an Aga kettle like you suggested."

Sylvia was still in bed, apparently. "One of her bad days," Robin had said.

He looked tired, Helen noticed and there were black shadows under his eyes, as though he hadn't slept well. It had to be difficult — really difficult — looking after someone who could do so little for herself. But never once had she heard him complain.

Helen had a brief glimpse of Robin undressing his wife at night. Helping her on to the lavatory. Sponging her down in the bath. Would David do that for her? Would Geoff have?

They were halfway through their second cup of tea when Robin had mentioned Sylvia. Until then, she hadn't come into the conversation but now she was there, like a third person at the table. Sylvia was in bed upstairs and she was downstairs, talking to Sylvia's attractive husband.

"I'd better get going." Helen sprang to her feet. "I need to get on with the mulching."

"Sure?" Geoff looked out of the window. "It's going to rain any minute. Looks like the weather people were right."

"Even more reason to get going. Thanks for the tea."

"I do understand, you know."

He was looking at her in an odd way.

She could feel her skin burning. "I just feel awkward . . ."

"I know. But it's understandable. This was your house. You miss it." His eyes were melting with sympathy. "And there's no reason why you shouldn't be here again, looking after the garden." He smiled. "It's got rather a nice sense of justice, don't you think?"

But she hadn't been thinking of the garden. She'd been thinking of Sylvia. For God's sake, woman. Get a grip. Striding down, away from him, across the lawn, Helen had to resist the temptation to run. What had she been thinking of?

"Dandy?" She whistled. "Dandy? Where are you?"

For a second, her heart stopped, just as when she'd lost Adam briefly at the playground once, and then she saw him. A black dot heading towards her, getting closer and closer with a big grin on his face. He loved it here.

And so did she. Especially now she had nothing to hide.

After Robin, she squeezed in Doris and another regular before finally heading home. There was nothing on the mobile from Becky. Any other time and Helen would have rung again but since that chance meeting in

Oxford with Monique, she felt cooler towards Becky in a peculiarly unmaternal way — which wasn't like her at all.

"You're being childish," she told herself.

Maybe.

David's car was already outside her cottage. Blast. She'd been looking forward to a quiet night in; maybe an early bed. That was one of the big pluses about being on your own or was it just because she'd got so used to having just herself to please? On the other hand, now the children had flown and no longer needed her — apart from the odd grandmotherly stint — did she really want to be on her own for ever?

"Hi." She forced herself to smile as she offered her cheek but — heavens! — David was kissing her full on the mouth as though they hadn't seen each other for weeks. It tasted different somehow (or was that her?) and she had to resist the urge to wipe it away.

"Did you forget?" He was standing with his arms round her waist, looking down on her.

She tried to contain the shiver of irritation. "Forget what?"

"You were meant to be cooking tonight."

"Was I?"

He loosened his arms. "You did forget." He looked down at her grubby hands. "You haven't been working late again?"

"I had to." She went across to the sink to wash. "Look, David. I'm sorry but do you mind if we forget it tonight? I'm absolutely bushed."

315

"I can cook." His voice sounded sulky. How could he switch so fast from being all lovey-dovey to this?

"It's not that. I just don't want . . . I'm shattered. I won't be very good company."

"Aren't you going to take your ring off?"

"What?"

He was standing next to her at the sink, disapprovingly. "Soap is bad for it. It will get into the stone."

Fuss, fuss, fuss. That was another thing about him.

"You're right." She gave it a twist and it came off easily; as though it had never belonged to her in the first place. "Here. You have it."

She almost threw it into the palm of his hand while washing her hands and drying them on the cloth hanging by the sink.

David held out the ring so she could put it back on.

"No," she heard herself speak.

David frowned. "Want me to clean it? It does look a bit tarnished. You need to look after it, you know, being an antique."

"That's not what I meant." She moved away, towards the back door, holding it open. "I'm sorry, David. I think I've made a mistake. I shouldn't have accepted the ring. You keep it."

He didn't move. "What are you saying?"

Helen felt herself beginning to shake just as she'd done all those years ago when she'd told Geoff she was leaving. "I'm not sure. Yes, I am. I'm not ready for a commitment. Not yet. I'm sorry, David. But I think I need a bit of a break."

CHAPTER
THIRTY-FIVE

Mel

Mel sat once again in the archdeacon's morning room
— as his assistant had referred to it — trying to get her
head in order. There were times when she almost
envied her daughter for lying there, peacefully, with all
that time to get her thoughts straight.

"Don't be crazy," she could hear Richard saying.
"How do we know if she's thinking anything?"

But she did know. She was Amy's mother. She might
not have got on very well with her in the last few years
but nothing — not even Kevin and his Cortina bumper
— could take away a mother's gut instinct.

Dear God, she prayed, looking straight ahead through
the casement windows which faced on to immaculate
nail-scissor cut lawns. Please make my daughter better.

You weren't meant to do that. Weren't meant to pray
for specifics like that because it could be God's will that
Amy didn't . . . no. She wouldn't allow herself to even
contemplate that. Positive thinking. That was what
counted. Indeed, that was probably the rationale
behind positive prayer. It worked because you believed
it and for some weird reason, that tipped life's scales in
your favour.

Not that that was something she could share with the archdeacon.

He was late. Ten minutes late. Mel shifted uneasily in her seat, wishing she hadn't taken that caffeine tablet of Josh's. "Keeps you awake" it had said on the packet. It was definitely doing that but in a weird scary way. Was she acting as oddly as she felt she might be?

Leaning forward, she took a sip of cold coffee which the assistant had left. It had been lukewarm when it arrived and now was barely drinkable. Her fault for thinking too much.

"Sometimes," Geoff had said during one of their runs the other day, "we think so much about something that it all gets out of perspective."

He had been trying to reassure her about Amy and the what-ifs. What if she never comes out of her coma? What if she was brain-damaged? What if (as she'd read about in the newspaper the other day), she regained consciousness speaking a different language like the man who spouted Spanish after being in a coma for four months, even though his wife swore he'd never even been to the country.

"Try to take one day at a time," he'd told her, stopping to tie up his laces.

She waited, keeping a professional distance. "I appreciate the advice, Geoff, but I thought we were here because you wanted to ask me something."

"I do. Ready?"

She nodded and they set off again. "It's about Monique. Well, marriage in general, really."

Why did everyone want to tell her about their marriages when hers was in such a mess? Mel wanted to laugh out loud. Her own husband thought so little of her that he'd taken a job away from home at a time when she needed him most. But just because she was a vicar, everyone thought she knew how to do it properly.

"Marriage," she repeated. "It's a big commitment."

"Exactly." Geoff was slightly ahead but he glanced back. She knew that look all right. It was the kind of look that men and women gave her when they'd booked their banns and, as the day drew near, began to wonder what exactly they had done.

"Monique and I," continued Geoff, "are very different."

"Yes," she heard herself say. "I've noticed."

"Have you?" Geoff hung back. "What exactly have you noticed?"

How about that she's a big hairy pushy lump and you're a kind good-looking man? No, Mel. Stop it. "She's quite a . . . a busy person." She tried desperately to choose her words with care. "Your fiancée has quite set ideas, doesn't she?"

Mel's mind flickered back to when Monique had laid down a list of what she did and didn't want at the service during one of their preparation meetings before she'd handed in her notice.

Geoff nodded. "But that's one of the things I like about her."

He stopped to lean against a tree, as though needing support.

Mel hated stopping. Far better to keep going but at a slower pace. She tried to keep the irritation out of her voice. "Then what are you worried about?"

He was still catching his breath. "That's just it. Can't really put my finger on it. I suppose it's just what you'd call bridegroom nerves, although you'd think at my age, I'd be too old for that."

"I'd be scared too if I was in your position," Mel heard herself saying.

"Would you?" He leaned forward again and for a minute she thought he was going to take her hand. "Really?"

"Yes." Mel tried to imagine marrying someone apart from Richard and failed. "It must be difficult when you've been used to someone else. How long did you say you'd been married to your first wife?"

That flicker in his eyes again. "Fifteen years. Nearly sixteen. But I've been on my own for over ten years."

"Then maybe," said Mel softly, "that's what you're scared of. Making the commitment to someone other than yourself. Trusting someone whom you haven't known that long."

Geoff nodded, his eyes not leaving hers. "That's true. And yet I just can't imagine life without her."

How many times had she heard that one before? From brides jilted at the altar (she'd had two to date); a woman whose husband had died unexpectedly just after retirement; from her own mouth as she watched Amy's chest rise and fall on the hospital bed . . .

"Then that's your answer," she replied crisply. "If you can't imagine life without her, you must love her.

And love is a gamble. There are no definites; no guarantees. It doesn't come with a twenty-eight-year return policy."

Normally the joke raised a few laughs but he wasn't smiling. "I know."

"Shall we walk for a bit?" He fell into a pattern beside her. "There's something else I need to tell you. I'm afraid I might not be able to take your service."

"What?" Geoff's raised voice caused a woman passing with her dog to look at them.

She flushed, wondering what the dog walker was thinking. A couple having a heated discussion. A potential pair of lovers. Not a vicar and one of her flock. Should have worn her dog collar.

"I might be leaving."

"You're being transferred?"

"Not exactly."

He shook his head. "I don't understand."

A picture of Amy's body on the bed shot into her head. "I need some time out. To reflect. To think. To be next to Amy just in case . . ."

"You're leaving the church?" Geoff's voice was incredulous. "You're giving it all up."

"Well wouldn't you?" She jumped off the branch. "My daughter has been run over. Run over by some kid who didn't stop. Amy had her life in front of her. What kind of God would do that?"

He was holding her now; holding her by her wrists. Forcing her to sit down on the hill. Handing her a proper handkerchief from his track suit pocket for the tears that were streaming down her face. "It's all right,

Mel. It's all right. Everything you feel is very understandable. You're being tested. That's what's happening. You're being tested. But you have to hang on in there."

"Why?" She spat it out like a child.

"Because if you don't," he continued, his gorgeous blue-grey eyes still fixed on hers, "there won't be any hope for the rest of us."

And now, here she was, waiting to see the archdeacon to say she'd thought it over and definitely wanted to hand in her notice because she couldn't be a hypocrite any longer. Couldn't hand out the holy sacrament every Sunday when every bone in her body was screaming, "Why, God? Why did you let this happen to us?"

"Mel." The archdeacon was opening the door and beckoning her in. "So sorry to keep you waiting. I had a domestic problem I needed to sort out, I'm afraid."

Domestic? Probably the milkman delivering one pint instead of two.

"Yes." The archdeacon sighed. "Please sit down. One of our daughters has found herself . . ." He coughed. "Found herself unexpectedly pregnant."

"Oh." Mel didn't know what else to say.

"Of course we want her to keep it but there are complications."

Had the archdeacon had some kind of transformation? She'd never known him to come out with something so intimate before.

"The father of the child is, you see, not the man she is married to."

Well done, God! No one can say life is boring when you're around. Mel tipped her head to one side in what she hoped bridged the gap between sympathy and curiosity. "Does her husband know?" she ventured.

"As from this morning." The archdeacon leaned back in his deep velvet padded chair and interlaced his slim fingers as though a solution might pop out from in between. "Hence the phone call."

He looked at her directly. "Of course, this is entirely confidential."

She nodded.

"As is our meeting this morning." His eyes still held hers. "When you rang to request this meeting, Melanie, I could tell you had made your mind up, despite our earlier conversation. Is that right?"

She nodded.

"And you're still going to leave?"

"I can't be a hypocrite."

He closed his eyes briefly; his eyelids were paper thin with fine blue lines. "You're being tested, Melanie. You do know that, don't you?"

"That's what a friend said."

"She was right."

She? Mel suppressed a smile.

"But a true Christian doesn't give up at the first hurdle."

"This isn't the first. There are other things too. My husband has taken a job in Leeds because he's been out of work for months and can't find anything else. My son is either being arrested in the name of conservation or telling me to go away in language that I wouldn't like

323

to repeat. And, even worse, I can't find it in my heart to forgive that kid who didn't stop when he ran over my daughter. Can't you see, archdeacon? I'm not fit to be a vicar."

"On the contrary, my dear." He was handing a plate of digestives to her as though she'd just discussed the new flower arranging list. "All those things you mention — and I agree they're not small — make you eminently suitable. You understand what people are going through. You speak their language. You don't come across as a pompous old codger like me."

She tried to politely disagree but he cut her off. "No, Melanie, I am well aware that people like me don't give the church a contemporary flavour. That is why we picked you. The church has to change, Melanie, and you can help us do it."

"But what about me?" Mel could hear her voice rise in despair. "What if I can never forgive this boy?"

"You will learn. Don't ask me how. God works in mysterious ways. But trust in Him, Melanie. People who are lost often come back. Besides, something tells me that it's not just this boy you need to forgive. It's yourself."

Counselling, the archdeacon had suggested just before she left. He was going to arrange for her to see a counsellor. Mel had wanted to say no but felt unable to. Maybe she'd go along to a couple of sessions and then say she was busy . . .

What on earth was that? A group of teenagers were sitting on the porch, banging drums. They were wearing what looked like white bedsheets, tied at the waist with cord. Their hair was shaved and they were chanting something. As she pulled up into the drive, Mel could see her next door neighbour looking through the curtains. Dear God. What are you throwing at me now?

"Mum." Josh looked up as she approached. He had a long stick of incense in his hand which he held out to her. "Welcome."

"What on earth are you doing? Josh, answer me."

Sometimes she wondered if he actually spoke English.

"We've decided to become Buddhists, Mum." Josh was smiling dreamily, as though he had taken something. God knows what. "We've been doing it in RE and it sounds really interesting. Here, have a smoke." He held out the incense stick and she realised it wasn't an incense stick after all.

"It will calm you down, Mum. Go on. Try it."

CHAPTER
THIRTY-SIX

Janie

"No," Janie said for the third time to the girl in the bank who looked about 15. "No, my credit card wasn't insured because I never have much in my account."

Why was it that banks made you reveal personal details like this through a glass screen, bang next to all the other customers who could hear every word? What happened to banks in the old days where there was a door to shut?

"According to this," said the girl, reluctantly turning to the monitor next to her which Janie couldn't see, "no one has used your card . . ."

Janie breathed a sigh of relief.

". . . but you're up to your overdraft limit so you can't take out any more, I'm afraid."

The girl slid a piece of paper under the screen and cast a suspicious look at her shocking pink and jade green skinny jumper with the matching mohair cloche hat she'd borrowed from Marjorie. "This is your current balance."

The figures swam in front of her eyes. "Sorry. I've left my glasses behind. Can you read that out to me?"

"£500 overdrawn."

Shit, shit, shit. Janie felt as though someone had drilled a hole in the pit of her stomach.

The girl pushed a piece of paper under the screen. "You'll need to fill this in."

She felt the usual wave of sick panic at the sight of a form with undecipherable instructions above each section. "But I need some money." Janie glanced sideways at the man at the next cashier hole who was listening. "I don't have any."

"I'm sorry. You'll need to see the personal banker about that. I can give you an appointment next Tuesday at 2.45."

Next Tuesday! That was nearly a week away. How was she going to manage until then? It would probably take her a week to fill in the form unless she got Marjorie to help.

Janie walked down the high street, her head spinning. Not only had she lost Lars' number on her phone — which she needed for business especially as Marjorie never heard the house phone when it rang — but she'd also lost her credit card and her Tesco loyalty card which was so useful and God knows what else. Every now and then, she kept remembering things she'd had in her purse. That gold chain which her parents had given her last Christmas and which she'd put there to take to the jewellers because the clasp had gone. A whole new book of first class stamps which wasn't cheap. A phone number from some old bloke who'd rung enquiring about a wedding. She'd promised to ring him back and now she couldn't.

He'd probably need their funeral division by the time she traced him.

Hang on. Didn't she have her postal account book still? With any luck, it might be in her bag. Yes. Here it was. Janie frowned as she tried to make sense of the bottom figure. £350? No, that couldn't be right. Must be £35 or maybe £3.50. Still, it was better than nothing.

The queue at the post office was massive. She'd be late for her telephone conference with Monique. Shit. The bride was meant to be ringing her but she wouldn't get through now her phone was gone. And Monique's number was on her missing phone so she'd have to get back to the house and ring Becky for her stepmother's number although she probably wouldn't get hold of Becky because she was bound to be in some high-powered meeting and . . .

"Hello, you."

Janie was so absorbed in her thoughts that she almost didn't recognise Mac. He looked even smarter than the last time she'd seen him: that navy striped tie made him look quite respectable.

Mac smiled at her, almost nervously. "How are you doing?"

The queue had shuffled forward and someone behind them coughed to indicate they should move up. Hastily, Janie gathered up her bags. "OK. You?"

"Better for seeing you. Here, let me take those. Look, I didn't get a chance to explain before."

"Explain?" Janie eyed him coolly despite her heart which was beginning to pound. "How exactly do you explain being in bed with someone else?"

The woman in front glanced back. Sod it. "Frankly, Mac, I don't want to see you again. Ever."

"I understand that." He began fidding with his tie. "Totally. But Janie, you've got to give me a chance. I've changed now. Tried telling you last time. I've got a job at an estate agents."

Janie snorted. "Perfect. You can test drive the master bedroom while showing round clients."

"I'm not seeing Carole . . . that girl, any more, either."

"Next!"

Janie grabbed her shopping bags. "Frankly, Mac, I'm not interested. Now excuse me, I need to get on."

Pushing the post office book under the counter, she appraised the woman on the other side. "I need to take out £30 please but I've hurt my hand so it's difficult to write. Would you mind filling in the withdrawal slip for me?"

It usually worked.

"I'm afraid not."

"Sorry?"

"You don't have £30 in here, love. You've got 35p."

No. Surely not?

"Well, I'll take that out then, please."

"Sorry, love. If you want to take that out, it means closing the account and you have to do that by post. There's a form to fill in, too. Here, take it away and bring it back later if you like."

Thirty-five pee! All she had left was 35p! That meant asking Marjorie for another advance on the small amount they'd already been paid. As Marjorie said, it

329

took time to get a business going, especially with overheads like printing costs.

"Need some money?" Somehow Mac seemed to be walking alongside her as she left the post office.

"Not from you, I don't."

"Come on, Janie. I owe you, don't I? Look at all the times you helped me out when I didn't have anything."

That was true enough. Free bed; free meals; free sex . . . Janie wavered.

"Marjorie said you'd set up business with her." Mac was walking alongside her again although at a slight distance as though worried she might push him away. "Things are probably a bit tough at the moment, I expect, until you've made a name for yourself. In fact, I might be able to put a bit of business your way. There's a bloke in the office who's getting married and . . ."

"It's not that," Janie heard herself saying. "It's because I lost my purse. It had my credit card in it and I've got to fill in this form to explain what happened and I can't fill it in because . . . well you know."

Mac nodded and she felt a surge of relief that she didn't have to explain. He'd been really cool and understanding about her difficulty with words and figures; never once treated her as though she was stupid.

"I'll do it for you. Come on."

Janie felt herself being steered into Starbucks. The wonderful smell of coffee and toasted sandwiches made her stomach rumble.

"Sit down. Please. I insist. What do you want to eat? I'm on an early lunch anyway. We'll do the form when we've had something." He smiled; a lovely warm smile that started something going in her chest and made her hand twitch into sketching a face on the paper napkin. "I'm starving, Janie. And it's so nice to see you again. Please."

By the time she got back home — dropping into the Body Shop on the way back for her free weekly squeeze from one of their lovely hand lotion sample bottles — Janie felt utterly confused. Was it possible for people to change so completely? Mac had even insisted on taking her into his office to introduce her to his line boss who had just popped the question. He'd seemed pretty impressed by the spiel she'd given him on For Weddings and a Funeral and had promised to get in touch, once he'd had a word with his bride.

He'd seemed to think quite highly of Mac too, from what he'd said. Mac even had his own desk and shared a secretary. A few months ago, he hadn't been capable of getting out of bed until lunchtime, let alone holding down a job with a pension!

"I've learned to use a computer too! I can back up and all."

Pity you couldn't back up boyfriends so you had a copy when the hard drive got corrupted.

"Good for you." She delved in her pockets for her bike security key. "Look, I've got to go now."

"Can I ring you?"

"No, you can't."

His face dropped and she almost felt sorry for him. "Well, how can you, if I don't have a phone."

331

He beamed. "How stupid of me. Listen, I can get you another . . ."

"No. You've done enough."

"But it's no problem. I've got a spare handset at home — I've moved in with my brother, you know — and I've got a mate at that new phone shop round the corner who can get you a sim card."

Janie glanced at the others in the office who were trying not to listen. "I don't want any favours, Mac. Get it?"

Later, as she got back to Marjorie's cottage, she wondered if she'd been too hard on him. Still, if she had been, he deserved it. Didn't he?

"Ah, there you are, dear!"

Marjorie was reclining on her sofa, a pre-lunch gin and tonic in her hand. "Thank goodness for that! I've had Monique ringing again and again, insisting that she had a telephone conference call with you and that she hadn't been able to get through on your mobile. I explained it had been stolen; in fact, I did exaggerate slightly and said you'd been mugged but that didn't wash. Said she'd ring here in ten minutes."

Janie groaned. "I was meant to have found out about ice sculptures and I did — except that I stored the information on the phone and now I've lost it."

"Dear, I've told you before. You should write it down. You young things use your phones far too much and then look what happens when you lose it."

I didn't lose it; it was stolen, Janie wanted to say. And I can't write it down which is why it's easier to punch numbers into my phone instead. "No one else rang, did they?"

Marjorie was topping up her glass. "No, dear, not for you. Expecting someone, were you?"

Only a sexy Norwegian who had probably forgotten her existence long ago in his quest to cut through the hordes of sexy Norwegian women who were doubtless queuing up for him. As if by magic, a picture of Lars appeared on her wrist in Biro.

"There's the phone!" Marjorie trilled, putting her hand in the air as though some unseen servant might answer it. "Are you going to take it or shall I? Oh, by the way, if it's about the wicker casket, I've sorted it. I found a wonderful little woman in Burford who sells those baby Moses baskets. She's going to make up a really big one. No one will know the difference."

Oh, God.

"I found the tape too," continued Marjorie happily. "Just as well since Ned could hardly do another one. Do you know, the dear man made a tape telling everyone how much he enjoyed life and that he didn't want anyone getting upset when he went. I'm going to have one of those at my funeral. Rather like a voice from beyond the grave, don't you think? Hadn't you better get that phone, dear?"

Fucketyfuck.

"Janie?" The bloody woman had her man's voice on. "I must say that I'm very disappointed. We had a telephone conference scheduled for over an hour ago. I've had to put a very important meeting on hold for this, Janie, and frankly I'm not impressed."

"Sorry but I lost my phone — in fact I got mugged — and . . ."

"I'm not interested in excuses. I want results. How are you getting on with the ice sculptures?"

"I've got some quotes . . ."

"Then email them to me. Immediately. We've only got another four months and frankly I'm not happy."

"I'm sorry." Janie fumbled for a pen. "Like I said, I've lost my phone and all my numbers were on it. Can you give me Becky's number too?"

There was a loud dismissive noise at the other end of the phone. "Well I could but you won't find her there. When I rang this morning, they told me she was recuperating after a major operation. Honestly! She hadn't even told her father. I can tell you, he's out of his mind with worry . . ."

There was an odd noise behind her as though Marjorie had hiccupped, followed by the sound of crashing glass. Janie dropped the phone. The old lady was lying slumped on the sofa, her mouth open and eyes shut. Around her were shards of glass on the carpet.

"Marjorie!" she screamed, racing over. "Marjorie! Are you all right?"

CHAPTER
THIRTY-SEVEN

Becky

"Thank you for finally coming in, Becky."

Brian was eyeing her appraisingly. It was a joke in the office that by the time Brian had finished looking you up and down, you could work out a page worth of coverlines, headlined with "How to cope with the office lecher who also happens to pay your salary."

Becky didn't feel like joking now.

"Please, sit down." He gesticulated with a chubby white hand at the leather-seated chair in green and chrome which was opposite his desk. No doubt the height had been carefully calculated to make the incumbent feel small. "You must be feeling rather drained after everything you've been through."

He was choosing his words carefully; she could feel that. Everything had a double meaning. Oh, Christ. This was going to be worse than she'd thought and that had been pretty bad. Steve hadn't been any help either. Normally, he gave her some good coping strategies for office politics but that morning, when she'd been in such a flap, he'd merely shrugged. "Tell him the truth, Becks." He looked away. "Otherwise it will just come out when you least expect it."

OK. So her husband was still shirty over Dan turning up but there was nothing to tell about that. Nothing had happened. Only in her head and everyone knew that didn't count.

"How are you feeling after your operation, Becky?"

Brian's crocodile voice sliced through her thoughts. He reminded her of a James Bond villain; oversexed, overweight and over-controlling. Good to have on your side. Scary if he wasn't.

She crossed and uncrossed her legs, wondering if that was possible if you'd just had a hysterectomy. "A bit weak. I have to take it easy. And I need to put my feet up as much as possible."

Brian's eyes were almost drilling a hole now. "Perhaps you should cut out the trips to Knightsbridge then?"

Shit-shite.

"My assistant saw you in Harrods last week, in the lingerie section. I remember when my wife had her hysterectomy, she couldn't go shopping for some weeks."

Honestly! It had been hard enough persuading one of Daisy's friend's mothers to have the children while she went shopping. No one would see her, she'd argued to herself. It hadn't even been lunchtime. "Yes, well, when you have a hysterectomy, it makes you change shape," she heard herself say.

Brian's eyes glistened and she steeled herself. God knows, she'd seen him in action enough times before but always with someone else. He was going in for the kill now. Think of something, Becks. Think of something.

"And tell me. Does a hysterectomy make you spend money too?" He pushed an invoice across the table towards her. "Money that doesn't belong to you?"

"I can explain." The figure on the cheque in front of her swam into a blurred papier mâché of black and white. "It was for a case history."

Brian's eyes narrowed. If they were still undressing her, they'd only have slit vision. "We never pay case histories as much as this. She must have been a very special case history."

"It was." Becky heard herself babbling. "It was for the story about Sally Smith. Remember. A real coup. We won the bidding war."

That was better. He ought to congratulate her now.

"But they didn't want paying. It says so at the bottom of the article." He slid a copy of the magazine over the table towards her. "Let me remind you. It says it quite clearly here in 12 point. 'Sally Smith would like to make it known that she has not received any money for this article.'"

"She changed her mind," said Becky quickly.

"Did she?" Brian's face was looming towards her as though they were in some awful film where the focus had gone out of kilter. "So why was it that the cheque was made out to a Monique Brown?"

Becky moved her chair slightly backwards. She could smell Brian's breath. "Monique is her agent. It was her that made them change their mind. She said they ought to be paid after all."

337

Great. Well done. Totally plausible.

"You know, Becky, I do think that after all our years together, you could tell the truth," said Brian softly. "It's really not very difficult to Google a name or to use other means to investigate people. It turns out, that Monique Brown is soon to be your stepmother. Isn't that true or might we be talking about a different Monique Brown?"

Fuck. Double fuck. "Well, there might be . . ."

"Don't play games with me!" Brian's roar almost made her fall off her seat. "I know bloody well she is. And my hunch is that you had a cheque made out to her so you could pocket the money yourself! You do know that's fraud, don't you?"

"No! No, it wasn't like that." Becky was torn between bursting into tears and running out of the room. "I'll tell you what really happened. Yes, this woman is going to marry my father. She's also a PR guru and she happens to handle Sally Smith. She said we could interview her without paying anything for it providing we gave her copy approval . . ."

"But we never do that." Brian hammered on the table. "It's not our policy. You know that perfectly well."

"Yes but it was the only way we could get the story. So I read it back to her but then we made some changes — including you, Brian, if you don't mind me saying — and when it came out in print, she was furious."

"So? What's new? We annoy people all the time. It's part of our job."

"Yes but she said she was going to sue us and then I got worried because . . ."

"Because you thought she'd tell me about copy approval and you knew I wouldn't be pleased."

"Exactly!" Becky felt a flush of relief that he understood. She should have come clean in the first place. Brian was an old pro. He knew what it was like. "She said she wouldn't say anything if I paid her that money. I know I shouldn't have but I was scared."

"Scared of me or of your father?" Brian had his fingers laced together in a prayer-like position and the light in his eyes was not unsympathetic now.

"A bit of both, I suppose."

"So you gave her the money."

Becky nodded. "I'm sorry."

"And she didn't share any of it with you?"

"No, of course not."

"So you're happy to bring in bank and building society statements to prove that?"

Becky felt a prickle of unease. "Well, yes if you want me to."

Brian leaned back. "Of course, she might have paid you in cash."

Becky could feel the heat rising. "I'm telling you, Brian, she didn't pay me at all."

There was a nasty silence. He didn't believe her. Christ. He thought she was a fraud.

"Tell you what, Becky." He spoke so quietly that she could barely hear him. "I should really call in the police. But you've been here a long time and besides," he looked straight at her abdomen, "you've been poorly. So I'll let you off on three conditions."

Becky held her breath.

"First, you post all your recent financial statements to HR. Second, that you don't take legal action for dismissal. And third . . ."

Another nasty silence.

"Thirdly," continued Brian standing up to indicate the meeting was over, "that you clear your desk."

Becky took a taxi home without realising it. It was as though someone else had stepped outside the building — almost colliding with one of those bloody cyclists — and given her address. Where were the kids? For a wild moment, she couldn't remember. Of course. School and nursery. Should she have picked them up by now? School wouldn't have finished but didn't nursery end at lunchtime or was it later now Daisy was almost four?

Later. Definitely later. About 2p.m., she seemed to think. Or perhaps 3p.m. Well, they could wait. That's what they were there for.

Clear your desk, Brian had said. Sod that. She wasn't going back into the office to do that with everyone looking at her. Fraud? How absurd could you get? Of course she wouldn't have taken the money although maybe, with hindsight, the hysterectomy had been a bad idea.

She ought to ring Steve. Or Mum. No. Not after last time. Janie wouldn't understand either. Her world was too different. Who then? Someone who could help her find another job. Her ex-secretary at *Cosmo*? But she'd know by now, wouldn't she? The magazine world was such an incestuous place. Everyone knew everyone because they moved around like on a giant roundabout. No good falling out with someone because sooner or later you'd end up on the same magazine with them again. What was she going to do?

"I'm sorry I can't take your call but . . ."

Great. Not even her husband was around to help her. Hang on. Wasn't he in Stockholm or was it Budapest this week? Becky sank on to the armchair which she'd just had recovered in Mimi Metzo, a new Japanese designer they'd featured on the At Home page. Mimi had done it free of charge and all she'd had to do was allow pictures to photograph it. No more perks like that now.

"Dan?"

Of all the people she could have phoned, her fingers dived for this one.

"Becky?" He knew her voice! She felt a ripple of hope flit through her. "What's wrong?"

Gisueppe's was packed at lunchtime, although not with the kind of people that Becky knew. At first, when Dan had suggested this place, she'd felt a tremor of misgiving. Where the hell was Clerkenwell, for goodness sake? Now she was grateful for the anonymity although it would be a lot better if Dan was here. Sitting at the formica table by the window so she could spot him coming in, Becky felt as though everyone was looking at her. Maybe the short skirt with the mock fur trimming hadn't been such a good idea even though it had come free from the sample cupboard.

And then she saw him. Weaving his way through the crowds as though they didn't trouble him. Towering over everyone else in his beige trench raincoat, broad shoulders and pleasant smile. Walking right past her on the other side of the window without realising she was watching him and then, as he came in through the door, looking around.

I'm here, she tried to say but nothing came out. For an awful moment, she feared he might think she hadn't turned up. Trying to get up, she caught her foot on the bar stool and almost tripped. The noise was lost in the general roar of the cafe but he turned round and saw her. Was that a flash of relief on his face?

"Becky?" He kissed her warmly on both cheeks. "I thought you might not have found this place. Bit of a backwater, I'm afraid. But I thought it would be private. Now what can I get you? A latte? I can recommend the toasties too."

Watching his back at the counter as he ordered, gently joking with the waitress whom he seemed to know, Becky felt herself relaxing. What was it about him? She barely knew the man yet somehow, she felt herself with him; more than with anyone else.

Even Steve.

"Right!" He returned, bearing two plates of toasties and two mugs of coffee. "Now. Why don't you start at the beginning?"

It was almost like their trip round Central Park when they'd talked and talked. Now, she did the same, although she toned down her feelings towards Monique in case he thought she was being uncharitable.

"So your boss thinks you stole the money?" Dan frowned and Becky felt a stab of panic.

"Yes. But I didn't."

"But you didn't have a hysterical-ectomy either?"

His eyes twinkled.

"No," Becky admitted. "Although the hysterical bit might be true."

"Have you contacted HR to talk about your rights?"

"I feel too embarrassed."

"What about the NUJ? You are a member, aren't you?"

"Yes but they're only going to say it was my fault."

"Not necessarily." Dan was scribbling on a piece of paper. "I'm the union rep at the company. Ring this chap. He gives free legal advice."

Becky took the number gratefully. "I don't suppose there's anything going at your company is there?"

Dan threw back his head and laughed. "What? You're so desperate that you'd work for a trade magazine that no one's heard of?"

"We need the money."

He picked up his mug of coffee and as he did so, she reached out for hers at the same time. Their hands brushed and she felt as though someone had electrocuted her.

"Sorry." He leant back in his chair, as though thinking. "What does your husband say?"

"I couldn't get hold of him. He's in Stockholm. Or maybe Budapest."

Dan raised his eyebrows. "Didn't get the wrong idea the other day, did he?"

Becky recalled the afternoon that Steve had got back early and found Dan there. She'd explained of course but he'd been horribly cool. "No. Not at all."

"That's all right then."

There was an awkward silence.

"And what about your partner?" she managed. "Karen, isn't she called? She doesn't mind us meeting up every now and then, does she?"

Dan's eyes twinkled again. Did he know how attractive that was? Nowadays, Steve was always moaning about everything — there had been a time when he'd just done that in bed. "No chance of that."

"So she's not the jealous type?"

"She most definitely is."

Great. So she wasn't even attractive enough for another woman to get jealous about. Dan had probably described her as an older woman with kids — that's if he'd bothered mentioning her at all.

"It's one of the reasons," he continued, playing with his fork, "that I finished it."

Finished it?

"Well, we'd been going out for three years and she wanted something more permanent." His eyes met hers. "I couldn't do that. Not when I'd suddenly found out what it might really be like."

The shop around them stopped. The talking and general noise seemed to come from a long way off. Becky's mouth went dry. Dan was looking at her, waiting.

Fuck. Not the phone!

"Mrs Hughes?"

"No, it's . . ." She was still in Becky Hastings mode. "I mean, yes. Sorry. Mrs Hughes speaking."

"This is Greenacre Nursery."

Omigod. Something had happened to Daisy. "Is everything all right?"

"Not really. Daisy's very distressed."

Distressed? Had her daughter fallen off the indoor slide/suffocated in the sandpit/been abducted by the caretaker — they'd covered all this and more on *Charisma*'s Real Life page. No wonder she was too scared to look after them herself.

"Nursery finishes at lunchtime on Wednesdays, Mrs Hughes. You're over an hour late."

Fuck. Double fuck.

"I'm just coming." Becky leaped up. "I'll get there as fast as can. I'm so sorry."

Dan was up too, putting on his jacket. "Problem?"

"I'm late for nursery. Got the time wrong. Nothing's going right." Hot tears stung her eyes. "I can't even be a good mother."

She felt a hand on her shoulder. "It's because you've got too much on, Becky. Calm down. It will be OK."

Will it? What did he know about kids or getting sacked?

"Hang on a minute." He was fumbling for his mobile. "Let me make a call and I'll drive you there. I'm parked just round the corner."

"Won't you get into trouble for taking time off?"

He grinned. "Not now they've made me publisher of the whole group. I was going to tell you about that. But let's save that for later."

He helped her with her coat. "You know, Becky, it's not all doom and gloom. There is something you could do . . ."

FOUR MONTHS TO GO

CHAPTER
THIRTY-EIGHT

Helen

Helen woke up with the sun streaming through her curtains at 6 a.m. Ever since moving into her cottage, she'd intended to line the curtains so the light didn't wake her but somehow she'd never got round to it and now she was getting used to it anyway.

Something wasn't right but it took her a few seconds to put her finger on it. Ah yes. David. Handing the ring back. A broken engagement.

For a brief flash, she felt a pang of fear, reminding her of that blanket panic which had gone on for so long after leaving Geoff. This was a mere pinprick in comparison but nevertheless, all the old uncertainty was there.

Should she have done it? David was a good man. Not the type to run off with another woman or even flirt the way Geoff used to and probably still did. Steady. A little boring at times but reliable. She would have been safe with him.

Is that what you want? she asked herself, swinging her legs over the side of the bed and heading for the bathroom before going downstairs and putting the kettle on the Aga. Surely you know by now, Helen Hastings, that safety isn't to be trusted.

The phone! Quick. What should she say? He'd be asking her to reconsider and why not? She could put the other day's performance down to premarital nerves. David would understand. He always did. And what would she get in exchange? A husband. Another person to consider in life when she'd got used to consulting only herself. Someone to talk to when it all got too much. Someone to talk too much when all she wanted was silence.

"Mum!"

"Adam!"

Any slight tinge of regret that it wasn't David disappeared. Her son! News from Adam, who was notoriously bad at communicating, made anything else pale into insignificance. "Are you all right?"

It was always her first question, even though it was clear that the very fact he had phoned, meant he was there. Safe (that word again). Not lost in the wilds of Queensland or wherever he happened to be that week.

"Fine, Mum. Chill out. I just rang for a catch-up."

His voice had a warm Australian twang to it and she glanced instinctively up at his latest photograph on the fridge door. A tall strapping smiling man who looked slightly older than his thirty-two years, especially now his blond hair was beginning to recede like his father's had at that age. This particular photograph had Adam with his arm around a small bright-eyed self-assured girl wearing an extremely scant bright orange bikini. No doubt she'd long passed on to his row of exes since the photograph had been sent.

"Where are you?"

350

"Right now?" He chuckled; a low lazy chuckle which was neither like her or Geoff. "Sitting by the side of Darling Harbour in the most fantastic fish restaurant with a friend. Here, Hayley, say hello to my mum."

"Adam, please, I . . ."

"Hi, Adam's mum!"

"Hello." Helen searched for the right words. Adam could be so childlike at times, making her speak to a total stranger.

"It's OK, Mum. I'm back now."

"Is that the girl in the photograph you sent me?"

Another low throaty laugh. "Probably not. Anyway, how are you doing?"

She leant against the Aga, cupping her hands round the mug of Redbush. "Fine, darling. Fine." She paused. "Did you know that . . ."

"Dad's getting married?"

He could always do that. Finish her sentences off for her. In many ways, she was closer to Adam than to her daughter. Becky was too like her, something which they both found infuriating.

"Yes."

His voice took on a more concerned edge. "And are you OK with that, Mum?"

"Fine."

Even as she said it, she was aware the word had a definite acrylic flavour.

"I see. Listen. Don't worry. I'll be there to give you support. I know it's not going to be easy for you but I'm going to look after you."

"You're coming home?"

"No need to squeal, Mum! Course I'm coming home. Well, not immediately obviously and only for a bit. But I'll be back for the wedding."

She could hardly talk with the lump in her throat.

"Mum? You still there?"

She nodded. How daft was that? "Yes. I just can't wait to see you, that's all."

"Me too. What's she like anyway, this Monique woman?"

"Fat. Thin hair. And boring. At least that's what Becky says."

"So you haven't met her yet?"

"Only briefly, by accident a couple of times."

"Well perhaps you should do it properly. It might make it easier for you. After all, Mum, it's been a while, hasn't it? And it would be nice if you and Dad could get along with your prospective partners. That reminds me; how's David? Becky said something about you getting engaged too. How come you didn't tell me?"

"We're not. Not any more. It's over."

"I'm sorry."

"Don't be. I called it off."

Another chuckle. "Like mother, like son. Listen, Mum. I've got to go now. But I'll see you in November. Promise."

By teatime, when she'd finished digging over Arthur White's potato patch, David still hadn't rung. He'd been away; she knew that much. Some job that required him to go to Norfolk for a few days almost immediately after she'd handed the ring back. At first, she'd told herself that was why he hadn't called; perhaps there wasn't any reception and besides, he was probably giving her time to think about things. That was so David.

But now she was beginning to wonder. Suddenly, the prospect of going back to her cottage which was bound to be cold with the boiler playing up (something David had been going to look at), no longer seemed quite so inviting. It reminded her of all those years after leaving Geoff when her main evening entertainment had been a solitary glass of red wine and a video while waiting for Becky to come back from a night out with her friends.

Purposefully, she kept her eyes ahead as she drove past the Old Rectory on her way back. If she glanced left or even behind in her wing mirror, like Lot's wife, she'd stop. And that would not be a good idea. Much better to go home, put on Radio 4, make a cup of tea and whip up a cheese and tomato omelette for supper.

So what the hell was she doing?

"Helen!" Robin opened the back door with a frown on his face that instantly turned to pleasure when he saw who it was. "What a lovely surprise. Please, come in."

You must be crazy, she told herself sternly. Absolutely barking mad.

"I only dropped in with the seed catalogue." She placed it on her old pine table, almost like a visiting card which gave her permission for turning up like this. "I won't stay — Dandy's in the car."

His back was to her as he filled the kettle from the old butler's sink which she had found at a reclamation yard all those years ago. Even from a few feet away, she could feel his voice warming her up. "You'll have a cup of tea, though, won't you?"

She hesitated. "I don't want to bother you."

"You never bother me. Besides, I could do with the company. Sylvia's had one of her bad days, I'm afraid. I've put her to bed early."

He spoke as though she was a child who had done something wrong but even so, Helen's heart went out to him. Frankly, she didn't know how he did it.

"I'm sorry."

"Why?" He put a mug of tea in front of her and a slice of carrot cake.

"For . . . well, everything. It can't be easy."

He shrugged. "She'd have done the same for me."

"Are you all right?" She looked across at the table where he was sitting opposite. "Your hands are shaking."

Oh, God. He was reaching over and taking both hers in his. "And yours are cold."

"They often are, I'm afraid."

She could hardly get the words out in her confusion.

He nodded slowly with sad eyes. "So was I, Helen, until you came into my life."

Quickly, she snatched her hands back. "Robin, please."

"No. Don't. Hear me out." He sat back in his chair, closing his eyes. "You have to feel it too, Helen. You can't say you don't. Electricity. Fireworks."

She giggled and he opened his eyes. "It's not that funny."

"It's not that. I used to tell my two that they shouldn't have a . . . well a physical relationship with someone unless they had fireworks. Becky used to ask if I meant Catherine wheels or sparklers. It was a bit of a joke when they were growing up."

"I know just what you meant." He leaned forward and grabbed her hands again. "Well for me, this is the finale. The last display. Fireworks are going off all over my head whenever I see you, Helen. It's Guy Fawkes day come early. And I need to know if you feel the same."

"But you're married!" The words came out too loud and she instinctively looked upwards as though Sylvia might hear through the ceiling.

"It's all right. She's asleep, like I said." Robin closed his eyes briefly again. "Yes I know I'm married and I hadn't meant to say anything but I can't wait and risk losing you . . ."

His eyes travelled down to her bare left hand. "Your ring. Where's it gone?"

"I broke it off."

His eyes sparkled. "Because of me?"

"How could it be? You hadn't said anything."

"But you knew your engagement wasn't right."

"Yes." What was the point in pretending? "But you're still married. I told you what happened before, Robin. Why I left Geoff. I couldn't do that again. Have an affair with a married man . . . that's right. It was wrong. Horribly, horribly wrong."

"Married?" he repeated quietly although sad, rather than disapproving. "But you were lonely. Besides, it was so long ago."

He was pulling her hands towards his mouth, covering them with small warm darting kisses. "This is different. One day, I'll be free. Will you wait for me, Helen? Please?"

"I don't know."

They were standing up now; bodies almost but not quite touching. "For God's sake, Helen," he was murmuring. "Just one kiss. What harm can it do?"

And suddenly his mouth was on hers as though it had always been. Robin's kissing me, she thought. He's kissing me. His lips melted into hers and her body fused against his chest.

"Come upstairs."

It was like a low growl and instantly a warm ginger-wine feeling flooded her body so that the bottom part of her body below the waist seemed to separate from the top like a train dividing in half.

"For pity's sake, Helen, come upstairs."

Later, she couldn't remember how she'd got home, let alone down the staircase with her legs shaking like that. He'd offered to drive her but she'd gently refused, needing the time to think. Dandy was frantic, having been left behind in the car but, thankfully, she'd left part of the window slightly open and his bowl of water in the back. Was that because she'd subconsciously known what might happen?

The cottage loomed up in front out of the darkness as though some unknown force had propelled her here from the Old Rectory; maybe some kind of force from the warmth which she could still feel inside. A secret all-consuming warmth which she wanted to wrap up inside like a gigantic secret, never to be shared with anyone.

"Come back tomorrow," Robin had whispered as he'd leant through the driver's window.

She'd nodded, scared someone would see them. How could she not return? But Sylvia would be there and — oh my God — all that guilt again! How could she have been so foolishly reckless as to repeat her mistake?

Now, fishing for her key in her handbag, she became aware of Dandy bounding out of the car, towards the cottage, excitedly pawing at the door. Bother. The light was on which meant David was already back.

Trembling, she slid the key into the lock and Dandy dashed in. What was this? Two small children's coats were slung over the banisters and two pairs of small red Start-Rite shoes were in the hall.

"Gan-gan," called out Daisy, racing out of the kitchen towards her. Helen bent down and scooped up her granddaughter into her arms. "Mum says we're all going to live with you now. Can I have your bed? It's bigger than mine."

What?

"Mum?" A tearful voice came from the kitchen. Instantly, Helen's heart sank. Becky. Something was wrong. Something was very, very wrong.

Still hanging on to Daisy, she raced through the archway. Immediately, her tall, beautiful daughter fell into her arms. "Mum, I'm sorry. I don't know where else to go and I had to get out. It's all so awful . . . so hopeless."

Automatically, she stroked her daughter's head, holding her close, just as she had as a child when Becky had still allowed her to do that.

"Shhh. Shh. It will be all right." In a way, she almost felt grateful for Becky's distress; her daughter had been so cold and dismissive for so long.

"No!" Becky looked up at her with wild burning eyes. "No. This time, it can't be. I've done something dreadful, Mum. Something really awful that no one can fix."

And that was when she saw him. A lanky man, exuding wiry energy just as Geoff had done when she'd first met him, casually leaning against the Aga with Daisy untying his shoe laces. Instantly, an electric current of terror shot through her as she realised. Becky had made her mistake; history had repeated itself.

"Hi," he said, holding his hand out to her. "I'm Dan. Good to meet you."

CHAPTER
THIRTY-NINE

Mel

How about a latte after the run, he'd suggested.

Why not?

But he'd got there after her and, dear God, he must have stopped off to buy a bunch of flowers on the way. An expensive mixture of roses and gypsophila, wrapped up with a pink ribbon.

"You really shouldn't have," she'd protested.

"Nonsense." He pulled out the chair for her and looked around for the waitress. "It's very good of you to spare the time. Coffee?" He looked closely at her. "If you don't mind me saying, you look as though you need something a little stronger."

And somehow — OK Lord, I can hear your warning bells — she found herself telling him about Josh's "incense sticks".

He leaned back, putting his hands in his brown corduroy jacket pockets. "I presume it was cannabis?"

"Probably. But I don't know. I didn't try it — neither when I was his age or when he offered it to me." She gave him another look across the small pink table at the coffee shop.

"How about you? Have you ever tried drugs?"

359

He gave a rueful grin. "I was at Leeds in the seventies." He spoke as though the two came hand in hand. "Besides, we went through all this with Adam."

"Really?" Sometimes Mel felt that parenting was a secret society where it was all right to talk about potty training and solids but no one discussed the darker side. "Richard had a word but I don't know if it went in. How did you handle it with Adam?"

Geoff snorted. "Badly. Helen freaked out and accused me of being too laid back. We'd split up by then and although I tried to be as much of an active father as I could, it wasn't the same as living there. I suggested we let him experiment until he came to his senses."

"And did he?"

"Not really. He went on to something a bit harder."

Mel shuddered. She could see Josh doing that all too clearly.

". . . but then he finished art school and went into advertising. I still think he smoked a bit but it didn't do him any harm as far as I know. He's coming back from Australia for the wedding. Did I tell you?"

No. Somehow, despite their meetings in coffee shops to discuss the wedding and other issues, this piece of information hadn't filtered through. Perhaps that was because they'd spent more time discussing Mel's situation. It wasn't right, she reminded herself. Her role was to act as an advisor to her flock; not the other way round.

"Another coffee?" He was standing up, feeling in his pocket for change and, not for the first time, Mel was struck by how big he was. Rather like a large cuddly bear with dancing eyes that made her feel . . . no. Don't go there.

"Not for me."

"Sure? I'm having one."

She shook her head, pretending not to watch as he walked up to the counter. How could his first wife have walked out like that? Geoff was such a warm man; funny and a good listener. Good father too. What on earth did he see in that Monique woman?

"Can't function unless I have at least three lattes at lunchtime," he said, returning. "Now, you were also going to tell me how you got on with the archdeacon. Or is that strictly secret?" He grinned.

"Definitely the latter, I'm afraid." She looked straight at him. "Besides, we're meant to be discussing you. How is it all going?"

Geoff shrugged. "I thought getting married at our age would be a doddle. After all, it's not as though we've got the parents to please. Instead, it's the kids to displease. Becky is still very cool about the whole thing."

"But you said Adam's coming."

"True, although he did make a comment about him being nearer to the bride's age group than the groom."

Mel put on her "Trust me, I'm a vicar" look. "And does that worry you?"

Pushing his chair away from the table, Geoff leaned back and stretched out his legs. "It's beginning to now. Monique has such high expectations. The whole thing

361

is costing me a bloody fortune. Sorry. Didn't mean to swear."

Mel shrugged. "I was in advertising, remember. In the nineties."

They both smiled at each other. "Touché."

"You know," said Mel, leaning forward, "it's probably just premarital nerves. Not just on your part but hers too. In my experience, brides take out their nerves on the flower arrangements . . ."

"Or in this case, the ice sculptures."

Mel raised her eyebrows. "Classy."

"Don't." Geoff groaned. "My daughter's friend is doing the wedding and to be honest, I'm beginning to wonder if she knows what she's doing. Monique wanted to hire some incredibly expensive wedding planner but Becky asked me to give the business to her chum, Janie."

She grinned. "And you thought it might save you a few bob but aren't sure."

"Exactly!" Geoff beamed at her. "We're rather good at finishing off each other's sentences, aren't we?"

She nodded, embarrassed. Stop, right now. "Look, Geoff, I'm glad I could help but I've got an appointment with the jumble sale committee before the hospital and I need another slogan for next month's church notice board."

"I love those signs."

"Really?"

"Honestly. What's the next one?"

She made a wry face. "Haven't a clue yet."

"How about 'EVERYTHING MUST GO!'"

She considered it. "I like that — funny but true at the same time."

He scrambled to his feet. "Anyway, sorry to have taken up your time."

"You haven't."

"Any news on Amy?"

She shook her head.

"Well let me know if there is, won't you?"

This had to stop, she told herself, walking back towards the car. At first she'd seen Geoff as yet another of the new breed of parishioners; the type who wouldn't normally go to church until something like a marriage or a funeral forced their hand. But he was different.

Another of your tests? Mel could never help glancing up at the sky when she talked to God. Crazy really because he was meant to be everywhere. Meant to be? Even in that boy's cell?

"Haven't you done with me? Haven't you tested me enough? First Amy and now . . ."

What was that? Mel started to sprint towards the car. A large woman in a huge fur coat (it was freezing for August but a fur coat?) was trying the door handle and peering in through the window.

"What are you doing?"

"Ah, vicar. There you are."

Geoff's fiancee? Mel felt the colour surging to her cheeks unnecessarily. "You were trying to get into my car!"

Monique turned a heavily made-up face towards her. The lines on her forehead and the side of her nose were

363

encased in a thick foundation which only made them worse and there was a gash of red lipstick below. "Getting into your car? Why would I want to do that?" She cast a disparaging look at Mel's dusty second-hand Fiesta which Josh had promised to clean in return for pocket money.

But you were, she wanted to say. I saw you trying the door handle.

"Anyway, you're here now." Monique spoke briskly as though she, Mel, was late for an appointment. "I wanted a word."

"I'm sorry but I've got a meeting and then . . ."

"This won't take long. Shall we sit in your car?" Monique narrowed her eyes. "Unless you want to go back to the coffee shop where you've just had three lattes with my future husband."

Had she been spying on them?

Uneasily, Mel opened the driver door and leaned across to do the same with the passenger. Not only did the car lack central locking; it also needed a good clean out on the inside. Kit Kat papers littered the floor (Josh) and on the back seat was a pile of school books which he should have taken to school that morning. Wrapped around the gear stick was one of Amy's black hair scrunchies which she'd found under the passenger seat the other day. Somehow, keeping it next to her made her feel closer.

"Sorry about the mess," she couldn't help saying.

Monique's expression indicated that it was no less than she expected. "You probably know why I'm here."

She tapped her white podgy fingers on a shiny, black clutch bag. "Geoff and I are going to get married."

Mel hadn't realised before how very black Monique's eyes were. She forced a smile. "I know. I'm meant to be marrying you. Remember?"

"Exactly." Monique's lips remained horizontal without the glimmer of a smile. "You're marrying us. You're not marrying Geoff yourself."

"I don't understand."

"I've been watching you, Mel. Or do you prefer to be called vicar? Not just at the coffee shop but when you go on one of your so-called jogs. Don't think I don't know about them. Geoff's so naive he actually expects me to believe you're only running even though you do it with your fancy earrings, make-up and pink shorts . . ."

"We are only . . ."

"Come on, vicar. I'm not stupid. Geoff's having second thoughts, isn't he?"

The serrated edge to her voice was chilling.

"No . . . I mean . . . I couldn't possibly comment on something that's confidential."

If they'd been in a public place, Mel would have got up and walked away but she was stuck. Just as Monique had intended. "You should be talking to Geoff about this — not me."

"Geoff!" Monique mimicked her voice. "Not Mr Hastings. Pally, aren't we? Well, vicar, I might just do that. And I might talk to some other people too." She leaned forward, putting a podgy hand on Amy's black velvet scrunchy.

"Don't!" hissed Mel. "Get off that."

Monique shot back as though she'd pushed her. "Don't you dare touch me."

Mel was quivering. "I didn't."

Monique's eyes were like little black hard boiled sweets. "Yes, you did. This time, vicar, you really have gone too far."

Grievous bodily harm? Don't be ridiculous. On the other hand, that woman could cause all kinds of trouble and trouble was the last thing she needed at this point in time . . .

Mel let herself in, checking the answerphone as she always did in case there was something from the hospital. Nothing. Just a message from Richard.

"Just wanted to touch base. Everything's fine this end. I'll try and catch you tonight."

Mel put on the kettle. If distance was meant to make the heart grow fonder, why did she feel so strangely detached at Richard's voice? She'd already got quite used to not having him around and when he returned at weekends, his presence often felt intrusive. She was pretty certain he felt the same which was maybe why he wasn't coming back this Saturday. A conference, he'd said. Well at least it gave her a chance to get on with her sermon. Josh was still out at yet another band practice. So it was going to be another late night, waiting for him to ring to say he needed collecting.

Was that the time? Sometimes, she didn't know where it went, especially when she was working. And still no sign of Josh. Maybe she'd tidy up his room while he was out.

As usual, clothes were strewn everywhere except where they should be. Fumbling with the controls on his hi-fi, Mel managed to turn down the music. Textbooks and dog-eared exercise books littered the floor along with magazines and a tome of a book entitled *The Unsigned Band Guide*. What was inside that box? Dear God. Penis Enlarger? Where had he got that?

Probably off the internet. In fact, his laptop was still on. She moved the mouse to get it off Sleep mode and see what was on it. OK, it was probably the equivalent of reading his diary but . . .

Oh, God. More Facebook pictures that she hadn't seen before. Amy smiling and laughing from the screen with a glass of something in her hand; her arm draped over a boy's shoulder. And another Amy. Wearing . . . very little. She could remember that outfit.

"You're not going out like that?" she'd protested at the time.

"Don't be boring, Mum. It's fine."

Mel could hardly breathe with the lump in her throat.

Loves: my family (including mum but don't tell her that!).

Favourite food: Chinese takeaways.

Ambitions: to travel the world.

Dear God! And how are you going to let her do that now? It wasn't fair. It wasn't fucking fair . . .

Mel gasped at her own use of an expletive just as the mobile went.

"Is that the Reverend Thomas?"

Something about the voice made her feel uneasy.

"Who is this?"

"My name is PC Gordon. We have your son Josh with us here. Don't worry. He's quite safe. But we need to ask you a few questions. Can you tell me how old he is?"

"Sixteen. Nearly seventeen."

"Actually, he says he's eighteen and he appears to have a fake ID on him which is an arrestable offence. He has also been found drinking in a public place. I'm afraid I need to ask you to come down to the police station."

She'd been here before, of course, but in another role. There'd been the woman who had asked to see the vicar when she'd been caught shoplifting. It turned out that the woman had really wanted someone from the Catholic church. Then there had been the drunk who'd insisted on seeing the local minister but who had been out cold when she'd arrived. And now her own son.

Josh was sitting sulkily on a plastic chair in a room without windows. He barely glanced up as she came in, ignoring the hand she stretched out to him. On the other side of the desk sat a sergeant and, next to him, the policeman who had apparently caught Josh swigging from a beer can in the high street.

"It's an offence," said the sergeant sternly. "The high street is part of the no-drinking zone. Having a fake ID is also an offence. You could be arrested for this."

"Please, sergeant," said Mel leaning forward. "We've been through a difficult time. My daughter — Josh's sister — is in a coma in hospital and . . ."

Josh sprang to his feet. "I don't need any fucking excuses! Piss off, Mum. I was drinking cos I wanted to. Not cos of Amy. I'm a teenager. It's wot we do."

There was a stunned silence. Mel knew exactly what they were thinking. Vicar allows her son to get away with bad behaviour and foul language. "Josh, apologise."

His eyes flashed. "Make me."

The sergeant coughed. "Perhaps it might help if his father came down?"

"He's away," said Mel quickly. Oh, God, they thought she was a single mother now. "Working away."

The expressions on their faces clearly showed they weren't convinced. "Look, I'm sorry. As both a mother and vicar, I'll make sure this doesn't happen again."

She could see them hesitating. It wasn't often she pulled the vicar card.

Finally, the sergeant nodded. "All right, sonny. We'll let you off this time. But don't do it again. Try drinking water instead."

Josh gave him a pitying look. "Did you know that in some places, water's been through seventeen humans before someone else drinks it?"

Despite herself, she couldn't help feeling proud.

"And can I have my fake ID back?"

Second thoughts, she took that back.

★ ★ ★

"I don't see why I couldn't."

Josh was still fuming as he sat in the front seat next to her on the way home.

"Couldn't what?"

"Have my fake ID back. It cost me twenty quid."

"How did you get it?"

"Amy did it for me. On the net."

Dear God, why did you make teenagers so difficult? Why was it that they wanted to be treated as children and adults but at different times which only they could decide.

"You shouldn't drink so much."

"Why not? I've decided not to go to uni now and everyone drinks there so I'm making up for it now."

Her hands tightened on the wheel. "I hope you never have a teenager like you."

"Thanks, Mum. Thought you were meant to be a vicar."

"Sorry."

It wasn't fair. They push you until you say things you shouldn't and then you end up apologising.

"And don't throw that crisp packet out of the window. It's bad for the environment."

"So's petrol, Mum. So why don't you stop driving?"

And why don't you stop driving me round the bend? No. Don't say it.

Short silence. This was worse. "I was going in to see Amy this evening. Want to come with me?"

"What's the point? She can't hear anything."

Mel gripped the steering wheel. "You don't know that!"

"Shurrup, Mum."

"It's shut up. Do try to remember your 't's.'"

"God, you really piss me off. Just like you pissed off Amy. She used to get really fed up with your nagging."

Sometimes the pain was so acute that they might as well have coshed her with an iron bar. "I'll drop you off first then, shall I?"

No reply. That was a yes, then. As Mel opened the door to let him in, she noticed the white envelope. "Mrs Thomas" it said on it. Not even vicar.

For a horrible moment, she thought it might be a letter from Monique. So much had happened since the afternoon that she'd almost forgotten. Now, her hands began to shake. That woman was weird; completely unpredictable. She might even have rung the archdeacon and . . .

YOU ARE INVITED TO "VISITS WITH A DIFFERENCE" DAY.

Visits with a Difference is a scheme organised by Bustead Prison to encourage visits from relatives and well-wishers.

It went on to give details of the time and date — about two weeks from now. At the bottom, in childlike capitals, was written: "My son wonts you to cum."

Kevin's mother. Kevin wanted her to visit him in prison? Mel felt her throat thumping. Upstairs, Josh's bedroom door slammed and the music became even louder.

371

Not the phone. Fuck. Sorry, God.

"Yes?"

"Is that the vicar?"

"Yes. Sorry. I didn't mean to sound abrupt."

"That's all right. Caught you at a bad time, have I?"

Yes. "Not at all. What can I do for you?"

"My name's Ann. I haven't been to church for years, to be honest. But I saw what happened at the fête the other week — the way your son was behaving."

Mel took a silent breath and waited for the inevitable criticism.

"I'm having awful problems with my own son who's the same age. And I wondered if you had any advice. It's really nice to have a woman vicar for a change — someone who understands."

Gimme five, God, as Josh might say. "I'm no expert, as you saw." Mel laughed drily. "But I know how difficult it is. Why don't you don't come round here some time for coffee?"

CHAPTER
FORTY

Janie

It had been some time since Marjorie's "funny turn" as she insisted on calling it, but it felt like yesterday. Janie had raced over to Marjorie on the sofa and shaken her which wasn't, in the circumstances, what she should probably have done. But it had worked and Marjorie had stirred, opened her eyes and — despite being somewhat spaced out — asked Janie to find the blood pressure tablets which she "should have taken but had somehow forgotten".

No, she insisted, there was no need to ring the doctor. She was fine. And indeed, she seemed that way. Even so, Janie still felt freaked out. Every time she left the house, she couldn't help fussing around and asking if she was sure she was all right.

"My dear girl," Marjorie would say, giving her a hug, "it's very sweet of you to worry but you shouldn't. It's happened before, you know. Before you moved in, I often found myself waking up on the sofa or the floor."

Sometimes the negligent attitude that Marjorie and her friends had towards life was breathtaking. "What does the doctor say?"

Marjorie waved a podgy ring-decked hand in the air in dismissal. "When I bother to see him, he just increases my blood pressure tablets."

Janie wondered what the protocol would be if she rang the surgery and told them about her landlady's condition. They'd have to do something, wouldn't they? But it might also annoy Marjorie and, in a strange way, her blackout or funny turn or whatever they chose to call it had ironed out some of those niggles about sharing a house.

Besides, now she had Becky to worry about as well — not to mention the wicker casket, Lars who hadn't rung, her empty bank account (they still hadn't sorted out the missing money) and Mac who wanted to lend her "a couple of smackeroons" even though she'd refused because she didn't want to be in his debt. Oh well, it would all probably sort itself out.

Apart from Becky. Now that had been a shock. "What do you mean, you've been sacked?" she'd asked when her friend had rung. "What did you do and why are you at your mum's?"

Intriguingly — and worryingly — Becky had ducked out of all questions, insisting instead that they met in town. "I need to get away from mum," she whispered. "She's giving me a really hard time and anyway, she's having enough problems of her own with that awful boyfriend of hers."

Would she be like that at Helen's age, wondered Janie as she strode through the indoor market to the coffee shop to meet Becky. Still unsettled in her fifties, without a permanent man in place? Yet at the same time, there was nothing wrong with that, was there? After all, Marjorie seemed quite happy. Why was it, even in today's world, that she still felt a need to have someone; someone to talk to; laugh with; cuddle up with . . .

A huge chasm opened somewhere at the pit of her stomach. She thought she might have had that with Lars until losing her phone.

"Auntie Janie, Auntie Janie!" Two small blond bombshells shot across the coffee shop floor — almost tripping up one of the girls — and straight into her arms. "Mummy said you'd be late!" Daisy's plaits swung defiantly. "Have you got something for us? Mum said you might if we were good!"

"Daisy! That's very rude." Becky stood up from her corner seat and leaned over to give Janie a hug.

"You've got thinner."

"Don't you start. Mum's been going on about it too." She opened her purse and took out a fiver. "Take this, Ben and go and choose a bun from the counter."

A whole fiver? For a minute, Janie felt another niggle of envy. What she could do with a fiver! If it wasn't for Marjorie, she'd have been down at the soup kitchen right now.

"I've ordered us the usual," said Becky.

Janie only hoped she didn't expect her to pay this time. "What's been going on, then?" She eyed her more closely. "I have to say that whatever it is, you look great on it. Even if you are too thin."

It was true. Becky's eyes were sparkling and her skin looked amazing. Janie made a mental note to find out

375

what foundation that was; with any luck, they might do free samples. She was wearing jeans too — something she hadn't seen Becky in for years. Normally, it was tightly cut designer trousers or suits signifying she'd come straight from the office.

Becky leaned forward as though trying to speak confidentially, though the sound in the coffee shop was almost as loud as the argument between the kids at the cookie counter.

"I want that one cos it's got peanuts in it," Ben was yelling. "Mum, did you know there are peanuts in dynamite? It says so on my computer."

"It's mine." Daisy was tugging Ben by the sleeve.

"Leave them," groaned Becky. "They'll sort it out themselves. Quick, before they get back. I was sacked because of that bloody woman."

"What bloody woman?"

"Monique of course. InaminuteBen. She got me a case history for the magazine but we sort of changed the quotes and then she got mad so I had to pay her off and then my boss found out and I've been sacked."

Janie was still trying to take all this in. "What did your dad say?"

Becky ran her hands through her hair wildly. "That's another thing. Inaminute, Daisy. He's defending her, saying it was a business decision and . . ."

Janie allowed the words to wash over her as she began to doodle a face on the pink and white checked tablecloth. Copy approval, flatplans, coverlines, all the words that Becky was coming out with meant nothing.

They'd moved so far apart, there wasn't much point any more. Apart, of course, from the children.

"Listen, Janie. Remember that stuff I gave you on dyslexia? I've been asked to do a freelance piece for some education magazine and that clinic has offered to treat you free if you'll be one of the case histories. How about it?"

"I don't know. I'd feel even more stupid if it didn't work and . . ."

"Auntie Janie, Auntie Janie, tell him I can have the bun. I saw it first!"

Daisy was tugging at her sleeve furiously, leaving a large brown gooey stain. Janie couldn't help grinning at her determined god-daughter.

"Go and sit on the other table," barked Becky.

What? She'd never heard Becky talk to the kids like that. Mind you, come to think of it, she'd never seen Becky in sole charge of both children before.

"There's someone else," she heard Becky say. Didn't she mean "something else"?

"No," repeated Becky, shooting a look at the children. "I mean someone else."

A horrible, nasty knife-feeling sliced through her. Couples split up all the time but not Becky and Steve. They were always there; always fine with their lovely Islington house, dual incomes and large loud noisy boozy lunches on Sunday which even Mac had loved.

"What do you mean?" she hissed. "Who is it?"

"Who is it?" chanted Ben. "Are we playing another game? Do you know, Auntie Janie, Mum didn't even know how to play I Spy! She'd forgotten and we had to teach her on the way down with Uncle Dan."

Becky whipped out another fiver. "Go and get an ice cream," she squeaked. "Now."

Janie's insides felt as though they were in an ice cream maker anyway. "Who," she growled, "is Uncle Dan?"

Oh, shit. Becky was going red which meant only one thing. "You haven't slept with him, have you?"

To her huge relief, Becky shook her head. "But we might as well have done."

Fuck.

"We can talk about anything, Janie!" Becky's eyes shone; so that explained the glow. "He makes me laugh. And he looks after me. And . . ."

"And he's not your husband." Janie surprised herself at the harsh tone in her voice. "I suppose you met him at work?"

Becky nodded. "He's an editor, well, publisher actually. Just a small magazine but it means he understands the pressures and the sort of stuff that Steve doesn't."

"And what does he say?"

"Who?"

Sometimes, Janie wondered if it was Becky who was thick and not her. "Your husband, Becky. Remember?"

"I've told him we're just friends but he doesn't believe me." Becky took a gulp of peppermint tea. "Besides, what does he care? He's never at home with all those work trips . . ."

"Nor are you."

"But that's my job — at least it was until I got sacked."

And she'd thought her life was complicated. "What does your mum say?"

"That's just it. She's furious with me. Says I'm making a big mistake but then she would, wouldn't she. She walked out on her marriage and now she's worried I'm going to do the same."

"And are you?"

"No. I don't think so. But Steve's still away and I can't do this, Janie. I really can't."

A strange, wild look crept into her friend's eyes. One she hadn't seen before. "I'm no good at looking after the kids, Janie. I can knock an issue into shape but I can't do the same with my own children. Steve doesn't help much and Dan . . . well Dan understands."

"Only because he hasn't lived with you. Can't you see that? It would be different if he did. Where is he now, by the way?"

"Gone back to London."

"Gone back?"

Becky coloured again. "Well he sort of drove us down."

"Sort of?"

Becky was going deep scarlet even down to her impressive cleavage which, Janie noticed, was far too prominent under the flimsy, summery-cream gauzy top which her friend wore.

"I was in a bit of a state, you see, so Dan offered."

"What did your mother think of that?"

"Not a lot." Becky laughed. "You should have seen her face."

"Becky!" Janie leaned forwards and clutched her hands. "This isn't a laughing matter. You've got to see that. This is your future you're talking about. And Steve's. And the kids' . . ."

Fuck. They both realised at the same time. Swivelling round, Janie's eyes darted through the shop. There were lunchtime shoppers everywhere, eating baguettes, soup, hot chocolates . . . But no kids.

"Where've they gone?" screamed Becky leaping to her feet.

Janie was already at the counter. "Did you see two children?" she gabbled. "They came up to the counter just now — well ten minutes ago — to buy ice creams."

The girl carried on dishing out food to the woman in front. "I told them. We don't do ice creams."

"So where did they go?" Becky's voice was behind her, getting higher.

"I told them about that new ice cream shop that opened near the centre. Maybe they've gone there."

Which was easier, Janie asked herself as they frantically fought their way through the half term crowds towards the centre? Keeping an eye on an elderly eccentric landlady or watching a pair of hyperactive kids?

"They've got to be here somewhere," she said clutching Becky's hand in support. She'd never seen Becky look so out of control. Her eyes were wild with terror and she was shaking. "Omigod, I've lost them.

Steve will never forgive me. What kind of mother lets her children go wandering off?"

"You didn't let them go wandering off. You just gave them some money to get out of our hair."

"Exactly." Becky was panting. "Supposing they're not there?"

"They will be."

They've got to be.

"It's not as though they've even got their mobiles on them!" Becky's voice rose in a moan. "I confiscated them because they were playing up."

They had their own mobiles? At that age?

"Nearly there." Janie's heart was in her mouth as they turned the corner. If the kids weren't there, what were they going to do? Ring the police but . . .

"Omigod!" Becky's voice couldn't get any higher. "They aren't here!"

Swiftly, she took in the ice cream parlour. The place was pretty packed but even so she couldn't see two small children on their own. There was a father over there with two kids and their backs to them, a crowd of teenagers at the bar — one with a huge gold cross round his neck — and some mothers with a party load of kids.

Becky clutched Janie's sleeve so hard she thought it was going to rip off. "Do something, Janie. Do something!"

"Auntie Janie!"

The dad opposite turned round, grinning. "Hello you! What took you so long?"

She marched over, furiously. "Mac! What the fuck — what the hell are you doing here with Becky's kids?"

"He was already here," piped up Ben. "He was in front of us in the queue. Daisy asked him what he'd done with the rest of his hair. It's really short now, isn't it?"

Becky already had Daisy in her arms, hugging her but almost shaking her too. "Why did you run off like that? You had Mummy really worried."

"Why? We've got lost before, haven't we, Daisy, when Auntie Janie lost us on the London Eye."

"What?"

"Ben, you promised not to split on me."

"'Sides, you told us to get some ice cream but you didn't give us enough money so Mac treated us."

Mac shrugged. "Not a problem. They're really cool kids. Did you know that snails walk an average of five miles in their lifetime? Ben told me."

"You should have told us they were here," hissed Janie.

"I texted."

Shit. She hadn't even looked.

"I thought your phone got taken, Auntie Janie. Mummy said you'd probably left it somewhere cos you're so disorganised."

"Actually, Daisy, it was taken. But Mac got me another."

"That's not all." Mac was grinning. "I've bought you some Shop-In and all. I know you like him."

Shop-In?

He handed her a CD.

382

"Chopin!"

She didn't dare look at Becks.

"I want to go shopping, Mum. I want to go shopping."

"Inaminute." Becky was still holding Daisy tight, as though she might run off again. "Look, we'd better head home."

"To London?" Janie felt a surge of hope. Becks had seen sense at last!

"No. To mum's. I'll ring you tomorrow. Thanks, Matt."

"Mac, actually."

Too late. She was gone.

"Your friend seems in a bit of a state." He was pulling up the chair for her but she remained standing.

"Yes. She's got stuff to deal with at the moment. Look, Mac . . ."

"Yes?" His eyes were locked on hers with that hopeful look she'd seen before; usually when he had his eye on someone else at the bar.

"I'm really grateful and all that. But it doesn't make a difference to us. I can't just forgive you like that, you know."

His eyes flickered and despite herself, she felt a twinge of sympathy for him. "I know that, Janie. I'm going to have to work on it. But I'm not giving up. You'd better know that. I've been really stupid and I'm going to make up for it. Know what I mean?"

In some ways, thought Janie as she made her way back to Marjorie's, she almost believed him. Besides, the new Mac was so very different from the old. Clean, reliable, in a job, polite, desperate to win her back . . .

Oh, shit. Not again!

"Marjorie." She gently shook the elderly woman on the sofa. Her mouth was slightly open although this time she could see she was breathing. "Marjorie, are you all right?"

"What? Who is it?" Marjorie sat bolt upright. "Ah, there you are, Janie. Sorry, must have dozed off there. Glad you're back. There are a couple of messages for you."

Something glad, joyous and spring-like leapt up inside her. "He rang, didn't he?"

Marjorie gave her a quick squeeze. "And very nice he sounded too. He gave me a number for you to ring back. Go on, you can use my phone."

Janie didn't need to be asked twice. No. That couldn't be right. Slowly, she redialled.

"It's unobtainable." The disappointment crashed into her. "Are you sure you took it down right?"

Marjorie's pancake foundation wrinkled in concern. "I think so, dear, although I did have to ask him to repeat it a few times. This hearing aid is getting a bit past it."

Janie could have wept.

"Don't worry, dear. I'm sure he'll ring back although I might have told him you were with your friend Mac." Marjorie beamed. "Nothing like a bit of competition to keep a man on his toes."

Oh, God. How had she known she was with Mac anyway?

"Because he rang here to say he'd got your friend Becky's children in an ice cream bar somewhere. Couldn't get hold of you on your mobile apparently. Now don't forget your second message, will you?"

Janie glanced at the note. Linda from the wedding shop? What did she want?

"Actually, she didn't sound at all happy, dear." Marjorie was already waddling over to the other side of the room towards the drinks trolley. "Said something about you taking one of her clients."

"Rubbish!"

"Well you'd better ring her back, dear. Apparently, it was against some agreement you signed. And she really did sound awfully cross."

THREE MONTHS TO GO

CHAPTER
FORTY-ONE

Becky

How was it possible to tip one's life upside down —
and everyone else's — so fast? Becky turned over in her
mother's narrow spare bed, bumping her nose against
Daisy's. Ben, on the other side, was hogging most of
the space or what there was of it. Helen had borrowed
a put-up bed from a neighbour for the children but
they both preferred snuggling up to her.

Not surprising when you considered what she'd put
them through.

"Why don't you just come back?" Steve had said on
the phone the other night. There hadn't been any
feeling in his voice; just an empty flatness which both
scared and annoyed her. A real man would have driven
down here and taken them back.

"You just think you fancy Dan because he's different
from Steve and seems like an escape from everything
that's gone wrong," Janie had said at the coffee shop
the other day.

Her words had had an uneasy ring of truth about
them. Dan reminded her of the kind of person she'd
been before. Before the children and before Steve. A
time when she could go to the loo when she wanted

without some small body yelling for her. A time when she didn't have that shaft of panic piercing through her chest when she realised the kids were there one minute and gone the next. A time when she'd been good at her job instead of being unceremoniously escorted out of her office like a criminal.

Becky eased herself into a sitting position against the wall so as not to wake the children and reached out for her mobile. Yes! Dan had sent a message during the night.

"How r u doing? Pls ring or text. Am worried. Do you wnt me 2 come dwn?"

Yes. No. Oh, God. Becky's heart hammered in her throat. Dan was so understanding! "Poor you," he'd said after they'd picked up Daisy from nursery that time she'd been so late. "Isn't there anyone you can go to, to get away from this for a while?"

And that's when she'd thought of her mother. All right, they'd had their fallings out over the years but a ridiculous childish part of her — the same bit that had made her ring Dan rather than her own husband who was in Frankfurt or was that Paris? — made her yearn to go home. To her bedroom (which mum had now turned into a spare room), that she'd had when she, mum and Adam had left the beautiful Old Rectory and all the security which that had represented.

"I'll drive you there," he'd said instantly when she told him. "You're in no fit state to do it yourself."

Of course her mother had got the wrong idea, just like Janie had. Now as she got out of bed, tiptoeing across the carpet while the children slept, she couldn't help thinking what it would be like if she was still at home. Steve would be up and about, making coffee or perhaps the children's breakfasts. Or else he'd be ringing from wherever he was that week to say good morning to the children and they'd be clamouring round the phone to talk to him.

"Where's Daddy?" Ben had asked a couple of times since they'd arrived at her mother's.

"On a work trip," she'd said. And because that was often the case, they hadn't questioned it. But how long could she keep this going?

"Mum! You're up!"

Her mother was putting the kettle on the Aga, still in the pink dressing gown she'd given her for last Christmas. There was something about her that was different; something livelier. Almost girlish in her air. What was going on?

The phone was on the table as though she'd just been using it and Becky felt tempted to pick it up. When her mother had left her father, causing such havoc all those years ago, Becky had constantly checked up on her; finding out what the last number was. Listening to her mother's conversations.

"Your mother must have someone else," her father used to insist when they'd met up every Sunday for a father and daughter lunch. "She wouldn't have had the strength to have left me if she hadn't."

"How's David?" she asked, reaching up into the cupboard for her special mug. It was a fine china one with pink roses that dad had given her one year.

"I'm not sure." Her mother had her back to her, looking for something in the fridge.

Becky found herself glancing back at the phone.

"What do you mean, you're not sure?"

"We're having a cooling-off period." Her mother carefully put a box of eggs on the table, taking what seemed like an inappropriate amount of time to choose one before breaking it into a saucepan of boiling water on the Aga.

She spoke in such a calm, measured way that Becky wondered if she'd missed something. "But you've just got engaged."

"Well, we're not now."

The egg spat and Becky jumped. Steve normally did the eggs at home.

"What happened?"

"Nothing really." Her mother took the saucepan off the Aga and covered it with a lid. "I just didn't feel ready."

Was everything falling to bits? True, she wasn't that keen on David; he couldn't have been more different from dad if he'd tried. But as Steve said, it was nice that she had someone instead of being alone.

"What are you looking for, Becky darling?"

Good question. Life? Happiness? Resolution? "My mug, actually. You haven't moved it, have you?"

"Sorry darling but it got broken. The other week. I was cleaning out the cupboards — long overdue — and I dropped it by mistake."

A wave of hurt smashed into her. "But that was my special mug. Daddy gave it to me."

"I know. I'm sorry. I'll get you another."

This was ridiculous and she knew it. But Becky couldn't help feeling petulant, like a child. It was yet another example of everything changing. Why couldn't dad break off his engagement with hairy Monique? She wouldn't mind that kind of change.

Her mother was already putting another mug of coffee in front of her. "Sit down, darling. I want to talk."

Here we go! She'd been waiting for this.

"I don't want to interfere but . . ."

"You're going to."

Her mother reached out and held her arm. "I just can't bear to stand by while you throw it all away." Her eyes were hanging on to hers. "Don't you see, darling? You'll make exactly the same mistake that I did. And all because of a . . ."

Her voice tailed off but not before she'd almost said the word. "All because of a man!" Becky was sure she was going to say that.

"All because of what?" she whispered.

"All because of a stupid feeling that life wasn't good enough." Her mother was standing up now, fussing around with the poached egg in the saucepan.

"It's not just a stupid feeling." Becky sipped her coffee. "I told you why I went. I got sacked for paying off Dad's girlfriend which, OK, I know I shouldn't have done but I needed to cover myself and anyway, she shouldn't have asked for it."

Her mother's lips tightened. "So I told your father when he rang the other day."

Good.

393

"Said he couldn't interfere with her business."

Becky nodded. "Just what he said to me. Coward."

Her mother returned to her seat. Becky preferred it when she stood up instead of looking at her so intently. "You've got too much to lose, Becky. A kind husband."

Becky snorted. "Who doesn't understand how much stress I'm under."

"That's what I used to think about your father. I was trying to bring you two up and studying for my horticultural exams. It was all too much." Her mother sighed. "And how are you going to manage for money if you and Steve don't get back together again? You've got a very high mortgage, haven't you?"

Becky shrugged. "We'll have to sell the house and I'll get another job."

"And what about the children?" Her mother's voice was rising, as it always did when she got agitated. She'd been the same when she and Adam had been little. Never able to cope. No wonder she, Becky, hadn't been maternal.

"They'll get used to it. Kids are resilient." Becky got up. All this was making her feel dizzy. She hadn't meant it to get this far and talking about all the practicalities made her feel as though she was standing on the edge of the Grand Canyon as she'd done on that press trip last year (no more of those for the immediate future!) and looking down. Why didn't Steve call? If he didn't, she certainly wasn't.

"Mum. Can I ask you something?"

Not a good idea, Becky. Not a good idea.

"Of course." Her mother put the plate of poached egg into the warming oven. "When you left dad, was it . . . was it because of someone else?"

"Of course not." Her voice sounded cracked. "Why?"

"Just wondered."

Her mother stood up again, flushed. "Goodness that Aga's getting hot. I must get it serviced. Is that the children I can hear upstairs? No, don't you go, Becky. Have a rest. I'll see to them. We could go for a walk."

"But it's raining!"

"A bit of fresh air won't hurt. You and Adam were always out in it."

Mum was gabbling. She always did that when nervous, even though she was always accusing her of doing the same. So she was lying. She had left dad for someone else. Just as she, Becky, would have to lie about Dan to Daisy and Ben when they were older.

True, she and Dan hadn't actually done anything but the pull between them was so strong that they might as well have done. It was only a matter of time, unless she called a stop to the whole ridiculous thing.

Reaching over, she picked up the handset and dialled the number.

"Steve Hughes' office."

"Hi, it's Becky here. Is Steve around?"

"He's away this week. Can I say who's calling?"

For goodness sake! "I told you. Becky. His wife."

"Sorry. I'm his new secretary."

New secretary? Steve hadn't told her that. Or had he?

"Tell him to ring me, can you, when he gets out of his meeting or wherever he is."

"It won't be for a while. New York is five hours behind."

New York? She was pretty certain he hadn't mentioned that.

"Shall I give him a message when he rings?"

"No, thank you."

What kind of marriage did you have if your husband flits off to New York without telling you or even the kids?

"Dan?"

She hadn't even realised she was dialling his number. "It's me. Becky. Your answerphone is on which means you're probably in some high powered editor's meeting." She laughed, trying to sound bright and not jealous. "About your texts. It would be great to see you if you're still free. I can leave the kids with mum and come up to London. Let me know. By the way, any luck with that vacancy you were going to check out?"

Becky put the phone down, hands shaking. She could hardly believe she'd just done that. Still, it was only a working lunch. Wasn't it?

Upstairs she could hear the children laughing with mum. They never laughed like that with her. She was hopeless with them. A useless mother. Not surprising really, considering she didn't spend enough time with them.

Becky listened to make sure no one was coming down the stairs. OK. 1471. Might as well find out who phoned mum last. My God! She knew that number!

Had grown up with it. What was mum doing, ringing their old house?

141. Then the number. Just so no one would know who it was if they did 1471 at their end. Besides, if someone answered, she could just put down the phone and . . .

"Helen! Darling! Thank God you phoned. I didn't like to, with your daughter being there but I've missed you so much and there's something I really need to tell you . . ."

Becky dropped the phone so it fell on the floor, scattering its batteries. *Helen darling?* The voice had been rich, deep, dark. Didn't like to ring with your daughter being there . . . And her mother had had the cheek to accuse her of being deceitful! What was going on?

"Mum!" A small body flew down the stairs and hurled itself at her. "What are you doing on the floor? Gran says she's going to take us to the mooseum. Can we go? It's got real fire engines you can ride on like the one that Jilly's mummy took us to at half term when you were working. Will you come too?"

"Inaminute. No. I mean I can't."

"Really?" Her mother had come in, holding Ben by the hand. She looked curiously at Becky holding the phone as though she'd caught Becky out rather than the other way round.

"No." Becky's cold voice cut into the air. "I was going up to London in a couple of days anyway. But if you're taking the kids out, I might as well go today. Mind if I stay the night and come back tomorrow?"

CHAPTER
FORTY-TWO

Helen

Much as she hated to admit it, it wasn't easy having four people in her tiny cottage. Everywhere she went, there were little pairs of shoes or toys or clothes. Becky had obviously come prepared to stay.

"It's crazy," Helen had whispered down the phone in furtive conversations with Robin. "She's making the biggest mistake of her life but she won't listen to me."

"Then there's nothing you can do about it apart from providing a solid family base." His voice washed over her in comforting waves. "I can imagine you're good at that."

Could he? How could he imagine anything about her? They hardly knew each other; not really. And yet he had this amazing ability to read her mind; to make her heart leap every time he answered the phone. The feeling that as soon as she heard his rich warm voice, she knew life was going to be all right.

"When can you come round?" he had asked urgently during their last conversation. "Today?"

She'd looked up, wondering if those were footsteps coming down the stairs. "Too difficult. I think Becky suspects. I've got a horrible feeling she might have done 1471 and discovered I'd rung you."

And then she'd had to put down the phone because Becky had come in, giving her the kind of look she had given her all those years ago when she'd been seeing Alastair.

And now — a few days later than she'd hoped — she was finally on her way to see Robin! Helen's heart had been beating like a teenager's ever since she had left the house. Even Dandy was excited, pawing at the window and making yelps of appreciation (not to mention smells) as they passed landmarks he recognised like the church — nice sign.

EVERYTHING MUST GO! was rather clever and so true. It was both scary and yet also hopeful in a funny kind of way. So much had gone in her own life and yet that wasn't necessarily a bad thing. It had to go, didn't it, to make way for the new?

Robin must have been waiting for her because the back door swung open before she even had a chance to knock on the large brass knocker that she and Geoff had unearthed in a local antique shop years ago.

"I've missed you," he said, drawing her into his chest and stroking the back of her hair. "Really missed you."

"Me too."

As she nestled into him, wanting to get inside his warm woollen blue jumper, she felt as though she was someone else. How could it be so wrong when it felt so right?

"Isn't that a famous song you're humming?"

She nodded happily.

His hold tightened. "Let's go upstairs."

"But Sylvia . . ."

"Hush." He held a finger against her mouth. "Next door. Asleep in her chair by the window."

"Let me see."

It wasn't that she disbelieved him; more that she needed to look. To say "This is the woman whose husband you are taking. Don't do it."

But as she took in poor Sylvia, slumped in the chair, eyes heavy in sleep and that lopsided mouth crashed against the side of her face, she saw something else. A limp doll. A woman who had, according to Robin, made his life deeply unhappy before the stroke. A woman who didn't deserve the pain and suffering she was in now.

Robin saw it too. She could read that in his face. And this time, it was she who took his hand. He needed this almost as much as she did; an intimacy born of two starved kindred spirits who suddenly recognise each other after years of battling with the wrong people, the wrong places and the wrong times.

Not the main bedroom. That wouldn't be right. Wordlessly, they walked hand in hand to the guest suite on the far side of the landing above the beautiful mahogany staircase. This had been the room they had put up friends and her sister, now in Australia. The curtains were different; white voile. But her carpet — sage green — the same.

She turned to face him. Sod that bloody cap, which she'd gone and left behind. If she couldn't take a risk at her age, when could she? "Robin . . ." she began.

"Shhhh." He crushed her words with his mouth and at the same time, started to unpeel her clothes, her body, her soul.

"Granny!" Daisy tugged at her legs. "You look all different. Have you been out on your bike? I want a bike but Mummy said London's too dangerous. If we came to live with you for ever, I could have one, couldn't I? And Daddy could have one as well."

Becky was looking at her sharply and for a ridiculous minute, Helen felt like a teenager who'd been caught by her parents, sneaking up the stairs late at night.

"I thought you were going to be back ages ago." Becky was still looking at her suspiciously.

Helen felt herself colouring. "I got caught at Doris's. I had to sort out her wallflowers."

"Mum rang her," piped up Ben. "But you wasn't there."

"Weren't there, Ben," interrupted Becky. "Doesn't school teach you anything?"

"You rang her?" Helen could hardly believe it. "How did you get her number?"

"From your diary." Becky's voice could have sliced the pizza lying on top of the Aga. "I told you. We were worried. Go back to the television, you lot. I'll bring supper in."

Helen waited for them to leave the room. "I was going to go to Doris," she began.

"Please don't, Mum."

"Don't what?"

"Tell any more lies."

A horrible creeping sensation took over her legs. "I'm not. It's just that . . ."

"I need to go up to London again. Tomorrow; just for the day. It's a sort of interview. Can you look after the children?"

"Well yes, although I do have a couple of gardens to do."

"Really?"

Becky had her "I don't believe you" expression on her face.

"Yes, really." Helen put the kettle on crossly. "But I'll take them with me. Fresh air will be good for them."

"Are you saying they don't get enough?"

Here we go again. It could have been 20 years ago except that then it was Helen who was always telling Becky to get out in the fresh air more.

"No, but they do live in London."

"With lots of parks."

Sod it. "Look, Becky." She moved towards her daughter. "Let's not argue. It's stupid."

"Don't touch me, Mum. I don't feel like a cuddle." She shot Helen a disdainful look. "I'm going out for a walk myself now. To get some fresh air. When the pizza's ready, give it to the kids, can you?"

She didn't mean it, Helen told herself. It was just that her daughter had been so used to giving orders to au pairs or nannies. If it weren't for those two snatched hours with Robin, she'd have felt awful but now she could feel a lovely warm internal glow from top to bottom. No wonder her granddaughter had thought she'd been out cycling!

How funny, she thought, slicing up the pepperoni pizza, that she should discover sex at her age! Finally, at 54, she could see what all the fuss was about. Robin had felt it too; she knew that.

"I love you," he'd said simply afterwards.

The polite answer would have been to have reciprocated but something stopped her. Now, as she dished out pizza to the children as they lounged on the sitting-room carpet (something she'd never have allowed in her day), she wondered. Did she love him? Did she really want to risk getting hurt all over again? And — more important — how could she love another woman's husband?

An hour later, Becky still hadn't come back from her walk. Every time Helen tried her mobile, it was engaged: An uneasy picture of Dan swam into her mind.

"Come on, you lot. Time for bed."

"We don't want to." Daisy didn't even move her eyes from the screen as she talked.

"We're waiting for Mum to come back." Ben's determined voice was staggering in its youthful authority. When, she wondered, did children start telling adults what to do.

"What are those scratches on your back, Gran?"

"Nothing." Hastily she slipped on a cardigan to cover up the low neckline. "Ah, here's Mum!"

Half-cross and half-relieved, she flew to the door. "Did you forget your keys . . . David!"

With everything that had been going on, she realised — ashamed — she'd almost forgotten about him. Now as he stepped into the hall, she could see he looked terrible. Thin and gaunt as though he hadn't slept for days.

"How are you?"

He shrugged. "OK. Look, I'm sorry but I was passing so I thought I'd pop in."

"Becky's here. With my grandchildren. Say hello children."

"Hi."

Neither looked up from the screen.

"Daisy, come and shake David's hand. You remember him, don't you?"

Reluctantly, Daisy got up. "Are you Gran's boyfriend?"

"No, silly." Ben nudged her. "He's gran's ex. Remember? She was telling Mum she doesn't want to marry him any more cos he's boring."

Helen suddenly realised the true meaning of wanting to be swallowed up by the floor.

"Sorry, David."

He was already heading for the door. "No problem. See you around."

Oh dear. Helen was still looking at the door long after he had shut it.

"Do you still like him, Gran?"

Daisy was looking at her worriedly.

"He's just a friend."

"Mum's got a friend," piped up Ben. "He's called Dan and he took us roller skating. Mummy fell over a lot but she thought it was funny."

"Really?"

Thank God. The phone. For one moment, it sounded like Steve. About time! If that son-in-law of hers had come down, or even phoned, he might have been able to make Becky see sense.

"Helen?"

At first, she'd thought the deep voice was a man's but now she realised it was a woman's. A woman who sounded like . . .

"This is Monique speaking. I hope I haven't rung at an inconvenient time."

"I'm just getting the children to bed."

"How are they? We had such a lovely time the other day, Geoff and I, when we took them to the park."

Becky hadn't told her that one.

"I'm actually ringing with an invitation, Helen."

Why was it that people often used your first name when they didn't really know you?

"You know that the wedding is just over two months away."

Yes, yes.

"Geoff and I are about to send out our wedding invitations, providing your daughter's friend gets her act together."

That wasn't very nice.

"Anyway, I thought it would be useful if you and I met for a coffee. I know we have briefly met but it hasn't exactly been under the most salubrious circumstances, has it?"

She said it like "salooobrious" as though it was a word she'd just looked up in the dictionary.

"No, it hasn't." What was the woman getting at?

405

"So I thought we ought to meet for lunch. I'm in Oxford next week. Shall we say that new restaurant in Little Clarendon Street? On Tuesday at one o'clock? Great. Sorry, my mobile's going. Must get that — it'll be the States. See you then."

CHAPTER
FORTY-THREE

Mel

It was odd, running on her own. Every time she passed the oak tree with the log underneath, she wanted to stop and have their usual catch up. She'd come to enjoy those conversations (almost like confessionals), even though when she'd first started jogging with Geoff early in the morning, it had been slightly strange getting used to the company.

A bit like marriage really. You got used to being on your own and suddenly there was another person, sharing the bathroom, leaving strange smells and socks; someone who never quite left you alone. It took a while to adapt and then suddenly you couldn't imagine life any other way.

But she wasn't married to Geoff.

That awful Monique was going to be.

Mel still burned with embarrassment when she recalled her conversation with that woman. "You've got it wrong," she had spluttered. "Your fiancé came to me for advice."

"What kind of advice?"

Mel had almost laughed. Surely she didn't really expect her to betray confidences? "I'm afraid I can't say. People come to me in privacy. I would suggest that as you are getting married, you have that conversation with him yourself."

"How dare you! I'll report you to your superior for being rude."

Sod it. Let her. Even if it did get as far as the archdeacon, she hadn't done anything wrong. Had she? Well, nothing physical. Just mental. What was it that the Bible said about that again? Something about lustful looks being as bad as the full infidelity stuff. Well if that was the case, most of the world would be considered unfaithful to its partners. Frankly, it was time the church got real. At least some people appreciated her, like Ann, the parishioner who'd rung up about her own difficult son.

Even so, she'd felt it was best to cancel her running sessions with Geoff.

"Why?" he had asked, confused.

Mel had hesitated, wondering whether to tell him about Monique. If she did, it might cause more trouble and it really would look as though she'd done something wrong.

"I need to be on my own. Sorry."

"I understand." The hurt in his voice cut. But it was true. She did need to be on her own, if only to keep that blessed woman quiet. And besides, maybe she had had a point. There were times when she looked forward to her one to ones with Geoff too much.

"How's your daughter?"

"No change." She'd swallowed. "I feel as though she's been away on holiday for too long and that it's now time for her to come back."

She had almost felt him nodding at the other end of the phone. "I can understand that."

Of course he could. Geoff understood everything. If only she could tell him now about the letter from Kevin. Her finger hovered over "G" for Geoff on her mobile. Yes. No. Was this what it was like, Jesus, when you were being tempted?

If she rang, it would sound as though she was asking for his advice again and that could so easily lead to something else. So it was a "no" then. OK, God, you've won. This round, anyway.

Besides, if she was going to tell anyone, it ought to be Richard.

She returned earlier from her run than usual — without their chats on the fallen tree, it didn't take so long — but Josh was still in bed. Richard usually woke him in the morning but now it was all down to her.

"I might as well be a single mother," she thought, angrily stomping up the stairs to Josh's room. A figure lay huddled under the duvet, the computer still on, which meant he must have got up during the night to turn it on again. "Josh, get up. You're going to be late for school."

"Five more minutes," he murmured, turning over. "I'm a teenager. We need our sleep."

It had been like this with Amy. She could remember that all too well. Now she wished she hadn't shouted and got cross — just like she was now. Calm down. Be the kind of mother you want to be.

"The important thing about parenting," Geoff said once during their early morning runs, "is to keep communication open. However difficult your teenagers are, make it clear that you are always there for them. I can't tell you how often Adam used to come home, drunk out of his mind. But it's no good reading the riot act until they're sober."

Josh drank too. He never used to. But since the accident, he often came home smelling of beer. "It's bad for you," she'd say.

"Chill out, Mum. Everyone does it. Even you."

That wasn't something she wanted to be reminded of. The same way she didn't want to think about that letter. Visits With a Difference. She ought to go. She knew that. That invitation — if you could call it that — had been sent for a reason. But she couldn't go. She just couldn't forgive.

By the end of the week, she almost wished Richard wasn't coming back for the weekend. "This is how couples grow apart," she told herself, stretching out on the sofa and switching on the *Wannabee a Singer* series. This was exactly what she warned others about during her marriage counselling sessions to young couples and — as in Geoff's case — the not so young. Even when she heard the sound of his car in the drive, she remained sitting where she was.

"Hi." Richard brushed her cheek. "How's your week been?"

Fine. I've virtually been accused of having an affair by one of my parishioners; I'm tempted to have an affair with another; and I've been told I'm here under sufferance by a third. Oh, and our daughter's would-be murderer wants me to visit him in prison.

"All right, I suppose. Yours?"

He threw his jacket on the hall chair instead of hanging it up. "Really getting into the swing of it. I've definitely got my quota of new customers this month which means I should be on target for the six monthly bonus and . . ."

Half-listening to his catalogue of triumphs, she turned her back and went into the kitchen. Not for the first time, she thought of the kitchen she'd left behind in Wandsworth. It had been three times this size and had a decent range instead of this ancient gas contraption. Stop. That's not the point, Mel, and you know it. If money had been important, you wouldn't be doing this and Richard wouldn't be forced to work away during the week.

"Mel, did you hear me? I said I'm starving. Didn't have time for lunch with that meeting. What's for supper, love?"

Good point. She opened the fridge. "Scrambled eggs? Cheese on toast?"

"You haven't got anything else?"

He didn't actually say the words "What have you been doing all week?" but the implication was there.

"Sorry. Haven't had time to go shopping." She opened a cupboard, which badly needed tidying, to see

411

if there was a stray tin. "It's been a bit hectic. Anyway, aren't you going to ask me?"

He frowned. "Ask you what?"

Mel shook her head in disbelief. "Amy? Our daughter. Remember? Aren't you going to ask if there's been any change?"

Richard was already taking a half-open bottle of Chardonnay out of the fridge. "If there had been, you'd have told me." His voice was flat like the wine, as he'd find out soon enough because she'd forgotten to put the cork back in the other night.

"That's right." Mel's voice was unnaturally bright as she cracked the remaining two eggs into a bowl. "I would have done."

"Come on, love." She felt his arms around her waist and wanted to walk away except the sink was in front. "I know it's hard."

"Hard?" She swung round, pushing him slightly backwards so she didn't have to be near him. "What do you know about that? You're away from it all, aren't you? You can have a normal life; talk to people who don't categorise you as the vicar's husband or the father of that poor girl in the hit and run crash or the father of that hard-to-control teenage boy. And you haven't even asked about Josh."

Richard was already on his second glass. "Give me a chance, Mel. I've just got back. I'm exhausted. Besides, you're doing what you wanted, aren't you? I didn't ask you to leave your 100k job in advertising or drag us out of London so you could be a woman of God."

"Bastard." The word came out of her mouth before she could take it back. Horrified at herself, she put her hand out. "Sorry. I didn't mean to say that."

"I'm going upstairs to change." Richard's voice had a "Keep Off" notice attached to it. "When I come down, we'll start the weekend again. OK."

He was the one who should have been a vicar. Not her. Richard was far more reasonable but then again, so would she if she could have a break every week away from everything. Mel crumbled a small remaining piece of Stilton on top of the scrambled egg to give it more flavour. There was only enough for one but that didn't matter. Since Amy's accident, she'd lost her taste. And not just for food. The thought of getting into bed tonight with her husband made her stomach turn over. She'd just have to pretend she was tired. Again.

"All right?" Richard was rubbing his hands to keep warm as he came down the stairs in his weekend jeans and sweat shirt. for a second, she had a vision of Geoff in his cords and plaid shirt. No. Stop right there.

"This is really delicious." He tucked in, glancing up as he did so. "Aren't you eating with me?"

"No." She turned her back, pretending to wash up. "I ate earlier."

OK, God. So I'm telling a white lie. Deal with it.

"Is this the post?"

Damn. She'd meant to remove the letter from the week's pile.

"That's nice."

She knew without turning round, what he meant.

413

"Nice?"

"Yes. I presume you've seen it. The envelope's open."

"And I presume you're talking about that boy."

"Kevin. Why don't you ever use his name?"

"I can't."

"But he's a kid, Mel. Not much older than Josh and Amy. Like he said at the trial, he's already had his real punishment."

Go. Go back to work and leave them all alone. "So you think I should go?"

Richard nodded. "Yes. I do."

She started to shake. "I don't want to. Can't you see that?"

Geoff had understood when she'd told him. He'd got it. So why couldn't her husband of 22 years?

There was the sound of the door slamming. "Josh?" Footsteps flew up the stairs. "Josh? Dad's back. Aren't you going to come and say hello?"

No answer.

"Leave him." Richard's voice was heavy with hurt. "He'll come down when he's ready. Here he is now. Hi, son. How are you doing?"

He's already speaking like an absent father, thought Mel. As though he didn't really know him.

"OK. Can you lend me a fiver, Dad?"

Richard already had a hand in his pocket.

"Hang on." Mel stopped him. "I only gave you £5 last night. You spent it on drink again, didn't you?"

"It's only lager. I'm a teenager, Dad."

"But isn't it illegal to buy it?"

"Not with my fake ID."

Mel groaned. "I told you. You're not meant to use that. Not after you nearly got arrested."

"Arrested? You didn't tell me about that. And I didn't know you'd got another earring put in, Josh. It's like a giant Polo! If you're not careful, you'll split your ear open."

"Fuck off, Dad."

"Josh!"

There was the sound of the door slamming. "See?" Mel almost felt pleased. "Now look what you've done. He's gone out without even eating supper."

"I didn't think there was any."

There was an empty silence, interrupted by a bleep on her mobile. Glancing down, she could see she'd received a text message from Geoff.

"Sure you dn't wnt a run tmorrow?"

No. Yes. No.

"What are you doing?"

Fumbling with the letters, she texted "Srry cnt do" before scrolling down to Josh's number. "Dnt dnk 2 much. Lv u." "Sending Josh a message. Then I'm going out." She pulled on her trainers.

"But I've only just got home."

"So?" Mel felt she was looking at her husband as though she hadn't seen him for months rather than days. He even smelt different. "Just because you're back, doesn't mean we all have to hover round you."

She stood on the doorstep for a moment, the door shut safely behind her, gulping in the anonymous dark cold air. Why couldn't she be nice to him? Richard didn't deserve this. Nor did she. But then again, that's what life was all about, wasn't it? Accepting the things you couldn't change and changing the things you could . . . like going to that so-called Visits With a Difference day.

Suddenly, she could feel the vibration of her mobile which she'd turned to silent.

"Mel?"

Great. This was all she needed.

"This is Tom here."

The AD?

"I just wondered if you were feeling all right, Mel?"

What? "Yes, thank you." She wondered what was the polite way to say, "Why shouldn't I be?"

"Because I've just received a rather odd text message from you." He coughed slightly. "It appears to be telling me not to drink too much." He coughed. "It also said you loved me."

God! "Sorry. I thought I'd sent that to my teenage son. He's drunk rather a lot of . . . Ribena recently and I was worried . . . I mean . . ."

There was the sound of something that sounded strangely like a chuckle. "It's all right, Mel. I do understand. Young men nowadays do tend to drink too much; even I, at that age, once had a rather embarrassing incident with rather too many port and lemons. But actually Mel, there was something else I needed to talk about."

Something about his tone filled Mel with foreboding. "I've just received a rather disturbing phone call from a somewhat angry parishioner of yours. At least, strictly speaking, it's her husband to be who is the parishioner."

Dear Lord.

"You probably know whom I'm talking about, Mel. A lady called Monique Brown. I have to say that she made some rather disturbing allegations. Too complex, in fact, to discuss on the phone. I'd like to arrange a meeting so we could discuss this."

CHAPTER
FORTY-FOUR

Janie

"Hello, you!"

She should have put the phone down straight away when he'd rung that morning. But instead, she'd found herself agreeing to lunch and now she was even telling him her problems.

"So Linda then accused me of poaching one of her clients!"

"And did you?" Mac was looking at her straight over the pub table. She still couldn't get used to his new haircut. It made him look so conventional. Rather attractive even. No. Don't even go there.

"Not really." Janie shoved a mouthful of pasta in her mouth. Becky was always asking how she could eat so much without putting on weight. At times of crisis, she ate even more.

"Not really?"

"Well . . ." Janie started doodling on her paper napkin. When she'd bumped into the Wilsons (or the Wilsons-to-be as they were then) in town, they'd remembered her from her previous job and asked what she was doing now. So obviously, she'd told them about For Weddings and a Funeral and all the rather unusual

418

trimmings they offered, as well, of course, as the discount which she had suddenly thought of on the spot.

So it wasn't her fault if they'd then asked her to arrange their wedding instead, was it?

"You could see it both ways." Mac was still looking at her in that odd way. The old Mac would have ordered another pint and told her not to be so daft. That business was business and good on her for getting on with it.

"Well what am I meant to do about it?" Janie felt herself going all prickly and she didn't like it.

"Offer to share the cut and all?"

That was ridiculous. "Marjorie and I work on a low profit as it is."

Mac shrugged. "Just a suggestion. You wouldn't want her taking you to court, would you?"

Janie felt another chill going through her. "She hasn't mentioned that yet but I suppose she might."

"Of course, there is another way of dealing with it."

"What?"

"Ask the Wilsons to tell their side of the story to your old boss. Let them explain that they bumped into you and got chatting and that they simply changed their mind without you influencing them. I mean, that's true, isn't it?"

"Yes." Janie wriggled uncomfortably in her seat. "I think so."

"That's it then." Mac got up.

Hang on. His glass was only half empty. "Aren't you going to finish that?"

"Nah. Got to get back to work." He touched her shoulder briefly in a gesture that might or might not have meant something. "I've told you, Janie. I've changed. By the way, I like your picture. Who is it?"

She glanced at her sketch of a bearded Norwegian who'd have doubtless forgotten her by now, thinking she wasn't interested.

"No one." She screwed up the napkin. "Just something in my head." She smiled weakly. "Know what I mean?"

"Wonderful idea," wheezed Marjorie when she got back. "Can't think why we didn't work that one out ourselves. Why don't you phone the Wilsons immediately."

Janie grit her teeth. It was all very well being deaf and having memory loss at that age but it really did get very wearisome repeating everything over and over again. "Because they're in Vietnam on honeymoon."

Marjorie was fishing in her handbag for something. "Vietnam? Isn't there a war on there?"

For God's sake! "Not any more. It's one of the hot spots now for tourism. You remember. We arranged it for them through that internet agency."

"Ah yes. Now you come to mention it, I think I do." "What's that?"

Janie was staring at the grey, cigarette-sized object which Marjorie was pulling out of her bag.

"This?" Marjorie was examining it as though she hadn't seen it before. "Just my new inhaler."

"Did you go to the doctor again about your wheeziness?"

420

"Yes but only because you kept telling me to, dear." Marjorie patted her hand. "Says I'm fit as a flea apart from this stupid chest."

"And what about the blood pressure?"

"Doing nicely, thank you. Now, on to more important matters. Everything set for the bonfire tomorrow?"

Oh, God, it was going to be one of those weeks. "You mean, the pyre."

"That's right, dear. Goodness me, I bet when Angus ordered one of those, he hadn't realised how fast they were going to catch on. Everyone wants one now. Only problem is that they need their own land. Remind me, dear. Who is it this week?"

"Gladys from your bingo club." Janie frantically leafed through her notes, trying to make sense of the words. "No, sorry. I've read the wrong column. She's getting married — not buried. Let's see. That's right. To Bert from your Tuesday Club."

Marjorie swigged back her g and t. "Better not get them muddled up, dear. They're confused enough at their age as it is. I simply can't think why she's doing it. Poor old Gladys wouldn't know one end of a man from the other. By the way, how's your friend doing? The one who can't decide between her husband and this young man she met in New York."

Perhaps she shouldn't have told her so much. "Still a bit wobbly. You won't mention any of this if you meet her, will you Marje?"

"Of course not, dear." Marjorie rose majestically to her feet. She was wearing one of her seventies kaftans

421

with a matching rose-pink turban to go with her Chinese-looking lacquered pink walking stick. "Don't worry. You can rely on me, although I do think that if she played her cards right, she could have them both. We often did in our day, you know. No wonder today's divorce rate is so high."

"Steve? It's me. Janie. Look, I know this is none of my business but can you ring Becky? She says you haven't called and if you want her back . . . well, that sounds more desperate than it is but . . ."

Fuck. Why can't you just erase messages when you got it all wrong?

". . . that is, if you want to make things up, you need to call her. She's at her mother's and it's been weeks now. She's scared, Steve, can't you see that? It's not easy when you lose your job and . . ."

Fuck and double fuck. The line had gone dead. That was the problem with Pay as You Go, especially when you were ringing abroad. Where was he anyway? Becky said he was always away. It wasn't good for a marriage, although that didn't excuse her behaviour. Couldn't Becky see how much she had to lose?

And why was it that every time she, Janie, found someone, they were never right? A picture of Lars flashed into her head, even though she tried to make it go away. There had been something there, she was sure of it. But if he really cared, he'd here tried to get hold of her.

As for Mac, well he'd really changed, hadn't he? What was it Marjorie had said the other day?

Something about life being a train and that if you didn't change platforms every now and then, you'd always end up going to the same destination.

Maybe it was time to give Mac one last chance . . .

The elderly gentleman at the altar was tapping his stick on the faded blue carpet. "I don't understand it. Why isn't she here?"

"Bert, don't fret. I'm sure Gladys will be here any minute. Her car's probably been delayed. Janie will go and check, won't you, dear?"

If she was Gladys, thought Janie as she went to the church door for the sixth time, she wouldn't turn up either. Bert was so fat, he looked as though he needed stuffing (although not the kind of stuffing in Mac's terminology). He was clearly on the wrong side of 75 and spat every time he opened his mouth to talk. Apparently he was a lucky Bingo winner and dealt a mean hand in bridge at the Tuesday Club but that obviously wasn't enough to get Gladys here on time.

The vicar — who'd told her to call her Mel although she still couldn't quite bring herself to be so familiar — was checking her mobile phone, presumably to look at the time. "I can wait a little longer but I've got another wedding after this, I'm afraid." She smiled apologetically. Really, thought Janie enviously. Couldn't God — if he existed — spread his favours a bit more widely? It must be wonderful being beautiful, married and not having a worry in the world because you knew Someone was watching over you.

"I've rung the driver but his mobile's off. I'm not sure what else I can do."

She hadn't meant to sound abrupt but it somehow came out that way and immediately she felt guilty. She hadn't given the driver the wrong time again, had she? And why was his mobile off anyway? Surely he had hands free? It came with the male anatomy, didn't it? Thank God. Here was the car now. Fuck. Gladys wasn't in the back.

"She got out." The driver was shrugging with a typical male 'Don't blame me it wasn't my fault' expression. "Insisted I stopped in town — Cornmarket, no less. Bloody nightmare with everyone hooting at me — and then she legged it."

"Where did she go?"

Another shrug. "Search me, love."

No, thanks. Not with that breath. Still, he might have his uses. Janie hopped in the back seat. "Take me to where you dropped her off."

McDonald's? Just round the corner from where she and Becky had found the kids the other week. Bloody hell, there she was sitting in the corner with a milkshake. Everyone was looking at her and no wonder. It wasn't often you found a silver-haired pensioner in a full-length cream white wedding dress sipping a vanilla milkshake under her veil.

"Gladys?" Janie slid into the seat next to her. "What's wrong?" There was a slurping sound which might or might not have been the milkshake. "Did you get cold feet?"

424

There was a slight nod under the veil.

"That's understandable." Janie's hand reached out for Gladys's velvet glove. Blimey, she's really gone in for the works. "But he seems . . . he seems a nice enough man."

"He is." It came out as a strangled cry from under the veil. "He's lovely."

Lovely? Had she seen his teeth? "I wouldn't go that far but . . ."

"I'm not good enough for him."

What?

"He's been married before and I don't know if we'll last. The previous one didn't."

Janie leaned back in her seat. "I know the feeling. How long was he married for?"

"Forty years."

40 years? The ex-wife deserved a medal with gnashers like those.

"And then she died." Another slurp. "Only five years ago so he's only just got over it. And now I'm worried in case I don't match up to Gloria."

Gloria? It got worse. Still at least she was dead and couldn't play the jealous first wife like Helen, even though Becky's mum was trying to hide it.

"Another thing." The gloved hand tightened on hers almost like a vice. "I've never . . . you know, dear. Been familiar with a man. Not really. Although I did once go swimming in the public baths in 1965 and I accidentally saw a man whose trunks had slid down when he was climbing out." Her voice rose almost to a silent strangled whisper in her ear. "I'm not sure what to do! Where it . . . where it goes. That kind of thing. It looked awfully odd. Rather like Marjorie's new inhaler but slightly bigger."

"Gladys. Listen." Janie's hand could almost circle Gladys's thin wrist. "Everyone gets nervous when they start a new relationship. But if Bert didn't want to marry you, he wouldn't be standing there at the church right now, wondering where you are. OK, it might not work. But life's a gamble. You've just got to be brave."

Gladys was picking something out of her front tooth. Weren't old people meant to have manners? "What's the bravest thing you've ever done, gal?"

What?

"Well . . ."

The old biddy was giving her a sharp look. "Or are you scared of something too?"

OK. Fair deal. "Actually, I am."

"Tell me."

"I can't."

"Then whisper."

What the hell.

"Really?" Gladys's ear was so close to her mouth that she could almost see inside. Ugh!

"Tell you what." Gladys gripped Janie's hand as though she was on the edge of a cliff instead of blocking the side of the table so no one else could get past. "You do something about that and I'll do this."

Anything to shift the old bird to the altar. "All right you're on. But only if you come with me now."

"But what if it doesn't work out?"

"Then you can get divorced like everyone else."

Another slurp. Or was it a giggle? "Maybe you're right. That would be one for the Tuesday Club, wouldn't it? They don't believe in that sort of thing. Besides, I don't want to die as a spinster of the parish. I promised myself that I'd get married before I was seventy and I've only got a couple of months to go."

"You don't have to have sex either," urged on Janie. "Lots of married couples don't."

"Really? You do surprise me, dear. If I'd known that, I might have done this years ago." Gladys rose unsteadily to her feet. What kind of milkshake was that? It smelt distinctly like . . .

"Want a sip?"

Gladys was thrusting a miniature Johnny Walker at her. "No thanks. Listen, Gladys, the car's waiting for us — in fact it's probably got a few tickets now — so shall we just make a move?"

Everyone was looking as they left, including a crowd of hoodies. "Going to a fancy dress party?" leered one of them.

"Piss off," hissed Janie. "She's getting married."

There was a round of wolf whistles. "Cool. Listen up everyone," yelled out one of the hoodies with a black metal twist through his left ear and a gold Star of David together with a cross round his neck. "These two are getting married! Gay wedding is it?"

"Very gay!" Gladys beamed. "Thank you so much, Janie. I'll never forget this."

★ ★ ★

By the time she got back to the cottage, having safely married off Gladys to Bert, Janie was exhausted.

Marjorie had decided to go on to the reception. ("Don't want to turn down a knees-up, dear; not when you don't know how long your knees will stay up at my age.") In fact, Janie was grateful. Right now, all she wanted was to chill out on the sofa and try to block out the image of Gladys and Bert on their wedding night.

Honestly! Why did people get married when it caused so much trouble. Just look at Becks and her mother before her, not to mention Monique — blast. That reminded her. Those bloody ice sculptures still hadn't been sorted.

"Hello you!"

Why did she feel quite pleased to see him? Didn't she ever learn either?

"Hi, Mac."

She weaved her way past him even though it meant squeezing against the front hedge so as not to brush against him.

"Just passing. Thought I might pop in with these and all."

Flowers? Mac never bought flowers. He spent money — when he had it — on booze and fags. And Stargazers too. Her favourite. Not that he'd know that.

"They're Stargazers. Your favourite. I remember you telling me once."

He was holding them out to her, pleadingly and something inside her lurched without permission.

"All right. You'd better come in." Ungraciously, she unlocked the door and motioned to the sofa. "Sit down. I've got to go to the bathroom. Second thoughts, you could put the kettle on while I'm gone."

She was longer than she meant to be. What are you doing this for, she asked herself as she freshened up her make-up from her last remaining free foundation sample and squirted some of Marjorie's Adore behind her ears. It wasn't as though she fancied Mac. Not any more. Besides, a leper never changed his spots as Becky always said. That was another thing. She needed to ring Becky to see if that message to Steve had worked.

Mac was standing up with the phone in his hands as she came in. "Cup of tea on the side," he said kindly. "You look as though you need it."

The old Mac would have handed her an unopened brown bottle.

"You can't use the phone. It's Marjorie's. I have to pay her."

"I wasn't. Someone rang so I took a message."

She flopped down on the sofa with her tea, hoping he wouldn't sit next to her. He took his mug and then seemed to hesitate before sitting down on the chair opposite. Absurdly, she felt disappointed. "Who rang?"

"Some chap with a foreign accent."

Her heart pounded and she leaped up. "Lars?"

Mac shrugged. "That might have been it."

"But didn't you take a number?"

"He said he'd ring back. I told him you were in the bathroom."

"You told him I was in the bathroom!" Janie felt the blood pounding in her ears. "Did he ask who you were?"

"He didn't need to."

"Why not?"

"I think I might have answered the phone saying 'Mac speaking'." He grinned. "It's what I do in the office. Habit, really. Know what I mean?"

Fuck and double fuck.

"You could always do 1471."

No shit, Sherlock.

"Except that, now I come to think of it, someone else rang just after. Someone called Monique. I did take her number because she insisted. Rather a pushy woman, I'd say. She wants you to ring her straight back."

The phone! He was ringing back.

"I'll get that." She almost pushed past Mac before he had a chance to do more damage. "Hello?"

"Can I speak to Miss Jones?"

Janie's heart sank. It wasn't Lars. "That's me."

"This is the police station here. Someone has just handed in your phone and purse. Would you like to come down to the station to collect them? Looks like you've been lucky. There are several credit cards and money still inside. A vicar's son handed it in apparently. Nice to know there are still some responsible youths around, aren't there?"

TWO MONTHS TO GO

CHAPTER
FORTY-FIVE

Becky

Becky turned sharp left out of Highbury & Islington, pausing briefly to drop £1.50 into the palm of the *Big Issue* man. Guilt. That's what it was. She'd never bothered before.

She'd seen the man the other week when she'd first come up to see Dan and, in her nervousness, had briefly wondered if the *Big Issue* vendor was a private eye hired by Steve.

For God's sake, don't be ridiculous. She wasn't going to do anything. Dinner, he'd said. And then . . . then she'd either get the train back to Oxford or maybe stay the night at her house which wasn't far away. Too close. Too easy for someone to spot them.

But it had been all right. Dan had been the perfect gentleman. They'd gone to a quiet Italian bistro; down some steps and into a basement with red candles which made it difficult to see each other, let alone be recognised by someone else. And they'd just talked.

Talking, mused Becky, as she strode along the Caledonian Road towards Dan's flat, could be so more sexy than sex. She'd told him about Steve and work and her parents and how insecure she'd felt when they'd split up which was why she'd married so young. Talked about her ambition at work which had stemmed from her mother who had never had a proper job until her gardening — which was hardly the same.

She'd confessed how terrified she'd been after the children were born because she didn't know how to handle them which was why, to be honest — and this wasn't something she'd ever dared to be before — it was easier to go to work and leave them behind with someone who knew what she was doing. And she'd sobbed her heart out about Dad getting married to the horrendous Monique.

All he'd done was listen. But not in a way that made her wonder if he was thinking of something else. No. It was the kind of listening that made her realise he really understood.

"I feel I've dominated the conversation," she'd said shyly at the end of the evening when he'd walked her back to her house (too late by then to get the train).

"Nonsense." He'd brushed her cheek as she stood at the door, wondering whether to ask him in. "I'll bore you with all my baggage next week." He'd looked at her quizzically. "That is, if you want to do this again."

Again? In a few weeks? Anything could happen between now and then. Steve might beg her to come back. Or she might listen to Janie and her mother and go back anyway.

But she hadn't. In fact that one night alone at the empty house without him or the children had made her swear that she wouldn't do that again. And here she was. Walking to Dan's house where he'd suggested cooking supper. And not even walking; almost stumbling because she was scared, so scared, about what might or might not happen.

Here it was. Not as bad as she'd thought, considering he'd told her he rented. A smallish terraced house which was, apparently, divided into two. Dan's was the front door in the basement down some black steps with wallflowers in a window box. Nice touch. Or was that the girlfriend he'd fleetingly mentioned but not referred to again?

"Becky!" He was there within seconds of her lifting the door knocker, wearing pale blue jeans and a black silk shirt, open at the neck. Something inside her caved in and she could barely make it over the doorstep.

"Careful." He put a hand out as she stumbled. "Sorry. It's a loose piece of carpet. Been meaning to get it fixed."

The touch of his hand burned her arm and to cover her confusion, she tried to take her coat off, fumbling with the arms. "Here. Let me take it."

For a minute, she'd thought he'd said "Take you". The tremor in his voice made her realise he was nervous too.

"Something smells delicious," she babbled awkwardly.

"M&S. I'm afraid I haven't been doing much cooking since I've been on my own. Please, come and sit down. We're almost ready to eat."

We should have gone to a restaurant, she thought, perching on the edge of a pale wooden sofa (mail order catalogue?). This was too intimate. And he was gabbling. Even worse, he was piling the food on her

435

plate. There was no sign of a dining-room table and it looked like they were going to be eating on their laps.

"Cod mornay," he said, watching her pick at it. "I know you're vegetarian but this is all right, isn't it?"

Why was it that people thought fish was different from meat?

He leapt up. "How stupid of me! You don't eat fish either, do you? I remember now. Look, I've got some cheese. At least I think I have somewhere. And there's definitely an egg. I could do a mean omelette!"

"Very mean with one egg!"

There was the split second of a pause before they both burst out laughing. "Listen, I'm too wound up to eat either." He put a hand on her shoulder and she almost jumped apart with the electricity. "How about toast?"

She opened a cupboard door. "You wouldn't happen to have some peanut butter, would you?"

He grinned. "Are you kidding? Adore the stuff. Providing it's the crunchy variety."

"Exactly!"

Relief flooded through her. It was going to be all right.

"So the children are with your mother?"

She nodded.

"And you don't have any plans to return home?"

Was he digging?

"I don't know, Dan. I just don't know. I feel Steve has let me down. He should have been more understanding. I've lost my job and the nanny has gone. What am I going to do?"

"I've told you. There might be something going at the magazine. An editorial assistant. I know it's not what you're used to, Becky. But at least it would be something until another post came up. Email me your CV and I'll see if I can pull some strings." He grinned again. "After all, I am the boss."

The publisher of some trade magazine that no one had ever heard of?

"Thanks." She helped herself to more peanut butter. OK, so she'd already put on half a stone since being sacked but so what? It wasn't as though Steve ever noticed her.

"Tell me about you."

He put the lid back on the peanut butter jar, carefully wiping off the excess round the rim. For some reason, that irritated her. "Me? Not a lot to tell really. After uni, I joined the company's trainee scheme and worked my way up. I wanted to get into music journalism but that hasn't happened — yet. You have to take what you get in this market."

No need to remind her.

"And your girlfriend?" There. She'd said it.

"Karen?" Dan stood up, to put the peanut butter jar back in the cupboard. "Not much to tell really. We'd been together for nearly nine months which is quite good for me."

"I thought you said it was three years!"

His eyes flickered. "We've known each other that long but it's only been serious for nine months.

437

Besides, it wasn't right." He sat down opposite her again on the sofa. "No one has been. That is . . ."

Becky stood up. "Sorry. Can you tell me where the loo is?"

"Of course." Immediately the stilted tone at the beginning of the evening returned. "I should have shown you before. This way."

The loo seat was up and there were only a couple of squares of loo paper left on the roll. Becky felt a lurch of longing for her own bathroom at home with the framed children's scrawlings.

Sitting on the seat (which she would have liked to have lined with paper if there had been enough to spare), she wondered what on earth she was doing here.

You're crazy, Rebecca Hastings. Absolutely crazy. Mum and Janie are right. You can't throw it all away just because you've got the hots for some grown-up kid who doesn't even have a dining-room table. Besides, if you were serious, you'd have let him say his piece about no one being right for him apart from you. That's what he was going to say but you hadn't wanted him to say it. Well you had but . . .

"Are you OK in there?"

Had she really been there for 25 minutes? "Yes, thanks. I mean, actually, not really." She coughed. That was it! That's how she'd get out of it. "Sorry but I don't feel that great. I'll be out in a minute."

He'd understood. All too well. Yes of course he'd take her back if she didn't feel well. No, he wouldn't dream of her going back alone. She didn't think it was the peanut butter, did she? He'd bought it ages ago . . .

Thank God. They were outside her own house now. She'd just say goodbye — brush his cheek if necessary — and then spend another night at home alone before going back to Oxford in the morning. After that, she'd ring Steve and . . .

"Steve!"

Omigod, it was her husband all right, fumbling in his jacket pocket for his keys and looking as startled to see her as she was to see him. His gaze flitted quickly from her to Dan who was helping her out of the taxi, hand on her shoulder. And she knew immediately from the look on his face that he'd got the wrong idea.

"Steve." She touched his arm but he stepped back as though recoiling. "I haven't been well. Dan, a colleague, brought me back and . . ."

Steve was fixing Dan with a gimlet look. "We've met before, haven't we?"

Dan nodded, his Adam's apple bobbing nervously up and down.

"Where are the children?" He was speaking to her as though she was a stranger.

"At Mum's. I'm going down in the morning."

"Fine."

Forget the stranger. More like the Inland Revenue.

"I'll book into a hotel until the morning and then come back."

"No. Steve. Don't be daft. It's not what you think."

"Isn't it?" He moved further back as though he couldn't bear to be anywhere near her. "My wife gets herself sacked by doing something incredibly stupid. Then she takes the kids off to her mother's and is never

439

there when I ring. I get a phone call from Janie, begging me to ring and telling me in coded terms that if I don't do something fast, it may be too late. And now suddenly, I realise what she means."

"Dan, tell him!" She glanced behind her but the taxi and Dan had gone.

"Steve, please." She pulled at his sleeve but he pushed her away.

"I'm sorry, Becky. But you're right. We both need a bit of breathing space until we decide exactly what to do."

Omigod. Whatamigoingtodo? Becky sat in the middle of the playroom, surrounded by the children's toys, listening to the silence. It was two o'clock in the morning. There was no way she could sleep. She'd never heard Steve speak like that before and it chilled her to the bone. If she didn't have him, she wouldn't have anyone. No one else would do; he was the father of her children. No one else could step into those shoes.

So that's how Mum felt. That was why Mum had never quite got over her father, even though she'd been the one who'd done the leaving. Suddenly it all made sense. Poor Mum. And she'd been so hard on her. If only she could ring her but a call at this time of night might wake up the children.

But she could ring Dad. For a minute, Becky felt like a child. Daddy. He'd come round. He'd hold her in his arms and say it was all right. He'd . . .

"Hello?"

Why did that woman always have to answer?

"Is Dad there?"

"Becky?" The voice had clearly been woken up. "No, he's away on business. Is something wrong?"

"Yes!" To her horror, Becky felt the grief pour out of her mouth. "Yes," she sobbed, hot tears running down her cheeks and into her mouth. "Everything. Everything's horribly wrong."

How had this happened? Within half an hour of that phone call, Monique had turned up at the front door, not in her usual perfect outfit with concrete make-up but in a kaftan-like thing without any make-up on at all. Somehow she looked more attractive than normal.

"You poor thing," she had soothed, taking her into her arms. Frozen, Becky had allowed her stepmother-to-be to hug her in a vice-like grasp that she couldn't have got out of if she'd wanted.

"Tell me what happened," she'd said softly.

So Becky had. And instead of saying anything, as she'd expected, Monique had just nodded and let her get it all out.

"Sometimes," she said slowly, "we do things we shouldn't do for our men."

Becky listened, stunned, aware this was the first time she had ever heard Monique speak naturally without making her feel as though she was putting on an act.

"That's why I needed the money."

What?

"Can't you see?" Monique pulled back her hair and almost pushed her face into Becky's. "I had my eyes

441

done and my neck. That's where I've been for the past few weeks. In Switzerland."

Talk about a facelift too far! No wonder her eyebrows now had a permanently surprised expression. Still, at least she didn't look like a bowl of Eton Mess any more.

"I did it for your dad because I wanted to look good for him at the wedding. I know I shouldn't have made you pay me over that magazine stuff. But it was business. Shit happens in business. And before you ask, I did give the money to my clients and I took a cut. In more ways than one."

Monique gave an almost-feminine smile. "Of course it also helped that they're finally sorting out my hormone problems. Turns out I've got something called polycystic ovaries. Don't be worried. It's treatable but it was responsible, as you might have noticed, for my weight gain and that facial hair which is — as you can see — all gone!"

She patted Becky's knee. "Now, as for your problems, I have a suggestion. Work for me! I need an assistant, and a journalist with your experience would be invaluable. Think about it, Becky. Think about it."

CHAPTER
FORTY-SIX

Helen

"I saw your daughter last night."

They had barely sat down before the wretched woman had launched into her stepmother one-upmanship.

"Did you?" asked Helen carefully, wishing she'd worn her smart black trousers instead of the mail-order cotton skirt that she should have sent back because the A-line shape really didn't suit her. And why did Monique seem different?

"Yes." Monique leaned over and patted her arm as though they were old friends. Helen flinched. "Seemed in rather a bad way, between you and me."

This was too much! "I'm well aware of that. Becky has been staying with me for the past few weeks along with my grandchildren."

That grin again! She could almost throttle it. "No need to sound so stiff, Helen. We're almost family now. We should work together, don't you think? Actually, Becky confided in me — no, don't look jealous. She rang to speak to her father and he wasn't there so I went round to the London house."

Helen felt dizzy. When Becky had rung that morning, she'd sounded perfectly calm. More in control in fact than she'd heard her for some time. She was getting the Oxford train that afternoon, if that was all right. Something about having another job possibility to look into first. It had meant Helen asking Doris if she'd mind looking after the children — she'd offered enough times — so she could keep her appointment with Monique. But now it was all beginning to sound quite a different picture.

"Having problems with her husband, I gather."

How could Becky be so daft as to confide in this woman? Helen's chest ached with hurt.

"Nothing that can't be sorted out." Helen reached for the menu briskly. Food was the last thing on her mind but she needed a distraction. "Every marriage has its hiccups as you will, no doubt, discover. You haven't been married before, have you?"

"No." Another Cheshire grin although there was definitely something different about it from their last encounter. Less wolfish, somehow. "I wanted to wait until I was certain, although I have had a couple of long-term relationships so I know what it's like."

That's like saying you know what it's like to have children because you have a nephew or niece, Helen wanted to say.

"Anyway," said Monique, crossing her legs which somehow looked less hour-glass-like than last time, "I know what it's like to have children because I have two nieces and frankly it's not for me. Stepchildren are a different matter because they're not a full-time commitment. By the way, I don't know if Becky's told you but I offered her a job to help her out."

444

"You offered her a job!" Helen had a sudden urge to yank the thin gold chain round Monique's neck.

"That's right. It would help me out too; Becky has some great contacts as a journalist."

"But she's always said she wouldn't consider PR. The dark side, I believe she called it. Selling your soul to promote products or people you don't always believe in."

Monique laughed with that silly little-girl trill that had grated on her nerves before. "Well, your daughter hasn't exactly turned me down. Said she'd think about it, which is perfectly fair, given the circumstances. Still, it's us I want to talk about today. Not Becky, although of course, she's part of the equation."

Helen was beginning to feel distinctly uncomfortable. She'd come here, determined not to let Monique take the upper hand but that's exactly what she was doing. Acting as though she was in charge instead of walking into a family which had existed quite nicely, more or less in its fractured state, until she'd walked in.

"I'd like us to be friends, Helen." Another tap of the hand although this time Monique had caught her by the wrist. "It's not as though you can see me as a threat. You and Geoff have been over for . . . how many years?"

Helen yanked her hand away. Ouch. It almost hurt, the woman's grip was so strong. "When you have been married for as long as we were, you are never 'over', as you put it. You are constantly tied together through children. You can never quite have the same relationship with someone if you haven't had babies with them."

Good. She could see Monique definitely wincing. At the same time, she felt a pang of guilt. Not being able to have children would have been something she couldn't have borne. It was one reason why she had felt such empathy for Robin the other day when he'd talked about the pain of not having a family.

"Ah, but I'm going to have stepchildren now!" Monique was still smiling but less confidently now as she clicked her fingers for the waiter. "And the wonderful thing about that is that they're grown up so there won't be the usual horrid spats and custody weekends. And I've got step-grandchildren too!"

She leaned over the table. "Aren't Daisy and Ben delicious? I could just eat them!"

Get off them, Helen wanted to yell. They're mine — not yours.

"Ah, good. Here's a waitress at last. What are you going to have, Helen?"

Taking charge again. Christ, this woman was insufferable. Geoff had hated pushy women when they'd been married. How did he put up with her?

"Just the soup, please."

"Not hungry?" Monique raised an eyebrow. Something was definitely different about her face. "I'll have a green salad, please." She winked at Helen. "Sticking to my pre-wedding diet, as you can see. I've managed to lose quite a bit."

If she was fishing for compliments, she wasn't going to get any from her.

"What I really want to know," said Monique before the waiter had barely left the table, "is why your marriage went wrong."

What?

"I know it might seem slightly intrusive but it would help me." Monique was sitting back now in her chair, eyeing her shrewdly. "Geoff said you'd just drifted apart. That you had the children and he had his work and you simply stopped communicating. Is that right?"

Was it? Possibly, although she hated the idea of Geoff telling Monique as much.

"Sort of, I suppose. Geoff was always back late and that didn't help."

"Difficult for him, though, if he was working. It's why I've never had children myself. I never had time to fit them in." Her eyes narrowed. "So there wasn't anyone else then, Helen?"

Was there no bounds to this woman's nosiness? Or the way she slung words like daggers.

"No." Why couldn't she have sounded firmer? "Why?"

"Just wondered." Monique was looking at her, not letting her gaze slip. "That's all."

"She sounds awful." Robin nuzzled her hair. They were lying in bed which was where Helen had fled to, straight after lunch with Monique. Of course, she'd dropped off at Doris's first to collect the children but they were making fudge in her kitchen.

"We don't want to go, Gran," Ben had said.

447

"Let them stay a bit." Doris, who was wrapped in a red and black apron, looked brighter than Helen had seen since her brother had died. "Maurice and I used to love cooking. I'd forgotten what fun it was."

She was becoming redundant, Helen had told herself before pulling up outside the Old Rectory. Her daughter was confiding in her stepmother to be and it probably wouldn't be long until her grandchildren did the same. Her former husband was getting married again and her son had built another life for himself in Australia.

As soon as Robin opened the door and gently shepherded her upstairs, she felt better again. Now, as she lay by his side, she felt complete.

"Sure Sylvia is all right on her own?" she whispered.

He stroked her hair again before bending down to kiss her shoulders. "I've told you. She's in the conservatory. Asleep in her chair. She likes it there because she can look out on to the garden. And it's so warm today, a real Indian summer."

In another life at another time, she could perhaps have been friends with Sylvia. Maybe they might have been neighbours. They could have swapped plants, had tea together. Once upon a time, she'd never thought she was the type to be the other woman. But then again, what was the type?

"What are we going to do?"

She'd been asking herself that question from the second he had touched her but hearing him ask too, made it seem more real. "I don't know."

"I could leave Sylvia but . . ."

"No. Sorry, I didn't mean to shout. It's just that . . . well someone else said that to me once. And he didn't. Men don't. It's the oldest line in the book and besides, I don't want to be the other woman."

"You're not." He was burying his face in her breasts. "I told you. Our marriage was over years ago . . . Christ, what was that!"

Robin was up before she had a chance to take in the noise. A strange screaming noise as though from a bird but not quite. Instinct made them both move towards the open window. A small dot was speeding in slow motion towards the pond at the bottom of the garden. A dot with what looked like a shock of red of hair on top.

"I left the door open! Christ, I left the door open because it was so warm."

For a second, they both stood there, frozen in shock. Then Helen found herself leaping down the stairs, three at a time, and out the back door, racing, running, her heart bashing painfully against her ribs. "Sylvia," she called out. "Sylvia!"

And then she saw it. A black shape in front of the chair. Dandy! But she'd left him in the kitchen. Had he got out too? Sweet Jesus. His lead was entangled in the chair. He was pulling Sylvia towards the pond!

"Dandy. Stop!"

Robin was with her now, as they raced down the lawn.

"It's Dandy," she gasped. "His lead. "No. *No!*"

There was a terrible splash as the chair hit the water.

"Get her out, Robin. Get her out!"

449

Frozen with cold, her hands disentangled the lead from the chair to release Dandy who was jumping around so much she could hardly see Sylvia.

"Let me help!"

She'd forgotten how deep the pond was. Frantically treading water, she tried to help Robin but it was so difficult. Once, twice, he almost lost her but then she could see him taking his wife's head against his shoulder and swimming backwards towards the shore.

"Is she all right?"

Robin was breathless, unable to answer. Sylvia was slumped on the ground, stomach down; desperately, she tried to turn her over but she was too heavy.

"Call the ambulance!" yelled Robin.

He had turned her now and was blowing through his wife's mouth, pressing down on her chest at the same time. Sylvia's face was a horrific mottled shade of blue and purple.

Where was her mobile? She had a dim recollection of leaving it by the bed. Horrified, she began running up the lawn towards the house phone, Dandy racing behind her.

CHAPTER
FORTY-SEVEN

Mel

"And that," said Mel, taking a finger of shortbread for Dutch courage, "is exactly what happened between Mr Hastings and me."

"I see."

The archdeacon ("I've told you before, dear, call me Tom") helped himself to the last piece and chewed thoughtfully. When he spoke, there was a small crumb left on the outside of his mouth and just like last time, her motherly intuition made her want to lean across and brush it off instead of concentrating on what he was saying. Anything to get away from what was happening. Perhaps that was how Josh felt. Maybe that's why he was so rebellious; to shut out the things he had to face up to.

"When I was your age," said Tom slowly, "there was a certain parishioner who took a shine to me."

And did you feel the same way, Mel wanted to ask.

"And at times, I felt the same way."

The silence was tangible.

"What happened?"

"It made me question my values." The archdeacon picked up his tea cup, made as though he was going to drink it and then put it down again. "I was engaged to my wife by then."

This time Mel made herself bite her tongue.

"Other people noticed." He smiled ruefully. "Parishioners tend to do that. And I was called in for a chat by my superior, much as we are doing now."

It was no good. She had to ask. "And you chose to give her up? The other woman, I mean, not your wife."

"No, I didn't." Another rueful smile and a dab of the mouth with the napkin which, slightly to her disappointment, removed the crumb which had made him seem refreshingly vulnerable. "I chose to give him up."

Wow. She hadn't been expecting that one. Tom was a big man; his voice was deep and he had black curly hairs on his arm. Somehow, this didn't fit.

"Not of course, that things had gone that far. It was all in the mind, you see, Mel. But I never quite forgot him. Loving someone mindfully can be far deeper than the physical type."

"And did you regret it?"

Now she really had gone too far. Or had she? The archdeacon was smiling wistfully into the distance, beyond the pale duck blue wallpaper and the framed photographs of his sons and grandchildren. "At times, yes, I did."

He was looking at her now. Really looking. "In this job, Mel, we need to be as innocent as doves and wise as serpents. So I would urge you to think carefully, Mel, before you make a decision. Weigh each side up. I can see you care for this man, whatever you are telling yourself and me. Does he feel the same way? And what effect would it have on both your families?"

Mel tried to answer but nothing would come out.

"More tea?" She had to hand it to him. Tom knew how to handle situations. Silently, she handed across her cup and saucer. He filled it carefully. "By the way, Mel, I've been meaning to ask you. Have you come to a decision about Visits With a Difference?"

The following day was Drop-In Day at St Giles. As usual, there were a couple of regulars, including the church wardens. Amy used to refer to them as traffic wardens, Mel recalled with a smile.

"I did ask some of the others to come but they were busy," apologised one.

Mel didn't need to be told this was code for "They won't turn up because they expect you to come individually to their homes and have a slice of stodgy fruit cake." Couldn't they add up? She had three parishes to cover for Lord's sake. If she had fruit cake with all the old regulars, she wouldn't have time to do anything else. And she'd weigh about three stone more than she did already.

"These Drop-Ins aren't working, are they?" she heard herself say.

The warden shrugged bravely. "Give it another month or so to see if it warms up. By the way, have you heard the news about the Old Rectory?"

"No." Mel glanced at her watch. Another half an hour and she'd call it a day. Maybe visit Amy early.

"There's been an accident." The churchwarden's eyes dropped but her voice sounded excited. "The new people — the Michaels — well, the woman, at any rate, drowned in the pond."

"How awful! But I thought she was in a wheelchair."

"She is. Was. Apparently the gardener's dog dragged her down the garden."

Dear God. What are you trying to do now? Or is this one of your "I'm not a puppeteer" moments?

"I'd better go over there now."

"Not sure it's worth bothering. He's gone apparently. Left the house after it happened and hasn't been seen since." The warden lowered her voice. "There is a rumour — and of course one shouldn't listen to these things — that he had something to do with it."

The warden was right. There was no one at home. Mel scribbled a note, pushed it through the door and set off for the hospital. En route, there was a bleep on her phone, indicating someone had left a text but she resisted the temptation to stop until she'd got there.

"Hvn't hrd fm u 4 ages. R u ok? G."

DELETE.

"Hello, darling, how are you?"

She smoothed back her daughter's hair and pulled up a chair. "Anything interesting been happening?"

Good thing no one was around.

"You've had some more messages on your Facebook; don't think I'm prying but Josh checks them for you and replies on your behalf. I can't tell you how many people are thinking of you."

454

This felt like praying. You know you ought to believe someone is listening but at times — quite a few times actually — you couldn't help thinking they weren't.

"Oh and the archdeacon called me in, accusing me of having an affair with a parishioner. I'm not, of course, so you needn't worry."

This was crazy but in a way it made her feel much better.

"Josh has got a tattoo on his right arm; I didn't even bother making a fuss about it this time in case it made a difference but it didn't."

Silence. What else did she expect?

"I know I probably shouldn't be telling you all this stuff but you're always saying I don't treat you like an adult. Well now I am."

Say something, Amy. Say something.

"In fact, there is something important I need to ask you." Christ, tell me how to say this. "Your dad thinks we ought to sign a form, agreeing that your organs can be donated in case . . . But I can't help wondering, if push came to shove, the hospital might save your organs and not you. Of course, that probably wouldn't happen but there was a big piece about that in the *Sunday Times* recently. What do you think? Chew it over. By the way, I've brought you the latest copy of *Charisma*. I read it first; I think I'm getting into it."

There was a noise outside, like the clinking of a trolley. "You'll never guess where I'm going tomorrow. Tell you what. Let's keep it a surprise and then I'll have something to tell you next time I come. Bye, darling, sleep well."

★   ★   ★

She'd been to a prison before during her student days when she'd signed up as a prison visitor. But she'd been assigned a middle-aged woman who had been imprisoned for tax fraud. Mel had found it hard to find sympathy for her and to her shame, had allowed her visits to dwindle. Still, it had been useful to put on her CV at the time.

This prison was different. Bigger with high walls with barbed wire on top. Following the instructions, she'd parked in the visitors' car park and made her way to the main gate. There were others waiting; a couple of women with green-streaked hair and baggy purple leggings clutching kids in shell suits. An older couple, in matching camel coats; she was in a skirt and he wore crisp grey trousers (Parents perhaps?). A young girl with an older man. And three teenagers who might or might not belong to the parents.

No sign, thank goodness, of Kevin's mother.

"How do we get in?" she asked the woman in the camel coat.

She could feel her eying her white vicar collar deferentially.

"Press the bell." The woman looked nervously at her husband. "We've already done that but no one's answered yet."

Mel shivered. How awful for visitors to wait outside in the cold for their visits. Did they do it every week or was it more limited? She glanced up at the security fence. How did anyone ever escape? Yet it happened sometimes.

A small wooden hatch in the huge gate suddenly opened and then shut again. The door opened and a grim-faced prison officer allowed them in, one by one. Mel stepped over the high doorstep and found herself in what seemed like an open lobby with a high ceiling. At the other end was another gate through which she could see a further space leading to what looked like the prison; a huge square building that might have been an office block built around the seventies.

"ID, please."

They were queuing up at the window and Mel fumbled for her passport which she'd been warned to bring. The prison officer on the other side eyed it sharply, her eyes travelling from Mel's face to the passport and back again.

"Thanks, vicar."

A couple of faces swivelled round. Mel was used to that.

It seemed an age until all their IDs were checked but finally someone said, "This way."

Through the gates, across the windy forecourt, through another pair of gates, each of which had to be unlocked by the prison officer in front (there was also one behind them) and then into a large Portakabin. Again the doors were unlocked before they went in and locked after they got in.

Mel was beginning to feel claustrophobic. What if there was a fire? Supposing one of the inmates started getting nasty. How would they get out?

She took a seat, nervously looking around. On the stage in front, sat a line of men and her eye travelled

457

along them, wondering, hoping he wasn't there. Was that him at the end? If so, Kevin looked different. His hair had been cut short. He was wearing bright green trousers like the others and a grey shirt.

"Mel Thomas?" A tall, distinguished man — about her age — in a grey shirt with a dog collar was hovering. "I'm Father John. I'm the priest here." He shook her hand warmly. "Heard you were coming. Please sit down again. Looks like we're just about to start."

"What actually happens?"

Father John bent his head to whisper. "They do this twice a year. The men choose a theme and then they read poems or show their art work."

"What's today's theme?"

"Sorry." Father John put his finger up in a shush gesture. "Looks like they're beginning."

Mel sat motionless. It had started with an extraordinary poem by a young man who looked as though he could have been the boy next door. He didn't read it out. He'd memorised it, word for word. And it wasn't trite or flannelly. It was about the different ways that people said sorry and about those who meant it and those who didn't. At the end, everyone clapped. How could she not join in?

"What did he do?" Mel whispered into Father John's ear.

He raised his eyebrows. "Best not to ask unless they tell you."

She felt reproved but at the same time, wanted to know. Sorry was all very well if he'd shoplifted but if it was something else . . .

The next group of men on the stage were holding up pictures. Two were watercolours. The one in the middle, charcoal. "These are the three stages of 'Sorry'," said the older one on the right. His eyes seemed to look straight at her and Mel shivered, silently thinking he definitely wasn't the kind of person she'd want to bump into on the high street at night.

"Sorry," he continued, his eyes still on hers, "is acceptance of what you've done wrong, like; promising you won't do it again; and trying to make it right, like."

The pictures weren't bad but she didn't applaud quite as loudly.

What was happening now? A band? They were grinning, laughing as they set up their instruments on stage. For a minute, she could imagine Josh amongst them. But when they started, she felt herself being transported into another world. One of them — the one playing the saxophone — was amazing.

"Armed robbery," whispered Father John.

"All of them?"

He nodded. "Apart from . . ."

They'd finished. Mel's hands were beginning to sting with clapping. But then the line of boys at the side stood up, including Kevin. Her chest began to pound.

That's the boy who ran over my daughter, she wanted to say.

What were they doing? Someone — an older man in a smart jacket and tie — was putting an empty chair in front of them on the stage.

"Good afternoon, everyone. My name is Frank and I'm the drama psychotherapist here. One of the exercises we do here is to imagine someone in that empty chair and talk to them."

What was he on, as Amy might have said if she'd been here.

"Today's theme, as you know, is 'Sorry', and the boys have each chosen an imaginary person in the chair to apologise to. So without any further ado, I'll let them get on with it."

The first boy — who looked younger than Kevin — stood up nervously. "I want to apologise to my nan." There was a little wave from a woman in front of her who looked more like her age than a grandmother.

He turned back to the chair. "Nan, you did so much for me, bringing me up and all that when my mum left. And I did nothing but give you a load of trouble. I'm sorry, nan, I really am and I'm going to make it up to you when I get out."

There was a choking sound in front as though the woman was trying not to cry. This woman had brought up her grandson. That couldn't be easy. He didn't look any older than Josh.

The second man was older; more like his early thirties. "I want to apologise to my partner, Sandie."

One of the peroxide women who had come in with her gave a little wave.

"Hi, Sandie. Didn't see you there for a minute."

He sounded relieved.

"Talk to the chair, Dan," said Frank quietly.

"Oh yeah. Sorry."

He faced the empty seat. "I want to say sorry, Sandie, for the stuff I did which meant you've been at home on your own with our lovely little boy. Being in here has made me realise I shouldn't have done that stuff and I'm going to try — I promise — to wipe the slate clean."

More clapping. Mel felt slightly sick. Saying sorry was easy if you ended up in a place like this.

"Do they mean it?" she whispered to Father John.

He shrugged. "Some do. Some don't."

Omigod. He was coming out now. Standing. Looking at her. Mel felt as though every pair of eyes was on her. That's the vicar. The one who can't forgive.

Suddenly she felt cold. Very cold. If it wasn't for the locked doors, she might have done a runner. Where were her trainers now?

"I'm Kevin." He was turning to the chair now, thank God. "I want to say sorry to someone who can't hear me. A kid called Amy who isn't much younger than me. She was crossing the road, see, and I was going too fast. I should have stopped when I heard her hit the car . . ."

Mel winced.

"But I didn't. I just went on because I thought that if I did that, it might not have happened. I might have hit the kerb or maybe a bird or something else."

There was a chilled silence.

"But then I did stop. I went back."

His voice quavered. "It was too late. I saw the ambulance. They said I couldn't have done anything about it anyway. She just came in front of me, see. But I should have stopped. And I shouldn't have been driving on my own because I hadn't passed my test properly. Only the theory, see. I wasn't insured either, like." He was crying openly. Not loudly. Soft sobs that wracked his body. "And I'm sorry, Amy. I'm really sorry."

"It's all right."

She heard herself speak as though it was someone else.

"It's all right."

Mel stood up, aware that all eyes really were on her this time.

"I'm Amy's mother. It wasn't all your fault, Kevin. It was mine too. I texted her, you see, at the same time she was crossing the road and that's why she wasn't concentrating. I wanted to know she had got there safely."

No one spoke, but the way he was looking at her!

"Sometimes, Kevin," she said quietly. "It takes two. I'm sorry too."

And as she sat down, she suddenly saw Kevin's mother, a few yards away, beaming, smiling, putting her thumbs up.

"You did the right thing." Father John put a hand briefly on hers. "Well done. Just listen to the way they're clapping."

CHAPTER
FORTY-EIGHT

Janie

Blimey. They don't build vicarages the way they used to. She could still remember a vicar living in the Old Rectory before Becky and her family moved in. That was a real house. This could almost pass for a piebald brick council place.

Janie glanced down at the address which the police had given her. Was this it? As usual, the words were dancing around as though challenging her. Just as well she'd memorised it. She'd learned, years ago, to use the parts of her that did work to make up for the bits that didn't.

Hope this kid liked the HMV voucher she'd got him. Maybe she should have got something boring instead, like a pen which might have been a more sensible present for the responsible son of a vicar. And perhaps she shouldn't have worn her fucshia-pink bubble skirt; it was a bit short.

Janie stood on the door step which, surprisingly, had a couple of cobwebs on the porch bit. Somehow you expected vicars to be perfect. The door bell didn't seem to work either and the knocker was one of those daft flaps which didn't make much of a noise and trapped her finger. Buck up or she'd be late for Linda who was still going on about their poaching, not to mention another telephone conference with Monique about the ice sculptures. Honestly, the sooner this bloody wedding was over, the better.

"Hello?"

Janie stared at the woman in front of her, wearing skinny jeans, grey trainers and a t-shirt with words that looked like Mum On The Run.

"It's you! Hi, Mel."

It still seemed odd calling the vicar by her first name but she'd insisted from their very first funeral.

"Janie?"

"I didn't realise Josh was your son. Is he in?"

To her surprise, Mel groaned. "What's he done now?"

"Nothing. I mean, he *has* but it's fantastic. Great. Look!" Janie held up her purse and phone. "I lost these weeks ago on a train and your son must have found it. Handed it in to the police station, he did, and everything was still inside it. Well, apart from a tenner which I must admit I could do with right now but no one's tried to buy anything on the cards. Amazing for today, don't you think?"

Mel nodded. She didn't seem that pleased, thought Janie.

"Want to come in? Sorry. It's a bit of a mess. I'll call him down."

Janie looked round the tiny hall which was littered with shoes and a tennis racquet and someone's jacket thrown over the bottom of the banisters. It made Mel seem even more human, just like the way she was yelling up the stairs, like her own mum had yelled at her at that age.

"Josh. Come down, will you? There's someone to see you."

As soon as this huge gangly teenager appeared, shuffling down towards her, Janie was glad she hadn't got the pen. What did his t-shirt say? I Rock Catholic Chicks. No. She must be misreading that one.

"Wot?"

"Josh!"

Janie had to resist a giggle. She could remember that tone from her own mum so well. It was a "Will you behave in front of guests" voice.

"I just came to say thank you," said Janie. "The police said you handed in my wallet and phone."

"Oh that. Yeah."

He addressed the ground so it was difficult to hear what he was saying.

"How did you find it, Josh?" asked Mel in what seemed like an oddly sharp voice.

"One of my friends found it, like, on a train. He had it for a bit cos we forgot to hand it in but then I sat on it in his room and thought we ought to do something about it. Sorry it's a bit late."

For someone who looked like that, the sentence sounded extremely articulate.

"It's OK. The important thing is I've got them back, especially the phone. I had all my numbers on it."

All her numbers including Lars which, for some reason, wasn't ringing out now. Typical. It clearly wasn't meant. At least that's probably what the *Big Issue* woman would say.

"I've got you a small present to say thank you." Janie held out the envelope. Whoops. She must have doodled on it without thinking. "Sorry about the face. It's actually an HMV voucher."

"Cool."

"And I'd like you to have this too."

Janie took out a crumpled ten pound note. She couldn't afford it but somehow it seemed right.

"No, honestly, I don't want that." He shook his head so his wild hair flew out.

"Please."

Another wild shake. "No. It's OK."

He was shuffling back up the stairs and Janie glanced at Mel who'd been standing, mouth open.

"Will you give it to him later?"

"He won't take it." Mel was still looking up the stairs. "He's very stubborn. And unpredictable. In fact, I haven't heard him say so much in one sentence before. Not since Amy . . ."

She stopped and Janie felt a pang of embarrassment. Marjorie had told her about Amy. She was the vicar's daughter who'd been run over in a hit and run and was still in a coma.

"I'm sorry," she said awkwardly. "Well, better go. See you at the next wedding or funeral, I suppose." Damn. Shouldn't have said the funeral bit. "I like your t-shirt, by the way. Mum On The Run?"

"Thanks. My daughter gave it to me. It came with a novel about school runs."

Her eyes fell on the crystal round her neck. "I like your necklace."

"Thanks. It was a present. Meant to have healing properties, apparently. Not that there's anything wrong with me, physically. But it can't do any harm, can it?"

"I wouldn't think so." The vicar's eyes had come over all dreamy as though she was somewhere else. "Healing comes in all kinds of ways, Janie. In fact, nothing would surprise me any more."

Maybe no one's life was easy, thought Janie as she headed for Linda's office in town. Not even a vicar's. You could have cut the atmosphere in that house with a knife. Still, she had enough problems of her own, like Mac who was still ringing her every hour and Linda who had asked her to come in for a "meeting" after that ridiculous poaching claim.

The couple in question had, they'd assured her, told Linda that they'd gone to her of their own free will, so what did she want now?

"Ah, Janie. Thanks for coming in."

Janie sat down in Linda's posh shop. If only she and Marje could have somewhere like this. A high street spot. They could really do something with it.

Linda had clearly slapped another layer of foundation concrete on, but underneath her crocodile smile was the same. "I asked you to come in because I have a proposition."

Proposition? What was she on about?

"Mr and Mrs Wilson explained the little misunderstanding so we don't need to go down that road now."

467

She might have known better than to have expected an apology. "But I'd like to suggest something. You've done very well, Janie. Very well. You and your partner, Miriam."

"Marjorie."

"Sorry."

That was one word she hadn't heard her use before.

"You have some very unusual ideas, Janie, which, I must admit, I didn't think would work at first but appear to be very successful. That Elton John theme the other month got a picture in the local paper, didn't it?"

Not surprising really since the groom insisted on dressing up as Elton and having Elton songs instead of hymns. Marjorie's idea to hire a grand piano for the church and also hire Elvis lookalikes for the ushers, had been a brilliant stroke. What a combination!

Janie bent her head in acknowledgment.

"That's why I want to suggest a merger."

What?

"Don't you see, Janie? We could pool our experience and share the profits. Not quite 50/50 obviously because, after all, the shop premises are mine. I was thinking more like 70/30. What do you think?"

"A high street shop!" Marjorie tapped her cigarette sharply against the side of her whisky glass instead of the ash tray. "That's not a bad idea, Janie."

"But she wants 70 per cent! Besides, she's a cow. She'd ruin everything; insist on making final decisions and then accuse me of getting everything wrong just like she did before."

Janie started doodling on her wrist. What would her own shop look like? It might have a pretty bow front and maybe some crystals hanging down for good luck. "I can't work for that woman, I really can't."

"Then no one's going to make you, dear." Marjorie patted her hand. "Now before I forget, ring your nice friend Becky, will you? She sounded in a real state."

It wasn't just Becky who was in a state. So was her mum's house and the kids and Helen herself. In fact, she hardly recognised any of them when she cycled round to the house.

"What's happened?"

Becky dragged her into the kitchen where she stepped gingerly over the kids' toys that were lying on the floor. "I haven't heard from Steve since . . . well since he saw me with Dan. Don't look like that. Nothing happened. But I had dinner with him and then he took me home in a taxi and he wasn't coming in but Steve saw us and thought the worst and I haven't heard from him apart from a cold text saying he'll see the kids when he gets back."

"Back from where?"

"I don't know, do I? And then Mum's in real trouble."

"Why?"

"She was doing some gardening for the people who used to live in our old house and Dandy's lead got caught up round this woman's wheelchair and dragged her into the pond."

Fuck.

"It was an accident of course but there's got to be an autopsy."

So that's why Helen had such black shadows under her eyes and had shot back upstairs when Janie had arrived.

"Look, you can't do anything about that but you've got to make Steve see sense."

"I know. But how?"

"Leave it to me. I need to think about it."

It had seemed a good idea at the time. In fact, Janie hadn't even stopped to tell Marjorie where she was going. She'd just got on a train, caught a tube to Steve's office (she'd been there before to meet the two of them for something once), only to be told by a snotty immaculate-looking secretary with pearl-pink acrylic talons that Steve had gone away on business.

She'd managed to convince them it was a matter of life or death — well, Ben could have peritonitis, couldn't he? — which just about persuaded the snotty bitch to tell her which terminal he was flying from and admit that, if she rushed, she might just catch him before boarding a plane to Stockholm.

Why didn't people keep their mobiles on?

The taxi to Heathrow cost a fucking fortune and took longer than she'd realised with the traffic. British Airways check-in desk, the girl had said. That was his flight! And there was the check-in queue! My God, he was there!

"Steve!" She almost jumped into his arms.

"Janie?"

It clearly took him a couple of seconds to register. "What are you doing here?"

"It's Becky." She was tugging at his arm. "She needs you. There's been a terrible mistake. She didn't have a thing with that bloke after all. And Ben. Well Ben's a bit poorly."

His face tightened. "What kind of poorly."

She thought wildly. What did kids get? "Sort of stomach pains. And a really weird rash with yellow spots. And maybe a dash of peritonitis, too."

"But that sounds really serious!" He caught at her sleeve. "Is he in hospital?"

"I think so. Please, Steve, you can't keep going away for work. It's one of the problems. Don't you see?"

He hesitated. "Ben's really ill?"

She nodded. Well, he might be for all she knew. Kids were always getting things. "It's an awful rash, apparently."

"All right. I'll come back with you to Helen's."

"Thank you, Steve. Thank you! You won't regret it, I promise you!"

"Well if you've come all the way up here to find me — which I have to say was a pretty remote chance in these crowds — it had to be serious. How did you get here?"

"By taxi but I can't afford one back so I'll get the express coach."

"Nonsense." He opened his wallet. "I'll call one of our drivers to pick you up."

What a nice man! Even with Ben being ill — or rather not ill — he still thought about others. Did Becky realise how lucky she was?

471

"That would be great! I'm a bit pushed for time to be honest and I've got various work problems to sort out and . . ."

Not her mobile again!

"Janie?" Monique's voice could have out-rivalled Heathrow's tannoy system. "Janie, where the hell are you? You're late."

Late?

"For our ice sculpture meeting."

Enough was enough. "Sod the ice sculptures. Sorry, Monique. But frankly you can find someone else to arrange your wedding."

ONE MONTH TO GO

CHAPTER
FORTY-NINE

Becky

If her mother wasn't in such a state, she'd have taken the kids back to Islington. That would have been the sensible solution. Why not just admit that she'd thrown it all away just because of one stupid fling — which had only been in her head anyway and wouldn't have happened if Steve had been around more.

And now this! Becky glanced at the latest email rejection. Trying to get back into the magazine world was clearly a lost cause. Brian had probably spread the word and now no one wanted to employ her. Making things up was fine but virtually embezzling the magazine budget was another.

She'd just have to swallow her pride and take up Monique's offer. Ohshit. Could she really go into PR? It wasn't just a matter of working for a woman she couldn't stand. It was also giving up that objective stance which journalism gave you and being paid to promote a product like a saleswoman.

Besides, anything was better than being with the children. She was a hopeless mother. Why else would they be running up and down the stairs when they should be asleep?

"Becky?"

Her mother's voice floated down the stairs from her room.

"Becky? Was that the phone?"

"No, Mum. Go back to sleep."

It was only 8p.m. but she'd tried to get everyone to bed early — including her mother. The doctor had given her sedatives which was just as well. And poor old Dandy hadn't left his basket in the corner as though aware that something terrible had happened. He hadn't even farted today.

She'd had to turn away some local reporters too. "Fuck off," she'd told one of them.

"Can't you give us a quote?" one of them had said. "Tell us exactly what happened about the pond tragedy?"

"No, I can't and get out or I'll set one of the kids onto you."

"Becky!" Her mother's voice floated down the stairs again. "Becky, I'm sure I can hear the front door bell."

Oh, for God's sake. Sighing heavily, she flung the door open. If it was another reporter, she'd . . .

"Steve?"

For a minute, she almost didn't recognise him. His face was taut and his eyes bruised — not physically but internally. He seemed to have aged at least five years.

"Can I come in?"

He was looking beyond her as though expecting Dan to be there.

"Sure." She stepped aside. "I've got nothing to hide."

He looked at her as though she was someone else. "I know. Janie told me."

"Janie told you what?"

"Everything." He took off his coat, slinging it familiarly over the banisters.

"About Dan and him not meaning anything. About me and my work. About you feeling awful about your job . . ."

"Well it doesn't take much to see that." She turned her back on him. "Only a husband who doesn't bother."

"I know."

She felt his arms encircle her from behind. "And I'm sorry, Becks. I'm really sorry."

She moved away. "A lot has happened. Did Janie tell you what happened to Mum?"

"Daddy!"

Daisy flew into her father's arms, followed by Ben.

Becky groaned. "I just can't get them to sleep when you're not around."

Steve put his arm round both of them. "It's OK, kids. Dad's back. How's the rash?"

"What rash?"

He grinned. "I had a feeling you might say that. Now tell me about your mother. What's she been up to this time?"

Somehow, after a bottle of wine and a takeaway curry, it was almost all right again. It was as though Sylvia's tragedy — if it could be called that because, as Steve pointed out, the woman had had a pretty lousy existence anyway — had brought them closer together. Even the kids seemed calmer and had actually allowed Steve to take them back to bed.

"So the autopsy's this week? Poor Helen."

Steve had always liked his mother-in-law and, at times, got on better with her than Becky did herself.

Becky nodded. "We had enough trouble with the local paper calling round but now I'm worried the nationals will get on to it, especially after that dog attack the other week. Poor old Dandy. It wasn't his fault."

Steve looked horrified. "No one's suggesting that he should be . . ."

"Don't even say that out loud."

"Sorry."

"No. I'm sorry. I shouldn't have snapped. It's just that Dandy's really getting on and I don't know what Mum would do without him. He's all that's left of the old life before it went wrong."

Steve poured them both another glass of wine. "And now that's what you want to do to our children? Take away the old life, as you put it?"

"No, it's not."

"But you left."

"Only because you were being so unreasonable."

Steve leaned back in his chair. "Don't let's go through all that again. It won't get us anywhere. I've told you. I know I've been travelling too much and I'll try and cut down. But you'll get another job soon."

"Hah! Will I? Take a look at this." She handed him a wodge of printed-out email rejections. "Not great, is it?

And you know what? Most people didn't even bother replying. These are just from the ones who did. I'm just going to have to take Monique up on her offer."

"What offer?"

"Another thing I forgot to tell you. That's what happens, doesn't it, when we don't see each other for weeks. Monique wants me to work for her. Clearly she's just trying to curry favour with dad cos she knows she's partly responsible for me being kicked out of *Charisma*. But it means doing something I never wanted to do, Steve."

There was a silence. Becky reached out to stroke Dandy's damp nose. He always knew when she was upset.

"We'll be behind with our mortgage soon," Steve said quietly.

"I know." Becky put her head in her husband's lap and he tightened his grip around her arm reassuringly. "I know."

As soon as she woke up the next morning, still in Steve's arms but this time in the spare bed with not a centimetre to spare, with the two children wrapped around them both, Becky knew it was going to be all right. The sun was streaming through the window as though it was spring instead of autumn. There was even blossom on the trees outside.

Bleep bleep. Please no. Not a text from Dan. She hadn't heard from him for days now and it would be so unfair if he'd texted just when Steve was there.

"What's that?"

479

She froze. "Just a text."

"Who's it from?"

He still didn't trust her. Shaking, she picked up the mobile and almost slumped in relief. "Janie! She wants to know if we've made up."

"Let me see."

He didn't believe her.

Reluctantly she handed it over.

"Hv u shagged and mde up yt?"

Smiling, Steve handed it back to her. "What are you going to tell her?"

Becky glanced down at Daisy and Ben who were sleeping like puppies.

"That it's time we moved back to our own beds. We need more room."

Steve held out his arm and she nestled into the hollow she knew so well, breathing in his smell gratefully. How could she have ever considered getting close to someone else?

"Hadn't you better check on your mother?"

That's what she loved about Steve. He always thought about others even if they'd both neglected each other in the past.

"You're right. I'll make her a cup of tea. Then we really ought to talk about getting back to London and . . ."

Steve groaned. "Doesn't that mobile of yours ever stop? And I've never known anyone to get so many texts. No wonder you get text thumb."

"Hello?"

This was ridiculous. Why did she keep shaking every time it went? And she could tell from that half-frightened, half-defensive look in Steve's eyes that he still thought it might be Dan. How long was it going to take to get over this? Maybe — a terrible panic gripped her — maybe never.

"Becky?"

For one horrible minute, she thought it might be Dan because the voice was so deep.

"Who's that?"

"Me."

Why did "me" people always expect you to know them?

"Hello, Monique." She could almost feel Steve's shoulders relax from behind. "Listen. I've been thinking. Your job offer. I'd like to accept it but I was wondering about the money side. What exactly would you be paying?"

Out of the corner of her eye, she could see Steve tickling Daisy's feet and making her giggle. Ben started to clamber over his father and she felt a wave of relief. The children needed him. They needed her. They needed two parents for a family just as she had.

"Mum?"

"Inaminute. Sorry, Monique, what was that?"

"I mean, Dad?"

"Yes, Ben."

"I've got something to tell you."

What was the little sneak going to say now? "Monique, can I ring you back?"

"Mum said she missed you when you were away. She cried."

Steve's arm crept round her shoulder. "I missed her too."

"And us?" Daisy elbowed her brother out of the way to take his place.

"Of course."

"But you love us more than her, don't you?"

"I love you all the same." He stopped, sighing. "Is that your mobile again, Becky? Can't you turn it off even in bed?"

"It's Monique again, silly woman." She wanted to laugh; burst into song. Leap out of bed and dance round the room. Steve had missed her! And now, thanks to the kids, he knew she'd missed him! It was going to be all right! "Hello? Hello?"

Later, Becky could remember seeing all those details — Daisy's pink nightdress and Ben's gappy front tooth smile — as though they were printed in her head like a caption, dated with today's date and exact time. The time her world sat still.

"What did you say again?"

All three turned to look at her as though they knew; as though they were actors in a play where the script was in front of them, even though they had to pretend they had never seen it before.

"Dad's had a heart attack," she whispered, dropping the phone. She watched it bounce over the carpet. "He's in hospital. And he's asking for Mum and the vicar."

CHAPTER
FIFTY

Helen

"It's all right, Geoff. I'm here."

The words came out of her mouth before she could stop them but somehow it seemed the most natural thing in the world. This was the man who was the father of her children. The man whom she'd virtually grown up with. The man whom she had stupidly — so stupidly — lost on the way through one simple daft aberration.

"Helen." He opened his eyes. "Thank you."

On the other side of the bed, that Monique woman was bristling and it gave Helen a childish sense of satisfaction.

"I need Mel too."

"Mel?"

"The vicar." Monique almost spat out the word. Goodness! Couldn't she see her husband-to-be was ill?

"I think someone's called her."

Geoff closed his eyes again and nodded. His face was grey and Helen felt a surge of panic. According to the doctor, it was only a mild heart attack but even so.

"You've never had heart problems before. What brought it on?"

"Working too hard." Monique cut in. "Stress. Those arguments over your daughter didn't help, even though I tried to make up by offering her a job."

"Please." Geoff's voice sounded exhausted. "I need to speak to Helen alone."

She looked at Monique. If that woman could shoot from the eyes, she'd be a gonner. "Very well."

Rising, Monique sauntered out of the room. Helen had to hand it to her. She definitely had something and she seemed slimmer too since last time. Almost attractive.

"Helen?"

She moved closer so she could hear him better.

"There's something I need to tell you."

"All right." She took his hand. "And then there's something I need to tell you."

As she left the ward, she almost collided with a tall slim woman with a white dog collar.

"Vicar?" Helen held out her hand. "I don't think we've met. I'm Helen, Geoff's wife. I mean, first wife. Thank God you're here. I mean, thank you."

She looked flummoxed for a vicar. Weren't they meant to be calm rocks of peace at times like this? And she really did look far too pretty for her role with that blonde hair and Dora Copperfield looks.

"Not at all. The nurse said he was in room 8."

Helen nodded. "He's waiting for you."

"Is . . . I mean is . . ."

Somehow, Helen knew exactly what she was trying to say. "No, Monique isn't there. She went out for a bit but she might be back soon."

The vicar nodded. Someone else who couldn't bear her either then. Interesting.

"Mum! Is he all right?"

For a minute, she'd forgotten about Becky. "He's with the vicar." Leading her daughter by the hand, she sat down with her in the side room provided for relatives. "He's talking and I know he'll want to see you."

Becky had clearly been crying. "Is he going to die?"

She'd asked the doctors that question herself. "I don't know, love. But he's stable. That's what they've told me."

"It's all my fault. I kept going on at him about that bloody woman he's meant to be marrying . . ."

"Becky, please." She held her daughter close to her, breathing in her warmth. "All my life, I've felt guilty but now I'm beginning to realise. Guilt doesn't help anyone. Least of all, yourself."

Blast. Not her phone. She should have turned it off. "Helen."

She turned away. "I can't talk."

"But I've got to tell you something!" Robin's voice was insistent. "I've just come from the inquest where they read the autopsy report. Sylvia had a stroke before it happened. They can prove it. She was dead before Dandy dragged her across the lawn."

"Not now, Robin. Please, not now."

"But don't you see what it means for us? We weren't responsible."

"Mum, come on. They're calling us."

"I'm sorry, Robin. I need to go. My husband — I mean ex-husband — needs me."

CHAPTER
FIFTY-ONE

Mel

His eyes lit up when he saw her. Oh, God. Anyone looking would guess immediately. And why did her own heart jump up like that? Do something, Lord. Right now.

"Mel. I'm so glad you're here."

"I only popped in to bring your running shoes. Someone told me you'd be needing them soon."

He tried to grin and then seemed to grimace as though it was uncomfortable. "Only if I get my running partner back. It hasn't been the same without you."

Flirty chat or did he mean it?

"Geoff, you've had a nasty scare. But the doctor told me it was a minor heart attack and you're going to be all right."

"So I gather — although it might mean postponing the wedding. Monique's not too pleased about that."

Yes. Yes. No. No.

"Actually, that's not what I needed to tell you." His smile stopped. "Shut that door behind you, can you? I don't want anyone else to hear."

She couldn't believe it. Yet why not? It was her life after all. And yet it wasn't.

Please let her still be there, she prayed. Great. She was. Sitting in the corner of the room with that ghastly woman — no, that wasn't fair — next to her. Mind you, something was different about Monique. Shock seemed to have changed the shape of her face. She almost looked pretty.

"Vicar!" Both women stood up but it was Monique who spoke. "How is he?"

Mel nearly burst out laughing. All three of them, outside the hospital room of a man who meant different things to all of them. God certainly knew how to pull a punch.

"Almost chatty, actually. In fact, Monique, if you don't mind, I need a quiet word with Helen."

The animosity almost scalded her back, as she led Helen out of the room. "You're a braver woman than me," whispered Helen.

Mel warmed to her. "Only because of my plastic necklace."

Helen smiled.

"Let's sit down here, in the corridor. Round the corner where there isn't anyone else." She led the way to a pair of steel chairs. "I think I ought to start by saying Geoff's told me everything."

Helen's smile instantly vanished. "What do you mean, everything?"

Mel took her hand. "He told me what you've just told him. About why you really left him."

"Oh, God." Helen took her hand away. "I feel so ashamed."

"No." Mel took her hand again and held it firmly. "You did what many of us would have done. You had a husband who didn't show you much affection. He admitted that to me. He was never there. He worked too hard."

"But it doesn't justify falling for someone else."

Helen's voice was so quiet that Mel could hardly hear. "I almost did the same."

"You what?"

Mel heard someone else speaking through her mouth. "I almost did the same. My husband works away from home. My daughter is in a coma. My son is a challenge. And I nearly fell for someone else."

Who was it, she could see Helen trying not to say.

"But you didn't."

"In my head, I did. According to the Bible, that's just as bad."

"But you didn't actually do it."

"No." Thank God.

"But that's not all, is it?"

Helen shook her head.

"Look, I heard about the autopsy. Sylvia didn't die because of the dog. She had a stroke first."

Helen lifted her head. "But you don't get it. I love Robin. We were . . . that's why it happened. Why we weren't there to stop it. We were . . . we were in the bedroom."

She hadn't seen that one coming.

"I'm sorry. But God forgives, you know."

"Does he?"

488

"Yes. Don't you see, Helen. You've got to give up this guilt or you won't be any good to anyone. Not to your children, not to Robin, not to yourself and not to God. Sylvia's dead. It was her time. And now, maybe it's yours — but in a different way. Time to start a new life."

Time to let go. Time to go on. Someone had had that poem as part of their funeral service the other month and it had stuck in Mel's mind. How very true. But now, as she walked towards Amy's room — just a floor above Geoff — she wanted to shout out loud.

"What kind of time has Amy got in front of her, God? What exactly do you have planned now? Time for her to live or time for her to go wherever you feel like sending her. And was that you making me tell Helen all that stuff. One almost-adulterer counselling another? You're really weird at times. Know that?"

She quickened her pace towards Amy's room. Sometimes it felt her daughter was the only constant in a life that just wouldn't stop changing. Since the accident, Amy had just been lying down in bed, blissfully unconscious of the fuss around her. Blissfully unaware of the donor form her mother carried in her pocket; the form she had found herself signing this afternoon. The form she was now going to hand in to the hospital because somehow, after that visit to the prison, it seemed right to save another person's life if push came to shove.

Dear Lord. What was that? Laughter, it sounded like. But not Amy's.

"Josh! What are you doing here?"

"Chill out, Mum. We thought Amy would like some visitors."

Visitors! He'd brought the Get Out Of My Rooms; a gangly collection of kids in black t-shirts and earrings poking out from their noses, their belly buttons, their tongues — almost anywhere except their ears.

"If you don't stop making such a racket, you'll wake her up." That's what she'd have said at home. That's what she did say when Josh brought the band round to practise. Now she'd give anything for that to happen.

"Hope you don't mind, er vicar."

Mel tried to smile welcomingly at the kid who'd spoken. None of Josh's friends knew quite how to address her even though she'd always told them to call her Mel.

"Not at all. It's really good of you to come."

"We played her our new song," Josh said eagerly.

She hadn't heard her son sound so enthusiastic about anything for ages.

"Want to hear it?"

Incredible they hadn't been thrown out.

"I'd love to. Hang on, Josh. What's happened to your right eyebrow?"

Someone giggled loudly.

Josh shrugged. "One of the boys put some of Amy's hair removal stuff on it." He made a face. "It really ponged."

"When?"

"At that sleepover the other night."

How come she hadn't noticed?

"And what's that thing in your ear? No, not that earring. The other one?"

"A safety pin." Josh grinned happily. "I lost the ink cartridge somewhere in my room so I've just put this in till I find it. Chill out. I'm a teenager. By the way, that tattoo you didn't go on about, was a transfer. Not real. I just did it to see what you'd do. Now do you want to hear this song or not?"

And suddenly, the most incredible sound filled the air. Music, it wasn't. At least not the kind of music she liked. But wow! All at once she saw Josh as a different child, just as she'd learned to see Amy as a different child from her Facebook and friends and all the things that had happened since the accident. Josh was holding his trumpet like a precious object. His face was different. His body was different. And so too were his friends.

"It's what they love doing," Mel thought to herself.

Josh could have been a Kevin. But — thank God — he wasn't.

You could take the spirit out of the bottle but not the bottle out of the spirit. That would be a great one for the notice board!

Then, as she looked at her son's shaven eyebrow and listened to the music which would — surely — bring the staff running even though it was doing nothing to wake up her daughter — she heard another sound. One she hadn't heard for a very long time.

The sound of laughter.

Her own.

CHAPTER
FIFTY-TWO

Janie

"I still don't understand what you were doing there." Janie looked at Lars, sitting across from her, and tried to separate her body thoughts from her mental ones.

As he reached over for her hand, he might as well have passed an electric current through her.

"I have instructed you, Janie. I finally excavated your address from your telephonic number and arrive!" He beamed. "It is what my father would, comment, innovative. Yes?"

Not really but sod it. Where did this man learn to kiss? From some Norse god? Janie's entire body felt as though it was going to melt like an ice block.

Omigod. Marjorie was back.

"Janie? Are you home?"

Quickly, she slipped into Lars' t-shirt which almost fell down to her ankles. If she didn't go out to find her, Marjorie might just come in to her room. She'd done that a few times already.

Lars was stretched out on the bed rather like a horizontal Rodin's Thinker which had always been one of her favourite sculptures. "Where are you venturing?"

"It's my landlady. I just have to tell her something. Won't be a second."

Now it was over, she felt almost itchy; as though she needed to do something else like ring Becks to see what had happened. Frankly, she felt a bit hurt. After everything she'd done to persuade Steve to go back, the least her friend could do was ring and give her an update. It's what they'd always done since they were teenagers.

"Hi, Marjorie!"

"Darling! What are you wearing?"

Janie glanced down. "What? This old thing? Listen, I've got something to tell you about Monique. I'm afraid I told her we couldn't do the wedding."

"I'm not surprised." Marjorie sat down in a puff on the sofa and leaned sideways to pour herself a gin without tonic. "Doesn't look as though there will be one now, does there?"

"What?"

"Haven't you heard? Your friend's dad has had a heart attack — just a small one — and they've all been at the hospital."

"Is he going to be all right?"

"According to his cleaning lady — who happens to belong to my Tuesday Club and who's got her name down for a purple and white funeral by the way with the Spice Girls music — he's out of danger but still a bit wobbly."

"So he won't be strong enough for the wedding?"

Marjorie was fishing out some pills from her purse which she swigged down along with the gin.

"If you ask me, it's made him stronger. According to his cleaner, there's been some kind of a tiff with his bride-to-be."

"Great! Well not great if we were doing the wedding anyway but great for Becks. She couldn't stand her and I know she's always secretly hoped that Geoff and her mum might one day . . ."

"Janie? You are arriving?"

Marjorie paused, mid-sip, at the sound of Lars' voice. "Do you have a guest, dear?"

"We're going out in a minute. Sorry."

"Not at all, dear. It's me who should be apologising to you." Marjorie rose unsteadily. "A young girl like you needs some privacy. Goodness me, I remember when I used to go to those wonderful country house parties, we were always getting lost in someone else's room. You carry on, dear. I'm just going to have a little rest."

Janie made her way quickly back to the room, hoping that Lars wasn't having one too. No. From the looks of it, anything but . . .

"I am so glad we are discovering each other." Lars looked down on her, his bare chest hovering above hers. That voice! She could almost get there just by closing her eyes and listening to him . . .

"Janie!"

What was this? John and Yoko's bed? Surely Marjorie hadn't sent him in . . . Stupid question! Grabbing the sheets, she covered herself up. Lars, she noticed, didn't bother. If anything, he appeared to move so his body was even more on show.

"Hello, you," she said. Whoops. Maybe that was a bit unkind.

Mac's eyes moved from her face to Lars' body. "I thought we were working this out." His eyes glistened

494

with pain and for a brief second, she felt horribly guilty. "I thought we were working it out. You need me. Need me to read and write for you. I can't believe you're doing this to me, Janie."

Hang on. "You did exactly the same to me."

Lars frowned. "So you are utilising me?"

"Yes," said Mac.

"No." If she'd been dressed, she'd have leaped up and pushed him out of the door once and for all. "We're not right for each other. So you lent me some money and got me a temporary phone. But that doesn't mean we're back together again."

Lars cleared his throat. "So do not think you can be going into the bathroom with her." He stretched back langorously. "I am doing that now."

"You've hurt me, Janie. You've really hurt me and all."

Something pulsed in her chest. She didn't want to hurt anyone. Ever. And that was partly the trouble, wasn't it. That's what the *Big Issue* woman had meant when she'd said "Be brave". Sometimes you had to be tough to make it out the other end.

"Sorry, Mac. But I'm with Lars now."

Even as she said the words, she realised she might have been taking this a bit far. "Aren't I?"

Lars nodded. With Lars, there was no need for words. English, Norwegian or dyslexic. And for the first time for a very long while, Janie didn't feel quite so stupid any more.

THREE WEEKS TO GO

CHAPTER
FIFTY-THREE

Becky

"Mum, I'm starving!"

The computer clock had to be wrong. Had she really spent two hours checking her emails? Since they'd got back from mum's a few weeks ago, it had proved impossible to do anything with the children around. Applying for jobs was a nightmare and so was trying to do the few freelance jobs she'd managed to get.

"INAMINUTE, BEN!"

"But Daisy's eaten all the crackers."

Crackers? But she'd bought a shepherd's pie from Waitrose. Couldn't they wait or, even better, freeze for a few minutes like the huge blown-up black and white photograph of Ben and Daisy pretending to leap from rock to rock in an expensive London studio with a beach backdrop? It was so easy to have kids if you could just permanently frame them.

Shit. Another rejection had just popped up.

If she'd known how difficult it was to be a freelance, she'd have been kinder to the girls who'd phoned in, desperate to get commissions or even be paid for work they had done. Even Bel, her showbiz friend, couldn't help. "Sorry, Becks, your new idea on Posh just wouldn't go down. She's been papped to death. And to be honest, Brian has told us never to use you again. See you."

Now she was reduced to writing stuff for some business magazine which no one had ever heard of. She could have rung Dan for more work — he kept emailing her with suggestions but a reply would have given him the wrong idea. She must have been crazy to have got so involved but sometimes you needed to stand on the edge to realise that.

Meanwhile, Monique's offer was "still on the table".

"Do what you feel is right," Steve had said but she could see the worried look on his face every time they checked their balance online.

But what would Mum say if she went to work for Dad's future wife? That terrible accident had really knocked the stuffing out of her and so had the shock over dad. "Still, at least it's made them talk again," she said to Steve. "The other night, when I rang, they were actually having dinner together. You don't think, do you, that they might . . ."

Steve had shaken his head in a "you don't give up, do you?" way. "Just be grateful your dad's so much better."

It was true. He was back at home and even insisting on going into the office a couple of days a week.

"I'm fine, Becky, really," he'd said when she'd rung.

"And how are the wedding plans going?"

She couldn't help it; that touch of acid that slipped out every time the word "wedding" or "Monique" came up.

"OK."

Something was up, whatever Steve said. Something was definitely up. Her dad didn't seem particularly excited about the wedding and he was seeing more of mum. Mum had split up with David. What could be more natural than them getting back together again. Miracles happened, didn't they? Just look at Janie.

She'd never seen her friend look so happy, although to be honest, she had her doubts. Lars certainly looked the part — no one could deny he was stunning-looking — but his English was hysterical. Given that poor old Janie could barely write her name, let alone fill in a form, they'd have their work cut out between them.

"Mummy, I'm still hungry. Daisy's eaten all the biscuits and there aren't any cheese straws left. And you did promise us pancakes."

Pancakes? When?

"Ages and ages ago. When it was pancake day and you said you didn't have any flowers."

"Flour, Ben. Flour."

Hang on. What was this? Becky groaned as another email popped into her box. Not Monique again! Probably pestering her about the job.

"Am having my hen night this weekend at Champneys in Bedfordshire. Would you like to come? Sorry about the late notice. I've also asked your friend Janie."

Hen night? Champneys? With Monique? Oh, God. On the other hand, a whole two days with her best friend?

Becky's finger hovered over the Reply button. It was certainly tempting.

501

"Mum?"

"Yes, Ben?" Couldn't she have a minute to herself?

"Aren't I meant to be going to a party this afternoon?"

And she hadn't even got a present! Where was the spreadsheet? Shit. Daisy was meant to be at ballet by now as well but the good news was that Ben's party was on Saturday, not today. Or was that another party? And what about their recorder class? Omigod, how did other mothers manage?

"Mum!" Daisy was tugging at her now. "I'm still hungry."

"Inaminute, Daisy. Tea's just about to bleep."

"You must go," Steve had said. "I'll look after the children. It's the weekend after all."

He was trying, she had to give him that. Really trying. So she'd found a newish-looking computer game of Ben's for the birthday present, wrapped it up in last week's *Charisma* cover and sent Steve off on the party run. And now, here she was, pulling up outside a gorgeous building which reminded her of a small version of the Old Rectory, and walking into the reception where she'd arranged to meet Monique and Janie and also — intriguingly — one of Monique's friends.

"Becky!" Monique floated towards her in a swathe of blue velour tracksuit. "I'm so glad you could make it. Janie's already in her room with my friend Patsy." She grasped Becky's hand. "I thought you and I would share a room as we're going to be related."

What had she let herself in for?

"Just sign in there, darling."

Darling?

Monique's podgy arm was round her shoulders; she had an irresistible urge to shake it off. "This is my future stepdaughter."

The girl at reception smiled back. "How lovely to meet you. Miss Brown is one of our most loyal guests."

Monique beamed back. "I do like it here and, of course, I can set it off against my tax. Now, Becks, let's get down to having some fun."

Despite the "Becks" bit (if only she could summon up the courage to say that only friends called her that), she could get used to this. She really could. The swimming pool was beautiful and reminded her of a Roman bath with its white statue on one side and chairs on the other with a tall, conservatory-type roof above and wide windows looking out onto the grounds.

Monique had booked them all in for facials and massages that afternoon and there were also various classes she could choose from, ranging from meditation to yoga. It was nearly possible to forget why they were here.

"I didn't think you'd come," she'd whispered to Janie when they were sitting in the chairs by the pool while Monique was swimming up and down. Every now and then, she'd give a little wave from under her purple plastic cap with matching anemones.

"I wasn't going to but Marjorie said I ought to, to make up for trying to get out of the wedding."

"Did you?"

Janie grimaced. "I told her to get stuffed over her ice sculptures. But then Marjorie said it would give us a bad reputation so I rang to eat humble pie and she was amazingly gracious. Said something about everyone getting upset over weddings and while I was on the phone, how did I feel about going to her hen party?"

"Didn't think you'd be able to tear yourself away from Lars!"

Becky expected Janie to laugh but instead, she looked away. "He had to go back to Norway for a few days anyway. He's coming back as soon as he can."

"So is this it, then?"

Janie shrugged. "You know me. Live for the moment."

For a minute, Becky felt a twinge of envy. No, that wasn't fair. Janie deserved some happiness and it was absolutely right that she now had a Norwegian god to make up for all those toads. "By the way, what's Patsy like, then? This friend of Monique's you've got to share with?"

"Actually, she's . . . shhh. Here she comes."

Becky sat up in her comfy, white dressing gown that everyone wore here. Although it was comfortable, it was generous and made her feel the same size as Monique. So it was difficult to tell if Patsy, who was making her way towards them, was of similar proportions to her friend. Judging from her slim, chiselled face, it was unlikely.

"You must be Becky!" She held out her hand. "It's so nice to meet you. I've heard a lot about you."

504

Somehow, Patsy — a gorgeous West Indian woman — wasn't what she expected. Younger and, something told her, less pushy.

"Mind if I sit with you?"

"Not at all." Janie jumped up. "I was just going anyway. I need to make a phone call."

Thanks very much. Still she might as well go in for the kill now she had a chance. "Tell me, Patsy. How long have you known Monique?"

Patsy crossed her impossibly long legs which were definitely a different blend from her friend's. "Years. I'm a make-up artist and she put some work my way when my career was going through a sticky patch and I was having trouble paying the fees for my dad's nursing home. She's been very kind to me."

Kind? Monique?

"In fact, she even lent me some money at one stage. Wouldn't let me pay her back either, even when she got into financial difficulties herself."

"Why?" Becky heard herself asking.

Patsy smiled. "Monique's always said that I remind her of herself when she was younger. She had a hard life too."

Becky leaned forward. "We know so little about her. Why hasn't she got any family coming to the wedding?"

"Didn't you know?"

Patsy glanced across at the pool, where Monique was ploughing up and down. "She was in care for most of her life." She lowered her voice. "Her mother left when she was two and then her father. That's why she needs someone to love so much."

"So why hasn't she married before?"

"She almost did. A few times, in fact. But poor Monique isn't a great judge of character. The last person she fell for was much younger than her. Totally unsuitable." She lowered her voice. "Into drugs, even though he was meant to have given them up. He hurt her badly and it took ages for her to get over it."

She glanced again at Monique who was waddling up the steps towards them. "Before him, she had a miscarriage, poor thing. She'd always wanted kids but hides the hurt by pretending it was an intentional career decision. That's why it was so wonderful when she met your dad. Amazing, isn't it? Everyone seems to meet on the internet nowadays."

The net! "But I thought they met through work!"

"Oh dear." Patsy's pretty little nose wrinkled up in concern. "Better not tell them I told you, then. Some people still feel there's a bit of a stigma about it. By the way, I hear Monique's offered you a job."

No pressure then.

"Yes. I'm still thinking about it."

"She's a great person to work for. Honest. Lucky you, having her as a stepmum. I've got two stepkids — Matt and Alice — and we get on quite well now, though it's still a bit sticky with their mum. In fact you might meet them at the wedding. My husband Antony's coming too."

"I knew it!" Becky felt gloriously smug as she walked along the corridor towards the dining room with Janie.

"They met on the net. It just goes to prove that there's something wrong with her."

"Sssh." Janie jerked her head over her shoulder where Monique and Patsy were walking a few yards behind. "She'll hear you."

"God knows what Dad was thinking of. Normal people find each other in the real world."

"Do they?" Janie sounded offended. "It's not as easy for everyone as it was for you, you know, Becky. Some of us have disadvantages."

"Don't be silly. I didn't mean that."

She had to stop as they came to the desk at the restaurant.

"Good!" Monique was rubbing her hands. "I'm starving. They do some great salads here. When I was here the other month, I lost five pounds."

Pity it didn't show.

"Now, Becky, I want you to sit next to me, here."

Clearly, footing the bill made Monique feel she was in charge. Still, she was right about one thing. The salads were delicious and it was so nice not having to do anything.

"Anyone for seconds?" Monique was already on her podgy feet. If she had lost five pounds, she was going to put it back on again. "No? Well, I'll just have to go on my own. Now, after lunch, I've booked us all in for a mud bath. How does that sound?"

She had never done anything so embarrassing in her life. Somehow she'd thought you took a mud bath on your own — instead, a lovely woman in a white coat

507

told them to strip off and wear a pair of paper panties each before going through to the mud chamber which was dark and dotted with silver stars in the ceiling.

"Look!" Monique hooted with laughter as she held hers up. "Mine don't even cover half of you know what! Come here, Becks. Let's slap some mud on you!"

No way! But Patsy had begun plastering it on to Janie and someone began to giggle and somehow they were all doing it.

"If only Lars could see you now!" she said.

"Don't." Janie rolled her eyes which were the only things not to be covered.

"Just as well your father can't see me!" chortled Monique, "or he might call the whole thing off."

If only. Still, she had to hand it to her. Any woman who could take the mickey out of herself deserved some kind of admiration. In a way, she reminded her of the class clown. Someone who had to act the fool because that was the only way she could get any attention.

Yet at times Monique was so much cleverer than a fool. Scheming, even. Just look at the way she was steaming ahead with this wedding, even though it was clear her father was getting cold feet.

What, Becky wondered, as she looked at Monique sitting back on the chair under the dome of silver stars, was this woman really like?

Had she misjudged the woman? After all, it was sad about the miscarriage and all the other stuff. Never judge a book by its cover, her mum always said. Well,

508

she'd try and give Monique the benefit of the doubt for Dad's sake. But who was she, really, behind that muddy, flabby façade?

CHAPTER
FIFTY-FOUR

Helen

She'd put it off for too long. Just a note might have done after the funeral. That had been weeks ago but maybe it was still appropriate for a short letter. "*Dear Robin, What can I say? It was such an awful accident and . . .*" No. What about, "*Dear Robin, I'm sorry . . .*" Even worse. Sorry for the fact that my dog got his lead caught round your wife's wheelchair while we were upstairs in bed?

If he'd been a woman, she could have sent flowers. Daffodils were her favourite even though it was the wrong time of year. Always cheerful; bouncy; happy; a wonderful, warm yellow. Wordsworth had got it right there.

"Stop it, Dandy. Stop it."

She should have left him at home but it hadn't seemed fair. It was a beautiful day — really the weather was quite bonkers — and he needed a walk. She wouldn't bring him in of course — that would have been too insensitive — but she'd leave him in the van. It would only take a minute to say what she needed to.

It took so long for him to open the back door that she almost went.

510

"Helen."

Instantly, she knew this was a mistake. "I just brought these." She held out some bulbs, shifting awkwardly from one boot to the other. "Snowdrops. Crocuses. I thought you might want to plant them near . . . well, you know. I find it helps people to do that sometimes. Plant something nice."

Her words were coming out in a mess. Stop it right now before you go any further.

"Don't go."

He put out a hand but she neatly sidestepped it.

"I've got to."

His eyes looked red and his hair a mess. His shirt was open and there was a stain down the front. "Why?"

"You know why. It was my fault."

"Our fault."

She shook her head. "I should never have left Dandy in the garden. But he knows it — knew it — so well. I thought he'd be all right."

He smiled and his pale blue eyes watered. "I should never have left Sylvia in the conservatory."

"Why not? She liked the sun. And you weren't to know that she was going to have another . . ."

She faltered, unable to say the word "stroke".

This time, his hand did touch her sleeve. "I don't want to lose you, Helen."

What was it that Mel the vicar had said? Something about guilt eating into your rational thoughts? For a second, she hesitated.

"I'm sorry, Robin. But I don't think either of us can see each other in the same light after this. Bye."

Quick. Get to the van. Don't even bother to kick off boots. Get the pedals mucky. Ignore Dandy who was barking in the back. Drive to the woods. Breathe in the air. Talk to nature. Pretend she was back in her garden — the Old Rectory garden — all over again.

"How are you doing?"

She could hear the children yelling at the other end of the phone which had started to ring as soon as she'd got back.

"Ok-ish."

"Really?"

Steve's voice crumpled. "To be honest, it's been hell. I've just taken Ben to a party which took place two days ago because Becks misread the spreadsheet and he's really disappointed. Daisy, will you stop stabbing your brother with a fork? I've run out of plasters. I'm coming, Ben. I said inaminute."

She remembered that desperation so very well.

"Why don't you bring them down for a couple of days?"

"Sure?"

She felt a warm feeling running through. "Course I'm sure. That's what grannies — and mothers-in-law — are there for."

She needed them as much as they needed her.

"Gan, gan!" screamed Daisy, hurtling out of the car. "Can we go riding? Can we go swimming? Tell Ben he can't come too. He doesn't deserve it. He kicked me all the way down. Look!"

Helen hugged her and then Steve. "I can remember Adam doing exactly the same to Becky. Car journeys were a nightmare — Geoff used to really lose his temper. Ben, come here, you little monkey. I've got your favourite lunch ready."

"Chicken and custard?" asked Ben hopefully.

"Exactly."

"Cool, Gran. Did you know there are more chickens than people in the world? It says so on my computer."

Steve grinned. "It's so good to see you, Helen. These two have been driving me mad at home. I don't know how nannies manage."

Had this generation really lost the ability to look after their own children? Or was it their parents' fault for encouraging them to be academic and then wondering why they couldn't do basic things like discipline their kids?

"Daisy, don't touch that, darling. It will break. Look, you can help me plant these bulbs, if you like. They'll be out by Easter if we're lucky." She turned to Adam. "Have you heard from Becky? Is she having a nice time?"

Try as she did, she couldn't keep that slightly bitter tone out of her voice.

Steve leaned back on the Aga. Everyone always did that when they got here. It was so warm, so comforting, so solid. "I think so. It can't be easy for you."

She hadn't expected that. "No. It's not. I know it's daft but I feel jealous of that woman. She's got my ex-husband who, all right, I left in the first place. But

513

now she's befriended my daughter and is giving her a job and . . ."

"Becks isn't sure she's going to take it."

"She'll have to, though, won't she? Unless something else has turned up?"

Steve shook his head as though to say "Maybe; maybe not." She knew that feeling too. Don't let them go through what we did. Working too hard. Not having enough time for each other.

"Gan, gan. Will you read me a story?"

Daisy was waving a book in front of her.

"In a second, poppet. I've just got to check lunch."

"I'll read it." Steve tore himself away from the Aga. "Hang on. Where did you get this from?"

"Under Gan's bed."

Helen felt herself turning cold. "Let me take that, darling."

"What's the Big O, Gan? Is it about Red Riding Hood when she says 'Oh Granny, what big eyes you've got'?" Daisy was jumping up and down, tugging her sleeve.

"I want to read it; I want to read it," chanted Ben. "How . . . to . . . get . . . an . . . organ . . ."

"Give it back!"

They were tugging at the book now like kids at war. Any more and she'd burn up with embarrassment.

"Give it to me, you two." Steve couldn't keep the mirth out of his voice. "It's just a book for grown-ups!"

"What's funny, Daddy?"

"Nothing. Now, come on. Let's lay the table for Granny and give her a hand."

Helen glanced at Steve. "I wouldn't want you to think . . ." she began to whisper.

Steve winked. "I don't, Helen. Why shouldn't you read what you want at your age?"

At her age? Was that what they thought of her? Why did everyone think sex ended after 30 when she'd only just discovered it in her early 50's? A pang of regret shot through her. Discovered and lost in only a few weeks. Would she ever find it again?

"This chicken," said Steve carving, "will feed us for weeks. Pity there isn't anyone else to eat with us."

He's missing Becky, thought Helen.

"I'm so glad you two have sorted things out," she said quietly while the children were still fighting over the cutlery. Maybe getting them to lay the table hadn't been such a good idea after all.

"It's not been easy."

"But she didn't do anything with this man," pleaded Helen. God, it was as though she was doing this all over again, all those years ago . . .

"I know." Her son-in-law spoke in a "back-off" voice that reminded her of Geoff's years ago. "Actually, Helen, there was something else I wanted to talk about."

"Yes?"

"How about asking Geoff over for lunch? We could do with someone else to eat this massive chicken and besides, it would be nice for the kids to see their grandfather too."

Helen couldn't remember the last time she and Geoff had been under one roof with the grandchildren. The christenings hadn't really counted: they'd each kept to their own corners, taking care to speak to each other as little and as politely as possible.

But his heart attack seemed to have changed all that. It scared me, realised Helen. He could have died. Somehow, life without Geoff seemed inconceivable, just as it had when she'd first left. Now of course, she'd got used to it; the odd glimpse of him in town. The stray bit of information through Becky. But not having him there at all . . . That was another matter.

Even so, it would be a bit awkward, wouldn't it, actually having him to lunch? Perhaps he'd decline Steve's invitation, but no. Here he was, only 20 minutes later, on the doorstep, clutching an expensive bottle of red. For a couple of seconds, her heart lurched. He'd always looked good in a crisp white shirt without a tie.

"Can I have some wine, can I have some wine?" sang Daisy dancing up and down.

"No, stupid," said Ben. "You've got to be at least eight. Mum says so. And even then, we've got to be French like my friend Xavier."

Geoff gave her something that looked a bit like a smile and which made her chest jerk. "Remember that time Adam helped himself to an open bottle at Christmas one year?"

She nodded. "He slept until Boxing Day."

"How old was he, do you think?"

She considered the question. Ten maybe. Or eleven perhaps. How could she ever have thought they could start again with all those memories behind them?

516

"How are the wedding plans going?"

Geoff shrugged. "I've left it all up to Monique. It's a wedding, that's all." He glanced up almost shyly at her. "Nowadays they don't mean so much."

She felt a small leap of triumph before trying to analyse his sentence. What exactly did he mean? That nothing could be as significant as their own wedding years ago or that, at his age, it wasn't such a big deal?

"Becky's with your . . . with Monique at Champneys for her hen night."

"That's right. More sprouts, Ben? No, I never liked them either."

"What's a hen night, Gan?"

"It's a sort of farmyard game," said Geoff in a very serious voice. "You do it just before you get married."

Steve spluttered.

"But what do they do?"

Helen looked helplessly at the two men but they were busy tucking into their food. "Well, when it was my hen night, I went out for a meal with some of my friends."

"Why did you stop being married to grandad?"

Helen shot Geoff a "You can answer that one look".

Luckily, Steve got in first. "It happens sometimes, Daisy. Now who's going to clear the table?"

"Me."

"No, me!"

"Where's the custard, Gan. You said we could have it with the chicken?"

She got up, glad of the excuse. "Actually, I thought it might go better with the apple pie."

"Apple pie!" Geoff sat back in his chair, rubbing his stomach. "What a treat!"

A treat? Didn't Monique cook?

Somehow, she wasn't surprised. Monique, she felt, was the kind of woman whose idea of cooking was to buy something from a "deluxe" range.

It took a bit of time to get the apple pie out of its dish. She normally lined it with baking paper but somehow, in the midst of everything, had forgotten.

"Want a hand?" Geoff's voice took her by surprise.

"It's OK, thanks."

Her hand shook as she began to whisk the custard. Say something. Anything to fill the gap.

They both spoke at once.

"I'm sorry about the . . ."

"Daisy and Ben are . . ."

"You first."

"No, you."

Geoff leaned against the Aga, just as Steve had done an hour or so earlier. History. Bloody history. Don't let it repeat itself. "I was going to say I'm sorry to hear about that awful accident. It must have been horrible for you."

Cut the pie. Neatly. Into five slices. "It was."

"But no one blamed Dandy, surely? I heard the autopsy showed the poor woman had died already."

Her hand shook. "Yes, it did."

"Here, let me do that." Their hands brushed as she passed the knife over and she jumped as though his hand and the knife were red hot. "What were you going to say?"

518

That I can't remember now why I left you? That it would be so much easier if none of this had happened. That I can't seem to recall you being unkind and difficult to me although that's what I felt at the time?

"I was going to say that Daisy and Ben are excited about being bridesmaid and pageboy."

"What? Oh, yes. Yes, they are."

"Are you going to be wearing morning dress?"

He'd done that at theirs . . .

"Sorry? No. No, I don't think so. Monique wanted me to but I wasn't keen. Listen, Helen, before we take that lot into the dining room, there's something I need to discuss. It's about the wedding . . ."

TEN DAYS TO GO

CHAPTER
FIFTY-FIVE

Mel

Two funerals in two different parishes. The drop-in morning which no one would bother turning up for, apart from the regulars. The usual Sunday services. The PCC meeting. A couple of sermons to write. Another noticeboard ad ("Three for the Price of One?"). And four weddings, including Geoff's.

In other words, an ordinary week ahead. Come on. Who was she kidding?

Why, she told herself severely, as she parked her bike outside the Memorial Hall, did she still feel slightly sick when she thought of Geoff marrying Monique?

Maybe in another life at another time, something could have happened. He seemed to understand her so well. Listened so sympathetically about Amy. Had said all the things other people didn't dare to say about missing the world of advertising.

"You came close to it there, God," she said, locking up the bike. "Very close. But I've come through. I didn't do anything. So what do you give me now? Brownie points? Another empty drop-in centre?"

Blimey, it was cold in here. No wonder no one came. Better keep her coat on and hope that someone from the coffee committee had got in some milk. Hang on. What was happening? No one told her the hall had been booked for something else. There were at least 50 people here of varying ages, including mums with toddlers and the Tuesday Club brigade. Doris — the older woman who was the main objector to the drop-in mornings and screens with the words on during the service — was bustling up to her importantly.

"This is our drop-in morning," Mel started to say. "I'm afraid that if you've booked it for something else, we'll need to sort out alternative arrangements."

"Something else?" Doris's little bird-like eyes glinted in amusement. "Only your usual coffee morning, vicar. Heard it wasn't going that well so thought I'd rustle up a few faces for you."

Mel felt her jaw drop with disbelief. "But I thought you didn't approve. You told me that people expected the vicar to call personally. Tea, fruit cake and balm for the soul on a one to one basis. I believe that's how you put it."

Doris sniffed. "Actually I said that you could hardly expect someone to bare their soul to the vicar if everyone else was listening. It's just like going to the bank nowadays when you have to give all your personal information through a glass partition with someone else listening." She sniffed again. "Still don't approve, if you must know, but I heard about the prison."

The prison?

"The Kevin boy. Heard you went to see him." Doris patted her shoulder. "Can't see the other vicar doing that — the one before you. Not if his daughter had

524

been knocked down by some teenage hooligan. Now that's what I call really Christian, vicar. We all did. That's why we're here."

Mel looked around. How many people were there? She began counting and then gave up. Most of them she'd never seen before, apart from an elderly couple — Gladys and Bert she seemed to recall — whom she'd married not long ago and now seemed virtually glued together.

I have to hand it to you, God. You know what you're doing, even when it looks as though you don't.

"There's only one problem." Doris's eyes were glinting again.

There always was.

"We've run out of milk. Still, we could always send those wrinkled lovebirds over there to go and get some."

It was amazing. Mel had never experienced such warmth before. Some of the younger mums had said it was a great idea to have a place where they could just turn up. "We've got mother and toddler but everyone's the same age," said one with a baby in one arm, a toddler in a chair and a small bump in front.

Mel glanced at it, wondering if it was the start of something new or post-baby bulge.

"It's nice to have older people here," added the woman. "My own mum lives miles away. Sides, it's nice to have a woman vicar. Someone who understands." She looked around. "I was wondering if we could have a quiet word somewhere about this." She pointed to her stomach. Mel tried to look understanding and neutral at the same time.

"My partner isn't too keen on having another one so soon but it just happened. I'm a bit worried now in case it all gets too much. You're married with kids, aren't you? So what's the best way of having a happy family life?"

In fact, it was almost lunchtime by the time everyone left.

"Leave the washing up," Doris had said firmly. "We'll sort that out. Not as though we've got much else to do. In fact, I was wondering if you had time to talk about something rather personal. Women's problems, actually." She nudged Mel lightly in the ribs. "Never thought I'd say this but there are some things you can talk to a woman vicar about that you couldn't do with a man."

To her surprise, Mel found herself singing as she cycled back. For the first time since she'd got here, she actually felt welcomed. Even the girl with two children and one on the way had seemed reasonably happy with her paltry advice (try to make time for yourselves as a couple). She might not have practised what she preached but that's precisely why she knew how important it was.

Wheeling her bike round to the back door, she let herself in.

"Mum!"

Dear God. Did Josh just say something? Something must have happened. His eyes were bright with excitement and he didn't even have his mobile to his ear. Amy! Could it possibly be that . . .

"We've been asked to do a gig in London! A real gig and they're going to pay us!"

Of course it wasn't Amy.

"Fantastic." Her heart started to beat. "When?"

"Tomorrow."

"But you've got school the next day."

"So?" The eyes got surly again. "I'll be back in time and if not, you can write me a sick note."

"No, Josh. I'm not doing that. School comes first and you know that."

"Piss off."

She gasped.

"Josh!"

"I don't care." He was already on the way out. "I'm doing this gig and you're not going to stop me. I'm a teenager."

Another drink. That's what she needed.

Some time later she heard the front door opening. "I haven't changed my mind so forget it," she called out.

"Changed your mind about what?"

She looked up. "Richard? What are you doing here."

Then she realised. "Great. You've lost your job, haven't you. That's all I need."

"No." Richard's voice was slow and steady, the way it always was when he had something to tell her. Oh, God. He'd found someone else then. Or else something had happened to Amy. Or . . .

"I've been transferred." He took her hands in his and pressed them to his mouth. "Isn't that fantastic! A vacancy's come up in Reading and I jumped at it. So I can come back!"

"Really?"

"That is, providing you want me to."

Did she? In one way, she'd got used to making decisions without consulting someone else. Doing the bins, mending that leaky pipe because they couldn't afford to get anyone else in and because it wouldn't wait until Richard was back at the weekend. Thinking about Geoff . . .

No. That would never have done.

"Of course I want you back. It's been so difficult without you."

"I know." Putting his arms around her, he cradled her head on his shoulder, just like he used to. "I bumped into Josh on the way back. He told me about his gig."

"Exactly! That's another thing to worry about."

"Actually, I've got a suggestion to make but let's put the kettle on first . . ."

To her surprise, Josh's year head agreed. Yes it was unusual but in the circumstances they would allow him to come in late to school tomorrow along with the other members of the band.

And now, here they were — her and Richard — being frisked by a rather large security guard on the door of some dubious hall in south London.

"I suppose you have to be careful with drugs," she ventured.

The guard nodded briskly. "It's the adults we get the most trouble with. Kids are pretty sensible on the whole."

"Hole?" quipped Richard. "Our son's got enough of those in his ears."

"Come on." Mel dragged him in before he could say any more. "Josh made us swear not to embarrass him. Remember?"

She had to admit it. It was much better than she'd thought. No smoke like there would have been in their day. Loads of kids. And, surprise, surprise, a couple of other awkward-looking adults.

"Are you Josh's mum?" asked one.

She nodded.

"I'm Mandy — that's Mandy with a 'y'. Darren's mum. He plays the bass. I think they came round your place the other night to practise. You must be very proud of your son. He's got real talent and he's polite too."

"Are we talking about the same boy?"

Mandy laughed. "They're always nicer to people they don't know, aren't they?"

I should have made the effort to meet them before, Mel told herself as she fell into conversation with Mandy. It was all very well trying to be a woman of the people but she needed to spend more time with her family too.

"Here they are." Richard nudged her.

All eyes were on the stage and there were catcalls and whistles as Josh and his band came on. Josh was wearing shorts — in this weather! — and nothing else.

529

But it was his face that made her look twice. It had the same look she'd seen in the kitchen when he'd told her about the concert. He was happy. Really, truly happy.

And as he lifted the trumpet in front of a crowd of swaying teenagers and began to make the loudest noise she'd ever heard — which, surprisingly, had quite a good rhythm — she realised something.

The archdeacon had been right. It was hard enough to cope with life when you do have faith.

But it was impossible without it.

CHAPTER
FIFTY-SIX

Janie

"This wedding is very important," said Marjorie, topping up her glass. "We've got to get it right or else that ghastly woman will ruin our reputation."

Janie eyed the bottle of Sapphire Blue distrustfully. Judging from its low horizon, her landlady had definitely sunk a few.

"I've told you, Marje. Everything's under control."

Why didn't anyone believe her? It wasn't her fault that the ice sculpture firm had gone into liquidation.

"I've found someone else who can do it."

Marjorie clinked the ice cube inside her own tumbler.

"He wouldn't be a Norwegian artist, would he?"

Janie plonked herself next to Marjorie on the sofa and began sketching a face on her mobile phone bill which she'd left lying on the coffee table. Oh dear, hadn't she paid that yet? "Lars comes from the land of ice. He'll know what he's doing."

Marjorie nodded sleepily. "I did do the right thing, didn't I? Sending Mac in. I thought it might get rid of him once and for all."

Well, she could think of more subtle ways. "It certainly did the trick. Back to the wedding, I'm just about to pick up the service sheets."

"And the flowers?"

"Those too."

Marjorie sighed. "I'm so sorry I can't help you more but this migraine is really awful."

"Do you think it's a good idea to have a drink, then?"

"Definitely not." Marjorie's eyes twinkled as she picked a piece of fluff off her mohair sleeve. "But at my age, we've done the sensible bit already and now it's time to break the rules! How about one for you, Janie?"

She shouldn't have. She really shouldn't. Not when she was cycling at the same time. Whoops.

"Hi." Phil the printer grinned at her. "Wondered when you'd be coming to pick this lot up. Thought you might have forgotten."

Why did everyone think she was so hopeless? She'd show them. Monique's wedding was going to be a real showcase, so long as no one looked at the bride.

"The wedding's not until tomorrow." She propped her bike against the wall. "Plenty of time — providing you've got the order right."

"Come and check for yourself."

He led the way into his studio brushing against her as he went past. Flipping cheek.

"Here we are. Take a look."

Janie pretended to read it but the words swam in front of her like black fish.

"I need to be paid."

532

Why was he so close to her?

"Send me an invoice." She tried to squeeze past him.

"Payment is on receipt." He was so close now she could smell his breath. He'd been drinking. That explained it.

"Well I haven't got my cheque book on me. Phil, can you let me past?"

He didn't move. "I've split up with my wife."

A few months ago, the news would have sent small fireworks shooting up her chest. Now she just wanted to get out.

"So? Let me past, please? Let me . . ."

"Janie?"

What was he doing here? "Lars!"

The look on his face said it all. His beautiful blue eyes held hers in a moment of sadness. Then he turned to stride off.

Be brave? Take new opportunities? Now look what she'd just done!

"Lars! It's not what you think!" Stuffing the pile of service sheets into her bike basket, she pedalled furiously towards him.

"Please wait!"

There was a screech of brakes, a brick wall looming up in front of her and then . . . black.

"Janie? You are still living?"

For a moment, she felt as though she might have gone to heaven; a heaven full of blond Norwegian gods looking down on her. Lars' face appeared to be duplicated in several places and there was a terrible pain at the back of her head.

She tried to nod but it hurt. "I think so. Shit. The service sheets."

They were scattered everywhere like confetti, all over the lane. "They're muddy," wailed Janie. "And creased. What am I going to do now?"

"I will be picking them up." Lars started to gather them.

"Wait. Stop. It's not important."

She tried to sit up but everything felt wobbly. "Just there. At the printers. It wasn't what you thought. He was coming on to me — trying it on."

"Trying what on?" Lars' eyes still looked sad like a rejected puppy.

"It's just a phrase. What I mean is that I don't like him. It's you, I want, Lars."

"You are being solid?"

"Lars, I might be a lot of things in life but I am truthful. Apart from the odd white lie."

"White? You tell lies in colours?" Lars scooped her up in his arms and Janie felt her heart flip back into action. "You can explanate when we reconvene at the house."

No, she didn't want to go to hospital to be checked. Besides, there wasn't time. They'd need to iron out the wedding sheets and dab off the mud but then they'd be all right. Well, OK-ish.

At least she didn't have to worry about the food — the hotel was doing that. Although she did need to pick up the cake. Now what time did the bakers close? Oh fuck. And the bouquet . . . Shit. She'd forgotten to pick up the bouquet!

"Janie dear?" A fragile voice called out from the main bedroom. "Is that you?"

Janie put a finger to her mouth, indicating that Lars shouldn't tell Marjorie about the accident. The last thing she wanted to do was worry her.

"Yes but I'm a bit busy at the moment."

"This is important, dear. Monique rang when you were out. There's been the most extraordinary change of plan. You simply won't believe it . . ."

TEN MINUTES TO GO

CHAPTER
FIFTY-SEVEN

Becky

Becky sat in the front pew, staring straight ahead. There was something very odd about seeing your parents getting married again. She'd once interviewed a mother who'd lost her child and been haunted by her words. "You always expect to live longer than your kids."

Well she always expected to get married long after her mother — or her father for that matter. Why hadn't they had the decency to get married in Cuba or even Vegas? And why did her father look so nervous — it was pathetic at his age!

"Did you manage to get Daisy to wear her dress?" whispered Steve.

"Only by promising she could stay up until tomorrow morning. And Ben refused to wear his waistcoat the right way round."

Steve took her hand in his and stroked it. "You look lovely," he said in a low voice.

"Thanks."

Becky glanced down at her green silk coat dress from the days when she'd had the run of the samples cupboard at the magazine. Besides, Steve didn't really mean it. Things just hadn't been right since that stupid Dan business. Maybe they never would be.

"Where's Adam?" She looked around worriedly. "He's always late."

"But he rang to say he'd be coming straight from the airport, didn't he, to surprise your dad. By the way, did Janie manage to sort out the reception problem?"

"No." Becky tried not to sound smug. "The hotel had expected her to confirm the date weeks ago and when she didn't, they took another booking. Looks like they're just going to have to put up with the village hall."

"It was fine for us."

Yes. It had been. When she and Steve had got married (she'd worn a beautiful Amanda Wakeley dress) they'd insisted they didn't want any fuss. Instead, they'd had a buffet in the hall which everyone then took outside to have as a picnic. Still, that had been summer. Today was absolutely freezing — good thing she'd brought a coat as well.

"I think there's something rather special about Christmas weddings."

"Do you?"

He squeezed her hand again. "Lots of holly and mistletoe . . ."

"Shh. Here they come."

540

Helen

Helen stood at the altar, shaking. It wasn't just nerves. It was absolutely freezing, even for November. Didn't the church run to heating?

What are you doing here, she asked herself. It was crazy. She hadn't believed it when Geoff had asked her.

It was because of his heart scare, he'd said. Her loyalty in dashing to his bedside and their frank discussion, had made him realise they still cared for each other, despite everything.

So when he'd asked her *that* question, it somehow, it seemed right — staggeringly right — to say "yes".

Mel

Oh my God, she'd forgotten her collar. How could she have? And there definitely wasn't time to go back. Mel screeched to a halt outside the church. It was only white plastic — she'd have to improvise. Frantically, she rifled through the side pockets of the car. No. Only chocolate wrappers and car park tickets. Hang on. There was a copy of a magazine in the back seat — it must have been Amy's. And at the back, there was a white margin of space around the Readers' Letters page. Perfect. If she carefully creased it and then tore along the line, she might just make a long thin shape . . .

541

Five minutes later, Mel was hovering at the altar rail, hand at her throat, trying to hide the makeshift collar. She usually loved this bit at weddings. Each face told a story. The expectant mother of the bride. The nervous groom. The best man, fiddling with his pocket. And then the organ music as the bride floated down the aisle.

Floated? She almost laughed out loud. More like clomped. In fact, here she came. Heavens. She'd seen some meringues before but this one really took the biscuit. Mind you, the makeover was impressive. Very impressive. You almost wouldn't think it was the same woman. Dear God, not her mobile. Hadn't she left that in the car? Quick, put it on Silent. And why hadn't she changed out of her trainers?

Janie

Fuck. Fuck. Fuck. No one would ask them to do another wedding now. First the stupid hotel manager who claimed she hadn't posted the confirmation form. All right. So she should have kept a record but she was certain she'd spoken to someone on the phone even though she couldn't remember her name. Or maybe his.

Then the ice sculpture. "I am apologetic but it appears it has disappeared," Lars announced that morning.

You'd think in this freezing weather, it would be impossible to melt although she hadn't reckoned on Marjorie turning up the heating.

542

The cake wasn't quite what they had in mind either. No one had told her the shop closed early on Fridays. Luckily, Marjorie — bless her — had come up trumps with a triple layer Victorian sponge. And it was a brainwave of hers to use the plastic flower arrangements that the Tuesday Club had left on the tables after their last lunch.

Still, it was the wedding that counted. Wasn't it?

Janie smoothed out her wedding sheet which, like all the others, was distinctly creased and had traces of dirt. Quickly, she sketched a face over the mud mark to hide it. Was it too late to dash up and tweak those altar flowers which didn't look quite right? Maybe. Time for the flute solo now.

"Who did you book in the end?" she asked, turning to Marjorie who was fetchingly dressed in purple silk and a large ostrich feather turban.

"Book for what, dear?"

"The flowtist. You were going to ask Derek from the Tuesday Club to cut costs. Remember?"

"Wasn't that on your list? Oh dear. You know, Janie, I think we'd better stick to funerals. At least they can't come back and complain afterwards. Let's hope the party goes a bit better. You did confirm the disco, didn't you? Whoops. Oh well, here comes 'The Queen of Sheba'. At least the organist got that one right . . ."

CHAPTER
FIFTY-EIGHT

Becky

"Mum, did you know that the world's biggest bird is an ostrich? It says so on my computer."

"InaminuteBen. And I told you to leave your laptop at home. It will get broken here with all these people and it looks so rude. Daisy! You can't take your dress off in front of everyone!"

Daisy scowled. "But it itches. And I need the loo."

"Inaminute." Actually, she did have a bit of a rash from that silk. Becky readjusted her daughter's sash. "Just wait until after the speeches and then you can go and play with those older children, Matt and Alice. Steve, can you hang on to the kids for a minute? I've just spotted my cousin Charlotte and I haven't seen her for years."

He nodded. "Any sign of Adam?"

"No. And his mobile is switched off, not like the vicar's. I couldn't believe it when it went off during the service. Honestly, Adam's almost as unreliable as Janie — did you hear about the cake? This wedding's a complete disaster."

"Shhh, she's coming."

Gritting her teeth, Becky forced herself to smile.

"Congratulations, Monique. Lovely wedding."

"Thank you!" The bride beamed at them. What kind of flowers were those? Surely they couldn't be plastic? Yes! They were. Probably cost a fortune from some designer shop.

"Mum?"

"Inaminute, Ben."

"Naughty me." Monique stooped down to his level. "I should have said thank you for your recorder performance with your sister, even though 'Three Blind Mice' wasn't exactly what I had planned." She glanced at Becky. "I was expecting a flautist but Janie managed to mess that one up as well. Still, a bit more practice, Ben, and you'll be a lot better. What do you think?"

Ben scowled. "Mum says you look like a velvet meringue and I think she's right."

"Ben!" Becky laughed gaily. "Good enough to eat. That's what I meant."

"Is that why you said she makes you feel sick?"

Omigod. Omigod.

"Mum!" Daisy tugged at her dress.

"Inaminute Daisy."

"But I've done a poo! Look!"

Talk about time and motion.

Monique's eyes continued to shine brightly. "It's all right, dear. I understand. But nothing's going to spoil my day. Come here and give your new stepmum a kiss."

Helen

"Lovely wedding," said someone, whom she vaguely recognised from Geoff's office. There had definitely been more from the groom's side than the bride's.

Helen nodded, swallowing her mouthful of veggie burger quickly. "I thought the children did very well. Jolly lucky there were some spare recorders from Sunday School at the back of the church."

"Bit unusual, though, wasn't it?"

"I thought it was a nice touch."

"Rather like the food, you mean?" The woman put down her plate of chips. "I've never been to a wedding with takeaways from McDonald's."

Helen dabbed her mouth with a paper napkin. "I believe there was a bit of a hitch with the food but I actually think it makes a nice change."

"You mean like having you as a best man?" She leaned towards Helen confidentially. "Not many ex-wives would agree to that. I certainly wouldn't."

Helen took a large swig of bubbly, suddenly remembering who the woman was. Karen or Lisa or someone who'd been Geoff's secretary from years back. She'd never really warmed to her.

"Why not?" Another swig. "Geoff and I get on quite well. It's the civilised way to do things nowadays. Besides, it's much easier for the children."

Where was Adam? She hoped nothing had happened to his flight.

"I must say, I didn't expect Geoff to marry someone like . . . I mean, Monique is rather different, isn't she?"

Don't be drawn. "Is she?"

Unable to help herself, Helen found herself looking at the voluminous cream bride who was laughing at something her new husband had just said to her. Husband. Geoff was now Monique's husband. Actually, that didn't feel as odd as she'd thought it might. It was as though now it was signed and sealed, as it were, there was nothing anyone could do about it.

Be honest. She and Geoff had never been suited to each other. It was only the shared history she missed.

"Are you here with anyone, then?"

No, I'm just a wallflower. What a nosy cow! Now she came to think about it, she always had been. In fact, there had been a couple of occasions, like a staff party when Geoff had stayed in London overnight, when she'd wondered if there'd been anything going on between him and his PA. "Not at the moment."

"Shame. Still, I'm sure you'll find the right person one day."

"Excuse me." Helen brushed past her. "I've just seen someone I need to speak to."

Mel

"Nice wedding, vicar," said someone she didn't recognise.

"Thanks."

"Liked the bit about change and how sometimes it took you by surprise. By the way, heard your son busking outside Oxford station the other day. Can't say the music was quite to my taste but it was different."

Busking? Oxford station? Dear Lord.

"He got told to move, of course. You ought to tell him to be careful or he might be arrested again."

Oh, to be back in Wandsworth without any village gossip. "Actually, Josh has never been arrested. I think you're probably referring to a time when he was cautioned by the police for drinking. As for his music, they're talking to a manager about being signed up. Scar music — that's what it's called apparently — is rather popular nowadays."

Thank God, Geoff's first wife was coming up to save her.

"Vicar. Can we have a word. Somewhere quiet?"

"Of course."

She weaved her way through the crowd to the back room where they changed for mother and toddler.

"There's something I've got to tell you."

They both sat down on small chairs from the mother and toddler session. Mel waited. It was often best that way.

Helen looked at the wall. That was something else people often did. "The reason I left Geoff is because I fell in love with someone else. I know I told you this before. But I didn't say who it was."

More silence. Helen was studying a crack in the wall. Mel understood that. It was a trick she'd perfected herself.

548

"I fell in love with Janie's father. And he with me."
She buried her head in her hands. "To be honest, I
suppose Alastair was a bit of a catalyst but I loved him.
I really did. But neither of us could bear to destroy our
families, so in the end he went to France — with his
wife who never knew for certain although I think she
suspected."

"You must have felt awful," said Mel quietly.
"Knowing Janie was a friend of your daughter's."

"I did. Especially as Janie has always been so fond of
me. I feel awful about it every time I see her."

"But her parents' marriage survived?"

Helen made a face. "Only just. They had problems
before; that's not just an excuse."

"But your marriage didn't cope?"

"No. I couldn't bear being with Geoff once I knew
what it was really like to be loved. And now this awful
thing has happened — that terrible accident with
Robin's wife."

"Which wasn't your fault. She was dead before."

"Yes but don't you see?" Helen lifted her head. "I'm
being punished. Punished by your God."

"No." Mel shook her head firmly. "You're being
punished by yourself. God forgives everyone. And he
forgave you a long time ago, Helen. What you need to
do now is forgive yourself."

She left Helen there a while to compose herself while
going back into the hall. It was true. So why couldn't
she do it to herself. Forgive herself for phoning Amy
when she was crossing the road. Forgive herself for
putting the family through all this upheaval when . . .

"MEL!"

Richard's voice cut through the air so that everyone else fell silent. Richard?

"Mel, come quickly."

The last time she'd seen him look like that was when Josh was about to be born. It had all been much faster than expected and she'd been rushed to . . .

"We've got to get to the hospital." He was white. Absolutely white. "Something's happened. I've been trying to call you on the mobile. Didn't you hear? It's Amy."

Janie

"Just get me one more, darling." Marjorie's voice was slurred. "If we're going to go under, we might as well go under in style."

"I am thinking that is not wisdom."

Lars cut in before she could say something similar. It was a habit of his, Janie was beginning to realise. A rather annoying one.

"Just one." Marjorie smiled weakly before flopping down on a metal chair. "And don't forget the ice! Sorry. Couldn't resist that one! By the way, how did you get hold of the buttonholes at such short notice? I thought we forgot to order them?"

"We did." Janie whispered something in her ear.

"Don't shout, dear. I'm not that deaf. What did you say again?"

550

"I SAID I NICKED THEM FROM THE GRAVEYARD."

There was a deathly silence. Just her luck to speak when the music had gone quiet.

"And the photographer?" demanded Marjorie, oblivious to the shocked silence. "When is he turning up?"

Oh shit. She had told him about the change of venue. Hadn't she?

Becky

"What happened to the vicar?"

"What do you mean?"

"Didn't you see how she shot off?"

"No. Listen, Steve, I've just been talking to my cousin Charlotte and she told me something really interesting."

"Mummy, Mummy, my skin tickles."

"Not now, Daisy. Charlotte's been asked to start a new . . ."

"Becky!"

Becky swivelled round. "Omigod, Adam! Adam!" Flinging her arms around his neck, she breathed in his smell. "You're here. I can't believe it. You're actually here!"

She almost hadn't recognised him with that tan. "You've put on weight! Suits you. But you're late. You missed it all."

"I know. Sorry. Missed the flight and all that."

"You're as bad as Janie."

"Janie?" He looked around interestedly. "The same Janie who has a certain way with words? Is she here?"

"Yes and keep your mitts off. She's got a man; a nice man at last. Besides, aren't you going to go and congratulate Dad and his new bride?"

"Suppose so but I'd rather see Mum first. Where are they all anyway?"

"Over there."

"Bloody hell."

"What?"

"It's Janine."

"Who's Janine?"

Adam took a step backwards as though he was going to run off again. "Someone I used to know. I thought you said Dad was marrying someone called Monique?"

"He is. Has. What are you talking about?"

"If we're talking about the same bride — the one in a large meringue — her name is Janine. Or at least it was."

Omigod. The hairs on the back of her neck began to prickle. "Please don't tell me that you . . ."

She couldn't even bear to say the words.

"Fraid so, sis." Adam was still staring. "We had, what you might call, a bit of a thing."

"A bit of a thing?"

He had the grace to look embarrassed. "I know. Not really my sort, is she? But Janine, or whatever she's calling herself now, is good fun. She knows how to laugh with the boys. A man's woman, I suppose, and

I've always been a sucker for dusky looks. Besides, she's actually amazing in . . ."

"*Stop.*" Becky felt sick. Talk about here comes the bride . . . "Too much information. What do we do now?"

Adam had already begun to stroll ahead. "I don't know about you but I'm going over to find out what the hell she's playing at. At least I am when I've said hello to Mum. Do you think I should tell her about Janine or keep my mouth shut?"

CHAPTER
FIFTY-NINE

Helen

It was so lovely seeing Adam.

"You've grown," she'd said, hugging him to her.

"Don't be daft, Mum." He kissed her cheek affectionately. "I haven't grown since I was sixteen. You've shrunk. You seem smaller."

"Don't be so cheeky. And what's this?" She stroked his cheek. "Growing a beard?"

"Not really. I just haven't had time to shave this week. Happy birthday, by the way. Typical of Dad to get married on what's meant to be your day."

She shrugged. "Perhaps he forgot."

"Yeah. Well he did that enough times when you were married, didn't he? Anyway, Becks and I are taking you out to a special birthday lunch tomorrow to make up for it."

How sweet! He was leading her now to a chair away from the throng. Any minute now and the speeches would start. She wasn't looking forward to that one.

"It's very big of you to be here, Mum." He looked at her, with that same "are you all right" little boy expression that he'd worn when she'd taken him and Becky and left all those years ago.

She shrugged. "Dad asked me. We're getting on better nowadays."

"Glad to hear it."

Something wasn't right. He was fiddling. Shoving his hands in and out of his pockets. Glancing around as though expecting something to happen.

"What is it, Adam?"

"It's Janine. I mean Monique."

She frowned. "What about her?"

He was staring at the ground. "It's like this. When I was in Australia last year, I . . . I sort of knew her."

A nasty feeling sliced through her chest.

"What do you mean?"

"You know what I mean, Mum. I knew her."

"Like that?"

"Like that. We met through some friends."

There was a silence. Poor Geoff. Poor, poor Geoff.

"She called herself Janine then. And she looked different. A bit slimmer, although she was always on the plump side."

This was impossible! "What did you see in her?"

He looked sideways at her as though this was an odd question. "She's fun. At least she was then. And she's cuddly; larger than life." He smiled almost wistfully. "No one can call Janine boring. Maybe that's why she changed her name."

Helen nudged him. "Why don't you ask her yourself? She's coming towards us."

Mel

Everyone was looking as they raced through the corridors. Looking as though they knew exactly what had happened. It wasn't surprising. Amy had been one of their unsung stars. The girl in the coma they'd all been rooting for. The vicar's daughter. The vicar who had to show she still had faith.

Amy was sitting up in bed, her eyes open.

"Mum?"

Oh, my God. Oh, my God.

"What are you crying for, Mum? And get Josh out of here, can you? I've told you before, his music's rubbish."

"Thanks very much." Josh brandished his trumpet in the air, defiantly. "If it wasn't for us, you'd still be in your coma."

Mel was still trying to understand even though the doctor had already explained Amy's so-called miracle recovery.

"We kept playing, Mum. Louder and louder. The nurses told us to shut up but we said it might help. And it did. It was our new song that did it."

The other members of the band nodded.

"In a coma? What's he talking about, Mum?"

Richard sat down next to her. "Amy, darling. What do you remember last? Before you went to sleep?"

She rubbed her eyes. "Some bloke. Coming to the house and asking for mum. Said he wanted to get married but he looked far too ancient. Then . . . then I think I remember getting in the car to go shopping with Sharon. I was crossing the road when my mobile rang to say I'd had a message . . . that's right. And then . . ."

Amy frowned. "I can't remember any more. What happened, Mum. What am I doing here?"

"It's all right, darling. It's all right. You had an accident. But you're going to be fine now."

Thank you, God. Thank you. No more Geoffs now, I promise. Honestly. But I have to hand it to you. You sure know how to deliver a punch.

Janie

If it wasn't for the pinch she gave herself, Janie would have told herself she was dreaming. But no. She was right behind them. She could hear every word. Thankfully, Geoff — who was at the other end of the hall — couldn't.

"What are you playing at?"

She'd always secretly fancied Adam but he was even sexier when he got angry. How funny. He looked rather like that imaginary face she kept drawing. In fact, he even had the beginnings of a beard, too . . .

"Adam!"

What was going on? Monique was white; she actually looked scared.

"I didn't think you were coming."

"Well unfortunately for you, I changed my mind at the last minute. What do you think you're playing at, marrying my dad? Does he know about us?"

"No." Blimey. Monique looked like a child who'd been caught in the act. "Listen. I can explain. You hurt me, Adam. You really did. And when I came back to England, I joined one of those internet dating sites."

Shit. She had a horrible feeling about this.

"And I found someone with your surname. So out of interest, I looked him up."

"You made a play for my dad to get back at me."

"All right." Monique's eyes began to blaze. That was more like it.

"I did to begin with. But then I fell in love with him. Honestly. And by that time, we were in too deep. I couldn't tell him the truth."

What? "But you must have realised that Adam would find out some time?"

They both swivelled round to look at her.

"Sorry." Janie twisted the chain of her crystal necklace round her finger in embarrassment. "Couldn't help overhearing."

Adam nodded. "She's right. You knew we'd have to meet up."

Monique nodded. "I hoped by then it would be all right."

Hah! "You mean, you hoped Adam wouldn't mention it."

The meringue nodded. "Yes. If you must know. I did. You wouldn't want to hurt your dad, after all, would you?"

This woman was a scheming cow.

"Know what?" Adam took a step back. "You're a scheming cow, Janine. But why did you change your name?"

"It's my middle name, darling." She emphasised the "darling". "Besides, you can never be too careful on the net. And then I thought I'd keep it. A sort of fresh start, you know."

This was unbelievable!

"I can't believe it." Poor Helen. She looked shocked.

"You're not going to go and tell Geoff now, are you?" Monique's voice had a slight quaver in it.

"Should we?"

Janie held her breath as mother and son exchanged questioning glances.

"His heart attack was due to stress," said Helen softly.

Adam nodded. "OK, Janine or Monique or whatever you want to call yourself. But remember. We're watching you. And if you ever hurt Dad, you'll have me to answer to me."

Wow! Monique was scuttling off like a wobbly blob of cream.

"That was fantastic!" breathed Janie. "You were amazing."

"Not really." Adam took his mother's arm. "You all right, Mum?"

Helen nodded. "I can't believe it."

"Nor me." He held out his other arm and linked it through hers. "But actually, I think she was telling the truth when she said she loved Dad. So maybe it might just work after all. Amazing outfit by the way, Janie. Just let me find my sunglasses. Come on — you know I'm just joking! Now, why don't I find us all a drink? Then we can have a dance."

He jerked his head towards the band that were shuffling onto the stage.

"Where did you get that lot from?"

"It's the Tuesday Club music group," hissed Janie. "They sing along to stuff from fifties vinyls. There was a bit of confusion about the disco so they've stepped in instead. We had to do quite a bit of improvising, actually. The photographer didn't turn up so I've just dashed out to get some disposable cameras."

Adam threw back his head in laughter. "You haven't changed, have you, Janie?" He gave her a quick hug. "You've no idea how good it is to see you again."

"Really?"

"Really. C'mon." He put a hand in the small of her back, guiding her to a chair. "The speeches are about to start."

"Wow!"

"What?"

Janie was staring at a good-looking man who was surrounded by a bevy of women.

"That man looks just like the actor Hugh . . ."

"He is."

"What?"

"Janine knows him quite well through her charity work. She mentioned it in Australia, although I'm surprised he's turned up here. Where are you going?"

She took a deep breath. "I always said that if I met him, there was something I had to tell him."

Adam grinned. "You're something else, Janie. Know that? And what exactly are you going to say?"

Janie hesitated. Everyone made mistakes, didn't they? Including her. And almost everyone here. "I'm going to tell him that I really loved that film. You know. *Four Weddings and a Funeral*. And while I'm at it, I might just ask if that fantastic car outside is his. Because if so, I know just what I need him to do with it."

Helen

She'd been dreading this especially since the best man always went first. Why had she agreed to do it?

Becky had asked her the same question. "To be honest," Helen had replied, "I was so surprised that I said yes without thinking."

Just as she had when Geoff had proposed all those years ago.

But there was something else, too. A feeling that she owed him one after running out on him like that.

"You'll look amazing on the top table, compared with Monique," Becky had said.

Well, yes. Maybe that had something to do with her decision as well. She might be older than Geoff's bride but, as Robin had said enough times, she didn't look her age.

Robin . . .

Oh, Lord. Everyone was looking at her now. Thank God it wasn't the hotel they'd first booked; that would have been far more intimidating. But somehow, the village hall made her feel at home. Quite funny really.

She had to hand it to Monique for smiling through the plastic flowers and McDonald's takeaway.

Helen glanced at her speech. There was an awful silence. Suddenly, the words she had prepared — wishing them happiness and so on — seemed quite wrong. She cleared her throat. Nothing came. Monique was frowning. Geoff was shifting on his seat, the way he always did when nervous. Was he regretting asking her? He certainly seemed to have got over his wedding nerves, judging from the way he was stroking Monique's thigh.

"The last time Geoff and I were at the top table was when we were getting married ourselves."

Nervous laughter. Silence from Monique. Oh, God. Too late to stop now.

"So when Geoff asked me to be his best man, I was very surprised."

More nervous laughter. She was clenching her fists now, under the paper tablecloth, so that nails dug into her palms.

"But actually, what could be more natural?"

No laughter now. Just silence.

"When you've had two children together, you can't erase the past."

She was looking in his direction now; forcing herself to concentrate on his button hole (a rather dead-looking purple-pink chrysanthemum) so she didn't do anything daft like burst into tears. "Even if you want to."

Whoops. Maybe she shouldn't have said that bit but the cheap champagne (apparently there'd been some misunderstanding over the original order) was putting up a mask between her and the outside world as though she wasn't really there. Meanwhile, Monique's black eyes, next to Geoff, were narrowing and her fixed smile was clearly wavering. Helen almost felt sorry for her. She couldn't have been very pleased that Geoff had asked her to be best man. Still, that would be nothing if Geoff knew about Adam . . . Perhaps they deserved each other.

"But life goes on. It changes. And often for the better. Geoff and I have moved on and the fact that we are here, sitting next to each other, shows how much we have learned about life."

There was a low murmur of agreement from a table in front.

"Most of you here, know that Geoff had a heart scare recently and in many ways, it did us all good."

"Thanks very much!"

He was laughing; that was all right then.

"What I meant was that it put life into context." Helen's mouth was beginning to feel less dry now. "It showed us what was important — like family. And you can still be a family, even after a divorce."

Someone gave a little clap at the back.

"Of course, Geoff might have asked me to be best man because it's my birthday today."

Geoff gasped. "Is it? So it is? I'm so sorry, Helen, I forgot."

She shrugged at the audience. "Some things never change. He was like that when we were married."

A roar of laughter rippled through the hall.

"So what I'm really saying is that I hope Geoff and Monique have all the happiness they deserve." She held out her glass towards the meringue blob. "Welcome to the family, Monique. Great party, by the way."

And as she sat down, amidst the clapping, Helen suddenly realised something. If Geoff could be big enough to forgive her by asking her to be best man, she should be big enough to forgive him — as well as herself.

TOO LATE NOW

CHAPTER
SIXTY

Becky

"I still can't believe it!" Becky took her daughter's temperature again. Miraculously, it was coming down now. Funny — a few months ago, she'd have freaked out at the whole idea of one of the kids getting chicken pox. But being at home more had made her feel more competent. "She kept saying she was itchy all through the wedding. I should have taken more notice. Daisy, come back. I said come back! I've got to put more calamine lotion on that spot. And stop picking it!"

"Nice." Janie sounded brighter than she'd heard her for a long time. Must be because the strain of the wedding was over.

"Actually, it's not too bad." Becky pulled Daisy onto her knee. "She's not as tetchy as she was being before — must have been because she was coming down with it."

"Mmm."

Janie definitely wasn't paying her full attention.

"Feeling better now it's all over then?"

"What's all over?"

Janie's voice had a slight edge of panic.

"The wedding, silly. What else?"

"Right. Yes. The wedding. Thank God it's over. They'll be in South America now — unless I got that wrong too."

Frankly, she wouldn't put it past her. Poor old Janie. Couldn't get anything right although she had to admit it was a stroke of genius getting Hugh to drive the bride and groom off to the airport when the rented limo hadn't arrived. On the whole, Janie had lousy judgment, especially when it came to men — although actually Lars wasn't too bad.

"How's your sexy Norwegian?"

"Fine."

Talk about lukewarm. "Sure?"

"Great . . . you know what. But there's a bit of a communication problem."

Not sure then. Pity, especially when she'd gone to the trouble of persuading Monique to throw her plastic bouquet in Janie's direction.

"Listen, Janie, I've got to take Ben to nursery now so I'd better dash. I'll ring tomorrow."

"Are you allowed to do that?"

"Allowed to do what?"

"Take Ben to nursery if you've got Daisy with you."

She was going to leave Daisy at home alone, watching a video.

"You weren't going to leave her at home, were you? Alone? Not after what happened to that poor kid in your magazine the other week."

Becky winced. "It's not my magazine any more and of course I wouldn't do anything like that. What do you take me for?"

568

"Sorry. Just being the over-protective godmother. That's all."

Janie knew nothing about bringing up children, thought Becky, bundling the kids into the back of the car. What gave her the right to tell her what to do?

"Come on, Daisy. Yes, we will go to Kidzone later on but we've got to get to school first. Ben, for God's sake. Where are your trousers? And what's happened to your other sock? InaminuteDaisy. Inaminute."

How did other mothers manage, she wondered as she drove over a speed bump, sending them all flying up to the roof of the car. And why don't they have enough parking spaces outside school? Ridiculous. How were they meant to do the school run? Sod it. She was only just on a double yellow; a couple of feet at the most.

"Hello? Can I help you?"

The girl in Ben's classroom looked up as though she didn't recognise her.

"I'm Ben's mother." Didn't she remember her from parents' evening? Not this year's. She hadn't been able to get to that. Last year's. Although, come to think of it, that might have been another teacher.

"Nice to meet you. Is Ben's nanny ill?"

"No." Becky gritted her teeth. "She's left."

"Really? Well, do introduce me to the next one, won't you, before she starts? We like to know who everyone is."

What gave her the right to assume she was going to get another nanny? And why had Ben run off without a second look?

"Goodness me, your little one doesn't look very well. Has she got chicken pox by any chance?"

"They came out a few days ago. At a wedding, can you believe . . ."

The girl's lips narrowed. "I'm afraid I'm going to have to ask you to remove her immediately. We don't allow anyone in here with infectious diseases. It means you've already infected the class."

What a fuss! You'd think it was the plague rather than common or garden chicken pox.

"And of course you'll need to take Ben back with you."

"But he hasn't got chicken pox."

"You mean he's had it?"

"No but . . ."

"Then he's at severe risk of getting it and passing it on. I'm afraid I'm going to have to report this matter to the head."

What a fuss! They'd just have to go home and . . . then what?

It was no good. She might as well admit it. She just wasn't a born mother. Of course she loved them but she needed to do something else as well. It was all Mum and Dad's fault. If they hadn't encouraged her to work hard at school and go to uni, she might have been more content with being a stay-at-home, like her own mother. Or wasn't that the point? Had Mum — an intelligent woman with a 2:1 in French from Durham — been frustrated too? Was that why everything had gone wrong?

Thank God she'd bumped into Charlotte — just goes to show you never knew what might happen at weddings (maybe she should write about it). At first she'd had doubts in case a nanny share didn't work out but today's little episode with school had made her mind up. How amazing that Charlotte had been asked to set up a new magazine and even more amazing that she was looking for someone to write a sprog blog and do a parenting page as well. That would give her two whole days at home with the children to learn how to do it. From now on, she'd be less self-centred and more kid-centred. Honestly.

"Mum, what are you doing? Those scissors are sharp. They might hurt you."

"It's all right, Daisy."

Snip, snip, snip.

"But that's our spreadsheet!"

Ben's little eyes stared at it with horror. "How are we going to know what we're doing now?"

Had it really got this bad?

"Because," said Becky, bundling them into their anoraks, "we're going to be more spontaneous in future."

"Wot?"

"It's 'what', Ben, not 'wot'. And spontaneous means we're going to do things on the spur of the moment, when we feel like it. Like going for a walk."

Both kids gave her a "Mum are you mad?" look.

"But it's raining."

"Exactly." Becky pulled on her own raincoat. "But a bit of fresh air will be good for you. It's what your uncle Adam and I did when we were children."

"That was centuries ago!"

"Can't we go for an in-a-minute walk?" asked Ben hopefully.

"Nope!" Becky shepherded both children through the front door. "Not any more. Now come on, you lot. We're going to have some fun."

Not the phone again! Just when she was really trying.

"Becks?"

No. No. No.

"Hi."

Why did her voice tremble like that?

"How are you doing?"

"Fine. Absolutely fine."

God, she'd forgotten how sexy he sounded.

"I've been worried about you."

"Well, don't be." She glanced ahead at the kids who were beginning to run down the road towards the park. "Come back, you two. Look, Dan, I've got to go."

"Did you make up with your husband?"

"Yes. Daisy, come back!"

"Because I've just broken off with Karen. Properly, this time."

"Ben!"

"And — this is why I'm really ringing — we've bought you out."

What?

"I know. Amazing, isn't it. Our group has bought out *Charisma* magazine and has made me MD. So if you want your old job back, you could have it."

The kids were becoming distant specks. She needed to run faster.

"Ben? Daisy!"

"So what do you say?"

Thank God they'd stopped now at the swings. How had she got so unfit? Maybe now she'd be at home more, she could start jogging.

"Thanks. But no thanks."

"You're sure?" Two months earlier, his disappointment would have excited her. But she'd come on a lot since then. Grown up. Got herself potty trained, rather late in the day. But clean, nevertheless.

"Quite sure."

"Mum!" Ben was waving at her. "Come and have a go on this — it's wicked! If we get really high, we can see the zoo. Did you know tigers have striped skin? It says so on my computer."

A swing? She hadn't been on one for years. But her son wanted her to. He wasn't calling for Laura or for Steve. He wanted her.

"Inamin — I mean, coming now, darling. Right now."

Janie

"Marje? Marje?"

Janie shut the front door of the cottage behind them.

Adam looked around at the low ceiling and pretty prints on the walls of the hall. "This is lovely."

Janie felt a rush of warmth. "Isn't it. I love it. And Marjorie's amazing. You'll really get on; I know it.

Marje? Are you home? It's me! Well, actually it's us and we've got something to tell you."

Janie reluctantly tore herself away from Adam's arm which was tight around her. "Wait there a bit, can you? It might be a bit of a shock if we both walk in. She's probably asleep on the sofa again."

No. That was odd. Maybe she was in her bedroom. Janie didn't like going in but then again, this was a special occasion.

What? No! No! "Omigod. Marjorie. Adam, quick. She's gone! Marjorie's really gone!"

CHAPTER
SIXTY-ONE

Helen

South America! That's where Geoff and Monique were going apparently. When he'd married her, they'd gone to the Isle of Wight for their honeymoon. It had been wonderful. Walking on the downs, running down the wooded landslip, walking hand in hand along the beach at Luccombe Bay.

Was Geoff remembering that? Or had he forgotten, like her birthday, which he hadn't so much as mentioned when he'd brushed cheeks with her at the wedding. Perhaps he was too busy now applying suntan lotion to his new bride to remember his first wedding. Mind you, one bottle wouldn't last long with the amount he'd have to cover . . .

In a funny kind of way, it didn't hurt as much as she thought it might. Maybe because it was all over now. Monique and Geoff were married. She and Geoff were finally over, even though they'd been divorced for years. That, together with her birthday — she still felt more like 35 in her head than 55 — had been a watershed. For the first time in years, she felt ready to move on.

But now what? David had been persistent with his phone calls, although he'd stopped calling round at the cottage unexpectedly. She was glad of that. He'd never been right but she wished she could have found that out in a different way. Poor Sylvia.

The ground was hard. Unyielding, rather like her guilt, despite what Mel had said. Helen pushed the fork into the frosted earth and the metal twisted as though it might snap. She usually liked this time of year, leading up to Christmas. So much to get ready. So much to look forward to, especially with Ben and Daisy coming down next week for a few days to give their parents a rest. And yet . . .

She was giving up. It was hopeless trying to dig Doris's little patch. She'd get back into the van, drive home and heat up some of that vegetable soup she'd made yesterday.

"Come on, Dandy."

He didn't need asking twice.

There was a diversion. Water works or an accident? Since the pond tragedy, she'd taken great care not to go past the Old Rectory but now with the yellow diversion signs, she had no option. Eyes ahead. Don't look. What?

Screeching to a halt, she reversed a few feet. There it was. Clear as the low winter sun.

A *For Sale* sign. Bang outside her old house.

"Why?"

She didn't bother with the preamble. Besides Robin knew exactly what she meant. She could see that from his eyes, when he opened the door. She'd gone to the front one this time as though to underline the fact that this time, their relationship was on a formal footing.

"I can't live here any more." His eyes sought hers. "There are too many memories."

Of course.

"And I'm not just talking about Sylvia."

He said this so quietly she almost didn't hear him.

"You ought to come in. Otherwise people will talk even more."

Dandy would be all right for a bit. "Is that what they're doing? Talking?"

"A bit. That's another reason why I'm going. A man whose wife had a fatal accident in the garden pond isn't going to be forgotten for a while."

"But they know it was an accident. The coroner said so."

He shrugged. "Doesn't stop the talking. Cup of tea?"

Don't. "No thanks. I didn't mean to come in . . . I mean, I saw the sign and . . . Where are you going, anyway?"

He was putting the kettle on anyway. "France. A small village near Nice. I used to go there as a teenager. I've been looking on the net: there are lots of places that might do. I'm going out this weekend to take a look."

Her eye fell on the brochures on the pine table. Stone clad cottages, rustic tables in pretty gardens, hills in the distance.

"Come with me."

What?

He was so close to her now that she could smell him all over again. Just as she had before in bed. The desire to touch him was overpowering. Don't. Don't.

"Come with me, Helen. You and your smelly dog. We can plant those snowdrop bulbs you gave me that I don't know what to do with. Please."

CHAPTER
SIXTY-TWO

Mel

"Mum, what have you done to my room?"

Amy's voice rang angrily down the stairs.

Mel glanced at Richard and together they shared a wry smile.

"Your mother only tidied it up a bit," called out Richard. "What else did you expect her to do? It was virtually crawling out of the house. If you hadn't been in bed for nearly ten months, you could have done it yourself."

"Very funny."

Dear Lord. What was that noise?

"Sorry." Richard continued stirring the cheese sauce for the lasagne tonight. "Forgot to tell you. I said Josh could have the band over for practice."

"Fine."

And it was fine. It was wonderfully fine. The four of them were together again; more together than they'd been for a long time.

Kevin would be out in five months and that might be a bit difficult. But she'd cope with that one when it came.

Mysterious ways? That had to be the biggest understatement of all time. Actually, that might make quite a good sermon . . .

Janie

It didn't seem possible. It really didn't. High blood pressure, the doctor had said.

"Apparently, she knew things were bad." Janie nestled into Adam's arm on the sofa. "But she wouldn't listen. Kept drinking because that's what she enjoyed doing."

Adam's arm tightened around her. "Sounds fair enough."

Janie felt his lips nuzzle her hair.

"She even left a tape. She kept saying how wonderful tapes were, after Ned's funeral. It gave you a chance, she said, to say things you should have said before. Listen to this."

Leaning over the side of the sofa, she turned on the music system.

"*By the time you hear this, darling, I'll be gone. Don't worry about me. It's time for a new life — something completely different. I'm too old for all this now . . .*"

Adam reached over for the remote. "Janie, do you really want to listen to this now? I know it was a shock but I need to talk about us. I've got less than twenty-four hours before my plane goes."

He was right.

"I really fancy you, Janie."

Perhaps her hearing was going along with everything else.

"And we're alike!" He cupped her face in his hands and she tried to find somewhere else to look apart from

580

his very blue, very piercing eyes. No. Hopeless. Especially when he kissed the tip of her nose like that. "We're highly disorganised; everyone thinks we're hopeless and we're shit at choosing the right relationships," he continued. "A perfect match, don't you think?"

Well Lars had apparently thought so which was why he'd gone flouncing back to Norway at the end of the wedding reception when she'd spent most of the time dancing with Adam. Funny how quickly you could go off someone — maybe it was something to do with running out of meaningful conversations.

"Yes but Marjorie . . ." She simply couldn't stop thinking about her. It had been such a shock. "Did I tell you that on the tape, she said everyone's got to wear bright colours and there's got to be Beatles music."

Adam stroked the back of her neck so she tingled. "Sounds like quite a woman. Wish I'd known her better."

"Well you will." Janie sat up. "We've got a few days before she and Godfrey come back for their 'Not-Getting-Hitched' party. I still can't believe that they just shot off to Godfrey's Spanish villa for two weeks like that, leaving the tape. So eccentric! Why couldn't they have just left a note instead? But Marjorie said it was because the doctor scared her. 'If I haven't got long, I'm going to enjoy every minute,' she told me when she rang the other day."

Adam ran a finger further down her back. "And they're definitely not getting married, even at their age?"

Mmmm. That was nice. "Marjorie says it wouldn't be fair on Godfrey with her poor health. Besides, she doesn't believe in it any more after the trouble she had with her steps. That's why she's not selling the cottage. I can have it rent-free while she and Godfrey live in Spain."

Adam's right hand was slowly progressing down her back, tingle by tingle.

"Thanks to your dad — who sorted out some legal hassle she had with her stepson."

"Instead of opening a shop, you could splash out on a ticket to Australia and come back with me. There are some really good deals on at the moment. What do you think?"

Right leg, higher up.

What did she think! She was drawing the picture right now, in her head. White sand. Sun. Someone who'd always known her; someone with whom she could finally be herself. Of course it was a gamble — men like Adam rarely settled down — but, hey! He was fun. And sexy. And, well, he was Adam. Besides, was she really cut out as a wedding organiser after the Monique and Geoff fiasco?

"I would," she heard herself say. "But I'm about to start something."

Be brave. Take new opportunities. Ok, *Big Issue* lady. You might have moved on but I finally get it now. Thanks. I owe you one.

"It's a course," she continued. "A rather intensive one that Becky has found for me." She took a deep breath. "I've decided to try and sort out my dyslexia at last."

"Good on you!"

Omigod! Not there! She'd read about it but this was unbelievable! No one had ever really got there before — it was like Edmund Hillary and Germaine Greer rolled into one!

"I need to do it . . ."

"Sure you do . . ."

"I promised someone, you see." A picture of Gladys in McDonald's shot into her head. If Gladys could conquer her fears, so could she. After all, the old dear had promised to get married if she, Janie, promised to do something about her dyslexia. "But I could come out afterwards. If that's OK . . ."

Becky

"Dad — just a quick question. What exactly do you see in Monique?"

Sometimes, Becky couldn't believe she'd had the gall to ask him that at the end of the wedding when everyone was about to go home. But, fuelled by the champagne, she'd suddenly burst out with it. After all, it was Adam who had sworn not to tell dad the truth about Monique/Janine. Not her.

He'd held her shoulders and looked down on her, full of love, just like she remembered as a little girl. "Because she's honest, Becky, and yet she's also got balls. She's not like the others. She's up front and straight. Monique doesn't try to hide anything or pretend to be someone she isn't. And to be frank, after all these years of being with superficial women, I find that refreshing. Why do you ask?"

She hesitated. How could she spoil it all for him. He'd find out one day for himself. Wouldn't he? It wasn't up to her to puncture the dream first.

Now, as she caught up with Janie on the phone, it almost seemed irrelevant. At least it did with Janie's news.

"Australia? Inaminute, Ben. Did you say Australia?"

Wow! Becky hadn't seen that coming. "With my brother? But I thought you liked Lars."

"Boring. And we couldn't talk much."

"Adam always fancied you, you know."

"Did he? I mean I know we were good friends but . . ."

"Daisy, stop doing that or I'll take you to nursery even if it *is* shut. Anyway, how long do you think it will last?"

"I don't know. We're going to take one day at a time."

"Not you two, silly. Dad and Monique. We're all taking bets on it. I say six months. Steve says five. Mum won't say but I've put her down for four. She's going on holiday to France, by the way, for most of January."

"Put me down for three months."

"And Adam for two?"

"I'll ask him."

"By the way, I can see why you don't want to do weddings or funerals any more. But do you fancy organising a christening in about seven months time? And yes, of course it's Steve's!"

Confetti

FOR WEDDINGS AND A FUNERAL
(AND KRISTENINGS TOO)

We'll make it a day you'll never fourget!

TRUE STORY: BACK FROM THE DEAD.

The girl who survived a nine-month coma —
as told by her vicar mum.

An exclusive from YOU TU, the new magazine for
women who want something different.
(Editor: Becky Hastings)

UNKNOWN BAND GETS SIGNED! (NME exclusive)
The Get Out Of My Rooms — the band that recently
hit the headlines for bringing a teenager out of her
coma — have been signed by a top American music
company. Senior executive Silver Golda said: "We
believe scar music is the face of the future."

Dear Daisy and Ben,

*We've almost finished decorating our new home.
It's very near a town called Nice. Ask your new
nanny — I mean mummy — to look it up on the
map — I mean, Google. We're so excited about*

you all coming down to see us next month.

Lots of love from Gan and Robin.

SECOND COMING? SECOND TIME LUCKY . . . Come and try out our new-style family service at St Mary's. "And here's a request here from Steve Wright's Sunday morning love songs. It's to Monique from her new husband Geoff who wants her to know that he loves her very much and can't wait for her to come back from . . . hang on, I'm not sure I can read this . . . it looks like a girls' weekend at Champneys. Lucky you, Monique!"

Hi Becks! Look! No spelling mistakes! (Not like our ad which I forgot to proof-read.) Will text soon — promise — but just off to Bondai. Your brother sends his love. J x

Josh,getupforschool.Anddon'tforgettotakethehomeworkyou haven'tdone.

AT HOME
Hugo and Angela Ponson-Ponsonby
cordially invite you to a housewarming party
at the Old Rectory on Saturday, March 17th.
Black tie. Carriages at 1a.m.

PR boss wins award for charity work.
Monique Brown, who recently took part in a sponsored walk for the NSPCC, says it's a subject close to her

heart.
(Taken from a report in *Public Relations Post*)

DON'T
'TILL DEATH US∧~~DO~~ PART
Looking for a lovely location for a wedding?
Try us first.
(Ad for St Mary's on YouTube).

"Ohmigodwhereisshe?Stupidstupidshareanannyshouldhave
beenherehalfanhourago.I'mgoingtobelateforwork.It'sabloody
nuisance,that'swhatitis."